PRAISE FOR

DEVLIN'S LIGHT

"Mariah Stewart leaps to the top with a work that will appeal to her myriad of fans as well as the audiences of Belva Plain, Barbara Taylor Bradford, and Anne Rivers Siddons. *Devlin's Light* has a luminance that leaves most other works pale in comparison."

—Harriet Klausner, Painted Rock.com

"With her special brand of rich emotional content and compelling drama, Mariah Stewart is certain to delight readers everywhere."

—Jill M. Smith, *Romantic Times*

"*Devlin's Light* is a must-read for you that like the romantic suspense of a Nora Roberts story, or the surprising twists and turns of a Mary Higgins Clark yarn. Mariah Stewart sated my appetite for a great read. . . ."

—Betty Cox, America Online

"A haunting tale of suspense and sensual delight."

—BarnesandNoble.com

"[A] magnificent story of mystery, love and an enchanting town. Splendid."

—Bell, Book & Candle

CAROLINA MIST

"A wonderful, tender novel with romance of a period past and love with a little mystery and adventure woven in."

—*Rendezvous*

"Contemporary romance lovers will find a lot to appreciate in this new offering from Mariah Stewart. All the good stuff is here. . . ."

—Cathy Sova, *Romantic Reader Web-Site*

MOMENTS IN TIME

Books by Mariah Stewart

Moments in Time
A Different Light
Carolina Mist
Devlin's Light
Wonderful You
Moon Dance
Priceless
Brown-Eyed Girl
Voices Carry

Published by POCKET BOOKS

WONDERFUL YOU

MARIAH STEWART

POCKET BOOKS

New York   London   Toronto   Sydney

This book is a work of fiction. Names, characters, places and
incidents are products of the author's imagination or are used
fictitiously. Any resemblance to actual events or locales or persons,
living or dead, is entirely coincidental.

An *Original* Publication of POCKET BOOKS

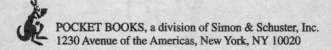 POCKET BOOKS, a division of Simon & Schuster, Inc.
1230 Avenue of the Americas, New York, NY 10020

Copyright © 1998 by Marti Robb

ISBN -13: 978-0-671-00416-3
ISBN -10:   0-671-00416-6

First Pocket Books printing July 1998

10 9 8 7 6 5 4

POCKET and colophon are registered trademarks of
Simon & Schuster, Inc.

Cover art by Franco Accornero

For information regarding special discounts for bulk purchases,
please contact Simon & Schuster Special Sales at
1-800-456-6798 or business@simonandschuster.com

Printed in the U.S.A.

To Mom and Dad,
with love and thanks

Grateful acknowledgments to—

Kathy Levine, the *true* diva of the shopping networks, with thanks for sharing her time and her humor, and for giving me a glimpse behind the scenes.

Loretta Barrett, my agent, who always believes and always encourages.

Kate Collins, for grace under pressure (and a special welcome to Connor and Declan!).

And to Lauren McKenna, who kept it all together.

Prologue

❦

A discordant sound from somewhere in the big, rambling house rattled the silence that wrapped around the sleeping child like a Band-Aid and shook her forcefully from her slumber. Pulling the covers up over her head to shield her from any stray Night Things that might be lurking about, she opened one eye to sneak a drowsy peek, just to make certain that nothing of questionable intent had, as yet, invaded the sanctuary of her room.

All appeared well.

A slow sigh of relief hissed from between her lips and she slowly inched the blanket away from her face. Drawing confidence from that small but brave act, she sat up quietly and leaned her back against the tall, carved wooden headboard, careful, for all her bravado, not to make the bed squeak and perhaps invite attention to herself. Not that *she* believed in Night Things. Her little sister did, but of course, her sister was only eight and *she* was almost eleven.

A sudden, nameless *thud* from the front of the house sent her scurrying back under the sheltering wing of her blankets, where she huddled in the cavelike warmth for a long moment, holding her breath to quiet herself as she strained to acclimate her ears to the sounds the house made at night.

Cautiously she slid to the edge of the bed until her head and shoulders hung over the side.

From somewhere in the night she heard voices.

She forced herself to remain there, suspended between the floor and the side of the bed, between fear and curiosity.

Curiosity, as always, won out.

Easing herself onto her feet without making a sound, she picked careful steps across the thickly carpeted floor, her feet making shallow wells in the deep blue wool pile. A deliberate finger bravely poked the bedroom door aside and she peered into the hallway, hoping neither to startle nor be startled. A glance up the long corridor to her right assured her that the door to her sister's room was closed. Employing great stealth, she crept into the hall, her destination the balcony that overlooked the dimly lit foyer below, from which the faint sound of muffled voices could be heard.

Someone was downstairs with her mother.

She paused at her brother's bedroom door, briefly considering whether to wake him. Her brother always treated her like a baby, even though he was only three and a half years older than she was. If she woke him up, he would think it was because she was afraid. Taking a deep breath, she crept past his door and continued alone down the hall.

Once at the railing she lowered herself onto the floor—oh so quietly—and leaned slightly into the space between the balusters, seeking the best view of the scene below.

Her mother, wrapped in her dark green chenille bathrobe, stood facing a white-haired man in a dark overcoat. Between them stood the boy, who was facing her mother, and it was to him that she spoke, her low voice but a whisper in the night. The girl wished she could hear what was being said.

No one looked happy, least of all the boy.

As her mother spoke, she brushed the hair back from his face with both hands, but he appeared to be looking not at her, but rather at the floor of black and white checkered marble. The man never spoke at all.

Finally the boy nodded, just the tiniest tilt of his head, and as her mother walked toward the study, the grandfather clock chimed a rude and sudden four bells. Trying to follow the drama and caught up in it, the girl leaned a bit too far to the left and banged her forehead on the wooden railing. The soft *bump* echoed, floating downward like carelessly tossed confetti through the darkness to the foyer below. The man and the boy both looked upward with eyes that seemed to tell the same story from vastly different points of view. The eyes of the boy burned dark and fierce, while the eyes of the old man held little else but sorrow. Both of them, she would someday realize, had appeared equally lost.

Her mother returned with the boy's jacket and held it open to him, helping him to ease arms heavy with reluctance into the sleeves. She hugged him then, holding him only long enough not to cause him embarrassment. The boy was almost as tall as her mother and the girl wondered why she hadn't noticed before.

She froze at the sound approaching from behind, a soft footfall on the plump carpet. Light fingers touched her shoulder to reassure. Without turning around, she knew that her brother, too, had felt rather than heard the disturbance. Together they watched, in silence, as the drama below played out.

Finally, her brother pointed at the old man in the foyer and whispered, *"That's* his grandfather. He's taking him back."

The girl bit her lip. As if she didn't know who the man in the dark raincoat was. "He doesn't want to go, Nicky. He wants to stay here. Can't we do something?"

"Mom said Ben belonged with his grandfather, Zoey. It's what his mother wanted."

"I wish she hadn't died, Nicky. I wish everything

3

could be just the way it was." The girl's bottom lip began to quiver in earnest. Her hero was leaving, and there was nothing she could do about it.

A nod from her mother seemed to imply a hesitant consent, and the man opened the front door. Before the girl could so much as blink, the man and the boy had disappeared. Her mother stood alone in the open doorway, wrapping her arms around herself against the chill of the night air, and there she remained long after the sound of tires crunching on stone had ceased.

A sense of overwhelming sadness drifted to the second floor and the girl leaned back on her haunches to ponder it all. The boy—who, unlike her brother, had never treated her like a baby, and had never been too busy to teach her how to climb trees and throw a fastball and catch frogs down near the pond—had vanished into the night, and there was, about all, a dense air of finality she did not comprehend.

"Nicky, do you think we'll ever see him again?"

He wanted to reassure her, to tell her yes, of course, Ben would be back. But having already learned that children were, after all, pretty much at the whim of adults, he merely shook his head and said, "I don't know."

Chapter

1

Zoey Enright leaned against the window and watched as, for the third day in a row, fat drops of water smacked and spattered against the wooden steps leading to the entrance of My Favorite Things, the shop she had opened but seven months earlier. April showers were one thing, she grumbled as she let the lace curtain fall back against the glass, but this was ridiculous.

Unconsciously she straightened a stack of hand-knit sweaters for the fifth time in half as many hours. Like all of the merchandise in her shop, the sweaters were exquisite things, made of hand-woven wool, one of a kind, and pricey.

Maybe a bit too pricey for this rural Pennsylvania two-mule town, her sister, Georgia, had ventured to suggest.

At the time, Zoey had brushed off Georgia's comment with a wave of her hand. What did she know, anyway? She's a *dancer,* Zoey had pointed out, not a shopkeeper, and Georgia had shrugged that she'd only been voicing concern.

Zoey had been convinced that her unique little shop would be the talk of Chester County, located as it was in a honey of a tiny renovated barn midway between Wilmington, Delaware, and Lancaster, Pennsylvania, just a pleasant drive from the country-chic of Chadds Ford and all those new upscale housing developments. The nearest shopping was a strip mall that was under renovation and had not been scheduled for completion until next year. By that time, Zoey had hoped to have her clientele all firmly locked up, and there would be a steady stream of repeat shoppers beating a path to her door to find all those very special goodies they could not find elsewhere.

Shelves laden with baskets of sweaters, wooden toys and dolls, pottery and jewelry, hats and afghans, painted boxes of papier-mâché and stained glass windows lined the shop and competed for the attention of the customer's eye. From old-fashioned clothes racks, satin hangers displayed dresses and capes, the styles of which dated from the turn of the century, some antiques, some reproductions. Authentic Victorian boots of softest black leather trimmed with jet beads sat next to nineties' style granny boots. Marcasite bracelets from the twenties and thirties shared case space with new pieces crafted by up-and-coming contemporary jewelry designers.

A glance at the calendar reminded Zoey that she had been open for business for exactly seven months today. With backing from her mother, Zoey had spent the entire summer preparing for her grand opening back in September. Georgia had driven up from Baltimore, where as a member of the famed Inner Harbor Dance Troupe, she worked hard to make a name for herself in the world of professional ballet. Early in the morning on opening day, Georgia had knocked on the front door and waited patiently for Zoey to admit her as My Favorite Things' very first customer.

"So," Zoey had ushered her sister into the shop, "what do you think of my little venture?"

Georgia had stood drop-jawed in the middle of the colorful, handmade rag rug that covered the center of the floor.

"Zoey, it's awesome. It's like . . ." Georgia had sought to do justice to Zoey's displays. "Like a tiny mall full of perfect little boutiques."

"Exactly." Looking pleased and somewhat smug, Zoey folded her arms across her chest, watching with pleasure as her sister lifted item after item and marveled at the variety.

"Where did all this stuff come from?" Georgia held aloft a small hand-blown glass perfume bottle to admire the workmanship.

"Here, there, and everywhere." Zoey grinned.

"Well, it's all wonderful." Georgia had lifted a black beaded shawl and draped it over her shoulders to cover the river of thick, straight blond hair that ran the length of her back.

"That's the real thing." Zoey's blue eyes sparkled with pride as she straightened out the back of the shawl. "Circa nineteen twenty. Those are real glass beads, by the way, hand sewn on silk."

Georgia glanced at the price tag.

"Ouch!" she exclaimed. "Are you kidding?"

"Nope." Zoey leaned back against the counter.

"Zoey, this is one pricey item."

"Georgia, that shawl is handmade, it's eighty years old, and it's in mint condition. I don't know where you're likely to find another like it, if in fact another exists. And the price, I might add, is barely marked up over what I had to pay to get it."

"It is gorgeous, there's no question that anyone would love to have it. I just hope that you'll be able to find a buyer for it. I'd feel a little more confident if you were a little closer to Philadelphia, or Wilmington—even closer in toward West Chester would help—but as far out as you are into the country, well, I just hope that you haven't priced yourself out of a sale."

"I'd be lying if I said that the thought hadn't occurred to me," Zoey admitted, "but that shawl was so perfect that I had to have it. It's like these sweaters." She held up a dark green woolen tunic. "The lady who makes them

7

wanted an arm and a leg for them, but they're clearly worth it."

"Zoey, I'm not the financial whiz in the family, but I don't think you'll make much money if you don't mark up what you buy."

"I know, but I thought that in the beginning at least, it would be a good idea to have some really eye-catching things."

"Well, you've certainly accomplished that." Georgia removed the shawl gently and carefully refolded it, placing it back on the shelf. "I just hope that the locals appreciate your style and that they shop here frequently enough to keep you in business. I'd buy this"—she patted the shawl—"in a heartbeat if I had a few extra hundred dollars I didn't know what to do with. You must have spent a bloody fortune on your inventory."

"Actually, the bloody fortune was Mom's," Zoey admitted. "She was as excited about this venture as I was, and you know how Mom is when she gets excited about something. Besides putting up the cash, she really got into scouting out the most unusual, the most exquisite things. That collection of Victorian mourning pins, for example . . ."

Zoey opened the case and removed a tray of pins, which looked, Georgia noted, strangely like hair.

"They are made out of hair"—Zoey grinned—"and yes, it's human hair. A hundred or so years ago, it was a popular custom to cut off some of the locks of a deceased loved one, and have them woven into rings or bracelets or pins, depending, I guess, on how long the hair was. There were people who actually did this professionally."

"Oh, yuck." Georgia made a face. "None for me, thanks."

"They're not exactly to my taste, either, but they are kind of interesting. Look at this brooch, Georgy. Look at how intricate the gold weaving is, and how the woven hair mimics the gold—"

"I don't care how intricate the workmanship is."

Georgia groaned. "The mere thought of wearing a dead person's *hair* gives me the creeps."

"Well, actually, not all hair jewelry was made from dead people's hair. Some people had the hair from a loved one—a spouse, a child—made into a pin or a bracelet or a—"

"Enough already with the hair jewelry, Zoey. I think it's creepy." Georgia handed the tray back to her sister.

"Mom was kind of drawn to the concept. She's probably thinking about how to use it in her next book. And besides, she thought that if we were aiming for an eclectic stock of merchandise, we should really go all out and find some things that probably wouldn't be available anywhere else locally."

Delia Enright had totally backed the efforts of her daughter. Zoey was her middle child and the only one of the three who hadn't—as Delia delicately put it— *landed* yet. Nick, her oldest child and only son, was a doctoral candidate who had found a contented life studying marine life on the Delaware Bay. He had met a wonderful young woman and before another year had passed, India Devlin would become his bride. Georgia, Delia's youngest, had never wanted to do anything but dance. Pursuing her goal with single-minded drive, Georgia had, at sixteen, been invited to join the prestigious Berwyn Troupe. Three years later, she had been asked to become a charter member of the newly formed Inner Harbor Dancers, where she had, for the past six years, worked hard and performed with blissful zeal. Only Zoey had yet to find her place.

It wasn't for lack of effort or desire on her part. Over the past several years, Zoey had tried her hand at any number of occupations, all of which she had mastered, none of which had fed her soul and promised her the kind of long-term gratification she craved. The joy that Georgia had found in dance, the satisfaction her brother had found in identifying and studying marine life, the pleasure experienced by her mother in crafting her novels, had eluded Zoey all her life. Many are called, few are chosen, aptly described Zoey's quest for a career she could sink her teeth into.

As a child, when asked what she would be when she grew up, Zoey would answer, "A teacher. And an astronaut. And a news lady on TV. And a fashion designer . . ."

And so on, and so on. There were few things that hadn't caught Zoey's imagination at one time or another. Over the years, she had, in fact, tried her hand at a goodly number of those things—except for being an astronaut, and there were times when she wasn't completely certain that she'd given up on that.

The problem was that for all the things that caught her fancy, and all the things she did well, nothing had sustained her for long.

"Zoey is a bit of a late bloomer," Delia would explain matter-of-factly when questioned about her middle child's current status. "One of these days, she will find her place, and she'll be an outrageous success and live happily ever after."

Delia would then pause and add, "It's just taking her a little longer to get there, that's all."

Zoey had on many occasions offered silent thanks that she had been blessed with a mother who understood *perfectly*. It had been Delia who, recognizing her daughter's sense of style, encouraged her to open the shop and fill it with all manner of wonderful things. Delia had had every bit as much fun as Zoey, shopping for all of those one-of-a-kind items that overflowed from every nook and cranny of My Favorite Things. All of those wonderful things that were *not* beating a path out of the store under the arms of the droves of happy shoppers who were all, alas, happily shopping elsewhere.

* * *

"Charming, Zoey." Georgia laughed as she entered the shop through the back door and shook off the rain. "Absolutely charming."

"Is this hat great with these amber beads around the

brim?" Zoey turned to greet her sister, grinning impishly as she pushed her long black curls behind her ears and plopped a wide-brimmed hat of brown felt upon her head.

Georgia dropped a heavy purse of dark green leather onto the floor.

"Ummm, I think it's the red rose that makes it." Georgia raised her hand to touch the huge red silk blossom pinned to the underside of the brim. "But there are probably only a handful of women on the planet who could get away with actually wearing such a thing. You just happen to be one of them."

"Nonsense. Just about anyone with some imagination could wear this." With a swoop, Zoey plunked the chocolate brown creation on her sister's head.

"Zoey, I look ridiculous," Georgia sought to remove the oversized hat from her undersized head.

"Silly." Zoey readjusted the brim, tilting it slightly to one side. "It's all in the attitude. There. See?"

"It's *entirely* too *extreme* for me. Too . . . *exotic.*"

"Well, it is an *extravagance,*" Zoey grinned, trading *e*-words with Georgia as they had often done as children, a game encouraged by Delia, who hoped to improve their vocabularies, "but then again, it is an *exclusive.*"

"It is an *excellent* hat," Georgia concluded the banter, "but I look like a female impersonator doing Bette Midler. And doing her badly, I might add."

Removing the hat with its glittering beads and huge floppy rose, Georgia replaced it on its stand.

"I'll admit that the hat is a kick, Zoey, but it may be a bit avant-garde for the territory. It's a shame there isn't more traffic out here. You really have the most delightful things."

Georgia picked the hat back off the stand and preened in front of a small mirror. "It does sort of grow on you after a while, doesn't it?"

"It looks great on you, Georgy."

"You know, you probably could sell ice to the Eskimos." Georgia told her. "I'll take the hat."

"It's yours."

"Zoey, you cannot hope to establish a business by giving away your stock."

"Consider it an early birthday. It looks too wonderful on you for you not to have it. And that hat won't make or break this shop." Zoey wrapped the hat in tissue before sliding it into a pale green plastic bag with My Favorite Things in purple script.

"The lack of traffic, as you noted, is the problem." Zoey straightened a basket of colorful scarves, hand knitted by a woman from Chester Springs who loomed and dyed her own wool. "That strip mall down the road just in from the highway is killing me. It wasn't supposed to be opened till this coming summer. When was the last time you heard about a construction project running six months *ahead* of schedule?"

"That was a tough break." Georgia nodded.

"And having those outlet shops open up out on Route One sure helped a lot, too." Zoey sat down on a little white wicker settee.

"Maybe you should consider taking some things on consignment for a while," Georgia suggested, "and give your cash flow a chance to build."

"The cash is flowing mighty slowly these days, " Zoey admitted glumly.

"What does Mom say?"

"I haven't had much of an opportunity to discuss it with her. She's been sort of holed up with her computer. You know how she is when she starts a new book."

"Underground" was the term Delia's children used to describe her single-minded drive to write.

"Well, if you need a loan . . ."

"Thanks, Georgy, but Mom's been pretty generous."

"As always." Georgia smiled, knowing that Delia had always maintained an open checkbook where her children were concerned. She had, over the past few years, purchased and decorated a charming condo for Georgia outside of Baltimore when she had joined the troupe. And two years ago, she had completely renovated an old crabber's cabin that Nick had found and purchased on the Delaware Bay. "Well, you know that if you need anything at all, I'm here."

"Thanks, Georgia."

"Look, if we're all going to have dinner together tonight, I'd better get back to the house and start now to blast Mom out of her office." Georgia slipped into her dark green down jacket.

Zoey grabbed a plum-colored scarf from a nearby basket and draped it around her sister's neck.

"Thanks, Zoey, but I think you've given away all the merchandise you can afford to for one day."

"It goes great with that glorious mane of hair, and the purple plays up the green of your eyes." Zoey hugged her sister in the doorway and straightened the scarf around her neck. "I'll just take a few minutes to close up here, then I'll meet you at the house."

Zoey watched Georgia dodge the raindrops on the way to her car, then closed the door and locked the dead bolt with the key. On the floor beside the counter she spied the plastic bag that held the brown felt hat that Georgia had left behind. It *had* looked great on her sister, Zoey nodded to herself.

Turning to flick on the switch that would turn off the outside lights at the front of the shop, Zoey paused to peer through the windows at the cars flying past on their way to the newly reopened shopping center a half mile down the road, and she sighed. She grabbed the bag holding her sister's hat and closed up shop for the night.

Chapter

2

Fingering the news article Georgia had so proudly sent from Maryland, Zoey rested her elbows on the glass counter and leaned forward to reread the feature that a local paper had run on Georgia's dance troupe. That the reporter had chosen her little sister as the focus of the article had provided Zoey with an unexpected and unwanted twinge of envy. Zoey studied the photograph that accompanying the article. A frail but happy Georgia in light-colored leggings and a long knitted shirt, sleeves pushed to the elbows, leaned against the doorway of the dance studio, her golden hair falling casually around her face, her legs crossed at the ankles. She looked pleased and sure of herself. Which she had, Zoey reminded herself, earned the right to be.

With a sigh, Zoey dropped the article onto the glass, where it fell upon the program from the ballet she and her mother had attended the previous Wednesday evening. While Georgia's role had been minor, she had danced with the joy and energy of one who clearly loved every step she took. Delia had made no effort to hide the tears of pride that had begun the second her youngest

14

had stepped onto the stage and illuminated it with her presence. Georgia was a fairy princess come to life, with her thick blond hair and round pale green eyes set in that tiny angel's face. Zoey recalled how hard Georgia had worked for so very long, giving up everything else for the sake of her dancing. Delia *should* be proud of her daughter.

For a moment Zoey wondered what it would feel like to find that kind of success in a job you loved, to earn that kind of pride from your family, to find your path and follow it to the stars. With each passing day, it was becoming more and more obvious that the path leading to My Favorite Things was veering farther and farther from success and happiness and closer and closer to one marked by a going-out-of-business sign.

"Damn," she whispered, *"it had seemed like such a good idea at the time. . . ."*

Forcing herself to shake off a feeling of gloom, Zoey chucked another small piece of wood into the small woodstove, having decided early that morning that she'd need a little something extra to dispel the dampness that seemed to permeate the old structure. The new heating system installed during the renovations just didn't seem to do the trick.

"Well, what we are lacking in heat, we make up for in *style,"* Zoey said aloud to her shop, empty of customers but crammed to the rafters with an endless array of wonderful things. "Yup. No one can ever say that Zoey Enright lacks flair."

"And *flair,* as we all know, " she noted as she draped a small round table with a lace cloth, giving a saucy little flip to the edges before smoothing it gently, "is one of those things you just have to be born with." She pulled a small settee up close to the table on one side, then set a small wicker chair at the other.

"Now, what do you say, Miss Maude?" Zoey addressed a large handmade stuffed mouse dressed in a calico pinafore and a large garden hat from which all manner of blooms tumbled over a wide brim to partially obscure the mouse's carefully embroidered face. The tiny faces of an entire litter of mouse babies peeked over the sides of the basket which rested in the mouse lady's arms. "Which tea set should we use today? Something painted at the turn of the century by someone's great-aunt Hattie perhaps? Yes, I think so, too."

Zoey lifted a stack of small, delicate plates, each decorated with spring flowers. "China painting, you know—now, Miss Felicity, I'm sure you will have a personal recollection of this"—Zoey turned and addressed an antique doll with a china head and a faded blue silk dress—"china painting having been such a popular pastime among genteel ladies when *you* were in your prime. So difficult to find acceptable outlets for one's creativity a hundred years ago. And it would appear that great-aunt Hattie—see, here's her name, Hattie Jerome, painted right here beneath the flowers—was fond of spring things. Or maybe it was the color purple, in all its shades and variations, that she loved. Look here at the plates . . . violets, hyacinths, lilac and pansies. Aren't they just too lovely?"

Zoey set the table for three, rinsed out the teapot, then filled it with coffee, which she poured from a small coffee maker that sat on a table behind the cash register. Zoey had thought to keep the pot filled to have something to offer her customers. It occurred to her that lately she had been drinking a lot more coffee than she was accustomed to, and that the pot was seeing a lot more activity than the cash register.

"Oh, yes, of course, Miss Felicity, I *am* aware that tea was the beverage of choice among ladies, but one must, on occasion, make do. I myself prefer a nice cup of Lemon Zinger, but I left the box at home, so it's coffee or nothing." She plumped a variety of handmade pillows, some needlepoint, some velvet patchwork, on the settee, then propped up Miss Maude at one end and Miss Felicity at the other. Zoey herself perched on the wicker chair. Opening a box of Girl Scout cookies, she placed one on each painted plate, explaining, "I get to keep the box because I'm the human and it's my fantasy. What's the matter, there, Maudie, cat got your tongue? Oops, sorry. How *totally* insensitive of me."

Zoey sipped at her coffee and munched first her cookie, then those she had placed on the plates of her silent companions, noting, "Well, the mints are my favorite, too, but the kid selling these door-to-door was all out, so I opted for the Trefoils, okay? If you don't like butter cookies, just say so.

"Okay, if you're going to give me the cold shoulder . . ." Reaching behind her, Zoey slid the morning paper from her tote bag. "I know it's rude to read at the table, but you guys aren't exactly holding up your end of the conversation, you know. Much as I love you all, this would be a lot more fun for me if one of you would *say something* once in a while, 'cause I love to talk, and not having anyone to talk *with* is making me crazy."

Leaning back in the chair, Zoey skimmed the headlines, occasionally reading aloud an entire item that snagged her attention. "Oh, listen to this." She brightened as she read the headline on the front of the business section. "'Valentine, Inc. Finalizes Purchase of Shop-From-Home Network.' Shop from home. Now, *that* is a concept I could get behind." She read through the article twice, once to herself, the second time aloud. "'Edward Bruce, spokesperson for Valentine, Inc., has announced the purchase of the station, which will be run by Val-Tech, the cable television company owned by Valentine. The station will be extending its broadcast hours from its present sixteen to twenty-four hours of continuous live broadcasting each day, and will mark a new venture for Valentine. The new channel, dubbed the Home Market-Place, will continue to offer viewers the opportunity to purchase items that will be displayed and demonstrated on their television screen. The Home MarketPlace will join several other shop from home stations already being broadcast, but will, Bruce promised, "bring ValTech's own special touch to this still relatively new retail outlet." The Home MarketPlace plans to begin interviewing this week for new faces to add to its on-the-air sales staff. . . .' "

Zoey sat silently staring across the table for a long moment, her eyes resting absently on the basket of baby mice.

"I know what you're thinking," she addressed her mute company. "You're thinking that this has my name all over it. And you're right. It does. I'm a natural. It's everything I love. Everything I do best. Shopping. Selling. Talking." She stood up, then slowly began to pace. "You know, when I had my brief run with the news, the only part of the job I really enjoyed was talking on camera."

Zoey turned on the small television set that stood at one end of the counter, and flipped along the dial until she found a shopping channel. She sat down on the high wooden stool and watched for several long minutes as the woman on the screen described a bedspread in the most careful detail.

"I can do that," Zoey announced. Picking up a pair of handmade copper earrings, she proceeded to sing their praises, mimicking the woman on the television screen. When she had finished her little sales pitch, she sat back on the stool and repeated, "I can do that," with unquestioned conviction.

Lifting Miss Maude and her basket of babies from the settee, Zoey held them to her chest and crossed the wooden floor to the window, where sheets of water distorted the view outside the shop, and contemplated the facts. My Favorite Things was a screaming failure. There was no way around it. The longer the shop remained open, the more money Delia would sink into it, and the more money she would lose. Not that she had ever complained. Money had long ceased to be an issue to Delia. Her daughter's happiness, on the other hand, meant everything. Zoey knew that she could keep the shop open forever, continue to lose money, and Delia would never chastise her for it, as long as Zoey was happy.

But Zoey was not happy, could not be happy, in a losing venture. The shop was perfect, its contents wonderful, but it had failed to thrive. Georgia had been right. It was, sadly, the wrong location for such upscale items. And isn't that what the real estate people say is the most critical thing—location, location, location?

She lifted the newspaper and read through the article yet a third time. The new station would be located less than twenty miles from where she stood. There was even a number listed to call to arrange for an audition. Were the gods telling her something?

Well, then, perhaps we should hear what they have to say, she mused as she lifted the receiver and punched in the numbers. The call was answered on the third ring by the light, pleasant voice of a young woman.

"Welcome to ValTech. How may I direct your call?"

* * *

Five days later, armed with written directions and high hopes, Zoey drove through the stone gates of her mother's home and headed toward Lancaster. With all the construction on Route 30, Zoey had missed the turn and driven almost as far as Soudersburg before she figured out where she had gone wrong, turned around, and headed in the right direction once again. Having successfully located the correct cross road, she had driven through one small town after another, past Amish farms generations old, as well as new housing developments, and fields that waited for the spring plows to turn over the earth. Zoey followed the directions she'd been given over the phone, taking what appeared to be one small backcountry road after another to a place called Lanning's Corner, which turned out to be every bit the one-horse town that its name implied.

Finally, she sighed with relief as she approached the drive announced by a sign: "ValTech—Home of the Home MarketPlace." Following its winding trail to the low-slung two-story brick and glass building, she parked in a visitors' spot and glanced at her watch. She was forty minutes late. Damn.

19

Zoey pulled the mirrored visor down and quickly studied her reflection. She touched up the blush on her cheeks and refreshed her lipstick. With her hands she fluffed up her hair, then took a deep breath and swung her legs out of the little sports car and stretched to get the kinks out.

Biting her lip as she smoothed the short skirt of her poppy red silk suit, Zoey straightened up to her full height of five feet six inches tall—in two-inch heels, that is—and gave the car door a slam.

She was here. She looked great. She would knock them dead.

Assuming, of course, that she hadn't missed her appointment.

"You do realize that you are forty-two minutes late," the young receptionist said by way of a greeting. "I'm not certain that there is anyone here now who can speak with you."

"I understand." Zoey forced a smile onto her face and raised her chin just a tad. "I got lost. . . ."

"Well, that is unfortunate, but I think Mr. Pressman has left the building—"

A girlish giggle from around the corner of the hall drew the attention of Zoey and the receptionist.

A shapely blonde bearing a startling resemblance to Marilyn Monroe rounded the corner, followed closely by a tall, lean, middle-aged man in a dark gray suit.

"Oh, Mr. Pressman," the receptionist addressed the man, "I wasn't sure if you were still here. Miss"—she looked down at Zoey's résumé—"Enright has arrived for her interview."

He looked across the hall and focused on Zoey momentarily, then smiled—a bit foolishly, Zoey thought, like a little boy who is trying to sneak out of the house to play baseball when he knows he is supposed to be practicing his piano scales.

"Ah . . . yes. Miss . . ."

"Enright. Zoey Enright."

"Ah, perhaps, Kelly," he addressed the receptionist, "ah, possibly *Brian* could interview Miss Enright. I was just on my way to . . . lunch, you see. . . ."

"I'll see if he is in." The receptionist's wary eyes followed Pressman and the giggly blonde as they passed through the front doors. She and Zoey exchanged a glance of having just seen the same ghost. "Have a seat, Miss Enright. I'll see what I can do."

Several moments passed before the elevator doors opened and a young man stepped into the lobby.

"Zoey Enright," the receptionist told him, pointing a ballpoint pen in Zoey's direction.

"Brian Lansky." He crossed the lobby in three strides. "You're here for an interview. Right this way . . ."

Thirty feet down the hall he turned to the right and led her through a doorway and flicked on the lights to reveal a set, which consisted of little more than a desk and a solid pale yellow painted backdrop.

"Tell me about yourself," he said to Zoey, "while I try to locate a cameraman. . . ."

"Well, I'm twenty-eight. I live in Westboro, Pennsylvania. I have a degree in English from Villanova, I am currently in sales—actually, I have my own business. . . ." She rambled on, despite the distinct feeling that no one was paying the least bit of attention to her.

Brian sat on the edge of the desk, punching numbers into a telephone, nodding and murmuring "Uh-hnn" every few minutes or so.

He put the phone down and said, "The cameraman must have left for lunch. I would hate to make you come back, so let's see if I can operate this myself."

He fiddled with the camera, then stepped out from behind it and took a quick glance around the room. He crossed the room and lifted an item from the windowsill and handed it to her before stepping back behind the camera. "What can you tell me about this?"

21

"It's a can opener . . . ?" a confused Zoey ventured.

"Right," Lansky said from behind the camera. "Sell it to me."

"Excuse me?"

"The camera is rolling, Miss Enright. Sell me the can opener."

And sell she did.

Flashing her best smile, she looked directly into the lens. Filled with the same sense of being *on* that she recalled from her news reporting days, Zoey launched into a sales pitch that would become the standard by which future auditions would be judged.

"When I was six years old, we had a snowstorm to beat all storms. All of the electrical lines in our neighborhood went down. We had to build a big fire in the living room fireplace to keep warm. We did have a gas stove, but everything else in that house ran on electricity. To keep us busy, Mom let us help bake bread in the afternoon and we ate dinner that night all huddled around the fire—this wonderful crusty homemade bread and chicken noodle soup. Even though the soup came out of a can, I remember that as one of the best meals *ever*. My brother and sister and I *still* talk about that day." Zoey held up the manual can opener. "It just goes to show that you can own all the latest equipment—God knows I like my gadgets as well as the next person—but you simply cannot do without the basics."

"Cut." Brian rose from his stool.

"How'd I do?" Zoey grinned.

"Would you mind waiting right there for a minute?"

"Sure."

Within minutes, Brian returned with an executive type—Ken Powers—and a cameraman.

"If you wouldn't mind . . ." Brian handed her a letter opener. "We'd like to run one more tape.."

"Sure." And Zoey proceeded to sing the virtues of the letter opener, convincing all who listened that without that little piece of polished brass, everything from Christmas cards to wedding invitations to letters from a favorite grandchild would forever be locked away. She had just launched into a discourse on paper cuts when Brian stopped her.

"Miss Enright, if you're not in a hurry, we'd like to take another look at the first tape. Perhaps just a short wait . . . ?"

"Not a problem," she assured him, inwardly raising a fist in triumph and shouting YES!, knowing it was in the bag.

"Let's see if I can find someone to bring you a cup of coffee."

"So, has there been a big response to the ad?" Zoey nonchalantly inquired of the young assistant who brought her a cup of dark and terrible brew.

"You wouldn't believe it." Eddie rolled his eyes to the heavens, and proceeded to tell her about the hordes who had come in to tape an audition.

He was interrupted by the ringing of the phone.

"They want you in Ken's office," Eddie told her. "This way . . ."

Zoey followed him out of the studio and to the bank of elevators. "Second floor. First door to the left off the lobby. Good luck." He winked and punched the 2 button.

"Ah, here she is." Ken stepped from behind his desk to greet her as she knocked softly on the partially opened door. "Miss Enright, this is Ted Higgins, vice president in charge of hiring our hosts and hostesses. We think that sounds more in keeping with the image we want to create. Now, *salespeople* can be found in any retail outlet, but *hosts* invite you in, hopefully, to shop. Miss Enright, we've all seen your tapes, and there's no question that you have a most inviting way about you."

A chair was held out for her and she sat in it.

"We think you have exactly that right combination of professionalism, charm, intelligence, poise—not to mention your natural gift of gab, if you don't mind my saying so. The camera loves you, and you have a great look—sort of a cross between Miss America and the girl next door. . . . We think you'd be very appealing." Ted Higgins all but beamed.

"We all agree that you're a natural," Ken added.

"Well, I do love to shop. . . ." Zoey nodded modestly.

"We're hoping you can convince millions of TV viewers that they will love to shop with you." Higgins smiled. "And from the looks of those tapes, I'd say you could probably sell just about anything to anyone. Relax, Miss Enright, and let's talk about your future with the Home MarketPlace. . . ."

Chapter

3

It was almost midnight when Zoey unlocked the front door to the apartment she had rented in Lannings Corner to give her a place to hang her hat while she went through the three months of training classes required by the Home MarketPlace. Had anyone suggested that the sessions would be downright rigorous, she'd have thought them deranged. The sales sessions were only the tip of the iceberg; selling techniques were important, but there were, in addition, hours of memory enhancement training and mock broadcasting situations. Zoey could not remember the last time she'd been so tired, or worked so hard. Why had she so blithely assumed that this new job would be *easy?*

Flipping through the mail just quickly enough to see that nothing but bills had been delivered that day, she tossed the stack of envelopes onto the glass-topped table in the hallway and headed toward the kitchen, turning lights on as she passed through the living room and small dining area, stepping around the moving boxes, which held her clothes and a few books and personal items she had brought with her. Zoey hated living alone, had always dreaded that feeling of solitude encountered upon entering an empty house. Perhaps because her mother had spent so many weeks over so many years away from home on book tours, Zoey had never quite gotten used to the hush, the slight echo of her footsteps on the hardwood floors, the ticking of a clock, the hiss of the heater. Even running water in the kitchen sink sounded like a waterfall to her ears. She was never comfortable with the silence.

She drew a glass of tap water and sipped at it slowly while she listened to the messages on her answering machine. Georgia had called to say hi and to let her know that she had seen Zoey's photograph in an article about the network that had run in the Philadelphia newspaper ('You looked gorgeous! I was so proud, I showed everyone at the studio! And Mom said you rented an apartment! Way to go, Zoe!'), and Delia called to ask her to think about what furniture she might want from the attic and to let her know that a retailer from Wilmington was interested in buying the contents of the shop and if there was anything in particular that Zoey wished to keep she should let Delia know before the following Tuesday.

Zoey saved all the messages, knowing that in her exhausted state she'd have forgotten anything important by morning. Flicking off the lights, she traveled the short hallway to her bedroom.

Stripping off her blue suit and pitching it toward the nearest chair, Zoey unceremoniously dropped facedown on the bed, shoving aside Miss Felicity, Miss Maude, and her assorted young ones, and immediately fell into a dead sleep.

"It's perfectly darling, Zoey," Delia had exclaimed when she had seen Zoey's apartment for the first time. "And you have a lovely deck," she added, having pushed aside the dining room curtains.

"Zoey, I want to take you shopping for some furniture," Delia announced from the kitchen doorway.

"Mom, that's very generous of you, but you don't have to do that. This time I'm actually being *paid* to shop." Zoey grinned.

"I know I don't have to, but I want to," Delia insisted.

"Mom, I'm not even going to be here all that long. It's a month-to-month lease. As soon as things settle down, I plan on looking for a little house."

"Hmmm. A little house will be fun. But, Zoey, just a sofa. Let me just buy a sofa so I'll have a comfortable place to catnap when I visit. I saw just the right thing at Bloomingdale's in King of Prussia last weekend."

"Just a sofa" had turned into "and just this one cozy chair and just this great-looking table and just this fabulous lamp." As Delia had intended all along. As Zoey had suspected she might do.

"Mom, did it ever occur to you that you spoil us too much?" Zoey had asked on the way home from shopping.

"Not for a second." Delia dismissed the thought with a wave of her hand.

"You don't think you're overly generous?" Mildly amused at the denial, Zoey leaned back into the luxury of the plush leather seat of her mother's big Mercedes sedan.

"Not a bit." Delia shook her head adamantly. "If I can make it possible for my children to pursue their dreams without having to worry about whether or not they can pay the rent, whether or not they can afford to live in a safe place, whether or not they are comfortable, why shouldn't I do that? Not a one of you been spoiled by it. And besides, it makes me happy to be able to help you along."

"We are all grateful for your help, Mom, but—"

"Please." Delia held up a hand. "I know you are grateful, darling. And *I* am grateful that you have all grown into such lovely, wonderful young people. I'd be happy to know and spend time with any one of you under any circumstances. It's just the icing on the cake that the three of you happen to be my children. And

27

besides, now that you are safely settled in that darling little apartment, I know I'll have a place to leave Gracie when I leave for the Midwest next week."

"My home is Gracie's home." Zoey laughed as they pulled into her driveway, knowing how Delia's much-loved old lump of an orange tabby cat had hated the kennel the few times she had been left there.

"And speaking of which, let me give you my itinerary, in case you need to get in touch." Delia dug in her purse for the carefully typed list of dates and hotels and bookstores and phone numbers for each.

Zoey smiled as she got out of the car and closed the door, knowing her mother would call her—and Nick, and Georgia—every other day until she arrived home.

"So, are you looking forward to this book tour?" Zoey leaned into the open window of the driver's side door and watched her mother sort through several pieces of paper until she found what she was looking for.

"Ah. Here we are." Delia handed the typed copy of her itinerary to her daughter, who gave it a quick glance before folding it and sliding it into her jacket pocket. "You know that I always look forward to my book tours. Always. I never get tired of it, Zoey. It rejuvenates me. And I've made friends in so many cities and towns over the years. Every time I go back, so many of the same people are there, at the same bookstores where I first met them when I toured that first time." Delia smiled at her daughter. "Like old friends, so many of them, the booksellers and the readers. I know a lot of writers don't like to tour, but when you've done it for as long as I have, it becomes an important part of your life. I like to hear what people think of my books. You know, there's a lady in Peoria who has been writing to me for almost twenty years now, another in Idaho about the same. They matter to me, Zoey. I look forward to seeing them, even if it's only for a brief time, once a year. It's always important to me to go back."

"Someday you'll get tired of all that traveling around and then your fans will have to come to you." Zoey leaned through the window to give her mother a fond kiss on the cheek.

"Not while I breathe," Delia grinned. "You just never know what you'll find out there, Zoey. You just never know."

"Hopefully, a lot of book sales."

"From your lips to God's ears."

"As if you need divine intervention." Zoey laughed as Delia backed out of the parking spot.

"My darling, we all need a little of that." Delia blew her daughter a kiss. "And may you have all that you need for your debut next Saturday. I'll be watching from my hotel room in Kansas City. I made certain that they had cable TV when I made the reservation. And don't forget to pick up Gracie on Tuesday morning. You know how she hates to be alone for too long. . . ."

It had been a week of changes and firsts, Zoey was thinking as she blow-dried her hair, the fourth time since she had gotten out of bed at 5 A.M. Her first real show was scheduled from 4 to 7 P.M., and she was a nervous wreck. She fussed with her hair until it swirled around her head in loose, shiny black ringlets, then turned her attention to her nails. Again. She stared at the polish. Too red.

With a sigh she plunked herself down on the stool in front of the dressing table she had brought from her room in Delia's house and unscrewed the top of the nail polish remover. Saturating yet another little cotton square, she attacked the offending color and wiped it away. She studied the row of small jars of polish that marched in a precise line across one side of the dressing table. Was there any color she had not tried and rejected at least once? Maybe this peachy shade of pink . . .

Choosing her clothes had been even worse. She had gone through seven outfits before only the ticking away of the afternoon forced her to settle on a dress of nubby peach silk and cotton knit with rolled-up sleeves and a slightly dropped rounded neckline, perfect to show off the gold necklaces she was scheduled to present in her first hour. At 2:30 she packed her makeup into a plastic pouch and turned off the bedroom lights.

"Wish me luck, you guys," she said aloud to Maudie and Felicity, who sat on the window seat at one end of the room. "And for heaven's sake, would you try to show a little enthusiasm? Sheesh, guys, this is a really big day for me."

She paused and looked at herself in the mirror from across the room.

"This is what it's come to. I'm talking to stuffed animals. To dolls. Out loud. I hope it's not a bad sign."

On her way out, she stopped in the little sunroom off the kitchen to scratch old Gracie behind the ears. The cat had made an uneasy adjustment. Clearly, she preferred Delia's big rambling house to the smaller confines of Zoey's apartment.

"Look, Gracie, it could be worse," Zoey reminded her feline houseguest. "It could be a K-E-N-N-E-L. Got that? So stop your sulking and be a good little guard cat. And cross your paws that I don't make a complete and utter fool out of myself today."

And with that, Zoey Enright set off to make her debut on national television.

The entry into the building that housed the Home MarketPlace was strictly utilitarian, a few large green plants near the doorway and a few outdated magazines the only effort made toward accommodating visitors. A sofa of bright green vinyl—not particularly uncomfortable, not particularly cushy—sat against one short wall, the only seating available.

You would have thought that someone would have made a little more effort to put a happy face on the reception area, Zoey thought as she checked in with the security guard at the desk.

That Zoey would make her debut was the very least of what was taking place that day. The Home MarketPlace was kicking off its new look, its new format, introducing its new program hosts in three-hour segments. There was a bustle, a heady electricity that surged throughout the building. From the valet hired for the day to park the visitors' cars, to the caterers setting up for the cocktail party in the CEO's suite, to the producers and product coordinators and lighting engineers—all seemed to move a little more briskly, with greater purpose and determination, to perform their tasks with a little more certainty than they had in the trial runs that had dominated every day and night of the past two weeks. Now, it was showtime.

"How's it going?" Zoey asked one of the technicians she passed in the hall.

"All things considered, we're doing pretty well." He nodded, his graying ponytail flopping silently against the back of his neck. "Your buddy"—he nodded toward the monitor—"got off to a little bit of a rocky start, but she's doing real well now."

Zoey crept to the corner of the stage where her new friend, Cecelia—CeCe—Hollister, a former Miss Montana, sat on a dark green velvet chair and exhibited the pantaloons of a porcelain doll. Sensing Zoey's presence, she glanced over and winked, made a face, and continued her on-air conversation with the woman who had called in to buy the doll. CeCe looked as if she was doing just fine.

Nervous energy propelled Zoey down the corridor and into the lounge where she could sit and fix her hair and makeup without interruption.

"There you are," Cara, one of the young production assistants, huffed and puffed as she poked her head in the door. "I've been looking all over for you. You have about twenty minutes before you go on. Do you feel that you need to come in the back and take one last look at the products you're selling?"

"Yes." Zoey nodded. "I want to make sure I'm as prepared as I can be. And there's so much to remember. . . ."

She rose on shaking legs and packed her makeup bag into her tote.

"You'll be great, Zoey. Everyone said you were the

best in the trial runs all week." Cara held the door open for her and allowed Zoey to pass through. The hallway was crawling with activity, florists and caterers, people moving furniture and people pushing carts of fine stemware and ice sculptures, preparing for the arrival of the CEO within the hour.

"That was then and this is now," she muttered under her breath. And *now* is when it counts. There was, she sensed, more riding on her airtime than how many items she would sell. She needed to feel sure of herself, needed to know that she had, after all these years, found her place. She suspected that, by the end of the next three hours, she might know.

"Zoey Enright, you kicked butt!" CeCe met Zoey with a high five as she danced off the set at the end of her three-hour run.

"WE kicked butt!" Zoey laughed. "And we survived our maiden runs. And . . . if the gods have been very good to us, maybe, just maybe, someone actually bought something that we were selling. Come on, let's see if there are any sales numbers available."

The two women descended upon the producer, who happily showed off the sales for the past six hours.

"The best we've had all day," he told them. "You are both either very good and very likable, or you're both very lucky. I haven't decided which as yet."

"We are all of those things," CeCe told him matter-of-factly. "We are good and likable and lucky. And now we are going to celebrate our good fortunes and our lively personalities with a few very cold beers and some very hot peppers at that little roadside bar a few miles down this old country road."

"Not so fast, CeCe." Zoey grabbed her arm and steered her down the hallway. "The bartender down the road will have to make do without our company for a little longer. Right now it's French champagne and all manner of other good things right on down the hall here."

"Oh, right. The CEO's picnic or whatever." CeCe

made a pouty face and ran her fingers through her thick dark auburn hair. "I'm from Big Sky country, Zoey, the good old American West. At the end of my workday, I want a cold beer and maybe, if it's a big night, a bowl of cashews."

"Later," Zoey promised, and flashed a smile at the guard stationed at the doorway to check IDs, making sure that no outsiders crashed the party.

Zoey's stomach reminded her that she had eaten next to nothing all day, her nerves having gotten the best of her early on. She made a plate of strawberries, melon, and icy cold shrimp. Stopping at the bar for a glass of sparkling water, she looked for a quiet corner in which to eat and collect her thoughts. Everyone in the room seemed to have watched her show, and had congratulated her on a job well done.

I did okay, she told herself as she settled near a window that had a ledge just wide enough for her glass. *Better than okay. I was good. And I loved it. I loved it. Once the camera stated to run, I was fine. It was great. It was the best time I ever had. It was . . . it was like dancing on my toes in a white dress, on a big stage with beautiful music swirling around me. Like pulling a story from my mind and writing a book about people who never existed and making them sound real. Like looking through a microscope and watching all of the life forms that share the space of one tiny drop of pond water.*

Zoey had landed, with both feet, and had made an enormous splash, exactly as Delia had predicted she would.

Chapter

4

Bennett Pierce set a steady pace as he headed for his destination. While in reality, he was jogging toward London's St. James Park, in his mind, he was slipping his race car onto the track and into its designated starting position, preparing for the line-up lap, the first step of a race. The cars would make one lap around the circuit, then line up, ready to begin. The line-up was the last chance for each driver to make sure that every component of his car was ready and working properly.

Oblivious of the traffic, still light this early hour of the morning, Ben crossed the street and followed the walkway that led down toward the pond, where the black swans had yet to waken to the day. Past sleeping forms on the benches, his feet kept up the rhythm, allowing his mind to keep him in the race. After the line-up would come the formation lap, which the race director would begin with a green flag, giving the drivers one full time around the circuit, at speed, to bring the tires, the water, the brakes, up to the right temperature for the race. This was also the drivers' opportunity to stake their ground, to try to psyche out the competition, maybe by getting

34

right up behind another entrant and not hitting the brakes until his gear box was practically in your face. Chances are that the spooked driver would be starting the race with his eyes on his rearview mirror instead of the cars in front of him. Which was just a means of letting everyone know that you were there to win. From that point on, it was a matter of waiting for the green light on the five-second board to signal the start of the race.

Every seasoned driver knew that the two most dangerous moments of a race were the start and the approach to the first corner. At the start of the race, the cars are too close together, with all the drivers trying to elbow their way as near to the head of the pack as possible, each of them well aware that the only driver who will be able to set up that first bend the way he wants to is the driver who is first into it. The cars behind him will have to brake earlier than they might like because of the bottleneck that will form at that first bend, making the driver who is last in line the first to brake and, being first, braking the longest amount of time. The first driver into the turn will be able to brake at the last second, saving him time that he will undoubtedly need later on if he is to have any chance of winning the race.

In two weeks, Ben would be driving in the Belgian Grand Prix at Spa-Francorchamps, considered by many to be the premier circuit of Grand Prix racing. As he ran, Ben tried to recall every inch of the 4.350 miles of track, every twist and turn his car would have to negotiate, planning every move he would make along the way. Spa climbed and fell through the picturesque Ardennes forest, with the legendary hairpin turn, La Source, the first bend on the circuit, leading uphill to the exhilarating Eau Rouge, one of the best-known curves in racing history. In his mind's eye, Ben took Eau Rouge steadily, then onto the straightaway to Les Combes, the bend at the top of a hill, which led into Malmedy, the next curve. From one kink and curve to the next, Ben Pierce mentally accelerated and braked, downshifting through the gears, calculating just the right gear ratio for each of the bends. With every step he took, he carried on a silent debate with himself on how best to complete each of the forty-four laps in the manner that would cost him the least amount of time.

He tried to avoid looking back on his last race, at Hockenheim, Germany, the previous month, where Gerhard Berger had won on a hot, dry track, and where another driver had clung to too much of the road coming out of a corner and wiped out, taking Ben and a third car with him. Fortunately, no one had been hurt beyond minor bumps, but it had been a terrible disappointment to Ben, who had made the best start of his career before he'd been blown off the circuit. Those things happened, he knew, and he knew that if he was to make a similarly good start at Spa, he would have to take the lessons he'd learned at Hockenheim with him, while leaving all the negative emotions behind. Part of the intense training was mental as much as physical, and Ben wasn't about to let the bad luck of his last race influence his performance in the next.

Glancing at his watch, he turned back toward his flat, where he would pack his weights into the back of his car and head out to join his old friend Tony Chapman for a swim at Tony's country estate, Stowe Manor. Ben would strap the weights onto his ankles, and swim for a full thirty minutes. Because during a race the heart will operate at 160 to 170 beats per minute, a smart driver will spend much of his spare time exercising to increase the heart's capacity and to lower the heartbeat at rest. Ben had established a rigorous routine two years ago, when it first appeared that his goal of driving in a Grand Prix would become a reality, and he had never missed a day, in season or off. Sometimes the exercise changed with circumstances. In the winter, cross-country skiing might take the place of running, weight-lifting might replace swimming, but always, there would be something with which he could challenge himself physically and mentally for several hours each day. His life could very well depend on his being prepared for the demands of the job, sitting in a narrow cockpit, essentially unable to change position for the length of the race, while maneuvering at high rates of speed and keeping his wits about him. The upcoming race would run for forty-four laps, maybe an hour and a half. Ben was not likely to forgo what he felt was an essential part of driving, the daily preparation that could make the difference between reaching his dream and losing it.

He tried to drive at a relatively slow speed on his way to Tony's, taking his time and allowing himself to relax. At one point he pulled over to the shoulder and hunted in his black nylon bag for the bottle of water he'd picked up when he stopped for gas before leaving the city. It was a typical English summer day, the earliest clouds of the morning having given way to a soft sunshine that spread across the rolling fields like a light blanket. Ben loved the smell of England, the rich, woodsy scent of the farm he'd just passed as well as the thick scent of the roses that formed the hedge just over the next rise in the road. Both reminded him of another country home, of another garden where roses had perfumed the air. *Long ago and far away,* he told himself as he started the engine and resumed his drive, jerking the car onto the road with more intensity than he'd intended, leaving behind the roses and the memories they'd stirred up.

* * *

"How many more laps?" Tony Chapman stood at the side of the pool, looking infinitely amused. During his own brief racing career, he had never trained nearly as hard as Ben did. Which may be one of the reasons why Ben had lasted into a third season, when Tony's career had ended with the fifth race of his second season. A nasty crash had left Tony glad to be alive and more than willing to walk away while he still could. He'd find another way to make his mark in the sport he loved.

"Four," Ben said as he passed by. Those two-pound weights he'd fitted onto his ankles earlier now seemed to weigh two tons. By the time he had finished his thirty minutes, he was relieved to take the weighted cuffs off.

Tony tossed him a towel and Ben gratefully wrapped it around him. It had grown cloudy and looked likely to rain before too much more of the day had passed.

"Mrs. Bridges tells me that Pamela called while you were swimming, but thought it best not to interrupt you," Tony said as he lowered his lean frame onto a lounge.

"Mrs. Bridges is a wise woman," Ben nodded as he sat on the edge of a nearby chair. Seeing the elderly woman about to enter the enclosed pool area, he raised his voice and said, "If I were the marrying kind, I'd have asked for Mrs. Bridges' hand years ago."

The housekeeper eyed him with a combination of practiced disdain and pleasure.

"I heard that, young man, as you'd intended. But you still have to dress properly if you want tea. I'll not be serving out here to either of you hooligans." She passed a portable telephone to Tony and said, "It's your sister."

Ben leaned back in his chair while Tony chatted with Sibyl, opening his eyes only when he felt the merest hint of sunshine on his face. The sun had peeked out briefly before sliding back behind the mounting clouds. Ben was glad to have gotten his swim in before the rain started. He hated a break in his routine.

"Sibyl says to warn you that Nicole Williams is in London and is planning to look you up," Tony told him as he turned off the phone and placed it on a nearby table.

"Remind me to thank Sibyl for the warning," Ben said without bothering to open his eyes.

"Yes, well, but all work and no play, Ben . . ."

"I had a date last weekend," Ben reminded him, "so don't start."

"Since when have you considered dinner with the formidable Cleo Abercrombie a date? Last I heard she was 'just a friend.'"

"She still is a friend."

"No offense, mate, but there's more to life than measuring the temperature of your engine and having an occasional night out with Cleo."

"There's no one else I'd rather spend time with right now. Cleo is smart, and she's interesting."

"For a country barrister," Tony muttered under his breath.

Ben laughed. "She's a nice woman, Tony."

"Oh, nice she is. You're forgetting that she's my cousin. Nice, however, isn't likely to inspire much in the way of passion."

Ben shook his head. "No time for that right now."

"There's always time for romance, Ben. That's what's wrong with you, you know. Not enough romance in your life. Never has been, if you ask me."

"Well, I didn't ask you." Ben sat up as Mrs. Bridges appeared with a tray of small sandwiches and a pitcher of iced tea.

"I thought we weren't getting served out here," Tony reminded her.

"I'm off to the market"—she straightened out the little black hat that perched above her tightly permed gray curls—"and I don't want the two of you crashing about in my kitchen while I'm gone. I thought perhaps you'd like a light lunch. Bring the tray in with you when you're finished. And you'll still have to dress for tea."

"Yes, ma'am," Tony said solemnly.

"Be sure you do," she told them. "And I'm buying chops, so I expect you both to be here for dinner."

"Yes, Mrs. Bridges," the two men sing-songed, earning a dirty look from the housekeeper as she closed the gate behind her.

"I was serious," Ben said. "I would marry a woman just like Mrs. Bridges. No loose ends to deal with. Things would always run smoothly."

"Ah, but no passion, Ben. No dancing in the moonlight."

"But dinner would always be on time. And these days, I don't have much time for dancing."

"More's the pity. There should always be time. Make time."

"I just haven't met anyone who . . ." Ben groped for words.

"Lit the spark," Tony provided him with a few.

"That's pretty close." Ben nodded.

"What are you looking for in a woman?"

"Right now, I'm not really looking for one. Right now, I'm looking for my first Grand Prix win, something I've waited years for."

"That's all that matters to you." It wasn't a question.

"Right now, yes. That's my goal."

"That's what I used to think, until Monte Carlo last year."

"Monte Carlo is one of the toughest circuits, especially in the rain," Ben said. "Running through the streets of the city, all those nasty little curves and turns." He shook his head. "You weren't the only one who has had bad runs in that race."

"That may be so, but it made me realize several very important truths, Ben." Tony lifted a glass of iced tea and handed it to his friend, then took the second and sipped at it. "Not the least of which was that as much as I love the sport, I never want to feel that particular brand of fear again. You can call me a coward if you like, but one close call like that was enough for one lifetime."

"Tony, I'd never call you a coward. I don't know how I'd feel if I had an accident like that . . . flipping the car over and then barely escaping as it burst into flames." Ben shook his head. "I don't know that I wouldn't hang up my helmet too, after something like that."

"Well, not wishing you similar bad luck, I don't want you to forget that Chapman-Pierce Motors is well on its way to becoming a reality." Tony broke into a smile. "I've found an old factory that might convert nicely into making our engines."

"Once we have an engine to produce," Ben reminded him.

"I'm working on it, mate. I recently got the name of an

engineer who used to be with Ferrari, who we might be able to talk into coming out of retirement. He's in Italy right now on an extended holiday, but as soon as he gets back, I'll be speaking with him. I think we have the right idea, if not the technical know-how to produce the sort of engine we want."

"Well, it is something to look forward to, having our own company." Ben nodded. "We've only been talking about it for the last six or seven years."

"And as soon as you've retired—not to jinx you with an early retirement, of course—we'll be on our way." Tony raised his glass to Ben's and said, "Here's to Chapman-Pierce. In its time . . ."

Ben tilted his glass in Tony's direction, hoping that *the time* for Chapman-Pierce remained a long way off. After all, there were still so many races to be run, and Ben was looking forward to being in the starting line for his share of them.

Later, after dinner in one of the small family dining areas of the palatial family home of the Earl of Stowe, Ben had taken his leave while the sun was still a ripple in the sky. Tony had a party to attend, and in spite of his encouragement that Ben join him, Ben was not in a party frame of mind. He drove through the fragrant dusk, back to the city and the brownstone where he leased a second-floor flat. After garaging his car, he took the steps two at a time, hoping that the delivery he anticipated would be waiting for him. Upon seeing the package wrapped in brown paper and propped against his apartment door, he broke into a grin. Whistling, he flipped the package from his right hand to his left while he fished his keys out of his pocket and opened the door.

This was the moment he hated, those first steps into the painfully empty apartment. Before moving to London, he'd lived in an out-of-the-way village, in a rented cottage he had shared with one very large dark brown dog he'd rescued from a busy city street on a rainy Sunday night five years before. He and Goliath had been the best of buddies. Over the years, they had shared many an early morning run down a peaceful country road, and many a warm fire on chilly nights in the cottage, which had been built long before the idea of insulation had caught on. Last year, a speeding van had caught Goliath broadside as he had tried to cross the road to reach his master. Ben's eyes still filled with tears every time he thought about his beloved mastiff, gasping for his last breath in Ben's arms. Ben had buried the dog in a nearby field and before two weeks had passed, packed his things and moved to the city. It had been just one more loss in a long series of losses that had defined Ben's life, one more place he'd left because it had hurt too much to stay.

He turned on the light with a casual flick of his wrist, and dropped the nylon bag that held his weights next to the door as he closed it, his attention focused on the package, which he placed on the coffee table at the same time he dropped onto the sofa. He reached behind him to turn on the floor lamp, then split the tape holding the brown paper together and let his prize fall onto his lap.

Crowning Glories, by Delia Enright.

Grateful that he'd made no social plans for the evening, Ben settled in and turned the book over, gently touching one finger to the photograph of the author on the back cover. It was a different photo from the one that had appeared on her last book, and he studied it for changes. Delia's eyes were still that deadly shade of sapphire blue he'd remembered, and still held the same spark. Her grin still saucy and her heart, he knew, was still the very purest gold. Though still the same shade of cool champagne, her hair appeared just a wee bit shorter. Other than that, as far as he was concerned, Delia hadn't changed a bit over the years.

In Ben's eyes, she never did.

Chapter

5

The early October sun blazed on a field of corn stalks that stood, pale and brittle, against a backdrop of bright blue sky. Zoey glanced at the clock on the dashboard as her little red car approached a curve in the road that outlined the field in an uneven black line of asphalt. The corn had long been harvested, but the crows were still picking through the remnants of the ears that hadn't made it to market. It was almost two, and the realtor's office was still another ten minutes away, out on Route 30. Zoey would be late for her appointment, but she knew that Peg Morris, the realtor, would wait for her. Peg had been assisting Zoey in her quest for a little house for the past two months, since Zoey had signed the contract that ensured her employment with the HMP for the next twenty-four months.

This house search was, Zoey acknowledged, a very big step for her. She saw it as nothing less than an act of self-affirmation. It spoke of her commitment to her job, to herself, to a future of her own making. It said that she could buy her own home with her own earnings, that she expected to be with the HMP for a long time to come. The realization of the enormity of the step she was taking, without having consulted either of her siblings or her mother, made her grin every time she thought about it. She had wanted to surprise everyone. Surely they would be as proud of her as she was of herself.

Zoey pulled into the parking lot of the little brick house that served as the office of one of Lancaster County's major real estate brokers. Inside, Peg would be waiting for her with a stack of color photos, perhaps a video or two of available properties. Zoey just hoped that there would be a few that were not center hall colonials with four bedrooms and two and a half baths in pricey developments that had years to go before they took on the appearance of a real neighborhood.

"I'm sorry I'm late," Zoey apologized as she slid her tweed jacket off her shoulders and sat in the chair next to the realtor's desk. "I should have left earlier."

"It's not a problem." The young woman smiled. "I was just organizing a few photographs of some new listings to see what you thought."

The realtor passed an inch-high stack of color photos across the desk to Zoey, who flipped through them quickly.

"No . . . no . . . no . . ." Numbers one through five were soundly rejected. "I think I'd like something with a little more *character.*"

"What about this one?" Peg handed her a photograph of a contemporary home perched high on a hill, from which an infinite series of decks led downward to what would have been the backyard had it been more accessible. "Gorgeous views."

"Ummm, not my style." Zoey handed the photo back. "It just isn't me."

"This one?"

"Not exactly . . ."

"How about this? It's a lovely little cottage, authentic Revolutionary War era."

"Is this one of those places where the ceilings are really low?"

Peg nodded. "The original section was built in seventeen thirty-two."

"That's out, then. My brother would have to crawl in."

"Well, then, would you like to look at this one?"

Zoey narrowed her eyes and inspected the photo. "Where are the trees?"

"There are trees." Peg leaned over and pointed to wispy shadows on the picture.

"What kind of tree is that?"

"I'm not sure," Peg, told her, "but this developer is known for his landscaping, so I'm sure it's a good one."

Zoey shook her head.

"I've decided that I definitely do not want a development house. I want . . ." Zoey placed the pile of photographs on the edge of the desk and frowned. "I don't know exactly what I want, but I'll know it when I see it."

"Well, how 'bout I take you out for a drive and we'll see what's out there that might catch your fancy?"

"I think maybe I should just wander about on my own. That way I won't feel guilty for taking your time if I don't see anything I like." Zoey checked her watch again. There was a meeting for all of the show hosts at 4 P.M. If she left now she'd have time to meander through the back roads while on her way back to the HMP headquarters. "I promise I'll call if I see anything that I think looks promising."

"Well, let me just suggest a few places." With a blue felt-tip marker, the woman drew a little map for Zoey on a sheet of letterhead. "There are a few small towns out this way." She made an arrow following a road to the right of the highway. "Of course, many of them are little more than crossroads. . . ."

"Crossroads could be fun," Zoey smiled. "I'll call you. And thanks for the map."

Once back in her little red sports car, Zoey followed the road back out to Route 30, drove south a little, then made the indicated right turn. Five or six miles down the road, she came to a crossroads, just as Peg had said. She rode the brake, driving slowly through the little town until she passed a sign that read, "You are leaving East Crawford." Three more miles down the two-lane road she passed another sign: WELCOME TO BRADY'S MILL.

Zoey slowed to the posted twenty-five-mile-an-hour speed limit and coasted down the wide main street. Gracious homes—mostly authentic-looking colonials—were set close to the road. A general store, a post office, a feed and farm equipment repair shop, and one gas station pretty much completed the center of town. A sign for the library—shaped like an open book—hung from the front porch of a small Queen Anne–style house. Set back off the road was a small white-spired church, architecturally plain except for its handsome stained glass window. Neatly tended rows of white marble headstones, glistening in the sun, marched behind the church in precise and neatly tended rows. Across the road weeping willows dipped lacy arms into a wide lake. Zoey eased her car to the shoulder and leaned across her steering wheel to watch two young boys in a small rowboat as they tossed fishing lines into the dark blue water. Irresistibly drawn, she turned off the car, got out, and walked to the edge of the lake.

On the roadside of the lake, a stone wall had been built, and Zoey found it to be just the right height for leaning on. Below the wall, the last few water lilies of the season floated and dragonflies chased lunch just above the surface of the water. A few brown ducks floated in the shade of some orange-leafed maples that grew near the bank, and along the shore, three young women walked frisky toddlers, holding onto their hands lest they venture too close to the water. Up a slight ridge to the right, several houses—newer than those nearer to the center of town—stood in the afternoon sun, their back-yards sloping slightly to the lake.

A slight shuffling sound behind her alerted her to company. She looked up and smiled at the old man in the worn straw hat and denim jacket who stopped and took a place next to her along the wall. He placed his arms across the broad top stones and leaned slightly forward and said, "Nice day, eh?"

The voice was like gravel, rough and gritty.

"Beautiful."

"Yup. Nothing like an early autumn day."

Several geese made a noisy arrival, feet first, startling the toddlers on the grassy slope with their loud honking.

"Noisy buggers, damned geese. Always complaining. Too many of them, nowadays. No predators, ya know. Oh, a hawk or a heron will get a few of the young ones, cuts the population a bit, but not so's you can tell the difference." He cleared his throat and took his hat off to wave it slightly in the crisp air. He ran a hand through thinning white hair before replacing the hat. All the time he spoke, his eyes never left the two boys in the rowboat.

"Isn't there a hunting season or something?" Zoey asked.

"There's sport hunting, but shooting those things"— he pointed a slightly gnarled index finger toward the birds on the bank—"tame as they are, would be criminal. Walk right up to ya. There's no sport in that."

"No, I would guess not." Zoey took a deep breath, deep enough to catch the scent of algae and slightly stagnant water. She leaned over the stone wall and saw that below the bridge, the lake narrowed somewhat to run into a culvert that disappeared under the road. Here and there, remnants of the summer's crop of cattails leaned toward the lake, their long fringed arms drooping like piano shawls into the still water.

"You wouldn't be Addie Kilmartin's granddaughter, now, would you?" the old man asked, still not looking at her.

"No."

"Didn't think so."

They watched as the small boat with its young fishermen floated toward them. One of the boys held up the small fish he had just reeled in. The old man waved to the boy to acknowledge the catch, then called to him, "Throw 'im back, James. He's too small."

The boy carefully removed the hook from the delicate mouth of the fish.

"What kind of fish do you suppose that was?" Zoey watched the boy as he gently slid the fish back into the lake.

"Trout."

"Hey, Gramps," James shouted up to them, "what do you think of this one?"

The boy held up another fish, noticeably larger than the one he had a minute earlier set free.

"Looks like dinner to me, son," the old man chuckled. "I'll be over to watch you boys clean them in another hour or so. Call your mother when you get home and tell her that we're doing the cooking tonight."

"Will do, Gramps." The older boy grabbed an oar and headed back across the lake.

From somewhere a church bell chimed three bells.

Zoey checked her watch. Three o'clock. She'd better get moving, or she'd be late for her meeting. Reluctantly she straightened up and said, "Thanks for sharing the view with me."

"My pleasure." The old man turned to look at Zoey for the first time. "Just passing through?"

"Just passing through." She nodded.

"Pass through again some time."

"I just might do that," Zoey called over her shoulder as she got into her car and started the engine, pausing for just a second to take one last look at the lake.

It really is a pretty little town, she thought as she followed the main street to the next crossroads, where one sign announced the end of the village limits and yet another the upcoming Brady's Mill Pumpkin Festival. She made a left turn and headed back to the highway. If she hurried she would just make her meeting.

* * *

On the following Sunday morning, Zoey hung over the railing of her small deck and watched a flock of Canadian geese fly overhead in a slightly ragged V and thought back to the geese on the lake at Brady's Mill. Sipping at the day's first cup of coffee, she inhaled deeply of the morning air, fragrant with the scent of clematis and sweetpea from a neighbor's deck, and wondered how she would spend this beautiful autumn day. A screen door slammed a few doors down, and she glanced over to see a young girl struggle to set a large orange pumpkin down on the deck steps without dropping it. Zoey glanced at the date on her watch. It would be Halloween in another three weeks. Maybe she would get a pumpkin at the local market and paint a clever face on it.

She thought of other Halloweens, long past, when her mother would take all four kids—Zoey, Georgia, Nick, and Ben Pierce—to the local farmers' market, where each of them would pick out their own personal Halloween pumpkins. She and Georgia would select small, perfectly rounded pumpkins upon which they would carefully draw cute and friendly little features on chubby orange-pumpkin faces. Nick and Ben, on the other hand, would seek out the biggest, most unperfect specimens, which they would later carve into grotesque masks of twisting scowls and ragged teeth that would glow demonically when lit candles were placed inside. Zoey laughed out loud at the recollection of the sight of the two ugly pumpkins, which the boys would set at the end of the driveway to ward off evil spirits and erstwhile trick-or-treaters.

The little girl disappeared into the apartment, returning minutes later dragging her father by both hands. Time to carve the pumpkin. The father gestured to his daughter, who spread a layer of newspapers across the top of the table. The prep work completed, the pumpkin was set atop the table and the serious debate of how best to carve began in earnest.

I want a pumpkin too, Zoey thought as she swished her coffee around in the bottom of the cup. Where had she seen something about pumpkins, about a pumpkin day or pumpkin fest?

Brady's Mill, she recalled. *Their pumpkin-something is today.*

What better place to find a perfect pumpkin?

Zoey finished her coffee in two gulps, and took the stairs to her bedroom two at a time. She slid into Sunday country clothes of slightly baggy jeans and a nubby crewneck sweater of palest gold, and bounced back down the steps as quickly as she had climbed them. Locking the front door behind her, she set out for Brady's Mill.

Traffic leading into the village was much heavier than it had been during the previous week. A middle-aged man in a black sweatshirt with a large orange pumpkin appliquéd on its front instructed Zoey to follow a short line of cars as they filed into a cornfield, now cleared to serve as a parking lot. She pulled into a makeshift parking spot in front of a row of tall evergreens, then fell in line behind a crowd of young pumpkin seekers who all seemed to know exactly where they were going. On the other side of the evergreens, a rambling stone farmhouse edged its way to the road. Behind it stood a barn, and next to the barn a windmill. In the open farmyard, large wooden cribs offered pumpkins of every size and shape, and long tables were laden with baked goods and produce. Zoey poked through the pumpkins until she found several that she liked, then tried to balance them while rummaging in her purse for her wallet.

"You planning on walking into town for a while?" a woman asked from the other side of a table upon which tidy rows of jars of relishes and butters—pumpkin, apple, and peach—were displayed, their labels neatly printed by hand.

Zoey hesitated momentarily. "What's in town?"

"Oh, the usual country fair stuff. Local crafts and food, games for the children."

"Sure." Zoey nodded. "It sounds interesting."

"Well, then, I'd be happy to mark these *paid* for you and set them aside so's you don't have to cart them around with you. You can just pick them up here on your way out."

"Thank you, I'd appreciate that." Zoey placed the pumpkins in a basket and passed them back to the woman, who instructed her to write her name on a slip of paper, which she stuck between two of the pumpkins before placing the basket on the ground along with other baskets similarly left under the table. She tallied up the cost of pumpkins, and Zoey handed her several bills to pay for them.

Zoey wandered along, glancing at the tables of baked goods, most of which had pumpkin or apple on the small white label stuck to the clear wrapping that covered all the tempting offerings. Pumpkin bread. Apple strudel. Pumpkin muffins. Apple turnovers. Pies. Cookies. Cakes. Zoey strolled along to the last table, where she bought a tall paper cup filled with icy cold apple cider, then followed the crowd meandering toward the center of town. The road was blocked off to traffic at either end, and shoppers and sightseers alike enjoyed the atmosphere of an old-fashioned street fair. A man on stilts passed by, followed by a woman on a unicycle. At a table under an enormous oak, a young woman painted tiny flowers on the chubby cheeks of a little girl. Someone was selling balloons in the shape of pumpkins, and farther down the street, someone else offered sweatshirts emblazoned with the same cheery jack-o-lanterns that smiled from the shirts of the festival volunteers. Makeshift stands along one side of the street sold water ice, Pennsylvania Dutch funnel cake, and cotton candy.

Sipping at her cider, Zoey walked the street with the crowd until she found herself back on the bridge overlooking the lake. She set her cup on top of the wall, and leaned her arms against the stone, just as she had done once before, and warmed by the afternoon sun, slid her sunglasses onto her face, and watched the activities on the lake below. Twenty or so rowboats, all manned by children who looked to be no more than ten or twelve, lined up along one side of the lake. Someone in a slightly larger boat popped a balloon, and the race toward the opposite shore began. Parents and friends shouted encouragement from both sides of the lake as the small boats made their way—some unevenly, some with practiced skill—toward the finish line. A whoop went up when a blue boat, manned by two young girls, slid past their nearest competitors for the win.

"So, then, if you're not Addie Kilmartin's granddaughter, it must be the lake that brought you back," a voice of grit and gravel said from behind her.

Zoey turned to see the old man in his straw hat who had sidled up to her. She smiled with genuine pleasure, tickled to be recognized by someone in this crowd where everyone else seemed to know each other.

"Actually, it was the pumpkins, but yes, I like the lake." She paused, then asked, "Who's Addie Kilmartin?"

"Was my next door neighbor." He took the place next to her, and leaning his arms on the top of the wall, added, "Died this past spring. Her granddaughter was supposed to come along this summer and tend to selling the house, but hasn't managed to get around to it. Wish she'd get on with it. I'm gettin' too old to keep mowing both her grass and mine."

"Hey, Gramps, did you see us?"

The young boy who had manned the fishing boat earlier in the week called from the boat, which bobbed up and down, so many boats making the lake a bit choppy.

"I certainly did. Could have won if you hadn't gotten so cocky there at the end and let your cousin Jackie sail right on past you."

The boy scowled as he rowed toward the shore.

"We're going to get lunch now. Besides, all the rowboats have to get off the lake now for the paddleboats," the boy called over his shoulder.

"Paddleboats?" Zoey asked. "I love paddleboats! Can you rent them here?"

"Yes, but right now, renting's for the race only. Course it's a two-person boat . . ."

She frowned.

". . . but in my day, I could paddle with the best of them. Say, I don't suppose you'd be up for a race this afternoon?"

"With you?" She grinned and nodded eagerly. "I'd love to be in a paddleboat race with you. . . . What did you say your name was?"

"Littlefield. Wallace T. Littlefield. Most people know me as Wally, or just plain Doc."

"You're a doctor?" She fell in step with him as he headed toward the slope leading down to the lake.

"Retired." He grabbed her elbow gallantly as the slope became slightly steeper. "And who might you be?"

"Zoey Enright." She paused and extended a hand, which he took with a grin.

"Zoey, eh? Used to have a maiden aunt named Zoey. Never did marry up, that one. Too independent. Thought she could do everything for herself." He looked at her slyly from the corner of his eye. "Are you one of those too independent women who wants to do everything for herself, Zoey Enright?"

"I'm working on it." She smiled, thinking of the plans she had made so recently for her future. "I'm definitely working on it. Now, do you prefer Wally or Doc?"

"Either one will do."

"I like Wally," Zoey told him. "You look like a Wally to me."

He motioned Zoey toward the end of a small dock where several two-seater paddleboats were secured.

"Sign me up, Henry." He handed over a ten-dollar bill to a burly flannel-shirted fellow who seemed to be in charge.

"Doc, you're not planning on racing one of these things. . . ."

"Plannin' on racing, plannin' on winning."

Burly Flannel Shirt opened his mouth to reply, then took a step back when Zoey, eyes twinkling with mischief, slipped her arm through Wally's. "Ready, Wally?"

"You betcha." Wally winked and with a frisky sidestep led Zoey to their boat, leaving his cronies behind to gape.

Once in the paddleboat, the old man burst out laughing, slapping Zoey on the back, saying, "Did you see the look on that old coot's face? Why, Zoey, he's still gasping for air. You're all right, Zoey Enright. Yessir, you're all right in my book."

"You'll be the talk of the town now, Wally." She laughed and slid her feet onto the wide pedals.

"Yup. Have every widow lady and old maid for miles around sending me pies and dinner invites." Wally laughed again, then pointed to the pedals and told her, "Now, then, let's get down to business. You know your feet are going to get wet."

"Not a problem," she assured him. "This will be fun."

"I take it you have done this before?"

"It's been a while," she admitted, "but last summer I rowed my brother's rowboat a couple of times."

"Well, this will require more leg muscle than arm or back."

"Not a problem," she told him. "I've always been a runner. I've got thighs like steel bands."

"Well, then, let's give it the best that we've got."

Another boat lined up next to them. "Say there, Doc, I heard that cocky little boast of yours back there on the dock."

"Facts are facts, Clifford. I call 'em as I see 'em. And what I see right now is me and my lady friend beating the pants off the nearest competitor."

"Well, now, Doc, you know, Betty and I have won this race five years running."

"Looks like the reign is over, Clifford."

"Wouldn't want to put a little money where that big mouth of yours is, would you?"

"I might. What did you have in mind, Cliff?"

Cliff rubbed his chin thoughtfully. "Well, the Youth Council is looking to build a new ball field."

"I've heard that." Wally nodded. "I've been thinking

about donating a few acres that I own on the other side of my woods."

"And I have a few acres back of our place facing Miller's Pond Park that I've been thinking might serve the purpose. Maybe the loser here gets to donate the ground for that new field."

"Hmmm." Wally appeared to think this over, then looked at Zoey. "Steel bands, you say?"

"Absolutely," she assured him.

"You up to a challenge?"

"You betcha."

"Well, then"—he turned back to Cliff—"my partner here says we can take you without breaking a sweat."

Wally turned the steering wheel slightly to the left and headed toward the starting line. "Cliff, I'm guessing that the next time we stand on that back parcel of land of yours, someone will be shouting, 'Play ball.'"

Zoey giggled as Dr. Wallace T. Littlefield cordially tipped his hat and paddled toward the starting line. It was clear that he—as well as Cliff and his wife—would enjoy the race, regardless of the outcome.

The starting gun was the puncturing of a large tightly filled blue balloon.

"Keep in sync with me, now, Zoey." Wally pointed to her feet. "Here we go, with the right foot. . . ."

Paddling like frenzied ducks, Wally and Zoey's boat shot out of the line like a bullet, headed for the red balloons strung across the water on the opposite side of the lake.

"I'm right on your tail, you old coot!" Cliff yelled from six feet behind them.

"You'll never catch us, Clifford, there's too much young blood in this boat."

Wally was still laughing as they crossed the finish line five feet ahead of their closest rival, and when he helped Zoey out of the boat amid whistles and cries of "Ringer! Ringer!"

The mayor stepped up to present the blue ribbon,

saying, "Let's hear it for Doc Littlefield and his great-great-granddaughter."

"Very amusing"—Wally grinned—"but this here's my date for the fete, Miss Zoey Enright."

Wally gallantly handed the winners' ribbon to Zoey, who on impulse leaned over and kissed him on the cheek to a round of catcalls and more whistles.

"Listen here, honey, you get the mind for a younger fella, you give me a call." The mayor, who appeared to be well into his sixties, patted Zoey on the back as she followed Wally down the rickety pier to the edge of the lake.

"You're a good sport, missy." He squeezed her arm. "I'd like to buy you some lunch."

"You're on, Doc."

"I hear the church"—he nodded his head to the right—"is serving their famed ham supper all day."

"You just lead the way."

They crossed the street and walked toward the white church Zoey had passed that first day she had driven through town. Up the long walk they ambled, toward a grove of trees under which long tables sporting red and white checked cloths spread out in clean straight lines. They were directed to their table by an ample lady with light blue hair and an apron that matched the tablecloths.

"So, then, Miss Zoey Enright . . ." Wally leaned back in his seat to look at her, as if seeing her for the first time. "What brought you back to Brady's Mill?"

"I wanted a pumpkin."

"No shortage of those around here," he agreed. "Did you find one?"

"Several," she told him. "I left them back at the farm where they're selling them . . . back that way." She pointed back down past the lake.

"Brady's Farm." He nodded knowingly.

"And then I just followed the crowd. Everyone looked like they were having fun, so I wanted to tag along, I guess, and see what else was going on."

"Now, if I were the nosy sort—which I'm not—I'd probably be itchin' to ask why a girl as young and pretty as you should be so lonely. But of course, I'd never—"

"Lonely? Me?" Zoey interrupted, pointing a perfectly manicured index finger into her chest. "I'm not lonely. I have a very busy life. I have a loving family . . . lots of friends. What makes you think I'm lonely?"

"Might have something to do with the fact that you've spent the last, oh, what, two hours or so of a gorgeous Sunday afternoon in a strange town, in the company of an old man and a number of other people you don't know."

Zoey pondered a retort as another checked-apron lady set a small Styrofoam bowl of salad before her. She avoided Wally's eyes while she dribbled pale orange French dressing—the only choice on the table—on the fresh greens, red onion, and halved cherry tomatoes.

"I wanted a pumpkin," she repeated.

"Could have grabbed one and been gone ninety minutes ago, by my calculations."

"It looked like a neat little town," she told him. "The kind of town I always wanted to live in. I felt it when I drove through the other day. Then this morning, when I was thinking about pumpkins, I remembered the pumpkin party—"

"Fest. Pumpkin Fest," he corrected her pointedly.

"Right. Pumpkin Fest," she repeated, a smile curling the corners of her mouth. "Now, is this an annual event?"

"Every year since nineteen thirty-nine," he told her.

"No way." She put her fork down.

"Yup. Next year will mark our sixtieth year."

"That's remarkable."

He shrugged. "Don't know 'bout that. But yup, fifty-nine years' worth of pumpkins and cider. Course, back in the early days we didn't sell much more than that . . . wasn't like it is today. Seems like every year, though, something new is added."

"What was added this year?"

"Why, you were, Zoey Enright."

Zoey laughed, and so did he. The salad bowls were whisked away to be replaced by plates of ham, sweet potatoes, and green beans as a jolly group of six joined their table. Wally made introductions all around, and Zoey smiled at the newcomers, all old friends of the old doctor's, as were, she guessed, ninety-five percent of those gathering in the old churchyard, waiting to be seated. After dessert—thick slices of creamy pumpkin pie—and steaming cups of pungent coffee, Zoey stood up and stretched slightly.

"I can't remember the last time I ate so much at one time," she told her companion, "or when I enjoyed a meal more. But I think it's time for me to collect my pumpkins and head on home."

"I'll walk you back to Brady's Farm," Wally told her. "That is where you left your car, isn't it?"

"Place with a weathered red barn and a windmill?"

"That would be the one." He fell in step beside her. "One of several working windmills in this part of Pennsylvania. Named the town after it."

"Do the owners use it for electricity?"

"That they do." He nodded. "As do some of our Amish neighbors, though many of them have gone to low-volt electric generators these days. They still use the windmills for backup."

"I thought the Amish didn't use modern technology."

"That's something of a misconception. The Amish thrive because of their ability to compromise with modern technology."

"In what way?"

"Well, for example, they don't own or drive cars, but they very frequently will hire a car and driver. It's not uncommon to see a telephone at the end of a farm's lane, but not in the houses. They use tractors around the barns, but not in their fields, which are plowed by modern equipment pulled by mules or horses. They have managed to maintain their own culture, but have adapted to progress when it best suits them."

"I've seen some Amish buggies on the back roads occasionally," she noted, "though I didn't see any Amish folk here today."

"You wouldn't," he told her. "It's the Sabbath."

The crowd was dwindling, Zoey noticed, the face painter's line reduced to a mere two or three children, the juggler having packed up his equipment, and many of the craft tables near empty of their offerings. The sun was dropping down a bit, and as they walked past the lake, Zoey noticed that only a few small boys fishing from rowboats and a teenage couple in one of the paddleboats were all that remained of the afternoon's flotilla, all of the others having been tied to the long dock at the far end on the opposite shore. The day was coming to an end, and unexpectedly, Zoey felt a little stab of regret at its passing. There had been something settling about the afternoon, something she could not define, and she wasn't ready to let it go.

"Here we are at Brady's," Wally said. "Where did you leave your pumpkins?"

"Right there." Zoey pointed to the basket that held her pumpkins.

"Well, then, let's see what you've got there."

Wally bent down and inspected the contents of Zoey's basket. "Nice," he nodded. "Now, are you a painter or a carver?"

"This year I will be both. I think I'll paint the smaller ones and carve the big one."

"Good choice," Wally nodded solemnly. He hoisted the big one and nodded to her to grab the basket where the small pumpkins still sat. "I'll give you a hand getting these to your car."

"Thanks. That big one's a two-hand pumpkin if ever I saw one."

"Exactly." He waited for her, then followed slightly behind her down the dusty rows through the cornfield. When she reached into her pocket and pulled out her car keys, his eyebrows rose.

"This yours? This little sports car?"

"Yup." She grinned as she popped the trunk and gently placed her pumpkins inside. "Hop in. I'll drive you home."

"Been years since I've had one of these little numbers." He chuckled.

"You used to have a sports car?"

He nodded.

"Convertible?"

"You betcha." He laughed.

"I just bet you were some hot stuff in your day, Wally."

"There are some who might say I'm still hot stuff, missy, and don't you—"

He leaned back hard in his seat as Zoey made a quick U-turn in the cornfield and headed out toward the paved road.

He cleared his throat. "They've added a few horses since then, it would seem."

Zoey grinned and asked, "Which way?"

"To the right, then take the first left. We'll have to go around town because the streets are still closed off." She did so and he pointed up ahead. "Now, you can take that left up there, and it'll take us to the other end of Main Street. Then you'll make another left onto Skeeters Pond Road."

She did as she was told, turning onto Skeeters Pond Road, then slowing down as the street narrowed slightly at a curve. Wide driveways led to houses of various vintage, from the tidy Victorians and long-slung colonial era houses closest to town, to randomly spaced homes that appeared to date from the turn of the century, to a sprinkling of 1920s-style bungalows, all set at different angles to the road on large deeply shaded lots.

"Slow down, here." Wally pointed to a slight curve in the road. "Third mailbox after the bend."

Zoey eased the little car to a stop on the shoulder of the road in front of a white clapboard two-story house with a porch that sat flush to the level ground and red shutters that looked as if they might actually close. At the end of a yellow gravel driveway sat a small barn, behind which several outbuildings spread toward a wooded area.

"Well, then, here we are." Wally unhooked his seat belt and turned to Zoey, saying, "This has been a real pleasure, Miss Zoey Enright. I've enjoyed spending the afternoon with you. You're a good sport, and good company. Easy on the eyes, too, though I've heard that women don't like to be told that these days. Want to be appreciated only for their minds, I've been told."

"I think you got bad information"—Zoey patted his arm—"and I thank you for the compliments, Wally, and for taking pity on a lost soul and making such a fine day of it for me. I can't remember the last time I enjoyed myself so much."

"Well, now, that doesn't say much for your social life, does it?"

"What social life?" She grimaced good-naturedly. "I'm a working lady."

"Take the time to enjoy the ride, Zoey Enright. It all passes by very quickly." His brown eyes deepened earnestly as he covered her hands with his own well-worked, callused ones.

Zoey gave a quick squeeze to his hands and nodded.

"Stop by and see me someday when you're out this way." Doc Littlefield pushed himself out of his seat and straightened himself up, then closed the car door with a soft thud.

"I would like that," she assured him.

"Well, then, I'll be looking forward to it." He stepped back toward the house as she pulled away from the side of the road, then into a driveway two doors up the road. She slowed on her way back to wave out the window to Wally, who stood where she had left him at the foot of his gravel drive. She smiled as he tipped his straw hat.

She was three-quarters of the way past the house next door before she saw the For Sale sign that sat back about ten feet from a plain aluminum mailbox upon the side of which *Kilmartin* had been painted in black letters with a shaky hand. She slowed slightly, then stopped to peer at the house, a bungalow with cedar shingles that had long since turned brown with age. Wooden steps rose to a wide porch that spread out from either side of the front door. No welcoming lights shone from the windows, no car stood at the end of the long drive. Along the left side of the house, on or near where Zoey guessed the property line might be, three large maples had dumped mounds of colored leaves, which gave a piebald appearance to the front lawn. All in all, Zoey thought the house looked outdated, but homey somehow. On a whim, she pulled paper and pen out of her purse and jotted down the name and phone number of the realtor.

After all, it couldn't hurt to look.

Chapter

6

Trying hard not to sound too hopeful, Zoey called Peg, her realtor, the very first thing Monday morning to tell her she'd found a place that intrigued her. Peg made the calls to the listing realtor and called Zoey back, asking hesitantly, "Are you sure you want to see *this* house?"

Zoey frowned. "Is there some reason why I wouldn't?" Zoey's ever active imagination summoned forth visions of malevolent spirits, carpenter ants, and possible holes in the roof. "Is it out of my price range? It didn't look as if it would be that expensive."

"Not at all. As a matter of fact, it's way less than anything else you've looked at. Properties in that area haven't been selling well over the past few years, so the prices have declined. And this is an estate sale, so someone will be able to pick this up for a song. It just sounds a little, oh, I don't know . . ." Zoey could visualize Peg biting her bottom lip while trying to find the most politic phrase. "It may need some work."

"I don't mind work. *Work* is not a problem." Zoey sighed with relief. Pale writhing figures beckoning her from the top of the stairs would be a problem. Walls

63

collapsing from insect damage, roof leaks causing her bed to float downstream, *those* would be a problem. *Work,* on the other hand, was definitely not a problem. "When can I see it?"

"Is ten o'clock tomorrow morning good for you?"

"It's fine. Great. I'll be there at ten."

Actually, it had been earlier than that when Zoey turned into the deeply ridged driveway of hard dirt and eased her little car carefully along the drive's entire length to the old garage. She sat in the car for a few minutes, windows down, taking in the sights and sounds and smells. All was quiet save for bird songs. Nothing more. No traffic sounds. No voices. She could close her eyes and be in the middle of a deep forest for all the sounds of modern life that reached her there at the end of the driveway at 27 Skeeters Pond Road.

The rear portion of the property was much more expansive than she had envisioned, reaching, she guessed, a good acre or so to the woods beyond, where trees stood like scarlet and gold sentinels in the autumn sunlight. The back of the house itself had a small shed-type entry and a small porch over which draped ivy in shades of tawny red and fading green. From the porch to an area parallel to the garage, a flat expanse of summer-weary lawn spread out, the dried grass having yellowed in the August sun and never quite recovered. A faded white picket fence that extended twenty feet or so from one corner of the garage ended in a tall arbor, the thick grapevines hanging heavily to obscure whatever might lie within the large rectangle beyond. Zoey got out of her car to investigate.

At the midpoint of the arbor, an arch led into a garden neglected and untended for at least one summer season, maybe more. Dried hollow stalks that once were graced by daylilies stuck out of the thick maze of grass and dull greenery like bony arms reaching skyward. Dense layers of vines—some with tiny white starlike flowers, some with pale blue morning glories, one of the few flowers Zoey could identify—seemed to cover all. Here and there, tall clusters of pink, white, red, and purple flowers, knee deep in gold and crimson drifts of leaves, fought the weeds for space. The air was redolent with the fragrance of flowers—which ones, Zoey could not say—and grapes fermenting on the ground beneath the arbor. Apples that had fallen from a tree on the other side of the fence now, brown and rotting, lay scattered like forgotten marbles throughout the yard.

I'll bet this was beautiful once, Zoey thought idly as she touched the pale pink petals of a rose that grew stubbornly despite the late season and the tangle of weeds doing their level best to choke it. *Someone loved this place once.*

She wandered around the various flowerbeds, wishing for the company of her mother or her sister, either one of whom could most likely have identified the remains of everything in the garden, despite their being dried and lifeless. Zoey smiled to herself, thinking of what fun Delia and Georgia could have sorting through the jumble to see what lovely things might be clinging to life beneath the thicket.

The sound of a car door, not particularly loud in itself, echoed across the silence like a shot. Zoey emerged from the arbor gate and waved to Peg.

"The listing realtor, Mrs. Beck, told me that this property . . . actually, all of the land from the corner down there out to past the old granary . . . used to be part of the original Davis farm, which predates the American Revolution. I was told that the Davises lost all four of their sons in the battle of Brandywine, and three of them are buried out there somewhere." The realtor waved a hand toward some vague place off in the distance behind the trees. "The farm passed into the hands of their daughter and her husband, whose name was McConnell."

"Interesting." Zoey nodded politely, though at that moment she was more interested in the house itself than in local color.

"This house was built in the twenties when descendants of the McConnells sold off some of the land. There's only been one owner"—sensing Zoey's eagerness to see the inside of the house, Peg gestured for Zoey to follow her towards the front of the house—"a family named Kilmartin. The husband was a professor at Lancaster College. Mrs. Kilmartin taught English at the district high school, and was a local historian of sorts. He died eight or nine years ago. She stayed here until she died last spring. The house has been on the market since."

"Isn't there a granddaughter?" Zoey thought back to her conversation with Wally.

"Yes. One, I believe. Mrs. Beck mentioned an heir."

"You learned all of that from one brief phone call?"

"Zoey, there's no such thing as a *brief* phone call between realtors." Peg grinned, then pointed to the side of the house and pointed to the shrubbery saying, "Lovely old hydrangeas. And masses of peonies. Lilac out front. Mrs. Kilmartin must have loved fragrant things."

"So does my mother," Zoey noted.

"Then your mother would be in her glory here next spring." From her pocket Peg produced a key for the lock box that secured the front door and dangled it. "Ready to take a look inside?"

"More than ready."

Swinging the heavy wooden door aside, Peg walked ahead of Zoey into the darkened entry and turned on a small lamp, then pulled back pale green drapes that shielded the windows in the living room beyond the small foyer.

"Looks to be chestnut." Peg carefully inspected the handsome grain of the woodwork around the door frames. "Nice."

Zoey stepped into the living room and sighed deeply. Along the long outside wall stood a large fireplace, the surround done in terra-cotta tiles, some of which appeared to have raised designs of flowers. Bookcases on either side were topped by long narrow strips of stained glass windows depicting what appeared to be scenes from the Middle Ages. The deep silled front windows overlooked the porch, which was shaded by a large Japanese maple tree, its lacy orange leaves shimmering in the morning sun, while the side windows faced a row of staunch pines and the house next door. Doc Littlefield's house. Zoey smiled at the thought of having the retired gentleman as a neighbor as she followed a wide arch at the far end of the room into the dining room, which had a lovely view of the grape arbor Zoey had previously inspected. A small kitchen, outdated and badly in need of everything, opened onto a small back shed and porch. On the opposite side of the hall were two bedrooms and a bath. A somewhat narrow door led to a flight of steps to the second floor, which was one very large unfinished room. Windows all around gave views on all four sides. It would make the most wonderful bedroom, with a spacious bath and one enormous walk-in closet. Zoey could close her eyes and imagine skylights that would open to bring in the night sky, or the first glow of a new day. She went back down the steps and walked through the house again.

The bedrooms could be a comfortable guest, bath, and sitting room suite for overnight guests, the sitting room doubling as a home office. The living room was just right for her curved and cushy sofa, which would wrap around the fireplace perfectly. She could see the bookshelves lined with books and that collection of American pottery her mother had started for her years ago. The dining room would be sunny and cheery, and even without closing her eyes she could see an old crockery tureen overflowing with lilac and peonies in the middle of a well-worn antique harvest table. There was no redeeming the kitchen, however. The counters, floor, and painted metal cabinets would all have to go, but since the room was small, it probably wouldn't take much to renovate. That and the bathroom—also well outdated—and the second floor makeover would be the big expenditures. The rest of the house—well, some cheery wallpaper would work wonders. The handsome millwork would be left untouched.

"It's perfect. It's exactly what I was looking for," Zoey announced.

"Are you serious?"

"Oh, yes. I love it. It's definitely me." Zoey grinned. "Or will be, once I'm done with it. Let's go back to your office and and talk over the numbers."

"You are serious."

"Absolutely."

"Fine. Great." Peg shook her head. She had been prepared to show Zoey two other older homes—larger and much more expensive—once Zoey had seen and dismissed the bungalow. And though there were larger commissions to be made elsewhere, one look at Zoey's face was enough to convince Peg that the sold sign would go up as soon as the paperwork was completed.

While Peg wrestled with the lock box, Zoey stood on the lawn beneath the trees, rustling the paintbox colors of the fallen leaves with the toe of her shoe, studying the front of the house that was, in her mind, already hers. It was a handsome little house, and had felt like home. It had just enough ground to give her space, and just enough room inside to spread out. Once she had completed the plans that were already spinning in giddy circles around and around in her head, the bungalow would be charming. And it would be hers, all hers. What a surprise for Delia, once she completed her tour and arrived back home.

Zoey bent down and picked up a large acorn that had dropped from the large oak that stood at the very end of the driveway and turned it around and around in her hand like a lucky coin.

Of course, Delia would love the house.

Of course, Delia would expect to take over the renovations, would most likely want to pay for the new furniture as well.

Zoey began to tap her foot unconsciously.

I want to do this myself. I want to hire the contractor and pick the wallpaper and argue with the plumber if necessary. I want to chose the new kitchen counters and floor by myself.

A cloud of guilt began to wrap around her, and the thought that perhaps she was, in a sense, betraying her mother tried to seep into her consciousness, but she pushed it back.

I'm a grown woman. I can do these things for myself. I want to do this for myself.

Zoey suspected that with her new job's generous salary, she could afford to buy the house, and still qualify for a loan to renovate it, but knew also that her mother would want to be involved with the process. She would just have to find the way to balance both, she decided, and she would somehow do just that. She nodded, as if in silent agreement with herself, and started to walk across the lawn to her car when the front door on the house next door opened and Dr. Wallace T. Littlefield stepped out.

"Thought that was you," he called and waved a greeting. "You weren't planning on leaving without stopping by to say hello, now, were you?"

"Actually, I thought I'd stop back when I finished up with the realtor," she told him.

"So. Whatcha think of the place?" Wally's eyes took on a hopeful shine.

"I love it." Zoey grinned and fought an urge to jump up and down and fling her arms around the old man's shoulders.

"That so?" He nodded happily.

"Yes. That's so. As a matter of fact, I'm going back to the realtor's office right now and we're going to talk over what it would take to buy it."

"Really?"

"Really. Thank you, Wally."

"For what?"

"If it hadn't been for you, I'd never have found this

road, I'd never have seen the house. . . ." Something in his eyes stopped her mid-sentence. "Wallace Littlefield, you wanted me to look at this house."

"Nonsense. All I did was accept your gracious offer of a ride home."

"You knew that if you helped me carry my stuff to the car, I'd offer you a ride."

"You're obviously a young lady who has good manners, it wouldn't be beyond the realm of possibility for you to—"

"You knew I was looking for a house. How did you know I'd fall in love with this one?"

Caught, he shuffled a little. Something caught his eye on the ground and he bent slowly to pick it up.

"That's from the tail of a red-tailed hawk." He handed her the deep auburn feather. "In the morning she sits out here and scans the fields for her breakfast. She's a beauty, she is."

Taken off-guard by the shift in conversation, Zoey turned the feather slowly between her fingers. "I know what red-tailed hawks look like. I went on a bird watch on Christmas Day with my brother and his fiancée in Devlin's Light down on the Delaware Bay. I saw a red-tailed hawk and a"—she sought to recall the name of the rare bird whose sighting had created such a stir that day—"yellow-crowned night heron."

"Really?" Wally took Zoey's elbow and guided her almost without thinking across the lawn. "A yellow-crowned night heron, you say? Haven't seen one of them in years. Used to be three, four of them that stopped over at the pond out back"—he raised a thin arm to wave toward the woods—"at the end of the summer. Migrating, I supposed. But no, I can't say that I've seen a yellow-crowned night heron within the past, oh, eight, ten years, at the least. Handsome devils, I recall."

"Very handsome. Regal." Zoey nodded knowingly, and the feeling of being home once again swept over her.

Wally stopped and pointed upward toward a hollow in an oak at the end of her driveway and said, "There's a family of raccoons that live up there. Three babies they had this year. Bad as can be, those bandits are. Cute as puppies, though, and I've spent many an early evening sitting on my porch, watching those rascals learn how to climb down the trunk of the tree." He stopped at the driveway and pointed toward the rear of the property. "There's owls in the loft of that old garage, and out back there, at the farthest end of the garden, there's a family of groundhogs, been here as long as I have."

"And how long's that been, Wally?" Zoey asked softly.

"I was born in that house." He nodded to his home. "Great-great grandmother was a McConnell, she and her husband built that house. Lived here a good part of my life . . . all seventy-two years of it. Parents both died from influenza. I moved back here with the wife after I finished medical school. Mae—that's the wife—died in seventy-eight."

"And you've lived here alone since then?"

"Yep." He pointed a crooked finger to the bungalow and added, "Course, Addie Kilmartin was good company over the years."

"Were you and Addie . . . um . . . companions?" Zoey's eyebrows rose.

"Maybe we were, and maybe we weren't. I've never been one to fuel the gossip mill, missy. And besides, a gentleman never discusses his relationship with a lady."

"I see." Zoey grinned. "I take it Addie was a single lady."

"She was a widow lady for the last eight years of her life." A slow smile tipped the corners of his mouth. "And a fine lady she was, too. I've missed her these past few months. I know she'd be pleased with you buying her house, though. She'd be real pleased."

"Why is that?"

"Just suits you, that's all." He waved a greeting to a passing car. "And you would have suited Addie. Well, then, missy, looks like the real estate lady there is ready to move on out. You'd better be following along if you're planning on making your interest in this house known. I

71

heard that Addie's granddaughter is leaving for a year's study in Germany in another month or so, so you'll want to get on with it."

"Good point. I'm on my way."

"Stop around and let me know how you make out, hear?" Wally patted her on the back before she took off down the driveway.

"I will!" Zoey practically skipped to her car, hopped in, and turned it around in a flash.

"And Wally . . ." She rolled down the window when she reached the end of the driveway.

He leaned forward a bit to hear her.

"Thank you. Whether by design or not, I love the house."

He saluted her with his right hand and a grin.

Wally watched both cars disappear around the first curve in the two-lane road, but stood there on the lawn until he could no longer hear the engine from Zoey's peppy little car. He walked toward the bungalow, where he pushed aside a scattering of leaves on the front steps before seating himself and stretching his legs out straight to catch a bit of sun. Across the road, trees the very color of sunshine spread a canopy of gold. He inhaled deeply of the last lingering scents of autumn, grapes and apples, sweet autumn clematis and phlox and Russian sage. Around the mailbox, brassy black-eyed Susans grew alongside the thin, dried arms of Queen Anne's lace, uninvited, all, but welcome. From a gnarled branch halfway up the oak tree, a squirrel dropped the shell of an acorn he had just opened and devoured. The sights and sounds were all familiar, all beloved. Wally sighed, satisfied with the season and the circumstances.

"Well, then, Addie, I'd say we did all right, wouldn't you?" He took off his baseball cap and scratched the back of his head. "Yep. I'd say we did just fine."

Six weeks later, after a quick settlement and nine days spent interviewing contractors, Zoey was pacing the hallway in her apartment, her cell phone jammed between her shoulder and her ear, talking to CeCe, who had become a close friend, and waited for the arrival of her mother.

"Zoey, I just don't think I really understand this," CeCe said. "I mean, if I called my mother and told her I had just bought a house, she'd be thrilled. Why do you think your mother will be upset? She didn't seem like a mean, evil person when I met her."

"She's not mean, and there's not an evil fiber in her body. It's just the opposite. She is too good to us. She wants to do everything for us."

"You don't think your mother will be upset that you didn't let her buy your house for you, do you?" Cece laughed.

"Actually, that's not as far-fetched as you might think." Zoey sighed.

"You can't be serious."

"You'd have to know my mother to understand." Zoey frowned, not certain that even she really understood Delia's need to do so much for her offspring. "Well, we'll soon find out. She's just pulling up. I have to go. I'll see you on Tuesday." Zoey hung up the phone with Cece's "Good luck" ringing in her ears.

Zoey grabbed a sweater and stuffed her keys into the pocket of her jeans.

"Hi!" She waved from the front steps, then turned to lock the front door behind her, taking a deep breath and admonishing herself for being so silly. Of course, Delia will be thrilled for her.

"Mom, I want to take a ride," Zoey hopped into the sedan and stretched across the seat to give her mother a kiss on the cheek.

"Fine, sweetie." Delia leaned back into the tan leather and smiled.

"I'll give you directions and you can drive." Zoey grinned with a playfulness she did not feel. "And while we're driving you can tell me what it feels like to have your picture on the cover of *People* magazine."

Delia laughed and rolled down the window, letting in

the crisp late autumn air while she turned the sedan around and followed her daughter's instructions.

"Zoey, have you spoken with your brother this week?" Delia asked, taking the indicated turn to the left.

"No, I haven't heard from him in over a week."

Delia raised an eyebrow. "Who is hiding out from whom?"

"I've been working odd hours, Mom. Sometimes I'm on the air at two o'clock in the morning, you know. I've left messages on his answering machine, and he's left a few on mine." Zoey put her passenger side window down and peered out, as if trying to check her bearings. "Take a right at the stop sign, please. And Georgia's been out on the West Coast with her dance group, so I haven't spoken with her either."

Delia made the right turn from one two-lane road onto another, wondering absently where they were going. Fields spread out on either side of the car, flocks of crows, large as hens, pecking along the tired rows of crops long harvested.

"It bothers me that the three of you would let so long a time pass without checking on one another," Delia said tersely, and Zoey turned to stare at her.

"Mom, it's only been a week and a half," she said softly.

"What if Nicky needed you? What if Georgia did? What if you needed one of them?"

"We would manage to get in touch if it was important. And Nick has India, and Georgia has the entire Harbor Troupe to look after her. Mom, what's the . . . ?"

"Staying in touch is important, Zoey. Staying in one another's lives is important. What if something happened to one of you?"

"Mom, settle down. Nothing's happened," Zoey said softly, watching her mother's face. It told her nothing. "Mom, what happened on that last tour that upset you so much?"

"Whatever are you talking about?" Delia attempted to dismiss her daughter with the wave of a hand.

"You're acting . . . odd."

"Odd?" Delia frowned. "How 'odd'?"

"I can't put my finger on it, but *distracted* might do. *Intense* would work equally well."

"Don't be silly. It was a long tour. I loved it, but I was tired, I admit, when I came back. Now I'm all rested up. And don't try to change the subject, Zoey. You know how I feel about you children keeping close."

"We are close." Zoey leaned over and patted her mother's shoulder. "We always have been. Always will be."

"Good. Family is important, Zoey. Everything else comes after. Don't ever forget it." Delia stopped at the stop sign and turned to her daughter. "Promise me."

"Of course I promise you."

"Fine. Which way?" Delia pointed to the intersection.

"Take a left, then slow down when you come into the town." The tension abated, Zoey leaned back and asked, "Got any chocolate?"

"Look in the glove box." Delia peered over the steering wheel as if looking for the telltale signs of civilization. "Town? There's a town out here? In the midst of all these fields?"

"Brady's Mill." Zoey nodded as she opened the glove box and peeked in. Seeing the gold foil box, she laughed out loud. "Mom, you are the only person I know who travels with a two-pound box of Godivas."

"Isn't that what that little compartment in the dash is for?" Delia grinned. "Fish one out for me . . . no, not that one, I want the one that looks like a shield with the tennis rackets on it. Yes, that one."

Zoey handed the piece of chocolate to her mother, selected a walnut of dark chocolate for herself. "Go slow past the lake," she said as she nibbled on the walnut.

"How picturesque," Delia noted, pointing to the lake.

"It is," Zoey agreed. "Now, take a right at the road up there, yes, right here."

Delia glanced up at the street sign on the corner. *"Skeeters Pond Road?"* she asked, her eyebrows raised.

"There's actually a place in this world called *Skeeters Pond?*"

"Yes, and we're almost there, Mom. Slow around the curve, it comes up on you quickly. Okay, now slow down just a little more . . . see the mailbox that says 'Kilmartin' on it? Pull in the driveway and stop the car."

Delia did as she was told, mystified though she was.

"Zoey, who are the Kilmartins?"

"They are the people who used to own this house," Zoey told her.

"And who owns it now?" Delia asked slowly.

"I do, Mom."

Silence.

"You bought a house?" Delia's eyebrows rose less than Zoey had anticipated. Not necessarily a good sign. It meant she was forcing control. And that was not a good thing.

"Yes, Mom. I did."

"Zoey, why?" Delia frowned. "I mean, you mentioned wanting to buy a little house, but . . . why didn't you tell me? Sweetheart, I could have helped you."

"I really wanted to do it on my own, Mom. I really had to do this for myself."

"But sweetheart . . ."

"Mom, I love you. I adore you, for that matter. I appreciate everything you have done for me. But I needed to do this for myself. I wanted to pick my own house, and pick all my furniture, hire the workmen . . . make my own choices."

"And are you saying that I would have tried to pick your house, pick your furniture, make your choices, for you?"

They sat in a silence as awkward as the truth.

"Oh, of course I would have." Delia raised her eyes to heaven with a wry smile. "Why waste both our time by trying to deny it? Of course I would have taken over everything. I would have tried to talk you into a bigger house. If you had chosen green walls, I would have tried to talk you into blue. Of course I would have . . ."

"Mom, it isn't that I don't value your opinion. . . ."

"Zoey, darling, the issue isn't whether or not you *value* my opinion." Delia reached for her daughter's hand. "The issue is that you wanted to do something for yourself, and you had to do it behind me so that I would not take over, isn't that right?"

"Oh, Mom, I hate to put it like that." Zoey squirmed uncomfortably.

"But that's the simple truth of it," Delia said in a soft voice. "Oh, I never wanted to take over your life, Zoey. I just always wanted to make it easier for you. For all of you. I only wanted for you to know that I was always there for you, in every way. I never wanted there to be a doubt."

"And there never was, Mom. Not for a second. This was just something I wanted to do. I didn't tell Nicky, or India, or even Georgia."

"Were you afraid they'd tell me?" Delia asked.

"No," Zoey told her first half truth of the day. "I just wanted to surprise everyone."

"Well, you've surprised me. And no doubt, you'll surprise your sister and your brother." Delia's face darkened. "I wonder if either of them resent what I've done in their homes. Georgia's condo. Nicky's cabin."

"I don't think so, Mom. Neither of them ever gave a hint that they did. But they're different, Mom. Neither of them had as much to prove as I did."

"What on earth does that mean?"

"Georgia and Nick have always known their way, Mom. I always thought of all the things you do for them to be your rewards for their hard work and for their accomplishments."

"And you thought that somehow you didn't deserve such rewards?" Delia's brow folded into deep creases. "That I felt you were not accomplished?"

"Let's face it, Mom, until recently I haven't even known where I was headed."

"And you thought that somehow that disappointed me?"

"Something like that." The admission was more difficult than Zoey had expected.

"What you *do* has never had a thing to do with who you are, Zoey. I have always been very proud to be your mother. Always. As proud as I am of all my children. It has never had anything to do with what you do to earn your living."

"Thank you, Mom." Zoey tried to speak over the lump that had grown in her throat.

"Well, then, Zoey Amanda, do you know where you're headed now?"

"I think I do, Mom. I'm happy. I like what I'm doing. Every day is different. It's fun. I'm meeting so many interesting people. Yesterday I worked with Alicia Green, the designer."

"I have several of her suits." Delia could not help but smile. The light was coming back in Zoey's eyes.

"And on Monday, my guest was Jackson Martin. Mom, I've been in love with Jackson Martin all my life. He is the greatest movie star of all time."

"Me too." Delia nodded, then asked, "What was he selling?"

"His autobiography." Zoey sighed. "And Mom—his eyes really are that blue."

"I've heard that." Delia sighed too. "I always wanted to meet him."

They sighed together.

"Zoey?"

"What, Mom?"

"Pass the Godivas."

Zoey opened the glove box and removed the lid from the gold foil box.

"Which one do you want?"

"Bring the box." Delia took the key from the ignition and stuck it into her pocket. "Next time we'll bring the champagne and toast your happiness in your new home. In the meantime, we'll just have to celebrate your independence with chocolate."

Chapter

7

~

Delia had clearly loved Zoey's house, even while admitting that, at first glance, she herself probably would have overlooked it. Had she been asked, she most likely would have tried to talk Zoey out of buying it, due to its seemingly small size and out-of-the-way location. Delia had followed her daughter from room to room, Zoey proudly pointing out the architectural details, the chestnut woodwork and the arched doorways, the many windows with their deep sills and the lovely views. Zoey produced both the architect's drawings for the second floor as well as the plan from the kitchen designer, and together they leaned across the old kitchen counter and peered over the sketches, Zoey showing her mother her well-thought-out vision of her new home. Bit by bit, Zoey had shared it all—the wallpaper selections, the carpets, the furniture. By the time the "tour" was over, Delia was enthralled.

"Heaven," she declared with a satisfied sigh. "This little house will polish up nicely, like a little gem. Oh, Zoey, I hope you're as proud of yourself as I am of you. Why, to have pulled all of this together in so short a time. Now, when does the contractor start on the kitchen?"

Zoey hesitated, and Delia laughed out loud.

"Sweetheart, I promise not to show up without invitation until they are all done. And if invited over while work is still in progress, I swear I will not tell the carpenters how to hammer or the plumbers how to plumb." Delia raised one hand to the sky.

"Mom, you are always welcome. You don't need an invitation." Zoey looped her arm through her mother's. "Now, come out back. Wait till you see my backyard."

Zoey slid aside the thin metal bar that served as the backdoor lock, and Delia eyed it suspiciously.

"Now, you are thinking about new locks, aren't you?"

"I hadn't," Zoey admitted.

"Well, right now, while the house is vacant and there is work being done on a daily basis, what you have there"—she pointed to the slide bar lock—"is probably sufficient. I'd feel better if you had dead bolts installed once you move in."

"I'll put it on the list."

Delia paused and looked up at her daughter. "Did that count as meddling?"

"Nah. We'll let that one pass."

Zoey pushed open the back door and stepped aside to allow her mother to precede her onto the tiny back porch.

Delia paused meaningfully on the third step from the bottom, as if about to say something.

"What, Mom?"

"Nothing, sweetie." Delia sighed, apparently having changed her mind about whatever it was that was on her mind and turning her attention to the wooden bower overflowing with vines. "Oh, a grape arbor! How wonderful!" She swept toward the garden. "We had a lovely grape arbor at the house I grew up in back in West Newton. Oh, and by the end of the summer, it would be laden with grapes. My mother made endless batches of grape jam every year, and gave them out at Christmas to the members of Father's congregation. As the minister's wife, she always took such pains to go a step or two beyond what was expected of her. Always. As if she would be judged by how many jars of jam she gave out, how many loaves of bread she baked for the poor, or how many new Bibles she raised the money to buy."

Delia stood so still, her face blank, transformed from the lively woman taking off across the backyard to a younger version of herself, frozen in time, robbed somehow of her jaunty, confident air and her strong presence. Some sadness seemed to sweep over her, transforming her for just a few seconds into a woman even her own daughter did not recognize.

"Mother always did exactly the right thing, Zoey. Always. She was a woman who never made a mistake. Never made a bad choice. She soundly—*staunchly*—professed on her deathbed to have had no regrets." Delia's body seemed to waver slightly, as if suddenly weakened from a blow delivered by an unseen hand, her voice lowered till it was barely a whisper. "None whatsoever."

"Mom." Zoey caught up with her. "Are you all right?"

"Of course, darling." Delia flashed a smile, shook off whatever demon had been perched upon her shoulder, and took Zoey's hand. "I can't wait to see what's inside the gate."

Zoey swung the wooden gate aside and Delia grinned happily. "Oh, yes, whoever Mrs. Kilmartin was, she kept a lovely garden. Now, I wonder if those hydrangeas will bloom pink or blue? And what color do you suppose the roses might be?"

"Well, there were still a few in bloom the first time I looked at the property. These were red"—Zoey pointed to a bush with long, tangled canes—"and very big and wonderfully fragrant."

"Were the petals a sort of velvet red, and was the scent more sweet and perfumey than spicy?" Delia asked.

"Yes, velvet is a good way to describe the flower. And I'd say a heady perfumey smell."

"Mr. Lincoln, perhaps." Delia guessed at the name of the rose. "And these, over by the fence?"

"Pink. Very pale pink. Those closer to the gate were a darker pink, but that's all I remember."

"That's more than I expected from you, dear, since you've never had much of an interest in gardening." Delia smiled. "Perhaps that will change now that you have your own. I've always loved to work in the dirt, myself. I've worked side by side with every gardener I've ever had."

"If you love it so much, why hire someone else to do it?"

"Because if I'd spent all my time gardening, I'd never have gotten a book done on time. But this"—she waved her hand in an arc to take in the garden that spread out before her—"is manageable. You'll have many happy hours out here, dear."

Zoey frowned. "I doubt it. As a matter of fact, I wasn't even planning on—"

"Oh, look here!" Delia swept past her, trotting off down one of the stone paths, a woman with a mission. "What do you suppose was planted in these beds? You know, if you stand back here by the gate, it almost looks like the garden was designed to follow an Elizabethan garden plot. Oh, what fun we'll have next spring when all of *this*"—she waved her arm in another wide sweep— "begins to green up. Now, Zoey, promise me you'll let me come back and work here with you in the spring."

"Mom, come next spring, the pleasure will be all yours."

"Now, look back there, sweetie. Running right across the back of the garden, where one would expect fence. What might that stone wall be from?" Off Delia went to investigate. By the time she was done exploring, they had found the remains of what appeared to be an old goldfish pond, an herb garden, and the groundhog hole that housed the family that Wally had mentioned.

"Seen enough?" Zoey crossed her arms over her chest and shivered slightly. The sun had begun to set behind a grove of ancient apple trees that formed a sort of boundary between the back of her property and Wally's, and the dusk brought with it a cool breeze that moved across them with a hint of even cooler nights to come.

"Not really, but if I can come back, I'll be happy for now."

"Of course you can come back. Let's just go inside and turn the lights off, then I'll take you to dinner."

It was on the tip of Delia's tongue to insist that dinner would be on her, but somehow she managed to resist the impulse, allowing for Zoey's earlier declaration of independence. "That would be lovely, dear."

Arm in arm, mother and daughter walked in the twilight shadows toward the back steps. Delia paused, and Zoey could sense that she appeared to be struggling with something, as she had earlier.

"What is it, Mother?" she asked as they went from room to room, turning off the lights.

Delia hesitated, as if about to speak, then not. Finally she gave in and blurted, "Just a deck, Zoey. Just let me build a little deck for you. A deck out there off the back of the house would be just perfect, sweetheart, don't you think? We could have dinner out there and sit and watch the sunset."

Zoey burst out laughing.

"My contractor has already drawn up the plans, Mother. He'll be starting on the deck when the kitchen and bathroom are done."

"I guess it would be out of the question to let me take care of that part of his bill."

"Mother, we went over all this. . . ."

"Maybe for Christmas then. Or a housewarming gift. Consider it a housewarming."

"Why can't you just bring a casserole or a bottle of wine like everyone else?" Zoey asked, trying to hide her amusement, lest Delia know she was on the verge of giving in.

Delia merely lifted an eyebrow as she lifted the lid on

the box of Godiva chocolates, which she had left on the living room mantel.

"One for the road, sweetie?" Delia tilted the box in Zoey's direction.

"All right," Zoey laughed. "But just the deck, Mother. And that will be my Christmas present. You won't buy anything else for me. Agreed?"

"Of course, dear. Just the deck." Delia smiled and draped an arm over Zoey's shoulder as they headed toward the front door, knowing that Zoey's presents, along with those of her other children, had already been purchased, wrapped, and stashed away. "I won't buy another blessed thing."

* * *

Frazzled from a three-hour special demonstrating exercise equipment, athletic clothing, and workout videos, CeCe Hollister flopped on a chair in the hosts' lounge where Zoey sat at a table giving her nails one last coat of dark pink enamel before her show began.

"Do I look as bad as I feel? Damn, three hours of trying to keep up with Michael McCall, the King of Fitness, and I'm ready to drop over."

"Ah, yes, how well I remember the day when this whole fitness concept was introduced." Zoey grinned. "Were you not the one who raised her hand and said, 'Oh, please, Mr. Producer, please let me host the exercise shows. I'm in great shape. Please, allow me to don the biking shorts and the sports bras and work out on national TV with the fitness guru.' That was you, wasn't it?"

"It was, and I may never forgive you for not stuffing something in my mouth."

"There wasn't any room. Your foot was already in there."

CeCe used the toe of one shoe—a heavily padded cross trainer—to slide the heel off the shoe of the other, then reversed the action before stripping off her white sweat socks. She wiggled her bare feet, then padded over to the small refrigerator and searched for the bottle of water she had brought in that morning. Leaning her head back, she took a long drink before asking, "So. How's it feel to be a homeowner?"

"Great. I love my house. I can't wait to move in. I go out there every day and see what the workmen have done, walk around the place, and just dream of how wonderful it will be when it's finished."

"When do you think that will be?"

"Probably not till February. I was hoping to be in by Christmas, since I have to work Christmas Day and I was hoping to have my family here for Christmas Eve. But there's no way that can happen. My mother and sister are going to Devlin's Light again this year to spend the holiday with my brother and his fiancé. India's family does a bird watch on Christmas Day, and they can't miss that. I went last year—I'm hoping to get down to the beach early enough this year so I can go again. It was fun. But apparently the electrical wiring in the house is more complicated than the electrician had originally thought, and it seems we've run into all sorts of little complications. But I expect I might be in by Valentine's Day."

"Let's have a party. A housewarming and Valentine's party."

"Swell idea, CeCe, why didn't I think of that?" Zoey glared. "And a swell party it will be. All single women, with perhaps one or two married couples thrown in for a little variety."

"We should be able to scout up some guys." CeCe frowned.

"Name one."

CeCe thought about it.

"Well, there's always Mike the King of Fitness. I think he's a hunk."

"If you like that beefy type."

"Oh, I do." CeCe grinned.

"Great. And I guess I can always count on Wally." Zoey grumbled.

"Your next door neighbor? I thought you said he was, like, seventy years old."

"He is. But he's the only single man I've met in the

past year who was the least bit interesting." Zoey slumped back in her chair. "This is so bizarre, don't you think? Here we are, two intelligent, decent-looking women . . ."

"Excuse me, but I believe that would be two *gorgeous,* intelligent, witty—"

"Judging by the number of dates I've had lately, I might just as well look like Granny Clampett." Zoey inspected her nails, then moved her fingers back and forth rapidly to speed up the drying of the polish. "And when was the last truly memorable evening you spent with a man?"

"Two weeks ago when I went home for Thanksgiving. My brother Trevor invited some cowpoke buddies of his to a skating party down on Russell's Lake back home in Larkspur, Montana. I met me the handsomest buckaroo you'd ever want to lay eyes on. Tall, dark, and to die for. Skated the night away." She sighed dreamily.

"What happened?"

"Nothing happened," CeCe told her dourly. "At ten o'clock, he skated off in one direction, I skated off toward the airport, and the next thing I knew, I was on a plane headed back east."

"Your brothers are really cowboys?"

"Yes, ma'am. Both of them. And three of my cousins, too."

"Think they'd be interested in coming to a Valentine's Day party?" Zoey said glumly.

"Only if we could find a barn to hold it in. The Hollister men aren't much for socializing. Not if it requires a shirt and tie, anyway."

"What was his name?" Zoey asked.

"What was whose name?"

"The skating cowboy."

"Dalt. Dalton Cahill. Deep blue eyes and dark hair, shoulders like this . . ." She spanned her arms to demonstrate how big Cowboy Dalt's shoulders were.

"Let me get this straight," Zoey twisted the lid of the

nail polish to close the jar tightly. "You met a tall, dark, to-die-for cowboy named *Dalton* and you left him to come back here?"

"I was scheduled to do a show the next afternoon, Zoey. It was the only flight I could get." CeCe stuck out her bottom lip to make a slightly pouty face.

They both sighed deeply.

One of the young production interns poked her head into the room. "Zoey, they're putting out the jewelry now. Amy wants you to come and take another quick look at the new products."

"I'll be there in a minute." Zoey held her left hand up for a final inspection. "Last I looked, there were a lot of rings in my first show. The nails can't be beaten up."

"They look fine," CeCe peered over Zoey's shoulder. "What else do you have today?"

"I have two hours of jewelry and one hour of cooking stuff. What a joke. Me, the queen of take-out, demonstrating cookware. This is definitely not a case of art imitating life."

"Still keeping the local take-out establishments happy?"

"If it's Tuesday, it must be Mexican." Zoey grinned, and looked toward the door as it opened again. The same young intern stuck her head in.

"Zoey, Amy said—"

"I'm coming, I'm coming." She slipped her feet into her low-heeled brown suede shoes. "Amy gets nervous when she has all that gold in one show. She'll be draping me with it."

"There are worse ways to earn a living," CeCe told her as she put her feet up on the end of the wooden table in front of her chair. "Worm farming comes to mind, taxidermy, perhaps . . ."

Zoey let the door swing closed with a bang, leaving CeCe to ponder alternative forms of employment.

"Oh, Zoey, there you are." The producer, Amy, met Zoey in the hallway. "There have been several product changes since yesterday afternoon. I want to make sure you are familiar with everything before you go on."

"What's new here?" Zoey peered over the jewelry, which was displayed on a long folding table covered with a plain white tablecloth.

"This bracelet"—Amy pointed to a wide, heavy gold chain—"was a substitute for the more narrow chain we had planned on. Someone had neglected to check the amount in stock. You always draw a large audience, and it was felt there wasn't sufficient quantity for the show."

Zoey checked the yellow cards, which contained all the product information—size, color, gram weight of the bracelet, along with the price, country of origin, how many times it had appeared on the air, including the last date, and how many bracelets were in stock.

"There aren't a whole lot of this one, either," she noted.

"But this one is a lot more expensive than the other one was, so there won't be as many orders."

"Good point." Zoey nodded, holding her right arm out so that Amy could fasten the bracelet on for her. "What else do you want me to wear today?"

"This gold bangle and the gold watch on your left wrist, and the big gold door knocker earrings. And this around your neck, " Amy lifted a very wide, flat gold necklace.

"Ummm, gorgeous." Zoey sighed as she lifted the necklace. "I'll bet there aren't a whole lot of this one either. This has got to cost a fortune, even at our prices." She leaned over and shuffled through the cards until she located the right one. "Wow. Is this right? Eighteen hundred dollars?"

Amy nodded and took the necklace from Zoey's hands.

"And to think they're actually *paying* me to wear this little beauty," Zoey murmured as the beautiful gold piece was fastened at her neck. "Not such a bad job at all."

* * *

The old man leaned back in the soft leather chair and stretched his stiff right leg into the void under the long walnut conference table that ran along one side of his spacious office on the twenty-fifth floor of the building that bore his name. Outside the window a scaffold swung unsteadily as the window washers prepared to do their job. The old man turned his head, not wanting to watch. Delaney O'Connor, CEO of Connor International, had a thing about heights, and watching someone walk around on a narrow platform—that platform being suspended from who knew where, or what—was not his idea of entertainment. Turning his attention to the financial advisers who sat in the third, fourth, and fifth chairs on his left, he frowned.

"Mr. O'Connor," a young man in a gray suit addressed him, "if I could just say one thing . . ."

"Go right ahead, son." Delaney sank further back into his chair.

"Televised shopping is the wave of the future—"

O'Connor held up a hand to stop him at that first thought and asked, "Now, stop right there and explain to me why someone would buy things they can't actually see in person, when they can go into a store and look things over—touch them, pick them up—before they make a purchase."

"Because there are a lot of people who can't get out to the store, sir. There are people who are ill or who have no transportation, people who work during the hours when most stores are open, and young mothers who can't get out of the house without a trail of little ones. . . ."

"What do you say, Paul?" O'Connor asked his senior adviser. "Is this a passing thing?"

"Not from all indications." He shrugged with the air of one who had done his homework on the subject. It could be a highly lucrative venture, but since it hadn't been his idea, he wasn't inclined to offer up too strong an endorsement.

"Humph." O'Connor pondered this, then gestured for the young man to continue.

"There are already several shop-at-home networks, all successful. It's a good investment, sir. The word on the street is that Valentine, who purchased the Home MarketPlace last year, is in trouble."

"How could they have gotten the financing to purchase a multimillion-dollar business a year ago if they are in trouble?"

"I'm sure that you have heard, sir, that Edward Valentine had a stroke two weeks ago."

"I was sorry to hear that, much as I can't stand the son of a bitch, but what makes you think his board is thinking about selling any of his holdings?"

"With Valentine incapacitated, the 'board' is controlled by his wife."

Delaney O'Connor "hmmph"ed once again, this time at the thought of Edward Valentine's wife of little more than two years. Dolly Valentine was likely to become a young widow. A very wealthy young widow. Some women just seemed to have the timing for that sort of thing.

"And you think she might be interested in selling off a company here, a company there, while waiting to see whether or not old Eddie makes it through?"

"I received a call yesterday morning, sir. There are several companies going up for sale." The young man slid several pages of data across the expanse of the wooden table and watched as Delaney O'Connor skimmed the numbers.

"Hmm. Interesting." Delaney swiveled his chair slightly.

"More than interesting, sir. If approached properly, this could be built into a multibillion-dollar business."

"You think so, do you, James?" Delaney looked at this latest hire on his advisory team, and swore to himself that they got younger every year.

"I do."

"Well, then, perhaps I should give it some thought."

Delaney stood and stretched his legs, a clear sign that the meeting was over. "Now, if you'd be kind enough to stop by at Mrs. Gilbert's desk and ask her to come in . . ."

"Yes, sir." Having been dismissed, the young man folded his notes and filed behind the others as they left the office, young James not knowing whether or not O'Connor had really heard a damned thing he'd said.

"Would you like your lunch now?" Pauline Gilbert stole a sideward glance at her boss as she entered the room and began to straighten up the conference table with practiced, efficient hands.

"In a few minutes." He lumbered over behind his desk and leaned his left hip against the edge to take the weight off his leg, which was throbbing unmercifully at that moment, an old horseback riding injury having been aggravated these past few years by arthritis. Anyone else might have opted for knee and hip replacement, as had been suggested by his physician. But not Delaney. Totally terrified of any medical procedure that involved cutting into his flesh, he had preferred to work around the pain, which he had, over the past few years, come to look upon as an inconvenience more than anything else.

Delaney O'Connor, at seventy-something, was still a large and impressive-looking man. From his thick white hair to his polished wing tips, he wore an unmistakable air of certainty, of power. Success. Clearly, he displayed the sure figure of a man who had the world by the tail.

Pauline Gilbert knew better.

Pouring a cup of hot water for her boss's tea gave Pauline a few seconds to observe him. Delaney was stressed, she could see that much. You didn't work for a man for sixteen years and not know when something was wrong. He was, she knew, deeply shaken by the fax he had received late yesterday from London notifying him of his grandson's latest car accident, in which he'd not only wrecked another of those ridiculously expensive race cars, but had managed to break one of his legs as well.

"The third car in as many years." Pauline had shared

this bit of inside information with her widowed sister, Josephine, who lived with her. "Delaney is sponsoring him, but of course, his grandson doesn't know it. Thinks his backer is a company that makes tires. Which it is. What he doesn't know is that one of his grandfather's subsidiaries bought the tire company a few years ago."

And Pauline had shaken her head, pondering the mental faculties of anyone who would risk life and limb—not to mention a small fortune—for the pleasure and privilege of getting behind the wheel of one of those whiny little contraptions that she had seen on ESPN. Those race cars looked about as substantial as the matchbox variety, and just about as safe.

"Pauline, pour a cup for yourself and sit down." Delaney gestured to the seating area of the office, where a sofa and two comfortable chairs were arranged in one corner.

He turned the television on by the remote and began to flip almost absently from one channel to the next.

Having fixed both cups, Pauline took a seat. It wasn't unusual for her boss to invite her to sit and chat for a few minutes, or to have a cup of tea and watch the noontime news with him. She knew that despite his wealth, and his aura of assurance, he was a lonely man.

"What kind is it today?" He looked into the cup and sighed.

"Apple cinnamon."

He grimaced.

"Pauline, how 'bout just one cup of coffee?" He winked and gave her his biggest smile.

"The doctor said it's bad for your heart."

"Half a cup?" he asked hopefully.

"I'm afraid not. I'm sorry." She looked up from her seat on the gray leather chair. They went through this same routine several times every week. "Dr. Bryson said—"

"What does he know?" Delaney grumbled.

"He knew enough to keep you alive after that last heart attack," she reminded him.

Delaney grunted an acknowledgment and turned to another station.

"You know what they said, Delaney," she reminded him gently.

"Right. No excitement. No stress. No cigars. No coffee. Now, what the hell kind of life is that?" He banged his teacup down on the wooden tabletop and sat himself down right in the middle of the sofa. "Cigars and coffee I can control. But what is life without a little excitement every now and then? And how the hell do you eliminate stress?"

Having had the same conversation with her boss on countless occasions, Pauline merely sipped at her tea and watched the channels change on the big-screen television on the opposite side of the room. He went right past CNN.

Amazingly, he stopped right at Pauline's favorite shopping channel, where at that moment a young dark-haired woman was displaying a wide gold bracelet.

"Pretty girl," he said absently.

"Zoey Enright." Pauline nodded, then added, "My sister and I watch at night sometimes."

"What?" The force of that one word seemed to punch the air.

"I said, Josephine and I watch at—"

"No, the girl." He pointed to the screen. "The name . . ."

"Zoey Enright."

Delaney sat mesmerized, staring at the monitor. *Zoey Enright. How many Zoey Enright's could there be in this world?*

"Delia Enright, the writer, is her mother," Pauline added.

Yup. That's the one, all right.

He leaned forward and rested his arms on his knees, watching the pretty young face on the TV screen, trying to sort out this new information and how best to use it.

Delia Enright's girl. After all these years. Imagine that.

Deep thoughts began to swirl around inside his head,

thoughts of Delia Enright, and her family, and the slender thread that had bound them together for so many years. Finally, a small smile began to play across his lips as he could see things falling into place. He hadn't become one of the country's most successful businessmen by not recognizing when a once-in-a-lifetime opportunity had presented itself. Delaney had never been afraid to follow his instincts.

"I'm going to buy it," he said aloud.

"The bracelet?" Pauline frowned. Could Delaney possibly have a lady friend that she didn't know about?

"No. The station." He pointed to the television. "Shop From Your Chair or whatever it's called."

"It's called the Home MarketPlace." She glanced over her shoulder, wondering if perhaps he'd gone a bit daft.

One look at Delaney's face confirmed it. He was grinning from ear to ear. He began to whistle.

Daft may not be quite the right word.

"Pauline, get Phillip on the phone for me."

Delaney stood in the center of the room, his hands folded across his chest, for just a brief moment not leaning on the cane to hold him up, staring at the photograph of his grandson that stood on the credenza behind his desk.

Well, now, buddy, looks like I may have finally found a way to bring you back for a while. God knows it's time, son, I'm afraid you'll never be whole until you've faced your old demons. I've done everything I could for you over the years, but that's one thing you'll have to do for yourself. And the only way to do that is for you to go back to where it all began. Forgive me, son, but I really think this is for the best.

Delaney studied the face of the young man he loved so fiercely, and indulged himself for a second, long enough to think that, with any real luck, he might even be able to keep him here, to someday take over the business that Delaney had spent a lifetime building. But of course, that was Delaney's dream, not his grandson's.

"Phillip is out of the office, Delaney."

"Find him, Pauline. Tell him I said I want him to buy that"—He waved his hand in the general direction of the television—"shopping thing. Lock, stock, and personnel contracts. Tell him I want it to be quick and clean and to use one of the smaller companies as a front. I don't want anyone to know that I'm the buyer until the sale goes through and I am sitting behind the CEO's desk. Tell him that, Pauline. Quick and clean and quiet. And tell him I said ASAP. I want to take it over ASAP."

He grabbed his cane and headed toward the door, with as close to a bounce in his step as Pauline had seen since before his arthritis had started plaguing him about seven years ago.

"Call Jackson and tell him I'm on my way over. Tell him I need a little legal advice today."

"Oh. And one other thing." He poked his head back into the room. "Call Walker in London and tell him we may be looking to sell Corona Tires."

Pauline, caught in mid-stride, stopped dead in her tracks. No—she shook her head as if to clear it—*daft* didn't even come close.

Chapter

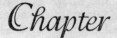

8

Looking out the window of his second-floor London flat, Ben watched the cars amble slowly past, their headlights like so many flashlights just being turned on, as the dinner hour rolled near and the workday came to an end. It was cold, even for early January, and the heating system in the old building left plenty to be desired. He turned his back on the dying day, thinking how a nice fire would warm the room, and how pleasant it might be to sit in front of such warmth with a tray of dinner and a good book. Unfortunately, with both his right leg and arm in casts, laying a fire could prove to be difficult, if not impossible.

With his good left hand, he grabbed his crutch and hobbled over to the sofa, where he flopped down awkwardly and managed to maneuver his right leg onto the big dark green hassock. He shifted in his seat to find the spot most comfortable, and picked up the book that had been delivered that morning from the bookshop two blocks away.

Only Footsteps Away, by Delia Enright.

For the third time that day, Ben flipped to the back of

the dust jacket to the color print of the author's face. Well into her fifties by now, he guessed, Delia Enright was still one hell of a pretty lady. She had been his salvation, his and his mother's, and he had never forgotten her. Deep inside, he had never stopped missing her and the home she had given them. But at fourteen, the trauma of losing both his mother and the only truly happy home he had ever known, had been unbearable. It had eaten a hole inside him that was so wide and so deep that he had never found a way to fill it, and so he had locked it all away, finding it much easier to push it all into the furthest corners of his adolescent mind and leave it all there, neatly wrapped and labeled. The night his grandfather had driven to Westboro to bring him back to Connecticut had been the last time he had seen Delia or her children or the house he had loved. Some-times, when he had let his guard down, he longed to go back, ached to see Delia and Nick—even the faces of Nick's sisters would have been like balm to a burn wound. But over the years, it had seemed that the pain of his loss had become greater than the sum total of his memories, and so he had chosen simply to close the door.

The only thread to that time in his life that Ben permitted himself to hold on to was Delia's books. Each new book, each photo on the cover, would bring back the day that Delia had first entered their lives, and just for a moment, before the memories began to throb, he would allow himself a fleeting look back.

Ben's mother, Maureen, had been working as a private secretary for a wealthy horse breeder outside of West Chester, Pennsylvania, when her employer's son decided he'd like to extend her private duties to include something more than dictation. Maureen had been waiting with the car packed and ready to go when Ben got home from school that day. Assuring him that his baseball glove and cards were safely tucked into the back of the old station wagon, Maureen had driven off toward parts unknown, looking for a new place to live and a new job, with no references, no savings, nothing but an old car, a few dollars, a ten-year-old son who would have to go to school the next morning regardless of where they spent the night—and a sense of humor.

They had stopped at a country store where Maureen had bought sandwiches and drinks for their dinner, and they sat outside at a small picnic table and ate, the cool November dusk settling around them. When they finished eating, Maureen had gone back inside to buy a local paper and some ice cream for Ben. She had peered intensely over the newspaper, squinting to read the small print of the want ads in the last light of the day, trying to appear nonchalant so as to not upset him, but the tension had been alive in her face and in her eyes. Ben had peeled the paper from the Popsicle in quiet little strips, hoping not to disturb her.

A long dark green car pulled up and parked a few feet away, and a handsome woman stepped out from the driver's side and smiled easily at him as she walked past. Her eyes had hesitated as she had glanced back a second time at Maureen, who in the fading light hunched closer to the newspaper. Ten minutes later, the woman came back out of the store, a bag of groceries under each arm. Instead of walking to the car, however, she had walked directly to their table.

"Excuse me," she had said. "It seems you've bought the last of today's paper. I was wondering if I could perhaps buy it from you when you've finished with it."

Maureen had looked up into the face of the woman, who stood not five feet away, and it seemed as if in that second the two women had sized each other up.

"Actually"—Delia set one of her bags on the end of the picnic table—"the only section I really need is the want ads."

"I've already finished with this page"—Maureen handed her a page from the paper—"so if what you're looking for falls between Advertising and Bookkeeping, you just might get lucky."

"Thank you, but I already have more *job* than I can

handle these days. I'm looking to hire someone to help me out, and thought perhaps I might find someone who is looking for something that would fit in with what I need." Her mouth had turned up slightly on one side and she added, "Though someone with a little advertising as well as a little bookkeeping in their background might do quite nicely."

"Could I ask what the job is that you're looking to fill?" Maureen asked tentatively.

"I need a wife." Delia smiled.

"Excuse me?"

"I'm looking for someone to run my house—to run errands, drive my kids around, do the shopping, cook, pick up the dry cleaning—all those things that wives do for their hardworking husbands—so that I can work."

"May I ask what you do?"

"I'm a writer. But I'm also a single mother with three children, and I'm finding that running a house and running with my children and trying to work seems to be a juggling act that I don't do very well. I'm afraid I've put the cart before the horse, if you follow. I've just bought a big house that needs tons of work—don't ask, it was exactly the house I always dreamed of owning, and it was, all things considered, a steal—and now I have to write the books that will pay for it. So I thought if perhaps I hired someone to do all those things that need to be done while I'm writing, that my home would run more smoothly, and I'd write better—not to mention faster—if I didn't have to worry about my family and my home being neglected. My children would be happier. I'd be happier. My editor would be happier. The mortgage company will be happier."

"How old are your children?"

"My daughters are four and seven, and I have a son who is ten." She turned to Ben then, and said, "Probably about as old as you are, am I right?"

"I was ten last month," Ben had told her.

"What a coincidence. So was Nicky. On the eighteenth."

Ben had grinned. "Mine's the seventeenth."

"Ha! Older than Nicky by a day!"

Delia had set her second bag down on the table next to the first and turned back to Maureen. "What type of work are you looking for?"

"Actually," Maureen had cleared her throat, "probably the same type of job you're looking to fill."

"Really? What a happy coincidence! Give me your number and I'll give you a call in the morning. I'm afraid I can't offer you much of a salary to start. That is, if you think you'd be interested . . ."

"Yes! Yes, of course I'm interested. It's just that, well, it would be better if I call you. I don't have a number. I mean, I don't know where we'll be. . . ." Ben could not recall ever having seen his mother so flustered.

"Are you new in the area?" Delia looked concerned, then asked gently, "Do you have a place to stay tonight?"

Maureen had sighed deeply, and looked up into the face of the older woman, and proceeded to tell her everything that had led them to that small picnic table near the parking lot outside Grover's General Store in Westboro, Pennsylvania.

"Is this your car?" Delia had asked when Maureen had concluded.

Maureen, clearly fighting tears but staunchly refusing to let them fall, had nodded.

"Follow me home." Delia lifted a bag. "It's getting cold and dark, and I have a feeling that we have lots to talk about." To Ben she had said, "How 'bout giving me a hand with these bags, son?"

"My name is Ben," He told her.

"And my name is Delia. Delia Enright."

"I've read four of your books," Maureen said.

"Really." Delia had paused, and turned back to Maureen. "Which was your favorite?"

"I liked them all, but I especially enjoyed the ones about Harvey Shellcroft, the detective."

"My very favorite guy." Delia had beamed.

Maureen gathered up the paper trash and discarded it

all in a large trash can at the side of the building. "Will you be doing any more books about Harvey?"

"Absolutely. I'm hoping he'll make me famous. As a matter of fact, I'm counting on it." Delia opened the driver's side door of the dark green car and slung her purse across the front seat.

"By the way, Mrs. Enright, " Maureen had called over her shoulder, "my name is Maureen Pierce."

"I'm pleased to meet you, Maureen Pierce. I have a very good feeling about you. I think we just might be able to work something out, you and I."

"I think I might like that."

"Then let's go home and figure out how we might help each other."

Over the next few years, it would have been difficult to assess who had actually been of greater service to the other. Delia had provided Maureen with a job she had loved and was perfectly suited to doing, that of running the handsome stone home Delia had recently purchased before she had become aware of just how much time and money it took to run so large a property. Maureen had tended to all those day-to-day tasks that, had Delia had to deal with them, would have distracted her from the business of writing. And in return, Delia had brought them into her home, and given them a family. It had been Ben's first real home, and the only roots, the only sense of *belonging* that he had ever known.

For a time, Ben and Maureen had stayed in the main house, though later, as Delia's career took off, plans were made for renovations to the old carriage house to serve as their own separate living quarters. Ben and Nick had taken an instant liking to each other, and by the end of that first week, had become close as brothers. Even Nick's little sisters weren't so bad. Georgia had been a somewhat shy little girl with long straight white-blond hair and a dreamy look who kept to herself a lot. Zoey, on the other hand, had been a bit of a tomboy, always struggling to keep up with her big brother and with Ben. Even now, years later, the thought of little Zoey tagging along valiantly, no matter what the game, could bring a smile to Ben's face. She had been such an earnest little girl, so determined to master it all. Anything the boys could do, Zoey wanted to do just as well.

Every once in a while, Ben would wonder what had become of her, and Nick, and their little sister. But then he would shake it off and force himself to concentrate on today, reminding himself that *that* part of his life was gone, along with his mother and the wonderful life they had had in Westboro. It had hurt too terribly to try to hold on to any piece of it, no matter how small. As a young boy, the first real security he had ever known had begun the night Delia Enright had found them, homeless and scared, in the parking lot of Grover's General Store, and had ended when his mother found the lump in her breast that so unexpectedly changed everything forever.

It seemed that the unexpected had a way of pulling his life off course every time he had started to feel comfortable, Ben though wryly, looking down at his casted right leg. Another symbol of things taking an unexpected turn just when you thought the breaks—*no pun intended,* he winced—were going your way.

His driving had been good, those last six months. Good enough to have qualified for some big races, though maybe not good enough to have won. Still, he had done well enough to have drawn some inquiries from the big boys at Ferrari and Benetton, Arrows and McLaren. He was just beginning to think that perhaps, after all the years of test driving, of waiting his turn, he just might have a shot at joining one of the big teams.

And then he had had the misfortune to slam sideways into a wall at eighty-two miles per hour on that second hairpin turn on the forty-third lap of the Portuguese Grand Prix—the last race of the season, and maybe the last race of his career.

Ben had awakened in a hospital, weights suspended from the leg that seemed to float before him through a dense haze of medication. Fractured in three places, his right leg had been pinned and casted, as had been his right forearm. *Lucky to be alive,* he recalled hearing through the fog that day, though at the time, he hadn't been certain that he agreed. It would be at least a year, at the very minimum, before he could even attempt to race again. And that was assuming that he would find a new sponsor, after missing an entire season. Recently, he'd heard rumors that the tire company that had been his biggest sponsor was considering the sale of its British operations to a Canadian company that expressed no interest in spending money on race cars. Ben wondered just how much worse his luck could get.

He did have his investments—a graduate degree in economics had served him well when it came to investing his mother's inheritance, which his grandfather had passed on to him when he had turned twenty-one—along with his London flat, so it wasn't as though he was desperate. But he sure as hell was bored. For years, most of his spare time was spent with other drivers and the members of the pit crews. These days, when it took him forever to get as far as the first floor of his apartment building, going down those narrow winding steps was an adventure all its own. "Don't get around much anymore" had taken on a whole new meaning.

And now his grandfather was on his way for a visit, something Delaney almost never did. Over the years, Ben had logged many a frequent flyer mile returning to the States to see his grandfather, but only rarely had Delaney made the trip to visit Ben. No one knew better than Ben just how much his grandfather hated to fly. Whatever it was that was bringing him across the ocean, it must be pretty damned important.

Well, Ben settled back with his book, *I guess by this time tomorrow night, I'll know.*

* * *

Delaney O'Connor paced the floor of his hotel room without any purpose whatsoever than to keep himself moving. Every fourth time past the mantel, he glanced up at the clock with its ornately painted face, annoyed to find that not even a mere *minute* had passed since the last time he had looked. The flight had left him anxious and weary, and he wished that he had put off this meeting with his grandson until the next morning. But the truth was he couldn't wait to see Ben. The only child of Delaney's own only child, Ben was also Delaney's only living relative, and the only person on the face of the earth whom Delaney truly loved.

Delaney had loved his grandson the minute he had first laid eyes on the boy. Understanding immediately that the boy's anger was a poor mask for the sheer terror he felt at knowing that his mother was dying, the sense of betrayal he must have felt when she had chosen to share her last months with her father as well as her son, Delaney's heart had gone out to the boy. The bonds of their relationship had been forged as they had, together, watched helplessly as Maureen had died, bit by sad bit every day, and had grown stronger still when she had passed away and the pain of it had wrapped around both of them so tightly. It had all but broken Delaney's heart when Ben had fled his home after Maureen's funeral, running back to the Enright home in Pennsylvania. Wisely understanding that it had been the reality of his mother's death that Ben had attempted to flee from, Delaney had vowed to do whatever it would take to help his grandson cope with his grief. When it became clear to Delaney that Ben was uncomfortable living in the house where his mother had died, Delaney had immediately closed up his Connecticut home and moved them both to a town house in Manhattan. And there they had lived until Ben had left for college in Arizona, then graduate school in London.

Though Delaney had always hoped—prayed—that someday Ben would express an interest in taking over Connor International, it had been difficult to ignore that Ben's real love was racing. Delaney had sighed with resignation when Ben became a test driver for a manufacturer of race cars, and then later, more recently, had taken the first steps toward establishing a career as a professional driver. Yet even as Delaney had secretly purchased a British tire manufacturing company and signed on as Ben's first sponsor, he had never given up his most cherished hope that one day, Ben would want to work for the business his grandfather had spent a lifetime building.

Delaney hated the feeling that he was manipulating the boy, even if it was, he felt certain, for his own good. For years, he had known that for Ben to block out the past was not a good thing. Delaney and Delia had spent many an hour on the telephone discussing Ben's refusal to return to Westboro, or even to see Delia. A deeply disturbed Delaney had consulted a renowned child psychiatrist, who had cautioned him not to force Ben to deal with memories he wasn't ready to cope with, to be supportive but to permit the boy to heal on his own. He would, Dr. Smith had assured Delaney, come to terms in his own time, reminding him that Ben had suffered a deep loss at a very vulnerable time in his life, and that he should be permitted to deal with it in whatever way was best for him. For Ben, the best way had apparently been to blot out as much as possible of those years before he had come to live with his grandfather. Delaney and Delia had stayed in contact throughout that time, both hoping that the time would come when Ben could make the trip back to Westboro and renew his old ties. It never had.

Well, maybe I should have followed my own instincts, Delaney thought as he paced, and said the hell with the damned shrink. Maybe I should have packed Ben in the car every damned weekend, sulking and moody or not, and driven him to Westboro myself. Maybe if I had, he wouldn't have chosen a career that kept him on the opposite side of the ocean from April through November every year.

And lately, Delaney had begun to fear that Ben's choice of a career was someday going to lead to something far more serious than a broken leg. The very thought terrified him.

Still, maybe it wasn't too late. . . .

Delaney wasn't a superstitious man, but he knew that there were times when Fate reached out a hand and made you an offer you couldn't refuse. He couldn't help but believe that this was one of those times. All the signs were there, and taken as a whole, they added up, in Delaney's mind, to one such offer. Ben's accident that took him out of racing for at least a year. That young pup from the finance department proposing that he buy that shopping thing that just happened to be located in eastern Pennsylvania. And there, as if a lucky charm, had been Delia's girl flashing that smile along with that gold bracelet. It just all fell into place too neatly to be ignored, and Delaney had learned a long time ago that an opportunity missed was an opportunity mourned. He had no intentions of mourning this one.

All he had to do, Delaney had reasoned, was to find a way to get Ben to come back to the States and run the Home MarketPlace.

Which Ben could, conceivably, offer to do, if, perhaps, he understood that his grandfather needed him.

Delaney would have felt a great deal more confident, would have been pacing a great deal less, if he had been able to figure out just *how* to do that. Playing up his illness a bit was the only thing that came to mind.

It might work. After all, he *was* an old man. And he did have a legitimate heart problem, though with medication and proper diet it was well under control and posed no immediate threat.

He was still trying to figure out how much of *that* hand he could play—after all, he didn't want to out-and-out *lie* when innuendo alone might do the trick—when simultaneously the clock struck a subdued eight bells and a knock was heard on the door.

"Come in, come in, Ben. Son. I'm so very happy to see you." Delaney stretched forth his hand, wondering for just a moment if Ben considered himself to be too old to be hugged by his grandfather.

"Delaney." Ben leaned heavily on the left crutch and took his grandfather's hand. "It's good to see you, too."

Delaney put his arm around Ben's shoulder under the guise of helping him into the room. The boy felt solid under his hand. Muscular. Strong. It was the closest Delaney had been to him in six months, since the racing season had begun, and he was in no hurry to end the contact, however brief.

"Sit, son. Let me get something for you to rest that foot on. How does it feel? Are you uncomfortable?"

"It's all right, Grampa. It only bothers me if I've been on it too much. I took it easy today, knowing I'd be coming out tonight."

Oddly touched by that admission, that Ben had planned his day around seeing him that evening, Delaney patted the boy's shoulder as he passed by.

"Let me bring this footstool over for you." Delaney dragged a heavy round cushioned stool over to the sofa. "Now, what can I get you to drink?"

"Club soda would be fine," Ben told him. "Alcohol doesn't mix well under the circumstances."

"Ah. Right you are. It wouldn't do to take another tumble now, would it?" Delaney went to the bar and spooned ice into a tumbler. He poured in some club soda, slid in a peel of lime, and walked back to the sofa, handing it to Ben and saying, "I've been unable to drink alcohol for so long now, I forget why I used to like it."

"Lost your taste for it?"

"Not really. I still love a good tumbler of fine Scotch as much as I always have. But, unfortunately, it's a poor mix with my medication," Delaney said, trying to look suitably concerned and yet blasé at the same time.

"What medication is that?" Ben frowned. Was his grandfather ill?

Delaney tapped lightly on his chest with his right fist and said, "Well, the heart's been giving me some problems, son." No lie there, Delaney gave himself a mental nod.

"What kind of problems?"

"Nothing I want you to worry about, son. Now, tell me, are you planning on going back into racing?"

107

"When I can. If I can. Delaney"—Ben turned around in his seat to face his grandfather—"is there something I should know? I thought that you had made a good recovery from your heart attack."

"Ah, Ben, I'm an old man." I *am* an old man, Delaney assured himself. Still on honest ground here. "Old men have old hearts. Old hearts are neither predictable nor reliable." All true.

Delaney had practiced this part all afternoon. He was going for *brave but philosophical,* hoping to come off a bit like an Apache chief he had seen in a movie once, who, knowing that death was impending, had announced stoically, "It is a good day to die." He stole a sideways glance at his grandson, wondering how he was doing.

Another knock at the door announced that their dinner had arrived. He excused himself to Ben and went to the door, slowing himself down from his usual pace, favoring his own arthritic knee just a little more than usual, going so far as to hunch his shoulders just slightly. Wishing he had eyes in the back of his head, he hobbled slightly on his cane to the door, and opened it.

"Would you mind setting up near the sofa?" Delaney asked, taking just a moment to lean against the door frame, as if weary.

"Not at all, sir." The tuxedoed waiter went about his business of moving the table closer to the sofa, where Ben sat watching his grandfather with anxious eyes.

"I hope you don't mind," Delaney said as he lowered himself into the chair with careful deliberation, "but I took the liberty of ordering for both of us."

"I don't mind at all," Ben replied, leaning back slightly from the table to permit the waiter to place a covered dish before him.

"Let's see now." Delaney peered across the table. "Yours does have the cream and herb sauce, does it not?"

"Yes. It smells wonderful."

"Ah, yes, so it does," Delaney's nostrils sniffed at the air wistfully. "Delightful."

"Did you order yours plain?" Ben frowned, noticing that his grandfather's plate contained a portion of broiled fish, naked without the fragrant herbed cream sauce, some sliced carrots, rice, and a few slices of lemon.

Delaney sighed deeply. "I'm afraid everything in that sauce except for the tarragon is off limits for me."

All through the superb dinner, which Ben barely tasted, he watched the old man and wondered if his grandfather's health was worse than he had been led to believe over the past few years.

"Are you in London on business, Delaney?" Ben asked, hoping to draw him into conversation.

"No, son," Delaney replied softly. "I just wanted to see you again."

"I'm sorry I couldn't make it home for Christmas this year." Ben pointed toward his leg.

"Tough to board a plane when you're strapped to an operating table." Delaney tried to smile, but the fact that Ben had had to undergo surgery two days before Christmas had made for a very lonely holiday.

"Knowing how you avoid flying under any circumstances, I'm surprised you didn't take the QE II." Ben had the uneasy feeling that he was only getting half the story. Delaney hated to fly, and yet for no apparent reason at all, he had flown to London, with no plans except to have dinner with Ben. Chilling thoughts began to form in Ben's mind. How much was Delaney not telling him?

"Well, you're right. I still do hate to fly, Ben, and I had thought about taking a ship. But, well, I just thought it might . . ." He paused, staring at his plate with what he hoped to be just the right degree of implication. ". . . take too much time."

The fish lay in Ben's stomach like a lump of sandstone.

"Grampa, are you sure you're all right?"

"Ben, I am closing in on eighty years of age. Need I say more?"

They ate in silence. The clock on the mantel chimed nine.

"So, tell me, son. What are your plans?"

"I don't really know, Delaney. I won't be able to drive for months. It may be a long time before I regain full mobility and control of my foot. The ankle fracture was pretty bad."

"That so?" Delaney knew just how bad the fracture was, having had Ben's X rays sent to his office immediately after Ben's accident. "What do you see as the earliest you might be back behind the wheel again?"

"Competitively?" Ben frowned. "Not for at least a year. If ever."

"I'm sorry, son. I know how much you love the sport."

"Thank you, Grampa. I appreciate that."

"What will you do in the meantime? Between now and when you can start racing again?"

"I wish I knew. There aren't many options."

"Hmmm. I wonder . . ." Delaney began, then stopped.

"What's that?"

"Ah, nothing. Just an old man's fancy."

"What are you thinking, Delaney?"

"Nothing, my boy." Delaney dismissed the thought. "Besides, I'm sure that it wouldn't work. You have established your life here. And besides, I really couldn't impose on you."

"What, Delaney?"

"Well, it seems that I've gotten myself into a bit of a bind." Delaney smiled what he hoped would appear to be a *sheepish* smile. "You see, I recently bought a company, one that has tremendous potential, in the long run, but it's been badly mismanaged. I have wonderful plans for it, and I know the right person could go in and turn it around."

"You've done it a dozen times before."

"This time it might be a little more of a challenge than I can deal with right now. I'm afraid I should have given

110

more consideration to . . . well, to *circumstances* before I gave in to the impulse. It was just such a natural reaction for me. After all these years, you know, of buying companies in distress and turning them around. I'm afraid I've bitten off more than I can possibly chew this time."

"Well, how long do you think it would take to make a go of it?"

"Oh, perhaps a year. Eighteen months at the most."

"That's not a very long time."

"Not for you, Ben. But for me, at my age, well, a whole *year* . . ."

A waiter removed their dinner plates while the other poured coffee for Ben.

"Aren't you having coffee?"

"Doctor won't permit it. Haven't had a decent cup of coffee in . . ." He paused, meaningfully. "Well, in some months now."

"So, are you going to tell me about this new business of yours?" Ben asked uneasily, watching his grandfather with wary eyes.

"Ah, yes. The entire concept is very exciting, innovative, challenging." Delaney's eyes took on a familiar shine as he settled back to cast the bait and reel him in.

It had been, Delaney later reflected, almost embarrassingly easy. Ben had opened the door for Delaney to give him the rundown on his new venture, and Delaney had smoothly stepped right through it.

Ben himself wasn't quite sure how it had happened, but before he had left his grandfather's hotel room that night, he had offered to give Delaney a hand with the Home MarketPlace, at least until his foot healed and he could resume driving again. For the time being, he would analyze sales and investment patterns from the computerized records that Delaney would have sent to him first thing in the morning. If Ben had any second thoughts, they had come only when Delaney had mentioned casually, as if an afterthought, that this new business was located near Lancaster, Pennsylvania—painfully close to Westboro and a past Ben had spent most of his adult life trying to forget. The dark thoughts could be pushed aside, to be dealt with when the time came.

After all, his grandfather needed him, and that was all that mattered.

Chapter

9

The news had hit the Home MarketPlace with all the devastating force of a tsunami. For the second time in roughly two years, the network had been sold.

The nerves of those whose offices lined Executive Row—particularly the nerves of those stalwarts who had survived the first sale—were frayed just about to the limit. And, to make matters worse, no one was quite certain who the buyer was. The sale had been crisply executed and smoothly accomplished, the paper trail long and twisted, with as many kinks and curls as a corkscrew. A company named Duval Industries had made the purchase, but seeking the principals had led to Kerry & Company, which in turn led to The Sikes Corporation. By the time the sun had risen on Connor International, Delaney O'Connor was on his way to the big office in the front corner of the second floor, and even as "ConnorCast" was being emblazoned on the side of the building, Pauline was guarding the door to the executive suite and preparing for Delaney's arrival.

"I'm sorry that I have so few hard facts to share with you." Ted Higgins stood at one end of the hosts' lounge and addressed the uneasy group that had gathered to try to sort out fact from rumor. "All I can tell you is that the new CEO will arrive here sometime this morning. He sent a memo to the personnel manager stating that he wanted to personally interview each one of you over the next week, starting immediately. His secretary is already in the building and has provided me with a schedule of the interviews."

"Are the interviews intended to weed out some of us?" John Dudley, the oldest in the group and a veteran of several shopping networks, fidgeted with his tie. It was no secret that his sales were mediocre and his ratings not much better.

"I don't have a clue, John. I wish I did," Ted told him bluntly. "Mrs. Gilbert—that's the CEO's secretary—said only that he wished to meet with his new employees as soon as possible."

"Maybe there's nothing more to it than that." CeCe shrugged. "For him to be moving in here so quickly, before the ink has dried, maybe he's just a real hands-on type. Maybe he does just want to meet us individually."

"I have no problem with the hands-on type, myself." Genevieve Cutler, the blond Marilyn look-alike, postured and pursed her lips.

"Unless those hands are placing a noose around your neck and yanking you out of your job," Dudley shot back.

"Some of us might have more to worry about than others." Garrett Wilson leaned against the wall with one hip, managing, as always, to look smug, his ever-present I-know-something-you-don't-know grin grating on every other person in the room.

"If, under penalty of death, you had to choose between John Dudley and Garrett Wilson, who would be the lucky fella?" Zoey whispered between clenched teeth into CeCe's ear.

"Oh, man, that's a tough one," CeCe whispered back over her shoulder while pretending to give careful consideration to her response.

"Might it not help if they switched toupees?" Zoey suggested thoughtfully.

"I don't know how all that blond hair"—CeCe pointed a discreet finger toward Dudley's shock of yellow hair—"would blend with Garrett's phony tan."

"Shhhh." Marly Campbell, a petite blonde known for her on-air chattiness, poked Zoey in the back.

"Well, I guess we'll have a better idea by the end of the day"—Ted held up the schedule and waved the paper slightly before the crowd—"since the first interview is scheduled for immediately after lunch."

"Who's the goat?" Someone asked nervously. "Who gets to go first?"

Looking down at the list, Higgins read the name. "Zoey Enright."

"Me?" Zoey gasped. "Why me?"

"Luck of the draw, I guess," Higgins said dryly.

"Does anyone even know who this guy is?" Garrett asked.

"By 'this guy,' if you mean the new CEO, yes. Of course." Higgins told him. "His name is Delaney O'Connor."

Zoey frowned and repeated the name aloud softly. *Delaney O'Connor.*

It picked at the threads of Zoey's memory, a loose strand from somewhere long ago.

Delaney O'Connor.

Where had she heard that name before?

With a lump in her chest that felt like a ragged stone, Zoey quickly checked her sales from the three hours she had just finished and grabbed her purse from under the technicians' desk where she had left it. She checked her watch and quickened her pace as she walked briskly toward the suite of offices that sat at the opposite side of the building from the sets. It would probably not be a good idea to keep the new boss waiting.

The handsome secretary, looking fiftyish and crisp, stood at Zoey's approach.

"Hello," Zoey smiled. "I'm—"

"Of course. Zoey Enright." The secretary smiled back. "Go right on in. He's expecting you."

The door to the office of the CEO stood partially open. Zoey tapped on it lightly.

"Ah, Miss Enright, come in."

Delaney O'Connor stood in the middle of his office, leaning heavily on a thick wooden cane, staring up at the oversized TV monitor suspended from the ceiling.

"Any guess where they might have found *her?*" he asked, skipping the formalities of an introduction as he nodded toward the television, where Genevieve was giggling her way through a VCR presentation.

When Zoey failed to respond, he added, "There's a rumor going around that Miss Cutler believes herself to be the reincarnation of Marilyn Monroe. I suppose you've heard that one."

Zoey nodded.

He dropped slowly onto one end of the long dark blue leather sofa that wrapped around one end of the room, leaned forward on his cane, and patted the seat next to him.

"Come sit next to me, Zoey." He smiled broadly, perhaps a tad more friendly, more *familiar,* than Zoey would have expected.

Warily, Zoey approached the sofa, and aware that he had barely taken his eyes off her since she had entered the room, chose the cushion at the opposite end and perched upon its edge.

Oh, great. Terrific. Delaney O'Connor is a dirty old man, and I got first dibs.

She crossed her ankles and tugged on the hem of her short skirt, trying vainly to stretch the hem to reach her knees.

Correctly reading her defensive moves, Delaney O'Connor burst into laughter. "Oh, my dear, I am so terribly flattered," he laughed. "But no, no, I only wanted to talk for a few minutes."

She smiled warily.

"Please, forgive me if I gave you the wrong impression," he said, still chuckling. "Please. Relax. Sit over there"—he pointed to a chair across the room—"if it makes you feel more comfortable."

Red-faced, she hesitated, then somewhat sheepishly leaned back a little against the arm of the sofa.

"Excuse me." The pleasant secretary poked her head into the office. "I've brought you some iced tea."

"Herbal, I'm afraid," Delaney noted, "since I'm not permitted any caffeine. And I miss it terribly."

Pauline placed two coasters—dried flowers under a layer of laminate—onto the table that curved into the arc of the sofa, then set down two tavern-style glasses and a pitcher containing cranberry-colored liquid.

"Raspberry Zinger." Pauline answered his unspoken question and winked at Zoey before disappearing from the office as briskly as she had entered.

"I read in the paper that your mother has just begun another book tour." Delaney leaned over and poured tea over the ice cubes in the glass closest to him, then handed it to Zoey.

"Yes. Out West this time." Zoey relaxed slightly, accustomed to having people ask about Delia, and impressed by the fact that the new CEO had apparently wasted no time before reading the personnel files. But, then again, one would expect someone like Delaney O'Connor to do his homework.

"Does she still enjoy the travel?"

"Yes," she answered slowly, the glass raised to her lips.

"I wondered if, perhaps, over the years, she had grown tired of it."

"No, she hasn't," Zoey replied, watching his face. "Mr. O'Connor, you speak as if you know my mother."

"We met, years ago." He cleared his throat. "Actually, our paths crossed for a brief period—a very brief, but very significant, crossing."

There it was again—the pricking sensation at the base of her neck. She waited for him to elaborate. A buzzer beckoned him from his desk, and he rose from the sofa with the aid of his cane to answer it. Excusing himself to Zoey, he lifted the receiver and after a moment's pause, said, "Yes. Please. Put him through."

Uncomfortable at having to sit through the intimacy of listening to a stranger's telephone call, Zoey's eyes began to wander around the room, which had been redecorated in record time. How intriguing, she mused, that a man like O'Connor would choose to set up shop there at all, rather than to simply rely on others to run the business for him. In little under a week, O'Connor had replaced the sharp-edged high-tech chrome and glass favored by his predecessor with plush carpet, rich wall coverings, and comfortable, cushy furniture, and the blacks, whites, and grays of the prior occupant had given way to jewel colors ... emerald green, sapphire blue, ruby red. The stark, edgy works of modern art had been removed. O'Connor had chosen instead to display photographs of various sizes, in frames of wood or brass or silver.

Zoey tried to be unobtrusive in her attempt to get a better look at the photos, which covered almost every inch of space along one wall. She leaned forward a bit, drawing closer to bring the pictures into slightly better focus. Every one had captured the same subject, a young man, dark-haired and handsome, in or near a sleek racing car. She stared at the one closest to her.

The young man leaned back against a Ferrari, his arms folded casually across his chest, his stance pure arrogance. His mouth quirked into a half smile and his dark glasses wrapped around his face like a blindfold, shielding his eyes. A jungle of dark hair tumbled over his forehead, and the orange overalls covered his body but did nothing to hide the muscular frame within. He looked, Zoey thought, every bit as sleek and dangerous as his car.

"My grandson," Delaney said, following her gaze as he hung up the phone.

"He races cars?"

"In Europe, yes."

"You're obviously very proud of him," she said.

He beckoned her toward him, and without saying a word, handed her a photo in a brass frame. Zoey held the frame into the light to get a better look.

The boy who had become the man who drove fast cars hung upside down from the bough of a tree, caught in the act of clowning, of showing off, his lopsided grin playful, his face animated.

Suddenly, she could see it, and for a split second, she was there—could smell the slightly rotted apples that lay about the base of the tree, could hear the boy's voice.

"Hey, Mrs. E.! Up here, in the apple tree. It's me! It's—"

"Ben," Zoey whispered incredulously. "It's Ben Pierce."

The old man nodded confirmation.

"You're Ben Pierce's grandfather?"

Again, a slight nod of the head.

"You came to our house once," she said softly. "I watched you from upstairs. You took Ben away. It was the night . . ."

"The night of my daughter's funeral. As soon as his mother had been laid to rest, Ben ran away. It didn't take much imagination to figure out where he'd run to."

"I remember. Something woke me up and I went to the stairwell because the lights were on and I looked down. Mom was there, and Ben—I remember feeling scared because Ben looked so angry. I had never seen him look so angry."

"Losing his mother had been a terrible blow to him, Zoey. Even though he had spent every day of her illness by her side, I don't think he really understood what was happening. I think he almost believed that if he went back there, she would be there, waiting for him." He turned and looked out the window, as if searching for something, before asking, "Do you remember my daughter, Zoey?"

"Of course." She nodded. "She practically raised us. Mom used to refer to Maureen as her clone because

Maureen did everything that Mom couldn't get to when she was writing."

"Ah, Zoey, I have blessed your mother in my prayers every night for giving Maureen and the boy a safe and happy place to live. Lord knows the two of them had long deserved it." O'Connor pulled himself up with the help of his cane and began to pace, somewhat uncomfortably, it appeared, back and forth in front of the sofa. "What do you know about Ben's father?"

"Nothing." She shrugged. "I never heard Ben—or Maureen, for that matter—speak of him."

"Jack Pierce worked in our stables. He was handsome and lazy and charming. Right or wrong, after Maureen's mother died, I kept the girl on a pretty tight string, to keep her out of harm's way, I told myself. What a fool I was. She was a normal, healthy, pretty girl, and Jack Pierce was neither blind nor stupid. As I saw it, he made it very easy for Maureen to fall in love with him. Of course, when she told me she wanted to marry him, I refused to hear a word of it. But worse than that, I told her the truth as I saw it. That Jack's only interest in her was in the money she'd inherit someday. That he didn't really love her at all. That he saw her only as a one-way ticket to the good life. So, of course, they ran away together." O'Connor's eyes narrowed. "Well, I figured they'd run out of money soon enough, and then she'd come home with her tail between her legs. Well, the money ran out fast enough, that was a fact. But she had no intentions of running home, not after Jack was struck and killed by a hit-and-run driver. Not after she found out she was pregnant."

"Didn't you try to convince her to come home?"

"Maureen was so angry with me, that she wanted nothing to do with me. I tried everything I could think of, but I could not talk her into coming home, or even to take my help. She would manage just fine on her own, thank you very much." He leaned back against the front of his desk as if very weary. "And for years, she did manage. But through all that time, Maureen could not forgive me for the things I had said to her. And I can't say that I blame her. What a terrible message to give your child, that she was not loved for who she was, but only for what she had."

"But surely you never meant . . ."

"Of course not. I only thought to protect her from someone who I believed would hurt her. But right up until the end, Maureen believed that Jack had loved her very much. And maybe he did, Zoey. Maybe I had been wrong about him from the start."

He ran his fingers through his still thick white hair. "I'd lost my wife when Maureen was three. I thought I understood pain. But then, one day, there was Maureen, in the hallway of that big house that had waited so long for her to come home. There she stood, my beautiful Maureen. My girl had come home." His voice dropped to a quivering whisper. "My girl had come home to die."

If she closed her eyes, Zoey, too, could see her. Maureen Pierce had been tall and straight when she'd first come to work for Delia, who had just moved her family to the "gentleman's farm" in Westboro. It seemed that Maureen and Ben had always been there with them, their best friends, part of an extended family. And then, before any one of them could really grasp what had happened, they were gone.

"For five months, I had my girl back with me. Five months while I nursed her and watched her grow weaker by the day. Five months for me to suffer with her, and to watch the anger and confusion and fear grow in the boy's eyes. We grew very close, Ben and I. I have been very grateful to my daughter, for bringing me the very precious gift of her son."

"So, you and Maureen were able to reconcile before she died?"

"Yes, yes. I have thanked God every day for every one of those minutes we were able to spend together. That she was able to forgive me. That, in spite of everything, she still loved me enough to come home."

"I don't know what to say, Mr. O'Connor."

"What is there to say?" He wiped his face with the fine white linen handkerchief he had pulled from his jacket pocket. "But I must tell you, when I found out that you were Delia Enright's daughter, so much came back to me. I know how happy Maureen had been in Westboro. How close she had been to Delia . . . how close Ben had been to all of you."

"Well, we all sort of grew up together." Zoey's eyes drifted back to the photograph that Delaney had rested on the table. *So this was the grown-up Ben Pierce.* She fought the urge to reach out and touch the glass, to reach into the photo and smooth the hair back from his handsome face. . . .

"Yes. So I understand."

"Maybe you could give me his address," Zoey said. "For my mother. I'm sure she will want to get in touch with him. And when you speak with him again, please give him my very best, and tell him"—she paused— "tell him that we have missed him very much."

"Oh, I expect that, if all goes well, you will be able to do that yourself. I'm sure he'll be around, sooner or later."

"Ben, here?" Zoey felt her bottom jaw drop, but was helpless to do anything about it. Surely, he didn't mean . . .

"Oh, yes." Delaney O'Connor nodded brightly.

"Ben will be here?" she repeated. "You mean *here?*"

"For a while, at least until he recuperates from his latest accident. I'm afraid he's done a nasty job on his leg. It will be some time before the fractures heal."

Delaney smiled and got up to answer the phone yet again. He said a few muffled words into the receiver, before turning to Zoey and saying, "I've just been reminded that I have another appointment. It's been a pleasure, Zoey Enright. You've grown into a very beautiful young woman. I'm delighted to have you on my staff."

"Thank you, sir." She moved across to his desk on numb legs and took the hand he reached out to her.

"Call me Delaney. After all, we're practically old friends, aren't we?"

He hesitated, as if about to confide something, then, appearing to have thought better of it, merely patted her hand and smiled. "Do give your mother my very best."

Zoey left the room in a bit of a daze.

Still holding the phone, Delaney walked to the window and looked out onto the rolling green landscape of Lancaster County, Pennsylvania. Off in the distance, on the next hill, he could see the old stone church that had stood since the days of the Revolutionary War. Earlier that morning, they had passed it, and he had had his driver stop and pull over. He had gotten out of the back of the car and walked among the flat thick stones marking the graves of soldiers whose names would never be known, the letters having been eroded a century or more ago. It had been a peaceful place, and he had gone into the little church and sat on one of the hard narrow wooden pews and stared at the stark altar. And there, Delaney gave thanks for having been given the ways and the means to bring his grandson home.

Then, being a God-fearing man who'd been raised in the bosom of the Church, Delaney O'Connor prayed for forgiveness for all the little half-truths he'd told to get him there.

Chapter

10

Zoey smiled graciously at Delaney O'Connor's secretary, nodding mindlessly in apparent agreement with whatever it was the woman was saying. It couldn't possibly be important compared with the news Zoey had just gotten from O'Connor's own lips. Ben would be here—sooner or later, Delaney had said—*right here,* under the same roof. Breathing the same air. Close enough to touch.

Maybe they'd bump into each other in the hallway.

No, no, better yet, in the parking lot.

"Ben?" she would call to him. "Ben Pierce, is that really you?"

"Yes?" He would stop in mid-stride and tilt his head slightly to one side, just like he used to do.

"It's me, Zoey. Zoey Enright."

And he would break into a fabulous grin and with a hoot lift her up off her feet and swing her around, just like she had dreamed he would do. She could see it so clearly, how his strong arms would lift her—in slow motion, with music playing in the background—and then he'd . . .

"Lady, for crying out loud, are you blind or something?" The delivery man yelled as she stepped mindlessly in front of the pallet laden with boxes.

"Oh. Oh. I'm so sorry." A flustered Zoey blushed. "I was just . . . I wasn't paying attention. Thank you for being more observant than I am."

She stopped at the front desk and leaned over the clipboard where everyone entering or leaving the building signed in or out.

"Is CeCe still here?" She asked Lee, the weekend daytime guard.

He barely looked up from his newspaper, where he was making his selections from the daily racing form, but merely pointed at the television set mounted on the wall to his left, where CeCe was selling a hand-stitched quilt in shades of rose and green.

"Thanks." She went back down the hallway and through the double doors leading into the studio, anxious to share this incredible news with her friend.

"Zoey," one of the producers called to her, "did you already meet him? The new CEO?"

"Yes," she called over her shoulder.

"Well? What's he like?"

"Oh, he's wonderful. It's going to be wonderful." She smiled dreamily.

Zoey stood just inside the doorway of the set, which was decorated with several beds upon which quilts of different styles were displayed. CeCe was, at that moment, stuffing pillows into shams that matched the pastel quilt Zoey recognized as one she herself had sold on-air two weeks earlier. She watched the dual monitors at the front of the set, waiting until the one on top—the one that displayed exactly what was appearing on the viewers' television screens at that minute—showed the linens only, then cleared her throat softly to get her friend's attention. CeCe glanced to the side of the stage, where Zoey stood, grinning like an idiot.

"What's up?" CeCe mouthed the words.

"How much longer do you have today?" Zoey whispered.

CeCe pointed to the lower of the two monitors, the one that showed the on-air host the next shot that the viewers at home would see, and said to the camera, "We're halfway through the first hour of this three-hour quilt special and I still have lots of pretty things to show you."

Zoey frowned and gestured to CeCe to call her later, then turned and all but skipped to the locker area where she had earlier hung her coat and her purse. Her head was buzzing. All she could think about as she walked from the building to her car was *Ben*. She had seen his face. His *grown-up* face, which was every bit as heartbreakingly handsome as, somehow, she had known it would be. Ben Pierce. Her very own Ben Pierce was coming home.

Humming, she started up the car, then pulled into the roadway leading out of the complex where the Home MarketPlace sprawled over three buildings connected by covered walkways.

She couldn't wait to tell her mother. Delia would be thrilled. She dialed the number on her car phone and waited impatiently while it rang.

"Hello, Mrs. Colson," she said when Delia's housekeeper answered the phone. "It's Zoey. Is my mother there?"

There was a long pause before the voice on the other end of the phone said, "Zoey, is something wrong?"

"No. Nothing's wrong. Why do you ask?"

"Zoey, you know your mother is in Tulsa at a writers' conference."

"Oh, of course she is." Zoey laughed. "I don't know what I was thinking. I'll call her tonight at the hotel. Thanks."

She hung up, then dialed another number. It rang four times before the answering machine picked up. "Hi. I'm not able to take your call right now, but if you leave your name and the date and time of your call, and your number, I'll get back to you as soon as I can."

"Georgey-girl, it's your big sister. I have the most incredible news. Call me the minute you get home."

Stopped at a red light, Zoey disconnected the call, then dialed yet again. Three more rings. Another taped message.

"Nicky! It's Zoey. Call me tonight. I have something so exciting to tell you."

She disconnected once again, still holding the phone in her hand, trying to think of someone else to call. She could not.

Sighing, she returned the phone to its base and drove toward home, trying to think of things that were more frustrating than having great news, and no one to share it with.

Even Wally's car was gone from his driveway when she got home. It was Saturday, so the workmen were gone as well. Slightly dejected, she parked near the back door and got out of the car. The steps to the new deck had recently been completed, and she took them two at a time. The contractor promised that his men would be back the following week to paint it, and to finish up a few details inside the house. She unlocked the door and stepped inside. Gracie stretched languidly into a large, loose apostrophe of orange velvet on the gold-colored carpet and raised one delicate feline paw straight up into the air, as much a greeting as an admonition for Zoey having left her alone for hours.

"Oh, you big old hairball." Zoey dropped her pocket-book and the day's mail on the kitchen counter to give the cat a scratch behind the ears. "Don't you have the life. No daily bread to earn. No traffic to deal with. No bills to pay—"

The phone rang shrilly.

"No phones to answer." Zoey pounced on it, hoping it was Delia. Or Nick. Or Georgia.

It was a wrong number.

Sighing, she pulled a chair out from the kitchen table and plunked down in it.

"Well, then, perhaps you'd like to hear my news." She turned to Gracie, who hadn't as yet bothered to open her eyes. "Well, that's too bad, because I'm going to tell you anyway."

Zoey decided she wanted coffee to accompany her telling of the tale.

"This is a story, Gracie, so pay attention." She rinsed the remnants of the morning's coffee from the pot, then refilled it. "Once upon a time, there was a little girl named Zoey . . . yeah, just like me. She had a little sister who everyone said was the most adorable thing in the world. That's because she *was* the most adorable little thing in the world, tiny and blond and graceful . . . and Zoey was tall and skinny and awkward and had dark stringy hair and was a tomboy. No one ever said that Zoey was adorable."

Zoey stuffed a white paper liner into the basket of the coffeemaker.

"Her name? Oh, we'll call the little sister . . . Georgia." She opened the cupboard and took down her coffee grinder. "And the two sisters had a big brother. His name was, what do you think, should we call him Nicky? Sure, why not. Anyway, Zoey and Georgia and Nicky lived with their mother . . . what? Sure, they had a father. But he didn't live with them." Zoey sorted through the bags of coffee beans in her freezer—which was where Mrs. Colson always insisted was the only place coffee beans would stay fresh—until she found the bag of decaffeinated beans she was seeking. "He had left them, a long time ago." Her voice lowered to a whisper. "No. I don't know where he went, or why he left them. He just did. And their mother had to find a way to make money to feed them all. Luckily, the mother—sure, let's call her Delia."

At the sound of her mistress's voice, Gracie raised a lazy head and opened one eye. "Ha! That got your attention, didn't it? Anyway, Delia was a very clever lady. She liked to tell stories . . . and she started writing them down. And people liked to read her stories. And before you could say 'catnip,' Delia had an agent and a publisher who was paying her to tell her stories. And Delia had lots and lots of stories to tell." Zoey dumped a handful of coffee beans into the bowl of the grinder and said, "Cover your ears, Gracie, you don't like this noise."

At the sound of the grinder, Gracie sat up and gave Zoey what could only be described as the feline equivalent of a dirty look.

"Anyway, Delia was very busy writing her stories, so busy that she decided that she needed someone to come and take care of them all, to cook and shop and be part of the family. And one night, she went out to the little local market for bread and milk, and she brought home Maureen. And Maureen's son, Ben."

Zoey stood with her hand still on the lid of the grinder, a faraway look on her face. "You didn't know Ben, Gracie. He left before Mom found you in that parking lot where you had been dropped off. But you would have liked Ben. We all did."

Zoey could close her eyes and see him as he had followed her mother into the kitchen that first night, carrying Delia's grocery bags for her. Zoey had been at the table in the breakfast room, just about to scoop some ice cream into a bowl for a snack.

"Zoey, this is Maureen, and her son, Ben," Delia had said by way of introduction. "Get another bowl, sweetie, and see if Ben would like some ice cream, too. Maureen and I are going into the study for a few minutes to talk."

"Would you like some ice cream?" Zoey had asked shyly. "It's cherry vanilla."

"That's one of my favorite kinds," he had said.

It had been very quiet in the kitchen then, as she could not think of anything to say as she dug a scoop into the brick hard ice cream.

"Let me do that for you," he offered gently, taking the scoop from her. She had noticed then that his eyes were dark green, darker than any shade of green eyes she had ever seen.

She had never forgotten his dark green eyes.

Nicky had come in while they were eating, and Zoey had introduced her brother to the stranger. After a few exploratory remarks, Nick asked Ben if he'd like to see the fish tank. Nodding enthusiastically that he would, Ben followed him from the room. Left behind, Zoey slowly picked up the ice cream bowls and rinsed them in the sink.

"Thank you for the ice cream, Zoey." Ben stuck his head through the kitchen doorway and smiled at her. "And I like your name. It's different. And pretty. It suits you."

And her seven-year-old heart had become his.

"I saw his picture today, Gracie. He's grown up to be the most handsome man you've ever seen. Like a fairy-tale prince . . ."

Zoey sighed.

"Gorgeous," she assured Georgia when she called later that evening. "He's gorgeous."

"Well, well, well." Georgia laughed. "Ben Pierce. That he would pop back into the picture after all these years! Isn't this the most amazing coincidence?"

No, no, not coincidence, Zoey wanted to tell her. *It's fate. He's come back for me. Just like I always dreamed he would do.*

Instead, she said, "Yes. It's incredible. I can't wait to tell Nicky. I left a message for him to call me."

"He probably won't get it till tomorrow night. He and India went to Paloma for the weekend. They were meeting with a realtor today to put India's town house on the market. She decided to sell it, since she has moved back to Devlin's Light permanently," Georgia told her. "But I know he'll be very happy. As Mother will be."

And of course, Delia was.

"Oh, Zoey, that's too wonderful! When will he be there? I wonder how he looks, all grown up."

"Delaney said in about a week or so. And he looks wonderful, Mom." Zoey sighed.

Delia hesitated just slightly before asking, "Really? And how would you know that?"

"Delaney showed me his picture. Pictures, actually. He had lots of them, all over the office walls."

"How did you know it was Ben?"

"Delaney knew who I was, Mom. He knew I was your daughter. He asked for you."

"Kind of him," Delia murmured.

"—and handed me a photograph you had taken of Ben once. In the orchard. Hanging—"

"Upside down from a tree limb," Delia said softly. "Showing off, the little rascal. I remember the photograph. I gave it to Maureen for her birthday that year. When she and Ben left us, I had another copy made. It's in my office somewhere."

"Well, it was that picture. Of course, I knew who he was the second I saw it. Mom, isn't it amazing? That Delaney bought the HMP and I just happened to be working there? And that Ben would be coming to work for him? Isn't it wonderful?"

"Yes. Yes, it is, Zoey. I know how much you always liked Ben." Delia spoke slowly, as if deep in thought. "Zoey, does he have a family now?"

"What?"

"Ben. Is he married? Does he have children?"

"I . . . I don't know. I didn't ask." Her words tumbled over each other.

The thought had never occurred to her. Could that be possible? Surely fate would not play such a cruel joke on her.

"I think maybe Delaney would have mentioned it, though. I mean, there were dozens of photographs of Ben. Just Ben. No woman. No children. Just Ben."

"Hmmm. That wouldn't seem likely if he had a family." Delia was thinking aloud. "And what do you suppose he will be doing?"

"What do you mean, 'doing'?"

"I mean, is he coming for a short visit? Is he moving here?"

"I think he might be visiting with Delaney for a while, but I'm not really sure. Delaney did say something about Ben being in the process of moving, but I was so surprised I forgot to ask where. Or when . . ."

"Well, of course, you must let me know when he comes back, Zoey. I do want to see him. But in the meantime . . ."

Delia paused, as if choosing her words carefully.

"In the meantime, sweetheart, just keep in mind that people can change over the years. We don't know who Ben grew up to be."

"What are you trying to say, Mom?"

"Just hold on to your heart, Zoey. The man may be very different from the boy we used to know."

* * *

Ben Pierce hobbled through the airport leaning his weight on a cane, not for a moment missing the irony that his lopsided stride perfectly mimicked that of his elderly grandfather, who was, Ben couldn't help but notice, a lot more adept with the cane than *he* was.

"You having a problem keeping up, son?" Delaney had stopped once to call over his shoulder.

"I'm still getting the hang of it," Ben told him. "I've never had to use a cane before."

"And with any luck and some physical therapy, you won't need this one for long." Delaney leaned on his own dark wood cane, as much to catch his breath as to allow Ben to catch up. "Are you sure you wouldn't like one of those little golf cart type things to ride in?"

"I'll be fine. I'm more concerned about you. Are you sure you should be doing all this walking?"

Delaney straightened his back. "The doctor told me I need some moderate exercise. I am more worried about your ankle than I am about myself."

Ben scowled and with his cane pointed ahead, indicating that they should proceed toward the exit.

"I'm having someone pick up your luggage and drop it

off at my condo," Delaney told him as they approached the escalator that would take them to the first floor. "But I wanted to pick you up myself. I left the car right at the curb, so we're almost there."

They went through electronic doors into the remnants of a deep, early morning mist that had wrapped about the Philadelphia airport. Too early yet for the commuters and the real hustle-bustle of a weekday morning, there were few cars and fewer buses. Delaney's Town Car was fifteen feet from the doorway, and Ben wasn't sure if he'd ever been happier to see a car parked and waiting for him. Maybe his first Ferrari.

Delaney unlocked the doors and Ben slid somewhat awkwardly onto the front seat. It had been a long time since he had been seated in the passenger seat of his grandfather's car.

"Still like the Lincolns, eh, Delaney?"

"Haven't found anything to beat it, son."

"Tried the Lexus?" Ben asked as Delaney started the engine and headed toward the airport exit and Interstate 95.

"Nope. Haven't bothered to try anything else. Seems to me that as long as I like what I have, there's no reason to waste time looking around. When the day comes that I'm unhappy with my Town Car, then I'll try something else. But for the time being, I'm happy as a clam."

Ben smiled and looked out the window as the scenery seemed to crawl by at a slow speed.

"Tell me what you'd like to do, son. Do you want to go back to my place and rest for a while? You know, you don't have to go into the office today."

"Rest?" Ben raised his eyebrows. "I've been resting for five months, three of which I spent in a full leg cast, the other two with a cast to the knee. Thanks, Delaney, but I think I've had all the rest I can tolerate for a while."

"I'm sorry that the ankle didn't heal better than it did."

"The doctors said that the screw through the side should help give me some stability. Fortunately, the break was high enough on the bone that I haven't had to have a fusion. I will regain mobility. It's just taking longer than they thought."

And longer than I can stand.

It had been a rough few months for a man accustomed to total freedom. Confined first to the hospital, then to his flat, Ben had learned just exactly what *cabin fever* really meant. With so many of his racing buddies out of the country for the holidays, he had few visitors. Unless, of course, he counted the girlfriends of several of his friends who stopped in to see if he "needed" anything. It annoyed Ben just to think about it. True, it had been a while since he'd had female companionship, and being restricted to his home had totally removed him from the lively London social scene, but still, he wasn't so desperate that he'd have accepted the offers—some more subtle than others—for comfort from another man's woman.

He leaned back in the seat and stared straight ahead through the windshield, trying not to think about the last time he'd been on this same road, in another big Lincoln, with his grandfather at the wheel. That time, however, instead of heading toward Lancaster and Delaney's newest corporate venture they'd been heading north, to the house his mother had grown up in, a house that for Ben held only the painful memories of watching his mother die.

And here we are, once again, my grandfather and I. Who'd have guessed that the years would bring me back to this place?

He read the names of towns, once familiar, from a sign at a stoplight, fighting back the panic that had started swirling inside his head, wondering just how far they might be from the house that *he* had called home. He had been tempted to find a map of Pennsylvania and see just how far Lanning's Corner, Lancaster County, was from Westboro, in Chester County, but wasn't sure he wanted to know. It couldn't possibly be that far. Even after all the years, he remembered that Lancaster was the next county. He watched the fields, frozen still in these last days of winter, as they rolled past the windows of the car, and wondered if Delia Enright still lived there, in that wonderful house that had offered him so much more than shelter so very long ago.

Ben having been in the hospital recovering from his accident, Delia's last birthday had come and gone without his sending his usual birthday card, which, along with reading her books, was the only contact with that part of his life he could permit himself to maintain. He wondered if she noticed. Every year the message had been essentially the same: I think of you often, and hope that you are all well and happy. He had rarely asked about her children, those near siblings of his. He had simply missed them too much. Merely writing their names could bring their faces too close, close enough to see their smiles, hear their laughter. For a fourteen-year-old who had lost everything that had mattered to him, it hurt too much to even think of them. After his mother had died, it had been so much easier to pretend that those days in Westboro—those days with Delia and her family, when he and Maureen had been happy and life had been so full, so wonderful—had never really happened after all.

And yet here he was, in his grandfather's Lincoln, headed north on Route 202 just outside West Chester. Which was, he recalled, just a few miles from Westboro.

Certain landmarks loomed familiar. The ragged stone wall that encircled the Friends cemetery on the corner they had just passed by, a small pond set back from the road where geese gathered, hunched and chilled, in the early morning air.

A small sign pointing to the right at the next intersection announced Westboro—three miles. He glanced at the street sign. Old Forge Road.

He studied the corner, searching his memory for something familiar, but there was nothing there that had existed back then. The intersection had, those many years ago, seen a field on each of three corners, a dense wood on the fourth. The gas station that stood on the far right was new. On the opposite side of the road, a housing development stretched as far as the eye could see. He wanted to say something, to comment on it, on how much the area had changed since he had left, but his throat had tightened so, he couldn't seem to get the words out. When the light changed and Delaney continued straight on the road ahead, Ben fought an urge to look far down that road that led to Westboro as they passed it.

Fought and lost.

Delia Enright lived two and six-tenths of a mile down that road.

He wondered if Delaney remembered.

Chapter

11

❧

That Zoey, who had no interest in cooking, had somehow been chosen to launch the first of the new on-air cooking shows was clearly someone's idea of a perverse joke as far as she was concerned.

"Zoey, you have a call coming in from a viewer." Ellen, the producer, spoke into Zoey's ear via a tiny transistor.

"Hi. This is Zoey. What's your name and where are you from?" She tried to sound perky as she broke an egg for an omelet into a pretty pottery bowl. The omelet was to be cooked in a pan that was part of the set of two that she was selling.

"Irene. I'm from Illinois." The caller sounded slightly nervous.

"Irene from Illinois," Zoey said cheerfully, since it was her job to make the customers feel welcome, part of the HMP family. "I'm glad to hear from you. How are you today?"

A large piece of eggshell was floating, noticeably, in the bowl. Zoey tried to grab it but it slipped through her fingers.

"I'm fine. Zoey, I have to tell you that you are my favorite person on the HMP."

"Thank you, Irene. You're my favorite person in Illinois."

She tried to lift the piece of shell with a fingernail, but it slid away and sank momentarily.

"Zoey, forget about the damned eggshell." Ellen's voice in her ear broke Zoey's concentration for a moment.

"Zoey," the caller was saying, "you know, if you used a larger piece of shell to scoop up that little piece, you could pick it right up."

"Really?" She had never heard that one. Then again, she hadn't spent too much time cooking over the years either. She tried it. "Hey, Irene, thanks. That worked really well. I guess you can tell I'm a bit of a fledgling."

"That's all right honey, everyone has to learn. You have all of us here to help you." Irene from Illinois offered maternal assurance.

"Well, thank you for calling in, Irene. And thanks for your help here this morning. . . ."

"Zoey, the frying pan's starting to smoke. Take it off the burner." Ellen tried to maintain her calm. "And mix up that damned egg, will you? Sell the pan and keep the show moving!"

"We're just going to whip up this little cheese omelet." Zoey glanced at the clock that was keeping time right above her own smiling face on the monitor. It was ten minutes past eleven. Fifty more minutes to go. She dumped the cheese unceremoniously into the frying pan.

"Zoey," Ellen said with some alarm, "the cheese is supposed to go into the eggs before you dump it into the pan. That cheese is going to—"

"Oops!" Zoey said aloud, realizing that the pan was very hot from having sat empty on a lit burner. "Well, now, here's a little impromptu test for this nonstick pan. Will it burn? Or will it stick?"

Using a spatula, she stirred the cheese quickly, then lifted out the globby mess.

"Wow. These pans *are* great. It didn't stick *or* burn."
Zoey held up the pan for the camera, trying to ignore
Ellen's laughter, which was, literally, ringing in her ears.

"Well, thank you, Irene, for calling in this morning."

"Zoey, can I tell you one thing?"

"Sure, Irene."

"Keep it short, Zoey," Ellen admonished her through
the earpiece. "You're running late. You should be on the
next size frying pan now."

"Zoey, you are the absolute image of a friend of my
daughter's from college. The *absolute* image of her."

"Really?" Zoey said absently, trying to flip the omelet
without dropping it onto the stovetop. Or the floor. "Did
your daughter go to Villanova? Maybe it was me."

"No, no. We'd have remembered you! No, they went
to school in Maryland, and are older than you are. But
you two could be sisters."

"Well, I hope you will tell her I said hello when you see
her. And I hope you enjoy your new frying pans." Zoey
bit her bottom lip, trying to concentrate on getting all of
the omelet turned over. "There! And now, let's look at
this bigger frying pan. What were we going to cook in
that?" Zoey checked her notes.

"Vegetarian stir-fry?" She groaned. "Is this someone's
idea of a joke?"

She kept up the constant chatter, as only one who truly
loved to talk could do, as she discussed the merits of the
large frying pan. She spoke with callers about how thick
the zucchini should be sliced, how much green pepper to
use, and when to add the mushrooms, all the while
keeping one eye on the clock.

"That was like doing penance," she muttered gratefully when the segment had concluded.

Ellen met her in the hallway. "You were terrible."

"Good. That means they won't make me do that
again. Whose bright idea was it, anyway, to have me
cook on the air? Me, the Queen of Take-Out, who has the
distinction of being the only person in eastern Pennsylvania with a reserved parking place at Boston Market."

Not waiting for an answer, Zoey untied the apron she had worn over her black tunic and leggings and headed for the hosts' lounge and a cold drink.

"Wow," Genevieve said dreamily as she walked into the room. "Did you see him?"

"See who?" Zoey said absently. Genevieve was always drooling over one member of the opposite sex or another. Visiting celebrities or stockboys, it was all pretty much the same to Gen.

"The hunk who came in with the old man this morning." Gen sighed and leaned back into the plush cushions of the sofa.

"What old man?" Zoey sorted through the assortment of soft drinks in the small refrigerator, looking for a diet something.

"Delaney O'Connor."

"He's a very, very nice man, Gen, but I'd hardly call him a hunk."

"Not him, Zoey." Gen giggled. "I mean the hunk that was with him. Tall, broad-shouldered. Dark hair. Gorgeous." She sighed. "To-die-for gorgeous. Even with the limp and the cane, he could . . ."

Zoey froze, the bottle, almost to her lips, suspended in midair.

Tall. Broad shoulders. Dark hair. Limp.

Car accident. Broken leg. Limp.

Her head began to swim.

"Which way were they going?" She grabbed Gen's arm.

"Toward Delaney's office. Say, you think maybe he's that actor who's supposed to be coming in to promote that new movie about the dolphins?"

Zoey flew out the door, her feet trying their best not to trip over each other.

"Mrs. Gilbert . . . Pauline." Zoey was huffing and puffing by the time she reached the CEO's office on the second floor. "Is Delaney here?"

"Oh, Zoey, you just missed him. He just left the building." Pauline looked up from sorting through Delaney's mail. Zoey appeared somewhat anxious, out of breath, and her hair uncharacteristically askew, as if she'd been, well, *running.* "Is something wrong?"

"No, no, of course not. I just thought, that is, I just heard, and thought that maybe . . ."

"Mrs. Gilbert, would it be possible for me to get a cup of coffee?" A male voice asked over the intercom.

"Of course. How would you like it?" Pauline asked with customary efficiency.

"Cream, no sugar," was the reply.

Cream, no sugar. Just the way Maureen Pierce used to drink her coffee. Zoey had prepared it for her that way a hundred times, years ago, late in the afternoons when she and Georgia would sit at the big farm table in the kitchen. Maureen would make a fresh pot of coffee and Zoey would fix a cup for her mother—black—and a cup for Maureen, cream, no sugar.

A wave of nostalgia passed over Zoey as she watched Pauline do exactly that for Maureen's son.

"Delaney's grandson." Pauline gestured toward the closed office door with her head. "Just back in the country." She paused on her way to the door and asked, "Did I hear that he was an old friend of your family's?"

"Yes." Zoey found her voice and, holding out a trembling hand toward the cup, asked quietly, "May I?"

The ever protective Pauline hesitated.

"I would love to surprise him," Zoey said casually, as if it was not the most important thing in her life at that very moment to see him again. "We practically grew up together, you know."

"I'm sure he'll be delighted to see you." Pauline opened the door for Zoey, then stepped aside for her to pass through it.

Zoey stood on the plush carpet and stared at the man who was hopping on one foot toward the desk.

"Thanks, Pauline. I really appreciate it. You've no idea how difficult it is to carry a hot cup of anything when you're—"

He looked up at her and stopped.

"Can I help you?" he asked uncertainly.

"I brought your coffee." She held up the cup and grinned brightly.

"Oh. Thank you. Here would be fine." He hopped around to the back of the desk and slid a coaster across the top of the highly polished wood surface. "Are you Pauline's assistant?"

"No."

"Are you my new secretary, then?"

"Nope." She knew she was grinning like an idiot, but she didn't care.

She walked slowly toward him, unable to take her eyes away. His pictures didn't do him justice. He was taller, more muscular, more handsome. His presence filled the room, and it filled her. He looked every bit a hero. *Her* hero.

"Is there something else?" he asked uncertainly, as he flopped solidly into the high-backed leather chair.

"No, no. Actually . . ." The awkwardness of the situation slammed into her like a fist. He had no idea who she was.

Happy reunions seem to lose something, somehow, when you have to explain who you are.

He leaned slightly forward to look at her, frowned, and said, "You look familiar."

"Oh, you recognized me! I knew you would!" Her eyes widened in surprise. She put her hand against her fluttering heart. "I am so glad. I was just starting to feel incredibly stupid. But you recognize me!"

"Of course I recognize you." He smiled a wonderfully crooked smile and her stomach flipped over a time or two. "You're the bumbling cook."

"What?" The one word popped from her mouth.

He pointed to the television. "I watched you this morning. You're the one who has trouble making eggs. I'm—"

"Ben Pierce." She said his name aloud.

"How would you know that?"

"I'm Zoey," she said simply.

For a long moment he did not react, and she thought that perhaps she had not spoken after all, that maybe being this close to him had addled her brain and she had only *thought* that she had spoken her name.

Finally, he said in a quiet voice, "I used to know a girl named Zoey."

"I used to know a boy named Ben," she whispered.

The color had seemed to drain from his face and he stared at her for the longest time.

"Zoey Enright."

"Yes." She nodded and tried to smile, but it seemed out of place, he appeared so strangely somber.

"Zoey. I don't know what to say. You've changed so much since the last time I saw you." His knuckles clutched the sides of his chair, and had, she could not help but notice, gone completely white.

"I would hope so. That was seventeen years ago. I'd hate to think I still looked like an eleven-year-old." She tried to make it sound like a wisecrack, but her heart wasn't in it. He looked, well, *stricken* was the only word that came to mind.

"No. No, you don't look like a child anymore." He repositioned his right leg, which was suddenly killing him, and leaned back in the chair, a swirl of thoughts and emotions whirling in his brain.

Why hadn't Delaney told him that Zoey Enright worked at the HMP?

"How is your mother? And Nick?" he asked, trying to sound cordial, nonchalant. "And your little sister . . ."

"Georgia."

"Right. Georgia." *As if I'd forgotten her name. As if I'd forgotten anything. . . .*

"Georgia is a dancer. She's with a Baltimore troupe."

"Ah, yes. She always talked about being a dancer someday. And your brother?"

"Nick is a marine biologist. He lives in New Jersey. He's getting married soon."

"Is that right?" His throat tightened and it was an effort to keep his air passages open. He was suffocating.

"Does your mother still live . . . in the same . . . in Westboro?"

"Yes. She's on a book tour right now, but she'll be back soon. She's dying to see you, Ben."

"Is she? Yes, I'd like to see her too."

"I hope you'll still be around by the time she gets back."

"Oh, I'll be around all right." Ben slammed the bottom desk drawer closed with a bang. The unexpected noise caused Zoey to jump.

"You will?" Zoey's eyes brightened at the prospect.

"Didn't Delaney tell you?"

"Tell me . . . ?"

"That he was bringing me in to give him a hand for a few months or so?"

She stared at him dumbly.

"You're going to work here?" She wanted to shout, to dance, to sing.

"Until my leg heals." Ben tapped his fingers on the top of the desk as something seemed to occur to him. "You said Delia was 'dying to see me,' but not that she would be 'surprised.' And you're not at all surprised that I'm here. Why weren't you as surprised to see me as I was to see you, Zoey?"

"I knew that you were coming back." Even as she spoke, she knew that somehow her words would make him angry.

"You did, did you?" He fought back his temper. "And how did you know that?"

"Delaney told me." Why was he so angry?

"When?"

When she didn't immediately answer, he looked up at her with eyes that were growing progressively darker. "When, Zoey?"

"It was a while ago."

"How long?"

"A month, maybe," she admitted.

"Interesting," Ben said dryly, "that you would have known before I did."

"I wasn't aware . . . that is, I didn't know that you would be working here, that you'd be staying."

"No, I don't suppose you did. It seems Delaney had a little surprise for everyone." He looked up and saw the crestfallen expression on her face. "I'm sorry. This has nothing to do with you. This is between my grandfather and me."

She stood watching him from the opposite side of the desk, watched his face grow darker, his scowl deepen, and watched her dream of a happy reunion evaporate like mist in the morning sun. He barely seemed to notice her at all. There was something bigger on Ben's mind than a reunion with the Enrights, and it had, as he so bluntly noted, nothing to do with her.

There was a soft knock at the door.

"Yes?" Ben called from between clenched jaws.

"Ben, Peter Bellows is here from the New York office. Delaney set up an appointment for you to meet with him at two o'clock." Pauline stepped into the room.

"Well, wasn't that nice of him? And where might my grandfather be right now?"

"I believe he had a meeting of his own at five. In Pittsburgh. He's already on his way to the airport."

"I see. Well, then. Please show Mr. Bellows in. And maybe before the day is over, someone will let me in on whatever else my grandfather has arranged that he neglected to tell me about."

Puzzled by his terse tone, Pauline all but backed out of the office.

"Zoey, I'm sorry. You'll have to excuse me. It appears that I have a meeting."

"Of course. I don't want to take up your time," she said stiffly. "I just thought I'd stop in and say hello to an old friend."

"I'm glad you did." Not looking at all glad, he tried to smile as he took the hand she extended to him across the desk, a hand that was small and soft, but strong. When he looked into her face, the sadness there all but overwhelmed him. "Zoey . . ."

"I'll give my family your regards." She took two steps backward, appeared about to say something, then apparently changed her mind, because she turned her back and walked through the office door without another word.

Ben leaned against the desk and cursed softly. After so many years of fighting off the memories, he was being forced to deal with feelings he had tried to keep buried for a very long time. And in his effort to protect himself, he had hurt someone who had wanted nothing more than to greet an old friend.

As for Delaney O'Connor, he had some explaining to do.

* * *

Zoey ignored what felt like a ball of wax in her throat, straightened her chin, and left the building without giving in to the urge to cry and to curse. She made it to her car, made it to the end of the parking lot before slamming on the brake and giving in to tears that made her feel almost as foolish as she had felt standing in Ben's office and realizing that Ben was not delirious with joy at seeing her again. If anything, he had looked positively *pained* when he realized who she was. Whatever had made her think that he would have been as happy to see her as she had been to see him? He had never known what special place he had held in her life, had no way of knowing that, all through her stormy adolescence, she had held on to his memory like a magic token, that she had always harbored the secret dream that someday, he would come back into her life, and make all her dreams come true.

Well, he was back, all right, but the dream seemed, somehow, to have run a tad off course. There was nothing to do but go home, cry it out, and figure out how she'd get through the next few months without making a complete and total ass out of herself.

And Ben himself simply wasn't at all the way he was supposed to be.

What had happened to the boy she had known, the one who had always been her champion, her buddy? She had found little of *him* in the man who had sat behind the big mahogany desk, his eyes smoldering with emotions that had seemed to run the gamut from sorrow to wrath in the blink of an eye. What had happened over the years that had stolen the joy from his eyes, the light from his smile?

And what would it take, she wondered without wanting to, to help him to find those things again?

Chapter

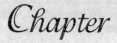

12

"When were you going to tell me that one of Delia Enright's daughters worked for you?"

Ben's words, clipped and cool, greeted Delaney as soon as he walked into the living room of the condo overlooking a broad stream that, miles away, fed into the Brandywine River.

Taken off guard, Delaney paused only briefly as he took off his overcoat. He opened the hall closet, taking advantage of the opportunity to look for a hanger and gather his wits at the same time.

"Ah," Delaney said, cheerfully, "so you ran into Zoey, did you? I thought that might be a nice surprise for you."

"I didn't run into her, Delaney. She came to the office. She knew I would be there." Ben shifted his leg, which had become increasingly more stiff and painful as the day progressed.

"I might have mentioned to her that you'd be around at some point." Delaney shrugged.

"Before you 'mentioned' it to me?"

"Well, I guess I may have let her know that I was hoping that you'd come back."

148

"Did you hire her, Delaney?"

"No. No, I did not hire her." Delaney sighed, partly from relief that this was one question he could answer honestly. "She was already working here when I bought the company. I bought her contract along with all the others."

Ben looked at him skeptically.

"I swear, son, that's the truth."

"Why didn't you tell me that she was here?"

"I thought it would be a nice surprise for you, Ben. I thought . . . that is, I was hoping that you would be happy to see her."

"It was a surprise, all right." Ben got up and tried to pace off his anger, but his leg slowed him down.

"Ben, you might want to see the doctor tomorrow, instead of waiting till next week. You're obviously in pain."

Ben looked out the window on the swift-moving waters of the stream, swollen from a week's worth of rain. He was in pain all right. But it had little to do with his leg.

"My leg will be fine."

"What is it, Ben? Why are you so angry?"

"You manipulated me, Delaney."

"Guilty." Perhaps the direct approach would be more effective.

Lightning shot through the night sky, a jagged metallic flash behind the woods.

"Why did you do it?"

"Because I thought it was time, son," the old man said softly.

"Don't you think that should have been my decision?"

"It's one that you didn't seem able to make." Delaney lowered himself into his favorite chair and stared into the fireplace at the logs that Mrs. Jackson, the house-keeper, had laid before she left earlier that day. The damper was still closed and the logs were unlit. "Ben, I think I understand why it's been easier for you to stay away. But sooner or later, you have to face up to the past.

149

It's all part of who you are. You can't cut and paste whole parts of your life, son."

Ben stared at his grandfather silently. That had been exactly what he had been doing for years. Cutting out the parts of his life that had hurt, hoping to make the pain go away.

How had Delaney figured it out, when he himself wasn't sure why he kept his foot on certain doors?

"Are you going to leave now, go back to England?" Delaney was asking.

Ben pondered the question. Of course, he could go. He could turn his back on all of it—on Westboro and all the memories that he had kept in the shadows for so long—and simply leave. It was his choice.

"Gramps, are you really sick?" Ben asked. First things first.

Delaney reached in his pocket and pulled out a tiny pillbox and tossed it to Ben from across the room. Ben caught it with one hand and opened it. Four tiny pills lay inside. He looked over at his grandfather.

"Nitroglycerin," Delaney told him.

Ben snapped the lid shut and tossed the pillbox back.

"I promised you that I'd help out for as long as I could. Until I can drive again." Ben met Delaney's gaze levelly. "I won't go back on that."

"Thank you, son." Delaney let out a breath he hadn't even realized he'd been holding.

"But, Gramps . . ."

"What, son?"

"The next time you want to surprise me . . . don't surprise me."

Later, after dinner had been served and Delaney had excused himself to turn in, Ben stood and looked out that same window. The rain had stopped and the clouds had given way to a cool, clear night. The moon, having made its appearance, cast a golden glow on the stream that ran little more than fifty yards away.

There had been another cool, moonlit night in March

when he and Nick Enright, both almost twelve that year, had slipped out of their beds and met inside the barn, prepared for adventure.

"Got the flashlights?" Ben had whispered.

"Yeah. Where are the oars?" Nick began scrambling around in the hay that covered the floor in one of the unused stalls.

"I already carried them down to the river," Ben whispered back. "Grab one end of the canoe and let's go."

"Wait just a minute." Nick took a flashlight and found the side door, which he opened. One of the horses, purchased along with the property, nickered in the dark. "Shhh, Jasmine. It's me, Nicky. Shhh, old girl."

"Come on, Nick."

"Right."

They had each grabbed an end of the long thin canoe and carried it through the open door, Ben balancing his end on his hip once outside, so that he could close up the barn. Once they had left the immediate area of the barn, the night became blacker and the woods deepened. The smell of damp earth that had yet to warm with the approach of early spring surrounded them as they walked down to the banks of the river. As quietly as possible, they slipped the canoe into the water, then climbed aboard and rowed unhurried into the dark of a Chester County night.

"There used to be Indians all along the Brandywine," Nick told him, still speaking in hushed tones.

"And British troops, too, during the Revolution," Ben said.

"Do you think General Washington ever floated down this very part of the river?"

"Probably. Him and Lafayette."

"You think there's ghosts here?"

Ben had nodded slowly. "I hadn't thought of it before, but yeah. I think there's plenty of ghosts. Indians and soldiers."

They had floated past some hanging rocks that in the dark had loomed large, both of the boys unconsciously paddling just a little faster.

"Are you afraid that we'll see them, Ben? The ghosts?"

"No," he had said, and he wasn't. "Are you?"

"No."

Their oars dipped into the water in perfect rhythm, making a warm, tinkling sound. Without warning, the moon emerged from behind the veil of clouds, the flood of light startling them with its suddenness. They both laughed nervously.

"What would you do if we saw one? What would you do if we rounded the next bend in the river and the ghosts of soldiers were standing right there along the bank?"

"I'd wave," Nick said, and they had both laughed, the sound of it echoing far along the banks of the river and long into the night.

Ben could almost hear them, those boys who had loved the river and had sought adventure. He and Nick had spent countless hours there on the Brandywine, exploring the rocks and the riverbanks and all the streams that fed into it, and had most likely even passed by this very spot, where Delaney's condo stood, at one time or another.

Suddenly, Ben missed Nick terribly. The feeling crept up and washed over him before he knew what was happening and could take his accustomed evasive action. Nick Enright had been the best friend he had ever had, and there were times when Ben could convince himself that that type of comaraderie came along once in a lifetime and he should be happy that he had had such friendship once, to chalk it up to a time gone by. And usually, he was successful in putting Nick back into that mental box labeled "Childhood Memories" and closing the lid. This, however, would not be one of those times.

Ben thought back to that afternoon, the look on Zoey's face when she had realized he was not only stunned to see her, but that he was not particularly happy about it.

She had seemed to all but dance into the room, her face lit with what he now acknowledged as joy at the prospect of seeing an old friend after so many years. He had been so overcome with so many emotions that he had barely been able to react to her. The woman who had come into his office bore no resemblance to the child he remembered. That goofy-looking little girl had grown into a beautiful woman, the kind who could take your breath away. Ben wasn't sure that perhaps she hadn't done just that, that maybe part of his reaction was shock at discovering not just that she'd grown up, but *how* she'd grown up. After all, the last time he'd seen her, she'd had braces. Her knees and elbows were constantly skinned and scabbed from falling out of trees or off her bike. And she'd been straight as a stick back then.

Ben had not been so overcome by emotion that he had failed to notice that she was no longer straight as a stick.

There had been long shapely legs inside those black leggings, he'd noticed *that* when she'd first come into the room. And over the years she had grown curves in all the most unlikely places—unlikely from his standpoint, anyway—this was little *Zoey Enright* he was talking about here. Somehow, he'd never thought of her growing up at all, and certainly had never thought she'd have grown up, well, like she *had*. And her hair, once little more than a ponytail high atop her head, now flowed around her face in dark waves. Zoey had grown up, all right, and she had, from all appearances, done a damn fine job of it.

The very first thing tomorrow morning, he vowed, he would seek her out and apologize to her for having let his own personal demons chase the light from her eyes. And maybe, one day soon, he'd find the courage to face those demons down.

* * *

"Mom, I made a complete ass out of myself," Zoey wailed into the telephone.

"Oh, sweetie, it wasn't all that bad. Actually, I thought it was, well, sort of cute the way the camera stayed on the bowl while you were trying to nab that elusive little piece of eggshell."

"Not that." Zoey sighed. She'd forgotten about her forced venture into televised cooking. "Later. When I went to see Ben."

"You saw Ben today?"

"You will never believe this. Mom, Delaney brought him here to help run the HMP."

"Ben is there? At the station?"

"Yes. And you were absolutely right about him. It was exactly what you said."

"And what was that?"

"The man is nothing like the boy, Mom. Ben grew up to be a cool, unfriendly man. He wasn't even happy to see me."

"Zoey, I find that really hard to believe." Delia frowned. "Ben was never cool and unfriendly, not to anyone, least of all to you."

"You yourself said people change, Mom."

"Most people don't change quite that drastically."

"Well, Ben did. I didn't like him very much."

"I'm sorry to hear that, sweetie." Delia bit her lip, wondering what had happened over the years to change him so. "I've been looking forward to seeing him again."

"Well, I wouldn't waste my time, if I were you." Zoey's sigh was heavy and weary. "I wouldn't even bother."

"That makes me very sad, Zoey. There has to be some explanation."

"Well, I for one am not so certain that I'd be interested in finding out what that might be."

Gracie strolled into the room, openly ignoring Zoey, then stretched what could well have been every muscle in her long feline body.

"Your cat has decided to make an appearance," Zoey told her mother.

"Ah, how is my sweet Gracie?"

"Sweet," Zoey said dryly. Gracie glanced up imperiously, then began to lick her paws and wash her face daintily.

"Well, I am infinitely grateful to you for giving her a home away from home. You know how she hates the kennel. Which reminds me, Zoey. Would you mind keeping her for just a few extra days?"

"Of course not. Did your publicist add a few more cities to the roster?"

"Not exactly. I just wanted to make a stop in Boston on my way back. It should only be a day or two."

"Stopping by to see Linda Lee?" Zoey shuffled through the day's mail. Linda Lee Patterson, Delia's best friend since first grade, now lived in a Boston suburb.

"Yes." Delia had seemed to hesitate just a little, prompting Zoey to ask, "Mom, is Linda Lee all right?"

"She's fine, sweetie. Oh, here's room service with my dinner."

"Staying in tonight, are you?"

"Yes." She put her hand over the receiver and called, "Yes. I'll be right there. Zoey, love, I have to go. I'll call you over the weekend. And let me think on this Ben thing. Something is just not right there. Oh—and kiss Gracie for me."

"Kiss Gracie?" Zoey raised an eyebrow. "I don't think so."

Delia laughed, then hung up the phone, going directly to the door of her hotel room, which she opened to admit both room service and the private detective who had, for the past several years, been a member of her private staff.

Tonight they would have a lot to talk about.

"Pauline, do you think you might ask someone to find Zoey Enright and ask her to stop down to see me today? At her convenience, of course." Ben had decided that the longer he put off apologizing, the more difficult it would be.

"I'll call downstairs and see when she's expected."

Ben tapped anxiously on his desk, wondering what exactly he would say.

"I'm sorry I was such an obnoxious moron" might be a good place to start.

"Ben, Zoey won't be in until Thursday," Pauline told him through the intercom. "She's off for a few days. Do you want me to try to get her at her home?"

"No, that's okay. Thank you."

Ben tried to visualize what Zoey's home might look like, how she might be spending her time. He had no clue, could not, he realized, even venture a safe guess. He had known her well as a child. Her tastes had been simple and eclectic. She had loved the out-of-doors, loved sports, loved to read. . . . She had pretty much loved most things, he recalled. But this grown-up Zoey was a stranger. What did he know about her?

Nothing, he thought dryly, *and I am not likely to get much opportunity to find out, since I so cleverly managed to morph into a jackass before her very eyes.*

Sighing with disgust, he turned his attention to familiarizing himself with the company's financial reports. By noon his desk was piled with spreadsheets and computer-generated sales reports. Before he knew it, the day had ended and Pauline was straightening her desk. He stuck his head out through the door and told her, "You can leave any time you like, Pauline. I have a few more reports I want to go over."

"I hate to leave you high and dry, as they say, but William is waiting outside to drive me back to New York." She smiled up at him. "I will be back on Thursday to interview a few more secretaries for you."

"Isn't this commuting starting to get to you? Two days here, three days in New York?"

"Having such luxurious door-to-door service makes it an easy pill to swallow. I sit back for a few hours, read a good book, perhaps watch a little television, take a nap, and leave the driving to William. Your grandfather always makes certain there's a lovely dinner waiting for me in the limo, and I am relaxed, well fed, and stress free by the time I arrive home." She patted him on the back. "And besides, I want to interview the last of the secretarial candidates before you do. Just to make sure that the skills are there."

"Well, anyone who passed your scrutiny would be fine, as far as I'm concerned. But tell me the truth"—he leaned over and whispered in her ear—"did Delaney tell you to weed out all the young, pretty ones?"

"No. Only the obvious gold diggers," she whispered back, and he laughed. "I did interview one woman today that I thought might be a contender."

"Why don't you call her back for Thursday, then, and we'll meet with her? I hate to keep imposing on your time when I know my grandfather depends on you so much."

"Oh, he's getting along just fine in New York without me."

"Pauline, he called here seventy times for you today. He can't function without you."

Pauline just smiled at him and continued to pack up the items she wished to take home with her.

"I'll see you on Thursday morning, Ben. If you need anything tomorrow, Betsy next door in Personnel will be happy to give you a hand. And of course, you have the number of the office in New York."

"I'll try not to bother you."

"It's no bother." She picked up her tote bag and swung her pocketbook over her shoulder. "Well, I'm sure I'll speak with you tomorrow."

"Good night, Pauline. And thank you for everything."

The building seemed very quiet once Pauline had departed. Ben returned to his office and folded up the papers he'd been studying all afternoon. He packed a few sales reports into his briefcase and started off down the hall, searching his pockets for the keys to the car that the leasing company had dropped off earlier that day. He signed out of the building and passed through the front door toward the parking lot. The BMW Roadster sat in the first reserved spot. He unlocked the door, tossed the briefcase onto the front seat, and climbed in, carefully folding in his right leg.

It had been some months since he'd driven, and he had missed it terribly. From the day he had turned sixteen, he had loved driving, loved cars. He took a few minutes to familiarize himself with the instrument panel and adjusted the seat, then worked both the gas and the brake pedals with his still stiff right foot, vowing to begin some home therapy that night in the whirlpool tub in Delaney's condo. He started the engine and gingerly stepped on the brake. There was still some pain, but he would overcome that. He'd been idle long enough. First thing in the morning he'd call London and have his X rays sent over, then he'd locate the orthopedic surgeon his grandfather had suggested. He'd make an appointment to have the foot looked at, and get a prescription for some intensive physical therapy. Before long, he promised himself, he'd be as good as new—or at the very least, as good as he was going to get.

He tried to ignore the nagging suspicion that maybe this was as good as it was going to get, but swept it from his mind. He wasn't ready to deal with the possibility that racing could well be a thing of the past.

He rummaged in the briefcase for the CD he'd brought with him that morning, anticipating having a car with CD player and Bose speakers again. He slipped in the disc, and tapped the button until he located the song he wanted to hear. The live version of Dire Straits's *Telegraph Road*. He pushed all those prickly thoughts from his mind and cranked up the volume and the car filled to the very seams with the sound of guitar, drums, piano, and thousands of hands clapping out the rhythm.

For just that momemt, he tried to believe that all was right in the world.

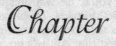

Chapter

13

"Addie would sure be pleased to see what-all you've done with the house, Zoey." Wally leaned over the fence that enclosed the garden in Zoey's backyard.

"Do you think so?" Grateful for a legitimate reason to take a break, she stood up and leaned against the rake she had been using to remove debris from the flower-beds, as her mother had firmly insisted she do.

"Give the soil some sun, for heaven's sake." Delia had frowned upon seeing that the several inches of leaves that had covered all back in October covered all still. "Let's see what's under there, Zoey."

Zoey had sighed and headed out to the nearest garden center for some implements with which to work. It was that or suffer having Delia show up early some morning with her gardener. Although right now, she reasoned, after three hours of raking leaves and picking up twigs and piles of yard debris, the gardener would be mighty welcome. The early April sun had been stronger than she had expected, and she peeled off the dark sweatshirt she had thrown over a long-sleeved T-shirt.

She stepped back to admire her work. It did look

better, she thought, though she still didn't have a clue as to what might grow there come summer.

"Next I guess you'll be wanting to restore Addie's garden." Wally let himself in through the gate and sauntered over to see how the roses had fared through the winter. Satisfied that Addie's favorite old-fashioned dusty lavender tea rose had fared well, he began an inspection of the grapevine. "I have some photographs somewhere that should help you out. Show you what she had where."

"I wasn't intending to restore anything out here, Wally."

He ignored her.

"Now, I'll just bet that you are burning with curiosity, wondering why the garden is laid out in four sections like that."

He pointed to the four big squares that were set off by overgrown paths.

"No, actually, I wasn't."

"Well, I'm going to tell you anyway." He sat himself down on an old stone bench, taking a moment to light his pipe. "Addie Kilmartin was a scholar of the Bard, you see, and she—"

"You mean Shakespeare?"

"Of course I mean Shakespeare." He gave her a stern look. "Who else is referred to as the Bard?"

"Does this have anything to do with why there are four square beds in the garden?"

"Has everything to do with it. And I'm going to explain it to you as soon as you stop interrupting me."

Chastised, Zoey tried to look contrite and began to rake the bed nearest the spot where Wally sat.

"Now then, being a scholar of the Bard, Addie spent a great deal of time reading his plays. She knew whole long passages by heart. Whole scenes."

"Was she an actress?"

"No. No, Addie was no actress. She chose to interpret his works in another way entirely."

"What was that?" Zoey felt compelled to ask.

He pointed to the garden's beds. "That, young missy, was the biggest, most complete Shakespeare garden in all of the Delaware Valley."

"I have this feeling that I should be impressed, but I have no idea what you're talking about."

"A *Shakespeare* garden," he repeated.

"I heard you clearly the first time. I just don't know what you mean."

"It's a garden that has only plants that were mentioned in Shakespeare's writings." He puffed on his pipe. "The Victorians called 'em literary gardens. Some used the writings of Chaucer, some used Spencer's, some used Shakespeare's. They're still popular in some parts of England, by the way. Now, many formal gardens, you might be interested in knowing, are marked by a hedge of English yew, but for some reason or another, Addie never seemed to have much luck with yew. So she bordered all her beds with English lavender instead. That's that dried, dead-looking silvery looking stuff there." He pointed to the edge of the nearest bed. "Cut it back and it will grow bushy again by summer."

"Wally, I'm not going to cut the lavender back, and I'm not going to restore the garden. I don't have the time."

"Oh?" His eyebrows rose in surprise.

"Yes. I'm very busy."

"Hmmph. Funny, I haven't noticed you doing much more than going to work these past few months. Guess something I don't know about has come along and kick-started that near dead social life of yours."

She didn't answer him, couldn't without looking foolish. She had no social life to speak of, and he damn well knew it.

"I don't like to garden," she told him.

"Funny. You just don't strike me as the type of woman who doesn't like to get her hands dirty."

"Getting my hands dirty does not bother me."

Wally peered into the bowl of his pipe, where the fire had gone out. He appeared to be debating whether or not to relight it before knocking the ashes out of the bowl by banging his pipe on the side of the stone bench.

"Spent many a fine spring afternoon right here on this bench, watching Addie bring that garden back to life after a long winter," he told her wistfully as he packed his pipe into the front pocket of his flannel shirt. "Yep, many a fine afternoon."

"Okay, I'll bite." Zoey gave up. "What exactly goes into a Shakespeare garden?"

"Plants—flowers, herbs, shrubs—that Shakespeare mentioned in his writings. I just told you that."

"And I heard that part. I'm asking *what* plants. What plants, specifically?"

"Now, Zoey, you're a smart girl. I'm sure you can figure it out." Wally stood and stretched. "I think I'll go in and check out the noontime news. Channel seven has one cute little blond number doing the weather these days. Then I'll take a drive to the post office, maybe stop at my son's and see what my daughter-in-law is making for supper. I'll see you later, Zoey. Have fun this afternoon."

Zoey frowned and watched him duck under the arch where the grape vine had yet to issue forth leaves or fruit.

"A Shakespeare garden," she muttered, trying to recall lines from plays she had read and studied while in college. "'Eye of newt, and toe of frog, wool of bat, and tongue of dog.' Nope, no help there."

She raked for a few more minutes, then stopped and recited, "'Ay me! for aught that ever I could read, Could ever hear by tale or history, The course of true love never did run smooth.' No, that doesn't help either."

A catbird landed on the arbor, and at the sound of her voice, turned his head this way and that as if hanging on to her every word.

"'We are such stuff as dreams are made on, and our little life is rounded with a sleep.'"

The catbird squawked and flew away.

"Everyone's a critic," Zoey muttered as she pushed

the wheelbarrow filled with leaves and twigs through the gate.

"'If music be the food of love, play on;
Give me excess of it, that, surfeiting,
The appetite may sicken, and so die.
That strain again! it had a dying fall:
O! it came o'er my ear like the sweet sound
That breathes upon a bank of violets. . . .'"

She stopped midway across the backyard and hooted, "Violets! Yes! *Violets!* That's one!" Zoey turned toward Wally's house in time to see his car back out of the driveway. She cupped her hands to call after the car, "Hey! I thought of one! Violets! *Twelfth Night!* Act One!"

She grinned as she bagged her yard debris, thinking that violets alone, while lovely and an old favorite of hers, would make a pretty boring garden. Maybe tonight she would curl up with an old volume of Shakespeare's plays and see what she could find. A few hours here and there spent outside would do her good, she reasoned—after all, she couldn't recall ever having seen a *fat* gardener—and whether she enjoyed it or not, at least she'd have some pretty bouquets for her pretty new house.

Zoey stripped off the garden gloves her mother had sent her for an Ides of March gift, and washed her hands in the powder room sink. She poured herself a cool drink, then took it out to the deck through the new French doors. The sun was pleasant and comforting, and she wished that she, like Gracie, could curl up in its warmth and snooze. Leaning over the deck railing, she looked out across her backyard. She loved the view from this very spot. Soon the grape arbor would green up and small green buds of fruit would appear. The roses were already thick with leaves, and it would not be long before they, too, would be covered with buds. She wondered what it would look like, what it would smell like, when everything was in bloom.

Funny, me ending up here, seventeen miles from the house I grew up in.

163

Funnier still, that Ben would be here too.

Yeah, she reminded herself. Ben had been *real* funny a couple of days ago. Just to think back on the encounter with him in his office caused her cheeks to burn all over again. Could she have made herself appear any more stupid than she had?

She squirmed, recalling how his green eyes had narrowed when he realized who she was. Why had he been so cool to her?

Well, then, so much for fate. So much for the man of my dreams. Guess his fairy godfather and my fairy godmother got their wires crossed. Guess it's time to stop believing in fairy tales. Time to let the dream go.

A little voice inside her protested softly. It had been the only real dream she had ever really wanted to come true. And it had been a wonderful dream.

She sighed, and wished that she could have held on to that dream just a little while longer.

* * *

Somehow Ben thought it would have taken longer to get there. But there was little traffic at that early hour of the day, and so it had been a mere twenty minutes from Delaney's condo to the gates of Delia Enright's home.

A gentleman's farm, people called it. No crops were grown and no animals raised to be sold for livestock or for food. The old farm had been purchased strictly as a family home. The acres purchased years ago must be worth a fortune now, Ben ventured. He pulled a little closer to the fence and leaned on the steering wheel hoping to get a better view.

The last tattered bit of morning fog floated over the fields. It looked eerie, somehow, and he almost expected to see fairies dancing on the slight ridge just to the left of his car. But then again, he'd always thought there was just a touch of magic here.

The pine trees that used to be little taller than he and Nick had once been now rose twenty-five feet into the air, totally blocking out any view of the house. Part of him wanted to back up and go right on past the old stone pillars that the original owners had erected at the foot of the driveway, right on up to the house. Another part of him wanted to run like hell.

For so many years, this place had appeared almost nightly in his dreams. He wasn't sure he was ready to face the reality of seeing it again for real. Perhaps another time. Tomorrow, maybe, or perhaps next week, after he'd gotten used to the idea of being there. But not right now. He put the car in gear and drove off down the road.

It was early when he arrived at the office. Pauline would still be in New York, and his new secretary was not to start until Monday, so he was pretty much on his own for a few days. Which wasn't necessarily a bad thing, he reasoned, since it gave him an excuse to wander around the building on his own. Seeking a cup of coffee, he stopped into one of the studios where a personable young man was on-air, selling electronics. The backstage area was more interesting and better organized than he had suspected, with tables displaying the products for the next several shows lined up across one wall. Everything seemed to be itemized and neatly arranged. He joined a flustered producer for a cup of coffee in the hosts' lounge, then sat with several customer service representatives and walked through the telephone ordering process with them. By the time he actually made it back to his office, it was well after noon, and his mind was filled with multiple images of this giant his grandfather had so recently purchased.

Ben requested the personnel files of all active employees so that he could review them and become acquainted with their backgrounds before he actually met them. He wanted a handle on who they were, where they had come from. The staff, he found, was diverse. Several former radio disc jockeys, former television news reporters. A few teachers. People with sales backgrounds, marketing, advertising. And then there was Zoey. He pulled her résumé out from the stack as if it was made of fine parchment. The list of her previous employers brought a smile to his face. She'd certainly run the gamut. It appeared that she had been at the HMP longer than she had been with any other job. He read the comments from the producers, one of whom described her as the backbone of the salesforce. Popular and respected by everyone, it seemed, she was also their top-selling host. No wonder they all spoke so highly of her. Her sales figures and percentage of items sold per number of items pitched were the highest at the network.

Ben leaned back in his chair and smiled. Zoey had done well for herself. He was happy for her, happy that she had found something she apparently enjoyed doing. Delia must surely be proud of her. He tapped his fingers on the desk blotter, wishing he could go back in time to the moment when she had stepped through the doorway with a cup of coffee in her hand. He wanted a second chance to greet her the way she deserved to be greeted by an old friend, with joy and welcome. The way she had attempted to welcome him, with open arms and an open heart.

And what had he done? He'd *grumped* at her, that's what he'd done, squashed that welcoming smile and chased the joy from her face.

And what a face it had been, he recalled.

Had her eyes been that blue when she was a little girl? Had she always had those deep dimples on either side of her mouth? And he hadn't recalled that her mouth had had that pouty *kiss me* look back in those days. And her legs hadn't been that long, come to think of it, and the rest of her body had been far from lush. . . .

Snap out of it, he chastised himself. It's obvious she still thinks of you as a big brother–type figure. After all, she was your best friend's little sister. You taught her how to throw a baseball. You climbed trees with her. You and Nick even let her sleep in your tent a few times.

He sighed. He owed her an apology. A big one. And she would have it. As soon as he could figure out what to say.

He walked to the window overlooking what had once

been a cow pasture and looked out at the complex that had grown up in the middle of nowhere. There was plenty of room for expansion here, more warehouses, more sets, if needed, more parking. Over the past few days he had spent hours in conference with Delaney's top staff members, more hours back at the condo going over reports and projections, trying to get a feel for the business. All indications led him to believe that his grandfather had been right. In time, with the right hand at the wheel, the company could become a major force in the retail industry, a cable giant that could dominate the field. All the right pieces were there. It would be a challenge to the one who tried to put it all together. He found himself almost regretting that he would, in all probability, be long gone by the time that challenge would be met.

Two long hours later, after sifting through the company's investment portfolio, Ben stood up and stretched. His right leg protested painfully when he attempted to put weight on it, reminding him that he'd been sitting for far too long. It was almost one o'clock. Maybe he'd drive out to the small sandwich shop he'd passed on his way in this morning and grab a bite to eat. It was a beautiful day, and he could use the fresh air.

Ben eased the roadster around one curve, then another, his foot testing the accelerator cautiously, wondering if he'd ever have that sureness again, that confidence in his ability to control a speeding machine the way he'd once done. It was an issue for another day, he told himself as he pulled into the dirt and gravel parking lot of The Well (Sandwiches to Go) at the corner of Everett and Lanning's Corner Roads, where the lunch hour had already peaked. He ordered the corned beef special to go, and grabbed a bottle of Arizona Green Tea out of a refrigerated case, paid for his purchases, and was back in the car in less than seven minutes. He started out of the parking lot, then pulled back into the space to put the convertible top down.

That's more like it. He grinned to himself as he slipped

a CD into the car stereo—Springsteen's *Thunder Road*—feeling all of a sudden like a man who had just about everything he needed at that particular moment—a sunny day, the top down, lunch in a brown paper bag, and music. He opened the bottle of tea and sipped at it as he drove off, looking for a suitable place to stop and eat his lunch.

He hadn't consciously planned on it, but he wasn't surprised when he found himself in front of Delia's house for the second time that day.

Delaney is right. It's time, he told himself as he drove very slowly to the entrance to the drive and stopped the car, pausing to look around. There was no sign of life, no cars, no sound other than birds excitedly circling a feeder half filled with seed that hung from the lower limb of a small oak tree. He drove a little further up the drive, then parked the car, and sat for a long time with his eyes closed, remembering the sounds and the smells. Then, still fingering his key ring, he got out and walked, slowly, toward the big stone house that Delia had bought years ago, mentally noting the changes the house had undergone through the years since he had been away.

The shutters, once black, were now chocolate brown, to blend better, he supposed, with the tans and gray-browns of the native fieldstone. Around one side of the house, an enormous addition stretched—home, he guessed from the condensation on the glass windows that formed two walls, to an indoor pool. New gardens led to the barn, which sported a fairly new coat of red paint, and a new addition there too caught his eye. More room for Delia's horses, he guessed. More pasture had been fenced in, and he leaned over the split rail to rub the muzzle of a curious bay that had come to investigate his presence. Overhead a hawk circled slowly, and from somewhere in the barn another horse nickered softly. Around one corner of the barn, a large black and white shepherd came flying, growling gruffly.

"Here, boy." Ben held out a hand for the dog to sniff. "It's okay."

The dog leaned into the offered hand, his tail wagging tentatively. Having decided that Ben was okay, the dog nuzzled his leg. "Okay, so we want our head petted, do we?"

He spent five minutes petting the dog, scratching behind his ears and carrying on a one-sided conversation, soothed somehow by the dog's presence. He took off his suit jacket and swung it over his shoulder, stopped and rolled up his shirtsleeves, then walked behind the barn to see if there were any remnants of the vegetable garden that was once the pride of old Tom Larsen, who had been the gardener there in Ben's youth. The weatherbeaten fence still stood to keep out the deer, and by peering over it he could see that the soil had been worked and readied for this year's plantings by someone, and he wondered if old Tom could still possibly be alive. He strolled down to the pond, the dog still by his side, and stopped to listen as the frogs splashed into the water at his approach. He sat on a large gray rock and watched several ducks dip their heads in and out of the water.

He walked back to the house and walked around outside, never thinking to knock on the door. He peered into the barn and walked around it one more time. He had rambled around the property for nearly an hour before he permitted himself to acknowledge what he had really come there for.

For a long, hard moment, Ben stood before the carriage house he and his mother had once called home.

His fingers unconsciously took the key ring from his pocket as he looked up at the second floor of the old stone and clapboard building, and his thumb and forefinger slowly rubbed the old metal key he'd never been able to bring himself to throw away. He touched the door, as if testing to see if it was real, then slid the key into the lock, wondering why he was not surprised to find that Delia had never had the lock changed. He pushed the door open and stepped inside quickly, lest he lose his nerve, and went up the steps.

Everything about it was familiar, and if he closed his

eyes, he might be fourteen again, or twelve. The smell was the same, a savory, herbal smell, and for a moment it overwhelmed him and stopped him where he stood. When he could, he poked into the kitchen to see if any of his mother's bunches of rosemary and coriander still hung from the window sashes. Entering the room Maureen had loved so much was like a walk back through time. Nothing had changed. From the wallpaper—now slightly faded—to the collection of small colored bottles on the wide window ledges, nothing had changed. It squeezed his heart until he thought it would rupture inside his chest, and he turned into the living room. There, too, the furniture remained the same. An old magazine—*House & Garden*—dated March 1981, sat on the end table, and an old blue sweater was folded neatly on the arm of the sofa. Numbly he followed the short hall to his mother's bedroom and stood in the doorway.

The first thing he noticed was that the charcoal drawing he had made of Maureen—a passable likeness, considering his young age at the time—still hung on the wall above the room's small corner fireplace. The pale yellow bedspread with the pink and blue flowers was still on the bed, along with a small square pillow she had made one year when she had taken a sewing course at the local community college. She had never made anything else. Having decided that she lacked both the skill and the patience to become accomplished at the pastime, she had plunked the pillow down on her bed after the last class and told Ben dryly, "Next semester, I think I'll try karate."

Ben sat on the edge of the bed and lifted the pillow. It was floral and had a deep eyelet ruffle, and felt weightless in his two hands. It occurred to him then that he was sitting in the exact spot he had been when his mother had told him that she was dying.

It had been winter and the first real snow of the year had begun to fall that afternoon. She had been to the doctor earlier in the day, and the week before she had been in the hospital for yet another round of tests. He had known that she was sick, but the thought that she could be seriously ill was not within the realm of possibility in his fourteen-year-old mind. He had come into her room—this room—to tell her that he and Nick were going sledding on the big hill across the road.

Maureen had been standing at the window, the fingers of one hand splayed against the glass as if to touch the snowflakes as they fell. The room was so quiet, that in retrospect, he had thought that his words had seemed to boom forth from his mouth in cartoon balloons to hang over his head. When she turned to him, he had stopped in mid-sentence. Maureen's face was wet with tears, her eyes big and frightened. And without even asking, he had known.

"No, Mom, you can't," he had whispered, suddenly terrified.

He sat on the edge of her bed because he had suddenly become as weak as a baby and he felt that an enormous boulder had smacked him in the chest and knocked him down.

"I'm afraid I'm not very good at this," she told him. "You know, as a parent, you would like to think that if the time ever came that you had to have this conversation with your child, you would be strong and calm. But I can't seem to stop crying, Ben. I don't want to leave you. I'm not ready, and that's the simple fact."

And he and his mother had cried together for what seemed to be hours, holding each other, both giving and taking what comfort there was to found. It had been the last time she had been solely his, the last time the two of them would have only each other to hold on to. By the time the weekend had come and gone, they had stood together on the front steps of her father's house, and from that day on he had had to share the rest of her days with so many others . . . his grandfather, her doctor. The private duty nurses who tended to her twenty-four hours each day. Old schoolfriends, tracked down by Delaney. Anyone and everyone, it seemed, who had ever known and cared for her had come by, so that from the day they had arrived at Delaney's big house in Connecticut, Ben and his mother were never alone. Even as she lay dying, he had had to share her. He had wanted to sit on her bed and cry with her, and hold her like they had held each other on that day when he had learned the truth about her illness. But the nurses wouldn't leave her alone while she still breathed. Unable to share publicly his grief, his pain, which had been, for him, something to be shared only with her, he had not cried again, nor since.

The funeral had been planned by Delaney, and before Ben had known what had happened, Maureen had been laid to rest beside her mother, there, in the family plot in Connecticut. Unable to go back into that house, now that she was gone, Ben had called a cab from the kitchen of his grandfather's house, and stuffing all of his savings into his pockets, took a train to Philadelphia, and from there, one to West Chester. He had hitched a ride to Westboro, then walked the rest of the way to Delia's, where, he had felt certain, he would awaken in his room in the carriage house to find that everything that had happened over the past five months had really been part of a long and very complicated nightmare that would, surely, end as soon as he got home. His mother would be waiting for him, and she would tell him that none of it had been real. Even now, as he sat on the bed, he could feel the same terror that had seized him that night, when he realized that it had not been a dream. If Maureen was not there, at the carriage house, then she was *not* at all. As if in a daze, Ben had locked the door and turned away.

Delia had met him halfway across the yard. His grandfather was on the way to pick him up and take him back, she had told him. She had tried to put an arm around him, but he had pushed her away. If Maureen had left this place, then he would leave, too.

And so he had made the long silent ride back to Connecticut in the front seat of his grandfather's Lincoln, and he had closed the door on his old life as quietly as they had closed the lid on his mother's shiny wooden coffin.

The past closed around him so tightly that he felt he was suffocating, and a very long moment passed before Ben had identified the water running down his cheeks as tears. They had been streaming down his face, falling onto the front of his shirt and soaking it without his even realizing he'd been crying. At once embarrassed and yet somehow relieved, he searched his pockets for a handkerchief to dry his face. As a boy who had not been quite a man when his mother had left him, he had not known how to deal with his grief, and so he had simply buried it. Now, back in this place, it welled up, and the tears he had been unable to shed for so long, now spilled over.

For just a moment he had felt Maureen's arms around him, and he felt both cleansed and at peace. The flood stopped then, and the pain that had pushed against his chest with such force began to ease. He leaned one hand on the bedside table to push himself up, and something small and sharp poked into his hand. A small stud earring, three colored stones on small gold-tone wires, pushed into the flesh of his palm. He turned it over and smiled. The stones were glass, but he had hoped that his mother wouldn't notice when he had given them to her for what had turned out to be her last birthday. He stared at the earring for a very long time before slipping it into his pocket.

"Thanks, Mom," he whispered.

A noise from the hallway drew his attention, and he looked up to see Delia Enright standing in the doorway.

"Welcome home," she softly.

"Thank you" were the only words he could manage to speak.

"What do you think?" She waved her hand around, as if to take in the entire apartment. "Is it as you remembered?"

"Nothing's changed."

Delia took a few steps into the room, and touched the wall. "Maureen picked out this wallpaper. She loved these little daisies. They were her favorite flowers, remember? I just couldn't bear to have it taken down." She traced one of the small flowers with the finger of one hand. "She picked out the furniture—I couldn't bring myself to take any of it out. Your mother was the sister I never had, Ben. In the end, I couldn't bear the thought of anyone else living here, so no one has. I moved my writing studio to the first floor." She did not say *to be close to Maureen,* but Ben thought that was what she meant. "But other than that, nothing has been touched since the day you left for your grandfather's house."

"I have to admit, that was a bit of a shock, seeing everything just as it was."

"Was it as difficult as you thought it would be?"

"Nothing ever is." He smiled wryly.

"Ah, true. Fear, unchecked, is a fearsome thing indeed."

"I feel so foolish now, having stayed away for so long. . . ." He shook his head. "I'm sorry, Delia, if I've hurt you over the years."

"You don't have to apologize to me, Ben. There's no one you've hurt more than you hurt yourself. I'm sorry that I wasn't able to have done something that would have comforted you. I think we all were in shock for a while after your mother's death, we all loved her so much, Ben. But I understand why you felt you could not come here."

"You do?"

She nodded. "You and Maureen had always been together. Losing her at any age would have been tough. At fourteen, it must have been devastating."

"You're not angry with me?"

She dismissed it with a wave of her hand. "You were a child. Now you're a man. And you have, after all, come back."

"Not of my choosing," he told her. "I'm afraid it was my grandfather who forced my hand."

"Then bless the man. But whatever it took, Ben, doesn't matter. The fact is that you're here."

"For a minute I felt that my mom was here, too," he said softly.

"Oh, I'm not surprised." Delia grinned. "Sometimes when I'm downstairs in my writing studio, I think I hear her footsteps up here. Of course, it's probably just squirrels on the roof or some such. But I prefer to think that she is nearby. It comforts me."

He slipped his fingers into his pocket and twisted the earring around and around.

"So. How long will you be staying?" Delia asked.

"I don't know."

"I thought Zoey said you'd be here for a while?"

"I'll be here as long as my grandfather needs me."

Ben walked to the window and looked out into the view of pine trees just feet from the window. Even through the glass he could smell the clean sharp scent.

"Smell the pine, Ben?" Maureen had thrown the windows up in a grand gesture on the day they had moved into the carriage house. *"There is nothing I love more than the smell of pine trees!"*

Sensing his distraction, Delia started toward the door. "Feel free to spend as much time here as you like, Ben. When you're done, come have tea with me. I think there's some pineapple upside-down cake in the pantry."

"You make it yourself, Delia?" He turned and asked, a weary smile tilting the corners of his mouth, remembering another day, when Delia had ventured to bake just such a cake. It had been a terrible cake, and he and Nick had secretly fed it to the ducks on the pond behind the house. It had been a lifetime ago, or so it seemed.

Delia laughed out loud, remembering, too.

"You're a sight for sore eyes, Delia," he said quietly, meaning it.

"As are you, my boy. As are you."

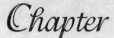

Chapter

14

Having slowed down to the posted speed limit of twenty-five miles an hour, Ben coasted into the town of Brady's Mill. At the lake he pulled over to the side of the road to check the map. That had been a left turn back there, hadn't it?

Satisfied that he was, in fact, in the right town, he eased back onto the two-lane road. The first right past the lake should be Skeeters Pond Road, and it was. He slowed even more to check the numbers and names on the mailboxes as he passed by. At the mailbox with the ivy and hand-painted daisies and the number 27 and the name *Enright* painted in blue, he paused. This would be the one.

He drove slowly up the driveway, then stopped behind a small red sports car with an HMP parking sticker on the rear driver's side window. A rake leaned against the wall of the garage, and a wheelbarrow piled high with dried leaves stood next to it. Ben turned off his engine, leaned across the seat to grab the peace offering of two dozen peach-colored roses mixed with some white, ethereal baby's breath and got out of the car, pausing for just a moment to observe his surroundings. The lawn that reached out beyond the house was wide and deep and green, bisected by a thick grape arbor that formed a sort of wall. In the distance, woods just beginning to green up for the new season fanned out as far as the eye could see. The air was fresh and crisp, cooler now than it had been earlier in the day. The serenity of the late afternoon tableau was disturbed only by an indistinguishable sound from beyond the arbor. Ben poked his head through the gate to see, expecting to find Zoey on the other side.

A white-haired gentleman in a red and white plaid flannel shirt was attempting to drag a concrete birdbath down a grassy path, inch by tedious inch.

"Can I give you a hand there?" Ben asked as he opened the gate and stepped into the garden area.

Startled, the old man straightened up sharply. "What makes you think I need one?"

"Well, you look like you're having a bit of trouble. . . ." Ben placed the bouquet of roses on the stone garden bench and pushed up the sleeves of his dark green sweatshirt. "Where were you going with this thing anyway?"

"What business would it be of yours?" The man's eyes followed Ben to the bench and back, then narrowed suspiciously. "And who might you be?"

"I'm Ben Pierce." Ben held his hand out to the man, who did not take it, but continued to watch Ben warily. "I'm an old friend of Zoey's."

"Funny, Zoey didn't mention she was expecting company."

"She wasn't . . . isn't . . . expecting me. I was in the area and thought I'd stop by. . . ." Feeling a little uneasy, like one who had been stopped by the highway patrol and as yet wasn't sure why, Ben put his hands in his pockets, wondering who this old man *was*.

"And just happened to have an armful of roses with you, did you?" The old man made a valiant attempt to lift the birdbath, which was clearly too heavy. Ben grabbed the heavy end of it.

"To your right! To your right!" The old man directed. "Keep 'er straight! Now, just let 'er down."

The birdbath properly placed to the old man's satisfaction, he nodded thanks of sorts to Ben for his assistance.

"What'd you say your name was?"

"Ben. Ben Pierce."

"Well, Ben Pierce, I don't know that Zoey's home, but I'll be sure give her your regards when I see her."

Ben laughed and asked, as the old man had previously asked of him, "And who might you be, sir?"

"Next door neighbor." He nodded toward the left, indicating the house beyond the garden, as he opened the gate and invited Ben to step on through it.

Ben turned back and leaned over the bench to pick up the flowers.

"Ha!" The single word resounded, loudly and triumphantly, across the yard as a screen door slammed.

Ben peeked through the grape arbor in time to see Zoey fly across the deck and down the steps. Holding an open book in front of her, she stopped midway across the grass and held one hand out in front of her, pointed to the old man and said, "'There's fennel for you, and columbines: there's rue for you: and here's some for me: we may call it herb of grace o' Sundays. O! you must wear your rue with a difference. There's a daisy: I would give you some violets, but they withered all when my father died.'"

"Ha!" She crowed again, then counted on her fingers as she repeated, "Fennel, columbines, rue, daisies. And that's not all! "She turned the page back. "'There's rosemary, that's for remembrance—'"

"'Pray love, remember,'" Ben passed through the garden gate, then completed the passage. "'And there is pansies, that's for thoughts.'"

Zoey's eyes widened with surprise, then slid into narrow slits of suspicion.

"What are you doing here?"

"I came to offer my apologies." He held up the roses. "Of course, if I had known that your taste ran more toward rue and columbine and daisies, I would have made sure that the florist put some of them in, too."

She crossed her arms defensively across her chest, holding the book in front of her like a shield. "A note in my mailbox at the station would have been sufficient."

"No, it would not have been," he said softly. "You deserved a better greeting than you received."

"How did you find my house?"

"Personnel records."

"If you could find my records, you could have found out that I'm scheduled to work tomorrow. You could have waited till I came in."

"I felt this was too important to wait till tomorrow."

Wally cleared his throat to remind them that he was still there.

"I take it you two have met?" Zoey turned to one, then the other of the two men.

"In a manner of speaking," Ben said. "Though I didn't catch your name."

"Wallace T. Littlefield, sir." Wally nodded, then turned to Zoey. "Ben was just telling me that he and you are old friends."

"Ben is an old friend of the family. He used to be my brother's best friend."

"I see." Wally looked from one to another, knowing there was more here than Zoey was letting on.

"Between Wally and my mother, I have been goaded into cleaning up the garden. Wally is trying to bait me into planting a Shakespeare garden." Zoey turned to Ben and waited for him to ask.

"Oh! You mean a garden that has only plants that are mentioned in Shakespeare's writings?" Ben asked.

"How did you know that?" Zoey frowned. *Why* would you know that?"

"I lived in England for years." He laughed. "They're not uncommon there."

179

Wally chuckled with satisfaction.

"Well, I might get around to doing it here." She closed the book and crossed her arms over her chest. "Then again, I might not."

"Well, you're off to a good start, there. You already have some of the plants you yourself just mentioned a few minutes ago," Wally took his pipe out of his pocket and fiddled with a pack of matches, as if debating whether or not to light up. "You've got roses growing over the fence, violets growing wild, and if I'm not mistaken, there are several old clumps of daisies that still come up. Now, that's the beauty of perennials, you know, they come back with or without your help. And come summer, why, that whole area back near the woods will be thick with rue. And then, you could—"

"Wally, I think I hear your phone ringing." Zoey said dryly.

"Hmmm?" He paused, about to strike a match. "Oh. Yes, I think you're right. Better try to catch it. Might be Alena Parsons. Widow lady. Caught her staring at me in church last Sunday. . . ." He continued his monologue as he walked briskly toward his house.

Her arms still crossed, Zoey turned her attention back to Ben, trying to decide whether it was anger or possibly something else that was causing her heart to bang against her chest the way it was suddenly doing.

Ben held the roses out to her. "You might want to put these in some water."

She tensed, pausing while debating whether or not to accept his flowers after the shoddy greeting he had given her earlier. He must have read her thoughts, because he touched her arm and said, "I'm sorry, Zoey. You deserved a much warmer welcome from me than you received. I was just so damned shocked to see you. I'm sorry."

"But I don't understand why. I had assumed that Delaney had told you. . . ."

"That you were working there? No. No, he did not.

But the surprise was nowhere near as unpleasant as I might have led you to think. It was unexpected, that's all. The truth is that I was delighted to see you, Zoey. I'm sorry I didn't say so then, but I'm telling you now."

She searched his face as if looking for something.

"You can tell me to leave if you want. It's okay, Zoey. I would understand if you did."

"Do I get to keep the roses anyway?"

"Yes," he told her solemnly.

She softened, in spite of herself. "They're beautiful, Ben. Thank you."

"I'm glad you like them."

"I do. But you didn't have to . . ."

"We got off on the wrong foot the other day, and it's bothered me ever since." There was more that he had wanted to say, but standing there in the quiet yard, with her looking up at him with those big blue eyes, it was the best he could do at the time. "And besides, I wanted to see your new house. Are you going to give me a tour?"

"It's still being worked on." She eyed him cautiously. "The carpenters are not quite finished yet."

"I don't mind the work-in-progress tour."

"Okay." She gestured for him to follow her. As they neared the deck, they heard a voice call from an open window next door, "Just leave the shades up, hear?"

Zoey laughed. "Wally's a little protective of me."

"I noticed," Ben followed her up the back steps, noticing too that she had a smear of dirt right across her backside. He had to fight the urge to brush it away.

"It's okay." She paused near the back door. "I sort of like it. I never did have a father to fuss over me, you know, to do all those things that fathers are supposed to do for their daughters. Tell them when to change the oil in their car and to interrogate their suitors. Not that I had any when I was growing up. Suitors, that is." She pointed to the side of the house and noted, "I just had the siding replaced. I think it will weather really nicely, to a sort of soft gray."

"I find that really hard to believe."

"No, it's true." She insisted. "Cedar changes color as it ages."

"I meant, I can't believe that every boy in Chester County wasn't beating a path to your door."

"Not hardly. I was the only girl in my graduating class who went the entire four years of high school without a date." She opened the back door and beckoned him to follow into the small back entry that led into the kitchen.

"You have to be kidding."

"If you had seen me back then, you wouldn't have to ask. Gawky, braces till I was sixteen, all leg, too much hair . . ." She grabbed a handful of the black silk that hung across her shoulders in a deep wave and shuddered. "Anyway, to get back to Wally, he sort of adopted me. He's been a good friend. Now, you wanted to see the house."

She gave him the downstairs tour, starting with the dining room.

"This is nice." He ran his hand appreciatively over the top of the smooth pine tavern table that stood in the middle of the room. "Beautiful. Antique?"

"Yes," she nodded. "And local. The dealer I bought it from told me that it was made right here in Lancaster County."

"I passed several antique shops on my way out here."

"This area is known for the number of quality antique pieces that still can be found. You just have to be careful, because there are a lot of reproductions on the market. You have to know what you want, and what you're looking at, or you could get duped. The good news is that the repros are top quality, so if it doesn't matter to you if something is really old or not, you can really get some great pieces at very reasonable prices."

"I'll keep that in mind." He paused to look out the window. "Beautiful view here."

"One of my favorites. I can't wait till those lilacs bloom. It will smell wonderful." She turned her back and led him into the living room, saying, "I've just had the fireplace tile restored. Some of them had come loose."

He bent to inspect the tiles, tracing the handsome Art Deco design with his index finger. She bent down to point out the differences, one tile from another. The faint trace of her perfume—a soft and dreamy rose scent—drifted around him, and her eyes took on a faint glow as she told him how she had managed to trace the maker of the tiles.

"He had started his career as a tile maker, took on a lot of local jobs to pay the rent, but what he really wanted to do was to make pottery, which he did, in his later years. I found two of his pieces, and hope to find more. Want to see?"

He had barely heard a word she said.

Could this really be the same Zoey Enright who had chased him and her brother through the fields to the cattail-lined pond to see who could catch the biggest frog?

"Ben?"

"What?"

"I said, would you like to see the vases?"

"Oh, sure." He nodded enthusiastically.

She stood up and reached to the shelves that flanked the fireplace, lifting a cobalt blue vase and handing it to him.

"He worked in a sort of free-form style, apparently, in the later stages of his career. His earlier pieces were made from molds, but the colors were always the same brilliant tones."

Ben turned the pottery piece around and around in his hands.

"The blue is almost the same color as your eyes." He'd been thinking it, but hadn't planned on saying it aloud. It almost seemed that the words had found their own minds and had made the decision to be spoken independently of him.

To her complete and everlasting embarrassment, Zoey blushed.

Flustered, she took the vase from his hands and returned it to the shelf. Crossing in front of him to the other side of the fireplace, she took down the second vase and held it out to him. "This is by the same potter."

"What was his name?"

"Who? The potter?"

He nodded.

"Elmer Langtree. Isn't that a great name for a country artist?"

"It is." He turned the vase to the window and turned it in his hands. "Interesting shade of green," he commented, adding, "but I prefer the blue."

He gave it back to her and watched as she stood on her tiptoes to replace it on the narrow shelf. Her movements were self-conscious somehow, as if she was aware that his eyes were following her.

"And through here"—she gestured for him to follow her through an archway leading to a hall—"I have a guest room, a bath and my little office."

He nodded his approval of the welcoming guest room, with its twin bird's-eye maple spool beds and two dressers, one with an attached mirror, and the small-scaled wing chair in one corner. A wreath of dried flowers hung on one wall, and over the beds marched a line of framed prints of roses. The lace curtains were tied back with what appeared to be small nosegays. The room was cozy and charming, and he told her so.

"Thank you. I planned it for overnight visits from my mother or sister, but right now, while the second floor is still being worked on, I'm using it as a bedroom. I do like it. It does feel cozy, as you say." She smiled and pointed across the hallway. "And this is the sitting room/office."

He stepped inside the room with its dark green walls and palest gold carpet. A small sofa with a bright floral print and a mound of decorative pillows stood along one wall, a curved desk fit nicely into an alcove on another. A third wall had two windows, side by side, with deep sills lined with pots of African violets, while the fourth had shelves that reached almost to the ceiling.

"I see you're still a reader," he said softy. "I remember how in the summer you used to lie in the hammock and read the latest Nancy Drew."

"Till two certain parties would come along to dump me out onto my butt."

"You remember that?" He grimaced.

"Do I ever." She laughed and rubbed her backside unconsciously.

"And I see you have what appears to be an entire collection of your mother's books." He pulled one off the shelf and flipped through it. *The Flute Maker.* An excellent tale of suspense. Ah, and here's *Over My Dead Body.* Another great favorite of mine."

He paused to read the dedication aloud.

For Ben—wherever he may be.

They stood in silence for a long moment before he said, "You will never know how much it meant to me to read those words."

"Perhaps you should tell my mother."

"I already have."

"When?"

"Right after I finished reading it. It was my first year at school in England." He sat on the arm of the sofa, his fingers tapping lightly on the back cover of the book. "I always made it a point to buy every one of Delia's books. They were my connection to . . . well, to a time that had passed. Sometimes, all of it—those days in Westboro—seemed to be nothing more than something I had dreamed, like none of it had ever happened at all. Then another of Delia's books would be published, and I would read it, and I would remember the places she wrote about. I remember the farmhouse in this book—it was out on Cross Creek Road. And the oak tree that she talks about hanging over the road 'like a giant parasol of the finest lace,' I *know* that tree. I've climbed it." He stood and walked to the shelf, laying a finger on the spine of yet another book. "There's a scene in this one where she describes two boys stealing out of a house in the middle of the night to go canoeing. Until I read that scene, I had no idea that she had known that Nick and I used to do that."

He returned the book to its place on the shelf, then turned to her.

"Your mother's books kept all those places alive in me all those years, Zoey, in spite of my best efforts to shut them all out."

Zoey wanted to ask *why* he should have made such an effort, but something in his face had tightened slightly, and she let it pass.

"I have read every one of these books many, many times," he added, "searching for whatever little tidbit of the past she had hidden there for me to find."

Zoey smiled. "Is that what you used to think? That she hid things for you in her books?"

"She told me she did. She said it was her way of letting me know that it was all still there."

"When did she tell you this?"

"She sent me a package right before I left for college. It was her newest book, let's see . . ." His eyes scanned the shelves until he found the book he was looking for. "Here we go. *The Devil's Light.*" He thumbed through it, searching for the page. When he found it, he looked up at Zoey and met her eyes. "Your mother had marked this page with a card. It wasn't difficult to find the passage."

He handed the book to Zoey and watched as her eyes scanned the page, then in a soft voice, began to read.

"'She wanted, more than anything, for the boy to know he could always come home. That the places he had loved would always be waiting for him, that it would never be too late.' I have read that ten times, and never made the connection," she told him. "And she did something like this in every book?"

"Every book." He nodded.

"She never told me." Zoey leaned back against the door frame and shook her head. "How 'bout that? She never told me. And *every* book held a message?" She repeated incredulously.

He nodded again.

"Amazing. Now I will have to go back and read each one again and see if I can find your passages."

"Most of them are pretty obvious, if you're looking for them. Mostly just a little something to let me know that I—and my mother—hadn't been forgotten."

"That was so lovely of her to do that."

"Yes. Yes, it was."

"When you see her, you'll have to tell her that you remember the passages."

"I already did."

"Did what? Tell her, or saw her?"

"Actually, both. I stopped out today to see . . ." He cleared his throat. "To see the place."

"This was the first time . . . ?"

"Yes."

"Nicky and I used to wonder if you ever came back. If, when no one was there, you would walk through the house, or go out into the fields or the barn."

"No. I never did."

"Why, Ben?" she whispered. "Why did you stay away from us for so long?"

He looked across the room and began to say something, then stopped, and gave a half shake of his head, as if what he thought, what he felt, could not be expressed.

"Come into the kitchen and I'll make some tea." She held her hand out to him, her instincts telling her that this was painful ground, that perhaps what she had perceived as rudeness had hid something much deeper than bad manners.

His soft chuckle was unexpected.

"What's so funny?" She began to withdraw her hand, but he reached out for it and took it before she could hide it in her pocket.

"That's the second time today that one of the Enright women has invited me for tea." He squeezed her hand lightly. "Except that your mother plied me with pineapple upside-down cake as well."

"Well, I'm afraid I can't top that. But I might have a cookie or something to throw your way."

"Better yet, why don't you let me take you to dinner? We could sit and talk and I can try to make up for being such a bozo the other day."

"I'm not really dressed to go out." She frowned, pulling at the front of her sweatshirt, which still bore tiny bits of leaves and dirt. "And it would take a while for me to get cleaned up."

"Well, you could always make one of those cheese omelets I saw you cook on the air the other day."

Zoey groaned.

"But you have to promise to keep the shells out," he added.

"That is a promise I could not keep. But I do a mean take-out." She pulled him by the hand into the kitchen, where the room was brighter and less intimate than the dark shadows of her office had been. Even Ben's mood seemed to lighten.

"Zoey, you weren't kidding, were you?" He flipped through the take-out menus Zoey had handed to him. "Chinese, Mexican, pizza, Italian, a deli, Thai . . ."

"Georgia calls it the 'culinary league of nations.'" Zoey laughed. "My sister does not understand the entire concept of *take-out* food. Georgia either cooks and eats in, or goes out to eat. She does not *take out* to *eat in.*"

"Well, which do you recommend?"

"Ummm . . ." She peered over his shoulder and pondered. "I usually have Italian on Wednesdays."

"Fine. Call in an order for two and we'll go pick it up."

She shook her head. "They deliver. It takes a little longer, though."

"You have take-out delivered?"

"Just about every night that I'm home."

"You have to be kidding."

"Well, I do eat out several nights, when I'm working, and usually my friend CeCe comes for dinner once a week."

"Ah, and you cook dinner for her."

"No, she cooks."

"You invite her for dinner and she cooks?"

"Usually she invites herself. She really enjoys cooking."

"Then why doesn't she invite you over to her house—"

"Because I have a great kitchen and she doesn't." She leaned back against the counter. "What is that look for?"

"I'm trying to figure out why you would have a beautiful kitchen like this built into your home if you never intend to use it."

"I *use* it. I eat here. I sit here in the morning and have coffee and watch the birds on the feeder out there. Wally gave it to me for a housewarming gift." She pulled a curtain aside and pointed out the window to a low hanging branch of a pine tree. "I just don't do a whole lot of cooking. But someday, I might. And besides, the contractor talked me into it. He convinced me that if I ever wanted to move, I'd have a better chance of selling the house if it had a kitchen."

Ben laughed, his face crinkling into remembered creases that had been mere pencil lines the last time she had seen them.

She handed him the menu with the flag of Italy on the front. "Any of the pasta dishes are wonderful, the chicken is to die for, and the shrimp wrapped in bacon with horseradish appetizer is a must."

They made their selections and called them in. "Forty minutes," Zoey told Ben when she hung up the phone. "What can I offer you to drink while we wait? I have diet Pepsi, sparkling water and tea—both iced and hot—and I think there's some wine."

"Actually, I think I'd like a cup of hot tea." He eased himself into one of the comfortable-looking chairs that stood around the small kitchen table and stretched his leg out, grateful to be off his throbbing ankle.

"So. Did you have a good visit with my mother today?" Zoey asked, wondering why her mother hadn't called to tell her that Ben had been out to the house. "And what did you think of the changes she has made to the property over the years?"

He frowned, trying to recall changes. The things that had meant the most to him had not changed at all.

She counted them off on her fingers. "The indoor pool, the sùnrooms, the exercise room, the new barn, the indoor riding ring . . ."

"Oh. Right. Wonderful," he said. "I think it's wonderful that she's done so much for herself. For her own comfort."

"No one can say that Delia doesn't take care of herself, as well she should. Of course, first and foremost, she takes exceptional care of others. We were delighted, actually, when she started to build on to the house. She takes great pleasure in her sun room. We call it Babel, for the Hanging Gardens, because of all the tropical plants she has growing in there." She glanced at him as she turned to the cupboard to get mugs for their tea. His stare was glazed, focused at the tile floor, though his mind was clearly elsewhere. "Of course, I personally thought that adding that tower was going a bit too far, but Nicky thought it might come in handy some day."

"Ummm. Right." He nodded.

"Next, I hear, she's planning on taking down the barn so that she can re-create the Temple at Jericho. Before it came tumbling down, of course. Nicky's talked her into building a sort of Biblical theme park right there in Chester County, though some of her neighbors who still ride to the hounds weren't real happy when they heard she was thinking about adding a scaled-down Dead Sea right there in the middle of the traditional hunt course."

"Um." He nodded and played with the silver spoon she had placed on the table next to the cup.

She waved a hand in front of his face.

"What? Oh, I'm sorry. I'm afraid that for just a moment, I was back at the house with Delia." He tried to think of a way to explain to her how good it felt to be home. To actually see the faces of those he had held in his heart for so long, including hers. Which no longer looked even remotely like the child she had been.

The teakettle whistled and she turned her back to

him, wondering why her mother hadn't bothered to call to let her know she had come back early from her tour.

"So, did you have a good visit?"

He thought about the carriage house, unchanged since the day he and his mother had closed the door behind them and left for Connecticut, and the sights and sounds and memories he had spent more than half his life trying to forget—the memories that a confused and frightened boy had convinced himself would be better off forgotten. The way that rugged branch of the Brandywine flowed behind the small barn, swift enough to take two young boys back through history or forward through time. Trees he had climbed and songs he had sung, forts they had built in the woods and snowmen they had built in the fields. Dreams he had dreamed while laying on his back and watching the clouds change shape. His mother tossing him his jacket on frosty mornings before he left for school . . .

"Yes," he nodded, "If I had understood I could have . . . *come home,* I would have done it a long time ago."

The wistful drift had returned to his eyes, and she wanted to ask why he had not, but she swallowed the words. Some other time, she might press the point and perhaps he would tell her. But not tonight.

"I was just lucky that Delia happened to be home while I was there," he added.

"You were. I was under the impression that she wasn't coming back until next Monday."

"She said something about going back early tomorrow morning."

Zoey frowned. "That doesn't make any sense. Why would she come home today and leave again tomorrow?"

"She said she had just come home to get something."

"She made a trip home just to *get* something? That doesn't make any sense. Did she say what it was?"

"No."

"That's odd." Zoey opened the freezer and popped a

few ice cubes into her glass. "If she had wanted something that badly, why didn't she just call me—or Mrs. Colson, the housekeeper? Whatever it was could probably have been sent out by overnight mail."

She twisted the metal cap off the soda bottle.

"Maybe she was bored." Ben shrugged.

"My mother is never bored." Zoey grinned wryly. "If there is no fun, she makes her own. How did she seem to you?"

Ben thought back to his visit with Delia.

"Vibrant. Warm, welcoming, loving. As I remembered her."

"Nothing else?"

"A tad more subdued, maybe a bit more, well, philosophical comes to mind, than I may have recalled, but then again, I haven't seen her in years, so that may not be an accurate assessment."

"Subdued." Zoey repeated thoughtfully. "Philosophical."

"Look, I could be wrong," Ben said. "I was a little distracted, understand, overwhelmed at being home again."

Zoey smiled. It was the second time that he referred to the Westboro house as *home.* She was about to mention it when the doorbell rang.

"That must be dinner. I'll get it." Ben pushed the chair back and unfolded himself slowly, favoring his right leg as he did so.

Zoey watched his lanky body move to the front door, and noticed the limp for the first time.

"How is your leg?" She asked as she laid green plaid place mats on the kitchen table when Ben returned with two brown paper bags.

"As well as one has the right to expect after crashing into a wall at a high rate of speed," he said as he began to unload white containers onto the kitchen counter.

"Ouch." She winced as she opened the cartons and transferred the entrees onto dinner plates.

"*Big* ouch." He nodded and sat down. "I will be

starting with a new therapist next week. I'm hoping my ankle improves enough for me to drive again."

"I thought you drove here." She pointed in toward the driveway and the roadster parked there.

"I mean race driving."

"You would do that again?" She opened a cupboard and reached in for two bowls, into which she divided the salad.

"Of course."

"Why?"

"Why, because that's what I most love to do. I love the speed, the excitement, I even love the noise."

She placed the salads on the table, then followed with their dinner plates before sitting down opposite Ben at the table.

"My mother always used to say that you were a boy with a wish for adventure. You and Nicky both." She smiled, then said, "Oh, you should call him after dinner. He'll be so happy to speak with you."

"I spoke with him earlier today. Your mother gave me the number. Hearing his voice again, well, it just made me realize how much I've missed him. Your mother invited me to the engagement party she's giving for him and his fiancée, by the way. I'm really looking forward to seeing him again."

"Oh, you will love India, we all do. She's wonderful. They are so perfect for each other."

"That's pretty much what he said. And it sounds as if it would be quite a party."

"Oh, it will be." She smiled, thinking about the killer black dress hanging in her closet at that very moment, just waiting for the right occasion, an occasion when she really wanted to get someone's attention. "Now, would you like more tea, or would you rather have wine?"

She wanted to pinch herself, unable to believe that she was really sitting there in her cozy breakfast nook with Ben really sitting across from her so casually, as if he belonged there, making her laugh with stories about his earliest days on the race car circuit, about dirty tricks that had been played on one driver or another by a rival, of working for years as a test car driver before getting the opportunity to drive, at first in the smaller races, then, finally, some of the more well-known circuits. He nearly brought her to tears with his simple, eloquent accounting of the drama-filled 1994 San Marino Grand Prix in Imola, Italy, when he had watched his idol, Ayrton Senna, crash to his death. It was the single most sobering moment of his life, he had told Zoey.

"But not enough to make you want to change careers," she noted, as she refilled his wineglass.

"No. Not enough for that. Racing is one of those things that gets into your blood, Zoey. You don't stop until you have to."

"I guess fear for your life doesn't count."

"I never feared for my life." He grinned wryly. "For some reason, I never feared dying in a crash. Severe injuries, however, are something else entirely."

"But you plan to go back to it."

"As soon as I can. Of course, everything depends on how completely my foot heals. A race driver with a bad accelerator foot is a hazard to himself and everyone else on the course."

"What will you do when you're done with racing for good?"

"Well, for years, a friend of mine and I have talked about starting a business together, when we've both retired. He stopped racing last year, and has been looking into several possibilities."

"Will it be related to racing?"

"Oh, absolutely." He nodded emphatically.

"And in the meantime, you're running the company for your grandfather."

"Yes."

"What do you think of it?"

"The HMP?" His eyebrows raised slightly and she nodded. "I think it's an interesting concept. I think the potential could be unlimited as far as revenues are concerned. I have to admit that, initially, I had thought

Delaney had lost his touch when he told me what he'd bought, but after going over the projections, I think he might be sitting on a gold mine."

"How are you making the transition from race car driving to corporate executive?"

"Better than I expected to. It's just a different kind of game," he told her.

* * *

Just a different kind of game, she later mused after he had left and she had gone into the closet and pulled out the black dress. She stripped off her sweatshirt and jeans and slid the long cool column of silk over her bare skin.

She stood in front of the long mirror and raised her hands to scoop up her hair and pile it on top of her head, wondering if she should wear it up or down, what jewelry to wear, and whether or not Ben would like her in black.

The countdown to Nick and India's engagement party had begun.

Chapter

15

‿

"What?!" Zoey shrieked, both fists landing in front of her on the small conference table like twin pistons. "Why me? I was *terrible*. Ellen," Zoey turned, white-faced, to the young producer who sat across from her, "you even said so yourself. I was *terrible*."

"*Terrible* apparently appealed to a lot of viewers." Ellen picked a piece of paper off the top of a tall pile of similar white pages.

" 'Watching Zoey cook brought back memories of teaching my own daughter how to cook. I loved that show! When will she do it again?' "

Ellen reached for the next sheet and read, " 'Watching Zoey Enright cook is great theater. The most entertaining hour of the day. Oh—and the stainless steel pots I bought from her are gorgeous.' "

"And another. 'After watching Zoey try to fry cheese, I bought the entire set of nonstick cookware. If it works for her, it will work for me.' "

"And that," Ellen told her, "is why you'll be doing the cooking shows from now on."

"But doesn't it matter that I hate it? That I'm no good at it at all?"

"No." Ellen shrugged. "People loved watching you. Look."

Ellen slid the stack of faxes and letters across the table to Zoey. "People from all over the country are sending you recipes. They're sending you cooking tips. They love you, Zoey. They want to help you."

"I get all the help I need from my friendly network of take-out establishments," Zoey wailed. "Ellen, give this to CeCe. She loves to cook. Why, she made me some buffalo chili that knocked my socks off." Zoey grabbed the producer's arm, her voice dropping a few octaves. "And that's not all. She makes great pastries. Ellen, she makes the most heavenly homemade cheese Danishes. The kind you like. With the strawberries on top of the cheese."

"Save your breath, Zoey. You're scheduled to start in two days."

Zoey's eyes narrowed. "Start what in two days?"

"Your new cooking show. It will run twice each week to start, Tuesdays and Thursdays at noon."

Zoey looked to the heavens. "I don't deserve this. I have tried to live a good life. . . ."

Ellen laughed out loud.

"And now you're going to let others help you, Zoey. This will be a more interactive show than most of the ones we've done in the past. The viewing audience wants to feel as if they are cooking with you. Just think of all those sweet little old ladies watching you, clucking over your efforts, offering advice. Your cooking segments have made the viewers feel almost protective of you, Zoey. You're bringing out their maternal instincts."

"I have a mother, thank you very much. The last thing I need is several hundred thousand more."

"You'll love it, once you get into it."

"I'll hate every damned minute of it and you know it."

"But I also know that on-screen, you will be the

smiling, happy show host who is far too professional ever to let anyone suspect that she'd rather be in traction."

"You really know just the right button to push, don't you?" Zoey grumbled.

"Thanks, Zoey. I knew you'd come around. Now, what we'd like you to do is to look through these recipes that people have sent in to you and see which ones interest you. We've already had the product coordinators go through them and pull out the ones that you could use with products we already have available for this week's shows. So if you want to cook a pasta dish, we'll schedule the pasta cooker for that show."

Zoey flipped through the stack of faxes, occasionally groaning. "No, I don't do lamb. I will not cook anything that comes from anything that was once cute and fuzzy."

"I didn't know you were a vegetarian."

"I'm not. I just don't eat cute things." She looked over another. "Yuck. Okra. Add that to the list. I will not do okra."

Ellen made notes on a pad of white lined paper.

"This doesn't look too bad," Zoey murmured. "Hmmm. Chicken with fresh rosemary and tarragon."

"Let me see that one."

Zoey passed the recipe to Ellen.

"This one would be good. It uses both a frying pan and a baking dish, both of which we have in inventory and can be scheduled for this week. Okay, pick two more."

"Two more? I have to cook three whole things in one show?" A horrified Zoey asked.

"Sure. You're cooking lunch for the camera crew, did I forget to mention that?"

"Someone is going to have to eat this?"

"Yep." Ellen grinned. "And it had better be good. You know how temperamental cameramen are. One bad meal and your good side will slip into the land that time forgot, never to be seen again."

"I'll have to take these home and practice," Zoey whined.

"I'll have someone call the people whose recipes you

select and tell them the good news." Ellen slid the more interesting recipes to one side. "Think of how excited these people will be to know that you will be cooking their recipes on national television. And we'll invite them to call in during the show."

"Oh, sure. Misery loves company." Zoey pulled a second recipe from the tall stack and placed it on the "deserves another look" pile.

"Hey, for some of these people, this will be a really big thing. Please don't forget that," Ellen reminded her.

"I won't. But promise me, if this is not a howling success, we'll drop it sooner rather than later."

"I promise."

Much to Zoey's amazement, her cooking hours were instantly and wildly popular.

"Doesn't it figure?" She had grumbled to CeCe after a quick cup of coffee in the hosts' lounge before Thursday's show. "Someone *up there* has a very perverse sense of humor."

"You could always complain to your buddy," CeCe had laughed.

"What buddy?"

"The tall handsome one who moved into the big office on the second floor." CeCe's eyes twinkled. "I've seen him every morning this week, since I've been scheduled for the eight to eleven shift, and I must say, he is one fine sight first thing in the morning."

Zoey, who had been thinking the same thing all week, groaned and said, "It wouldn't help. I saw Ben yesterday and the first thing he said was how much he liked Tuesday's show. That he never knew how *entertaining* it could be to watch someone fumble around in the kitchen—his words—and what a great sport I was for doing something I really didn't like." She slipped her sweater over her head and picked up her purse. "And besides, I couldn't take advantage of our friendship that way. I couldn't use Ben to influence the producers to give me only shows that I like. It wouldn't be fair. Which is not to say that I haven't been tempted. But I couldn't do it."

CeCe watched, an amused grin on her face, as Zoey stuffed the latest batch of faxed-in recipes into her briefcase. "Light reading for the weekend?"

"For next Tuesday's show, Ellen wants a main course, a salad, and a dessert this time." She smiled devilishly. "Do you think I could get away with sneaking in the leftovers from my brother's engagement party?"

"Probably not. Anyway, you'll be too busy dazzling the boss to be thinking about food."

"Now, where would you get the idea—" Zoey began to protest weakly.

"Well, you said that he had been invited to the party. And since he has watched at least one of your shows from the set every day this week—with the cutest little grin on his face, I might add—I just naturally assumed that—"

"Really?" Pleased, Zoey blushed. "Ben has been in the studio?"

"Every day. Didn't you know?"

"I saw him yesterday when I was doing that clothing show, but that was the only time."

"Every day, my little chef-meister," CeCe assured her. "And besides, when I was at your house on Tuesday night, your black dress was hanging on the bedroom door."

"So?" Zoey asked innocently.

"In the right hands, that dress could be a lethal weapon."

Zoey laughed and swung her bag over her shoulder, heading toward the door.

"Hey, Zoe," CeCe called to her. "Don't make the same mistake I did with the cowboy."

"What was that?"

"Don't let this one skate away."

* * *

"Zoey, speed it up a little, will you?" Ellen's voice pleaded into Zoey's earpiece. "The carrots don't need to be sculpted, just chopped. It's stir-fry for the crew, Zoey. It won't be photographed for the cover of *Bon Appétit.*"

Zoey smiled sweetly at the camera and said, "My producer thinks I'm not chopping quickly enough. But we know, don't we"—she winked at the viewing audience somewhere out there—"what happens when we chop too quickly. We don't want to bleed into the stir-fry. Oh, we have a call. Hello."

"Hello, Zoey. I'm so happy to talk to you."

"I'm happy to speak with you, too. What's your name and where are you calling from?" Zoey pinned a *hi, neighbor* grin onto her face.

"My name is Evelyn and I'm calling from North Carolina."

"Evelyn, are you calling in with a cook's tip?"

"Well, I was watching you chop that onion and seeing your mascara run . . ."

Zoey flinched and peered into the monitor to see if she had raccoon eyes. She grabbed a paper towel and blotted away the telltale black circles.

". . . and I wanted to tell you that, if you run that knife under cold water before you slice into the onion, it won't make your eyes tear."

Now she tells me.

"Really? Does that work?" Zoey tried to sound chipper.

"Oh, yes. Every time."

"Well, thank you, Evelyn. I will add that to my list of things to remember. Thanks for calling in with that tip."

"Oh, Zoey, I wanted to tell you that you are a dead ringer for someone I met on vacation last year in Maryland."

"Really?" Zoey measured olive oil and slid it into the electric wok, the product she was selling, where it sizzled angrily and immediately began to smoke. "Oops. Too hot, I guess."

"Turn the temperature down, Zoey," Ellen sighed into Zoey's ear.

"She could be your sister," the caller continued.

"Well, then, give her my regards. And you have a good day, Evelyn." Zoey glanced down at her cards, trying to figure out what to do next.

Slice chicken breasts.

"Okay. Now we slice up the chicken into thin strips and throw it into the wok, then we add the peppers and the onions. Or is it the other way, veggies first, then the chicken?" She flipped through her notes, frowning.

A chuckle drew her attention to the side of the set. Ben stood in the doorway, looking handsome and casual in khakis and a loose knit sweater the color of amber. Zoey flushed, and her hands began to rattle.

"Ah . . . I think we add the wok to the peppers first. I mean, the *peppers* to the onions. In the *wok.*"

"Zoey, I think the rice is burning," Ellen warned.

"Ellen the producer says it's check to time the rice." Zoey muttered to the camera, momentarily flustered by Ben's presence .

"Time to *check* the *rice,"* Ellen corrected her impatiently.

"That's what I said." Zoey turned to face Ellen who stood across the set from her. "And time to take another call."

Ben leaned against the doorway to the set and shoved his hands into his pockets. He hadn't meant to stop in every day on his way out to lunch, just occasionally. And he tried to convince himself that the fact that his visits to the set just happened to coincide with Zoey's noontime show, well, that was nothing more than coincidence, wasn't it? He smiled to himself, knowing that if Zoey's show was switched to two in the afternoon, he'd probably find himself eating later than had recently become his habit. Only to himself could he admit that he had begun to look forward to these few minutes every day, when he could just watch her. She had grown into so beautiful a woman, and he regretted not having been around to have watched her metamorphose from her self-described gawky teen stage into the beauty she now was. He wished he had been there to take her to those dances she never got to go to, wished he had been her first date. Her first kiss. Her first lover.

Where had *that* come from?

He shook himself out of his reverie, grateful that she could not read his mind, that she would not know he'd thought of little else but her for the past week, since the night he had sat across from her at her little kitchen table and talked like the old friends they were.

And that's all I am to her. An old friend. Nothing more. Best not to think beyond that. As soon as the foot is healed, I'll be on my way back to England, whether to race or go into business with Tony. Either way, I'll be leaving.

But *friends,* he acknowledged, was better than nothing.

Zoey turned unexpectedly and flashed him a smile when the promo shot for another segment began to run. He felt dazzled, the way he felt after a race when the photographers all aimed and shot at the same time. He returned the smile and waved, then left the set quietly, afraid to overstay his welcome. Returning to his office, he checked his phone messages absently, then glanced at the calendar. Nick's engagement party was in three days.

He walked to the window and looked out at the flat expanse of turf that grew between the building and the two-lane country road beyond, where an Amish buggy, drawn by a single horse, trotted past at a nice clip. There were times when he could not help but envy what he perceived to be their simpler life. How much less complicated when the day-to-day living is reduced to a lower denominator. Rise early. Tend the animals. Tend the fields. Love your wife. Love your children.

He knew it was more complicated than that. The Amish way of life had its own brand of stress and its own problems. But sometimes, he thought, a simpler routine might be welcome. The Sunday paper had run an article about farms in the area where one could go and stay for a weekend or a week, or two weeks, sort of like bed-and-breakfasts with a twist—the twist being that the guests would take part in the normal activities of the farm. He mused momentarily about doing just that one of these days.

He could see himself, mucking out the barn and pitching hay. Riding the tractor, plowing the field in the spring. Harvesting the wheat at the end of summer. He'd be wearing one of those big black hats he'd seen the Amish men wear in the fields. And when he went back to the farmhouse for the noontime meal, it would be Zoey who would smile a greeting at him from her place at the stove in the big kitchen. She would be dressed in a homemade, loose-fitting dress of coarse dark blue cotton, a black apron tied around her slender waist, a black cap snug over her dark hair, which would be pinned back into a tight bun. Her eyes would sparkle and she would be humming as she set a plate piled high with chicken and wide noodles before him.

Of course, the chicken would most likely be as tasty as truck tires, and the noodles like glue. . . .

He laughed out loud at the very thought of it, then sobered somewhat, thinking there were worse ways a man could spend his life than living on his own land and raising a family with a woman like Zoey Enright.

Chapter

16

~

The red sports car flew into the driveway, stopping on a dime three feet from the garage door. Zoey ripped the keys from the ignition and hopped out. Nick and India's engagement party was starting *now,* and she was already late, having had to work until five.

Running through the house, she discarded her purse, her shoes, and her blouse—in that order—before she hit the bathroom and turned on the shower. Stripping off her skirt while she rummaged in the linen closet for her favorite oversized bath towel, she next pulled off her panty hose and underwear as she fled into the shower stall. She turned the nozzle to allow for more and hotter water, trying to catch her breath and calm herself down at the same time she squeezed shower gel onto a bath sponge. She lathered shampoo onto the top of her head and worked it through the long strands of thick dark hair. She rinsed the froth out thoroughly, as quickly as she could. She turned off the water and opened the glass door, grabbed a towel to wrap around her head and another to dry her body with.

She brushed her hair straight, then turned on the dryer, impatiently moving the hot air through the long tangles of hair. When finally—finally!—it had dried sufficiently, she skipped into the bedroom and reached for her dress.

"Come to Momma," she whispered to the narrow bit of silk she dropped over her head. She snuggled into it, smoothing the fabric over her hips. She leaned over and hit the replay button on the portable CD player that sat on the edge of the bedside table with that morning's choice of music still poised and ready to play. She cranked up the volume and filled the small house with the passionate sound of what she considered to be one of the all-time greatest songs of love and longing.

Layla.

The original version.

Nothing got her going like Clapton.

She spilled some hairpins into a small antique celluloid dish on the dresser and began to put her hair up atop her head in a sort of knot, allowing a strand here and there to ease loose. Then makeup. Smoky dark lavender shadow on her eyes, plum on her cheeks and mouth. Diamond studs in her ears, a single diamond in a thick bezel of gold on a thin chain around her neck. A wide gold bangle bracelet that coiled like a snake around her upper left arm. A wide gold band set with emeralds—her birthstone—on her right ring finger, a thin plain gold band on the middle finger of her left hand. Strappy high black heels. She broke a piece of baby's breath off a stem that remained in a small vase on the bedside table—the last of the flowers Ben had brought her the previous week—and tucked it behind her right ear.

She hit the replay button and stepped back to look at the finished product.

The thin straps of the dress came up around her neck to form a low U in the front, then crossed once across the small of her back. Other than that, the dress was essentially backless. Zoey had found it in a designer's boutique on a Saturday afternoon trip to Manayunk, a once industrial but now trendy Philadelphia neighborhood. The dress had called to her and Zoey had been unable to resist it. It was a *knock 'em dead dress* if ever she had seen one. And someday, she had mused at the time, she might want to do just that.

Well, tonight's the night. She smiled nervously at her reflection, realizing, as she turned off first the CD player, then the light, that she had waited for this night for most of her adult life.

Now that it was here, she could not get on with it fast enough.

The valet waved her forward through the gate flanking the entrance to her mother's home. She never passed between those tall twin pillars of stone without wondering if there had ever been a fence or a wall around the property. After all, what good is a gate if there is no fence? She stopped her car and put it in park, requesting that it be left around the back near her mother's garage. The young valet, seemingly struck dumb at the sight of Zoey emerging inch by long cool inch from the small car, complied with a few quick nods of his head.

Taking a deep breath, Zoey picked her way on high thin heels through the loose white stones in the driveway and forced herself to walk, not run, toward the house, where the party was obviously in full swing. The cars were parked all the way back to the barn and music spilled out from every door and window. Shades of lavender and gold backlit the old stone house as the last remnants of the day slipped into the horizon. The small candles in every window made the house sparkle. She stepped up her pace and entered the house through one of the French doors opening off the dining room.

Walking briskly through one room into the next, she greeted old friends, all the while admiring the ambience her mother had created with white flowers—lilies, roses, and lilac—that spilled from vases on tabletops and mantels and scented the air. How very *Delia,* she mused, as she strolled into the front hallway, her heart pounding and her palms sweating, wondering if in fact *he* had arrived.

"Zoey's here! Yay! Zoey's here!"

The rapid sound of excited little feet fled down the steps, and the small curly-haired child flung herself into Zoey's arms.

"Corri!" Zoey affectionately hugged the child that India, her soon-to-be sister-in-law, was in the process of adopting. "I was wondering where everyone was!"

"We were upstairs with Delia and Aunt August, see?" She pointed a small finger skyward to where Delia stood at the top of the stairs in deep conversation with Augustina Devlin, India's aunt. Zoey waved, and both women came down the steps.

"Hello, August. It's wonderful to see you again." Zoey fondly embraced first August, then Delia. "Hello, Mother. And aren't you pretty in pink tonight."

"It *is* a flattering shade, isn't it, this silvery pale pink?" Delia held out a soft section of her silk skirt. "So kind to fifty-something skin, wouldn't you say?"

"I would indeed." August nodded. "It's lovely. As is the party. Everything is perfect."

"Well, of course. My boy and your girl deserve perfect." Delia patted August's arm gently. "Have you seen the cake, Zoey? Mrs. Colson totally outdid herself this time. Ivory buttercream frosting, with palest pink frosting roses and candied violets. To die for. If she isn't careful, Mrs. Colson may get roped into making the wedding cake."

"I'm sure she'd be thrilled. Nicky was always her favorite," Zoey remarked.

"Zoey, I saw your little cooking show last week." August's blue eyes sparkled with amusement.

"Oh, I'm sure that a world-class cook such as yourself must have been appalled." Zoey cringed.

"On the contrary. I thought it was fun to watch."

"Fun?" Zoey sighed. "You thought it was fun?"

"Absolutely. Everyone makes the same mistakes as

you did, dear. Everyone has to learn the same things you are learning. It's refreshing, really, to watch you, you are so natural. However, if I might mention one thing . . ."

"Anything." Zoey looped her arm through August's and leaned closer. "When it comes to the kitchen, August, you are The Man in my book."

"Well, dear, I just thought that the chicken recipe you made on air the other day was a bit complicated for a"— she sought a suitable word—"a novice such as yourself. If I might recommend one. . . ."

"Recommend away."

"Perhaps I'll fax something to you. India's new computer has a fax capability, and I find that fascinating. I'm tempted to invest in my own."

"Before you leave this weekend, I'll write the fax number down," Zoey assured her. "We have been soliciting recipes and helpful tips from our viewers—the response has been overwhelming—but I suspect that some of them may not be much more skilled than I am. It would be wonderful to have your recipes, August. I would be grateful for any help you would be willing to give me."

"Well, then, I'll be sure to send a few off to you this week."

"Oh, sweetie, excuse us. There's Angela Weston. I wanted August to meet her, they have so much in common." Delia pecked Zoey fondly on the cheek, then dragged August off to the next room.

"Delia is so fun," Corri piped up. "I read a book one time and it said that a lady *swooped.*" She emphasized the word. "Delia *swoops,*" she told Zoey, who laughed and gave Corri's little shoulder an affectionate squeeze.

"Corri, you are absolutely right. My mother does indeed *swoop.*"

"Delia is nice. She gave India a pretty little necklace to wear at the wedding. It has pearls and a silvery blue stone like the ring that Nick gave to India."

"I'll have to see it. It sounds lovely." Zoey smiled at Corri and bent down to give her one extra little hug for good measure. "I missed you, child. I'm glad you're here."

"Me, too. I got to ride the ponies this afternoon." Corri leaned over and whispered this last into Zoey's right ear, touching the small white flowers with her index finger as she did so. "Nicky let me. Aunt August didn't want me to because she didn't want me to smell like a horse for the party, but Delia said I could take a bath. And I did." She held her arm up to Zoey and said earnestly, "See? I don't smell like ponies at all."

"Why, you're right. You don't smell at all like a pony. You smell like"—Zoey sniffed at Corri just as the child wanted her to—"like . . ." She sniffed again, unable to place the fragrance. "What *do* you smell like?"

"Bubble gum." She announced solemnly. "It was in the bubble bath."

"I see." Zoey straightened up, suppressing a grin. "Oh, so much better to smell like bubble gum than ponies."

Corri nodded. "Especially if you are going to a fancy party."

"And this is a fancy party, I would say." Zoey laughed—bubble gum, the fragrance du jour—as she took Corri's hand. "Now, you wouldn't happen to know where Nick and India might be, would you?"

"They were in the big sun room." Corri grabbed Zoey's hand and tugged on it. "I'll show you. It's this way."

Corri led her through the crowd, having forgotten—as excited six-year-olds might tend to do—that Zoey, being Delia's daughter, had grown up in the house and knew exactly where the solarium was located.

"India!"

"Zoey! I've been watching the door for the past hour. Delia said you had to work today and that you'd be a little late." India excused herself from the small circle of guests to greet Zoey with an eager hug. "Oh, wow! Don't you look gorgeous! Oh, my, what a dress . . ." India whistled, her violet eyes widening as Zoey turned around to give her future sister-in-law a back view of the dress.

"You look quite the knockout yourself," Zoey laughed and stood back to admire India's long dark teal blue sheath that started with a high neck and followed India's curves until it ended at the ankles. "Those jewel colors really do set off your hair and your eyes."

Zoey reached a hand up to touch India's strawberry blond curls.

"And where is my big brother?" Zoey asked.

"The last I saw him, he was headed out through the back door with an old friend." India leaned closer and whispered, "This is your Ben, isn't it? Nick's old friend, the one you told me about once. The one who left and went away for years, is back now. . . ."

Zoey bit her bottom lip and nodded.

"I met Nick's friend, Zoey. He's nice," Corri chimed in. "He has a little car and the top comes off. He said I could have a ride tomorrow with the top off if it doesn't rain." Without pausing for breath, she went on. "Isn't the lake beautiful? I saw Delia's swans. India said I could be in the wedding. You and Georgia and Darla, too. And we get to wear dresses that reach all the way to the floor."

"Breathe." India admonished the child just as she appeared to be ready to launch into another round. She handed Corri a cookie and said, "Here. Eat something. Give your mind a rest. Go get some punch to drink with it."

Zoey laughed along with India as Corri skipped off to find the punch bowl. All the while, Zoey's eyes were darting from one side of the room to the other, then trying to see over the crowd onto the front hallway, scanning the group, hoping that no one would notice.

India did, and knew exactly whose face Zoey sought.

"He's with Nick," she told Zoey quietly. "In your mother's study."

"Who?"

Ignoring Zoey's feeble attempt to appear nonchalant, India laughed. "Is he as wonderful as he looks? Your Ben?"

"He's not my Ben."

"Oh, but how could he resist you?" India's eyes sparkled. "You look absolutely stunning, Zoey."

"Well, I admit that I was hoping to get his attention." Zoey lowered her voice.

"Oh, I don't think getting his attention is going to be a problem." India tilted her head slightly toward the doorway, where Ben was poised to enter the room behind Nick. He stopped dead in his tracks when he saw Zoey, as if stunned.

"Whatever you paid for that dress, it was worth every blessed penny," India whispered in her ear as Nick approached them, oblivious to the fact that his friend was in a state of suspended animation, stuck somehow between one footstep and the next.

"Hello, Duchess. I'm glad you finally made it." Nick hugged his sister and placed a kiss on her forehead, then stepped back to look at her. "You look beautiful."

"Thank you, Nicky."

"Pretty," Ben had managed to make his feet move those few steps forward and stood in front of her feeling awkward and gawky and somehow the two syllables had found their way out of his mouth. He touched the flowers in her hair, wishing he could think of something besides that one word. *Pretty. I sound like Tarzan. Or Franken-stein.*

Zoey smiled. "Actually, I should be thanking you for them."

He looked puzzled, so she added, "They were in the bouquet you gave me last week. I dried them."

Feeling very pleased but not quite sure why, Ben merely nodded, still having difficulties in making his tongue understand that one of its primary functions was speech. He wasn't certain, but thought it might have something to do with the loud buzzing between his ears, which had seemed to begin the second he walked into the room and saw Zoey.

India laughed and tugged Nick's arm. "Let's get a drink. Then you can introduce me to that crowd over there in the corner."

Nick glanced behind him. "That's my mother's agent and her editor."

"Well, their conversation is obviously far too deep for this occasion. Introduce me and let's see if we can lighten them up a little."

Zoey turned to Ben and was about to say something when a waiter passed by with a tray of fluted glasses glistening with champagne.

"Would you like a glass? Ben asked.

"Actually, I think I would rather have a glass of Chablis."

Her smile having nearly knocked him out, Ben grabbed Zoey's elbow and headed in the general direction of the bar. At least he hoped that's where he was going. He'd been so dazzled that, for a moment, he almost felt the urge to blink, like one whose eyes had stared into the sun and needed time to adjust to normal light. He managed somehow to find the bar, order two drinks, and pass hers along to her without spilling either.

"So, I see you and Nicky had a few minutes to talk together," she said to break the silence. "How was it?"

"How was what?"

"Seeing Nicky after all these years."

"Oh. Great. Wonderful. Nick is one of those people who never changes, you know? He seems to be the same good guy I knew when I was fourteen."

"He is. The same, I mean. And you will adore India when you get to know her. She is just wonderful."

"Now, tell me who the older woman is? The one with your mother."

"That's India's Aunt August. She raised India and her brother after their mother died."

"And the little girl?" He asked as Corri blew in one door and out the next.

"That's Corri Devlin. India's older brother, Ry, had been married briefly to Corri's mother, and had adopted her. When Ry died, India became Corri's guardian, and started the proceedings to adopt her."

"What happened to the child's mother?"

"That is a long story," Zoey remarked, not wanting to waste precious moments talking about Maris Devlin, India's former sister-in-law and persona non grata in the Devlin household. "But we all adore Corri. My mother positively dotes on her."

"Your mother positively dotes on everyone, it seems."

"That is an understatement." Zoey sipped at her drink and waved to one of her mother's neighbors who had just arrived. "She mentioned that she offered to let you move into the old carriage house."

"She did."

They had gravitated through the French doors leading out to the small back porch that overlooked the pond.

"And you said . . ." Zoey leaned back against the porch railing and crossed her legs, leaving one to dangle from the knee of the other, her skirt hiked halfway up her calf.

"That I'd think about it." He licked his lips to moisten them, as they seemed suddenly almost too dry for speech.

"Are you?"

"I'm trying to." *Trying to think about anything except what you're probably not wearing under that dress.*

"Trying to think about it?" She asked, aware of his plight and pleased by it.

"I have a lot on my mind right now," he mumbled, not daring to permit his eyes to drop lower than her chin.

"Oh, I imagine you do." She smiled sweetly. "New job, new home—and I'll bet you miss racing."

"I do," he nodded, trying to snap out of it.

"What's the fastest speed you ever drove?" she asked.

"A little over two hundred miles per hour. Thereabouts."

"Really? What did it feel like?"

"It feels like nothing else. Nothing."

"Hmmm." She traced the rim of her glass with the tip of her index finger. "What do you miss most?"

"That feeling of being on the edge," he answered without hesitation.

"You mean, of danger?"

"That, and of life. You know how very much alive you are when you are most aware of how little it would take to end it. And when you are rounding a curve at top speed, there is no question in your mind just how little it would take to send you hurtling into the next dimension."

"A sharp turn of the wheel?"

He shook his head. "Not even. A small twist of the wrist is often all it might take."

"You really would have to have a lot of control to keep yourself on the road."

He nodded, wondering if he should mention that he was, at that moment, exercising as much self-control in keeping his hands to himself, as ever he had in a race, but decided to let it go.

From the big solarium, where an artificial floor had been placed over the pool to permit dancing, soft music flowed as the band resumed their play. Ben reached into one of the nearby floral arrangements and snapped an orchid off its stem. He presented it to her and asked, "Would you like to dance?"

Zoey slid off the porch rail, her heart pounding in her chest, and rested her arms around his neck. His hands encircled her waist and drew her body close to his. They swayed slowly as the music surrounded them. He hummed in her ear and the skin on the side of her face nearest his mouth prickled with the closeness of him. She twirled the orchid between her thumb and her forefinger to focus on something besides the tension that was building inside her. Ben glanced down and studied her apparent fascination with the flower.

"If I had taken you to your prom, I would have brought you a corsage," he told her. "Probably a white orchid. It suits you."

"You said that about my name, the first time I met you." She reminded him.

"It suited you then, and it suits you now. It's different.

Exotic. Sensual. I just didn't know those words back then."

She ran the orchid petals along her bottom lip, still looking into his eyes. *If he doesn't kiss me—right now—I think I'll . . . I'll . . . I'll . . .*

It didn't matter that she couldn't think of an *or else,* because at that moment he touched the side of her mouth with his, then brushed his lips slowly, agonizingly slowly across hers. She turned her face completely up to his, and tugged slightly at his neck to urge him closer. Her lips parted slightly as he kissed her, tentatively, then deeper, deeper still, until she thought she'd pass out from the sheer delight of the sensation that spread through her. She pressed herself into him and his arms slid down her bare back, sending waves of shivers from her neck to her ankles.

"Careful, Zoey," he whispered. "I'm not feeling very big brotherly right now."

"Thank God," she sighed, and pulled his mouth back to hers.

Oblivious to everything else, she backed toward the porch railing and danced him around slowly, still kissing him, as she eased him against the rail and leaned into his embrace. She fought the sudden urge to rip his shirt off, to run her hands down his chest, touch his bare skin, and . . .

"Zoey?" Georgia's voice called from the hallway.

"Zoey, someone is calling you." He disengaged his mouth from hers.

"It's my sister," Zoey grumbled. "Her timing has always been lousy."

"Actually," he whispered, "her timing couldn't have been better. A few more minutes alone out here with you, under the moonlight, and I would not have been responsible for the consequences."

"Zoe?"

Zoey sighed and called, "Out here, Georgia."

"Oh, there you are." Georgia stepped outside and stopped at the sight of her sister, with her flushed face and swollen lips, and was torn between being embarrassed at having interrupted an intimate moment, and wanting to see who it was who had her sister all but panting. Not that it was her business.

Which of course did not stop her from continuing across the porch deck to hug Zoey and see what she could see.

Zoey returned her sister's affectionate greeting. "Georgia, you remember Ben Pierce."

"Ben? I heard you were back!" Georgia reached behind Zoey pointedly to offer Ben her hand.

"Little Georgia!" he exclaimed. "I can't believe it. Look at you."

Georgia grinned. "All grown up now, Ben."

"I'll say you are. You look wonderful."

"So. Did you just arrive?" Zoey asked her sister.

"A while ago. I was schmoozing with the guests." Georgia made herself comfortable on the railing next to Ben as if oblivious to the current that ran between the couple on the porch. "Nicky tells me you've been racing cars in Europe. How exciting. I want to hear all about it."

"And one of these days, you shall. Now, don't you think you should see if Mom needs any help?"

"Help doing what?" Georgia pretended not to understand.

"With whatever it is she is doing."

Georgia dismissed Zoey's concern aside with a wave of her hand and a perfectly innocent straight face.

"Mom is fine. Isn't it a lovely night? Look at the pond, the moon is reflected so totally perfectly in the water."

"It was perfect up until about sixty seconds ago," Zoey hissed.

Unable to contain herself, Georgia tilted her head back and laughed.

"Actually, August sent me to find you. Mother is going to make the formal announcement of Nick and India's engagement now, and wanted you both to be there."

"Oh. Of course." Zoey nodded with little enthusiasm.

Georgia grinned and said, "Can I tell Mom three minutes?"

"Better make it five."

"But no more than five, okay? I think there were some guests who were preparing to leave and Mom convinced them to wait just a few for the toast."

"We'll be right in," Zoey told her, all but shooing her sister toward the door.

"Georgia looks terrific," he said.

"Yes. She does."

"And she's right about the moonlight there on the pond," he continued, drawing her back to him inch by inch. "It's almost magical, don't you think? A moon that big and bright . . ."

"Ummm. Magical." She permitted herself to be encircled in his arms and nuzzled the side of his neck, catching the trace of aftershave that hinted of musk, then toyed with his bottom lip, just to give him something to think about later, after the party when he was back at his grandfather's condo. "Peter Pan."

"What?"

"My father used to call it a 'Peter Pan' moon."

He held her at arm's length for a second, then said, "I've never heard you—or Georgia, for that matter, mention your father. Nick used to talk about him, but I don't recall that you ever did."

"He's not been a factor in our lives. You know that he left us and closed the door a long time ago, Ben. Right after Georgia was born. She has no recollection of him at all. My memories are very sketchy. Being the oldest, Nick would remember him the best. We just don't have much reason to talk about him anymore."

"Do you ever wonder where he is? If he's alive?"

Zoey shrugged noncommittally. "Not really. Other than to wonder why he walked out on my mother and his three children and just never looked back."

"Do you know for a fact that he never did?"

"What? Look back?" She shook her head. "He remarried eighteen years ago. He has another family. We don't exist as far as he is concerned."

"It's a very strange thing, don't you think?" He ran his hands slowly up and down her arms as if to warm them in the cool spring air, an almost unconscious yet familiar gesture. "Why he left, why he cut all ties . . ."

"I used to think it was because of something that I had done," she whispered into his chest, as if afraid to face him with the admission. "Then, a few years ago, Georgia said she thought it was because of her. That since he left so soon after her birth, it must have been because of her. Nicky, however, was convinced that somehow it had been his fault."

"Funny, isn't it, that as children, we think we have this huge power, that everything that happens is somehow a result of something we had done or thought. That somehow we were responsible, even though we rarely ever are."

"Well, as adults, we all understand that now. But it has taken a long time to have come to that realization, for all three of us."

"And none of you ever asked your mother?"

"I never did. I suspect that Georgia has not, either. If Nicky did, he kept it to himself. I always felt that there was something very deep there, something she could not talk about. That if she could have, she would have."

"Zoey, everyone's waiting for you," Georgia called from the doorway.

"We're coming." She disengaged herself from Ben's arms reluctantly. It had been comforting, for just a moment, to have someone to share an old deep hurt with. She tugged on his hand.

"I hate to waste such moonlight." He looked back over his shoulder at the pond, where the shimmering light caused the shadows of the trees to reflect on the mirrored surface of the still water. "Maybe we can steal out for just one more dance before the night is over."

"Maybe," she grinned, walking backward toward the

open doors and taking him with her. "You never know what a night like this might hold."

* * *

Delia stood on the third step from the bottom of the handsome, wide stairwell, and watched as family and friends gathered below, the black-tied waiters circulating with silver trays of champagne in fine fluted glasses of delicate crystal. She cherished each face that her eyes set upon, her children, several of her cousins, several of their children. Longtime neighbors and friends. All of the people who were most dear to her, most important in her life.

All but one.

She sighed the thought away. In good time, the picture would be complete. Only not just yet. It hurt her terribly to see that empty place where someone else should be standing with Georgia and Zoey and Nicky. She would have given anything to have had that last link returned tonight, after all these years.

Soon, she reminded herself as she bit back the tears she had cried every night, every morning, for thirty-five years. Soon, they would be tears of joy. Soon, the canvas will be complete.

But not tonight. Tonight was Nicky's night. Nicky's and India's. The rest can wait. Her eyes glistened as she looked into the face of her son, and a look of such deep compassion and love passed between them that she wished for just the briefest moment that she could be alone to weep, to cry it out. Nicky was the only one who knew her secret, the only one she had told. He had wept with her, *for* her, the depth of his understanding nearly breaking Delia's heart.

She looked for her daughters, and found them huddled, faces tilted toward each other, whispering and giggling together, as so often she had seen them do through the years.

Will they be as understanding as their brother, when they find out that I have lived a lie for all these years?

These thoughts were not for tonight. She pushed away

her fears and forced herself to stand just a little taller, forced gaiety into her smile as she tapped her fingertips on the side of her glass to signal she was about to begin. This moment belonged to his son and this wonderful woman who would become his wife.

She flashed the smile she had become famous for, and raised her glass slightly as she proposed a toast to the happy couple.

There would be time enough to weep later.

Chapter

17

A narrow sleeve of morning sunlight elbowed through the gauzy white curtain, and Zoey stretched in its warmth like an overgrown cat, momentarily disoriented when she opened her eyes and found herself in her old bed in her old room in her mother's house. Knowing that the party would most likely last till the wee hours, she had packed an overnight bag and planned to stay. Besides, she had wanted to spend as much time this weekend with her mother and siblings, her future sister-in-law and her family. Her nose caught a whiff of something wonderful being prepared for breakfast. Sausage and pancakes, most likely, one of Nick's favorites. She smiled. Mrs. Colson always did love to spoil Nicky.

She flopped back on the pillow, and raised her arms above her head. It had been a lovely party. She sighed, remembering it all.

Had that really been her, dancing in the moonlight with Ben Pierce? And had that really been Ben, kissing her like he meant it?

It had! It had! A little voice inside her head crowed.

She grinned, then laughed out loud.

Kissing Ben was every bit as wonderful, every bit as exciting, as she had known it would be. His lips were *that* warm, his tongue *that* knowing and clever . . .

Just thinking about it brought that coil of anticipation back to her gut and caused her breath to catch in her throat.

"Careful, Zoey," he had said. *"I'm not feeling very big brotherly right now."*

"And *that* is the best news I've gotten in a very long time," she said aloud to the menagerie of her old stuffed animals that crowded a shelf on the opposite side of the room, "particularly since *sisterly* is the last word I'd use to describe how I feel about you, Bennett Pierce."

She hopped out of bed and into the bathroom, all but dancing. Delia had invited Ben for brunch. He would be here in less than an hour.

Maybe, before the day was over, she'd get the chance to kiss him again.

* * *

"You're in an awfully good mood this morning," Georgia noted as Zoey bustled into the dining room where she sat alone at the long table, still laden with the elaborate centerpiece from the night before.

"Umm." Zoey patted her sister on the back on the way to the buffet, where all manner of delectable dishes had been set to tempt the diners. "Oh, wow, eggs Benedict."

Zoey opened the door leading into the kitchen and called, "I love you, Mrs. Colson."

"I love you too, Zoey," came the cheerful reply. "Enjoy your eggs."

"I will, I will."

"Where is everyone?" Zoey asked Georgia, who was sorting through the basket of herbal tea bags on the sideboard. "Has everyone else eaten already?"

"August just went down to the barn to get India and Corri, who, being Corri, wanted to give the ponies each an apple for their breakfasts. Mom and Nicky are outside." She waved a hand toward the window, where,

223

beyond, at the foot of the garden path, her mother stood with her brother.

Zoey glanced out the window, then resumed pouring her first cup of coffee, but something drew her eyes back toward the garden as she turned to walk to the table. There was something in her mother's face as she looked up into Nick's, something Zoey could not quite identify. *Sorrow,* the word echoed in her head. Sorrow and pain and regret, all in their purest forms.

Drawn closer to the glass by the sharp awareness that what she was witnessing was the breaking of another's heart, Zoey pushed the curtain all the way back. Nick had his arm around Delia and was bent close to the side of her face, as if whispering something that was meant for no ears but hers, even though there was no one else around, and his look held such tenderness that for a moment it appeared that he had assumed the role of gentle parent and Delia that of the child who was being comforted. Unexpectedly, it disconcerted Zoey, this thought that her mother, Delia the ever strong, ever mighty, would require such ministrations from anyone, least of all one of her children.

She watched from the window as Nick ran his thumbs ever so gently under Delia's eyes, and it was then that Zoey realized that her mother was crying.

This, too, was a foreign concept, and she tried to recall when she had last seen her mother cry. Oh, there had been a few random tears over the years—a woman with a flair for drama always had a tear to shed for a sentimental birthday card or maternal pride—but this was different. These were real tears. Real enough to shake Delia's shoulders. Zoey wished she could see Nick's face.

Turn around, Nicky, she whispered, but he remained with his back to the house and his face hidden from her scrutiny.

"Did you say something, Zoey?" Georgia asked as she poured hot water into a porcelain cup.

"What?"

"What are you looking at?"

"Mom and Nicky are in the garden." Zoey bit her lip.

"I told you that." Georgia dipped a tea bag—Peach Orchard—into the cup.

"Have they been out there long?"

"They were there when I came down about five minutes ago."

"What's wrong with Mom? She looks so upset." Zoey frowned.

Georgia shrugged. "It's probably the wedding. You know how Mom is about these things. Losing a son, and all that."

That could be it. Zoey stole one more look out the window, then set her cup on the sideboard while she opened a packet of artificial sweetener. *Maybe Mom is just feeling nostalgic about her only son getting married.*

Sure, that's it. Zoey nodded uneasily to herself, wanting to believe it, and took her place across the table from Georgia and began to chat about who had worn what the night before, what relatives had shown up and who had not.

"Georgia, are you all right?" Zoey asked after ten minutes of mostly one-sided conversation.

"Why do you ask?"

"You're not yourself." Was Georgia somehow clued in to whatever was bothering her mother? "You're not feeling nostalgic about Nicky getting married too, are you?"

"Me? No. I'm delighted for him." Georgia reached behind her head with both hands to secure the pins that held up a waterfall of thick blond hair. "Nicky and India are like two halves of a whole. It's very romantic."

"It is very romantic," Zoey agreed. "And it's true, they're so perfect for each other it's like something out of a romance novel. But that doesn't answer the question."

"What question was that?" Georgia sipped slowly at her tea.

"I asked if you were all right. You seem distant."

Georgia sighed heavily and put down her cup. "I'm

just distracted, that's all. I have an audition on Tuesday for a role I have always wanted. I'm just nervous because I know I won't get it. I don't even know why I'm bothering to try out."

"Why would you say that? You're a wonderful dancer."

"'Wonderful' is probably not enough, sweetie, but I appreciate your saying so." Georgia smiled wryly. "This particular director likes his principal dancers to be very tiny."

"Georgia, if you were any tinier, you'd disappear."

"I am three inches taller and twelve pounds heavier than the competition. I look like a cow compared to some of the other dancers." Georgia nibbled on a slice of cantaloupe.

"Georgey, you are not a cow." Zoey put her fork down on the side of her plate, her voice rising. "And I would be totally suspect of anyone or anything that made you feel, for even one second, that you were. If anything, you're so thin you're about to fade into next week."

"Zoey, please don't start," Georgia pleaded, recalling the arguments she and her sister had had over the past year or so over what Georgia ate or did not eat. "I burn a tremendous number of calories. I dance for hours, every day. I jog. Some days I swim."

"Why do you do all that?"

"I like to."

"Then maybe you should take in a few more calories." Zoey could not help herself. She had to add, "A few hundred more every day might help."

"Please, Zoe. Not today."

"Okay. Just promise me you'll take lots of vitamins."

"I take vitamins. In fact, I probably eat a healthier diet than you. What did you have for lunch yesterday?"

"I don't remember." Zoey averted her eyes and shifted uncomfortably in her seat, thinking about the hamburger and French fries she had shared with CeCe.

"Ah, that bad, was it?" Georgia's eyes began to

twinkle. "I'll bet it was loaded with animal fat and sodium."

"Don't try turning the tables on me. I'm the big sister here. And as the big sister, it's my job to look out for you." Zoey's voice softened. "Besides, I love you, Georgey, and I couldn't bear for anything to happen to you."

"Nothing is going to happen to me. And I guess as the big sister, you're entitled to throw your two cents in every once in a while. And for the record"—she leaned over and kissed the top of Zoey's head—"I love you, too."

"Thanks, sweetie." Zoey gave Georgia's hand a squeeze. "Now, do you think I should go down to the barn to get the Devlins?"

"Ben did that."

"Ben is here?" Zoey asked. "You didn't tell me that Ben is here."

"I thought you knew. I thought that's why you were up early and down for breakfast on time for a change instead of making everyone wait for you." Georgia shrugged.

"Very funny." Zoey plunked her cup down on the table and set off for the barn. "I'll be right back. Tell Mrs. Colson to hold the hollandaise."

Zoey fled through the back door, then stopped as she saw him coming around the side of the carriage house, one arm draped comfortably over August's shoulder as he pointed up to the carriage house that had once been his home. He would be telling them about his mother, about how they had come to live there. He turned and pointed down toward the trees, beyond which flowed the Brandywine. Now he would be telling them about the adventures that he and Nick had on the river as boys. Corri jumped up and down, excited by the tale, and Zoey smiled at the sheer exuberance of the child's animated response.

The four of them walked toward the house, and she watched each step he took. That he was there, *really there*, was a miracle that she still could not comprehend.

As a boy, Ben had won her heart the first time they met. It seemed that now, as a man, he had come back to claim it. It had always been here, waiting for him. All he had had to do was come home.

And now he was there, and it was all just exactly as it was meant to be.

She watched his face as she walked toward him, watched the smile that started with his eyes, then moved to his lips. *He knows, too,* she thought to herself. *He knows he belongs here. He knows he was meant to be with me. He knows . . .*

It was all she could do to keep herself from dancing.

"Zoey!" Corri took off across the yard, a six-year-old bundle of love and joy, and caught Zoey around the hips.

"Corri, don't wipe your hands on Zoey's nice pants," August called to her. "You've been feeding the ponies with those hands."

Corri froze and stared in horror at her open palms.

"Did you smear pony slobber on my butt, Corri Devlin?" Zoey asked, trying her best to appear stern.

"I did." Corri turned her pixie's face up to Zoey. "I didn't mean to, but I did."

"It's okay." Zoey laughed to assure her. "These pants aren't all *that* nice. And besides, I have another pair with me, just in case."

"Good. Me and Ben are going canoeing after we eat. And maybe Nicky, too."

"If we can find the canoes," Ben told her.

"I think they're still in the garage," Zoey looked over the head of the child into the eyes of the man who could turn her knees to jelly with nothing more than a smile.

"Would you like to join us?" he asked, close enough now to tuck a wayward strand of her hair behind her ear. She all but melted at the touch of his fingers on the tip of her earlobe, her fears for her mother being pushed aside by the tingling that started in her head and traveled through her body down to her toes.

"Sure," she squeaked.

He took her elbow, then trailed his fingers the length of

her arm until their fingers touched, then locked. Buoyed by the intimacy of the simple gesture, she all but sang.

". . . but I only had enough for the ponies," Corri tugged at her other arm. "So, do you think we could?"

"Could what, sweetie?" Zoey tuned back in.

"Could go back after lunch and give the horses some apples."

"Oh. Sure." Zoey nodded.

"Yippee!" Corri skipped ahead, and spying Nick and Delia in the garden, started off for them. India's hand shot out and caught her shoulder and pulled her back.

"Not now," she told Corri softly.

Zoey turned and looked at her future sister-in-law, and knew in that instant that, whatever it was that was disturbing her mother, India *knew*.

And whatever it was, Zoey sensed, it went well beyond Nick's impending wedding.

* * *

"You know, we'll never get anywhere as long as you refuse to paddle." Ben sat on one seat of the canoe, Zoey on the other.

She leaned over the edge of the aluminum vessel, her fingers skimming the surface of the water like a dragon-fly. It was peaceful on the river. It had been years since she had let it just take her. She liked the feeling of drifting. Especially since the other occupant of the canoe had her total attention.

"Zoey"—he leaned forward—"don't you want to catch up to the others?"

"Nope." She grinned lazily. "No place I want to go to, no place I'd rather be."

He looked around slowly, deliberately, as if studying his surroundings.

"I think that's the tree where Nick and I used to have a tire hanging from a rope. We'd swing out over the river, then jump in." He pointed to a tall maple tree that stood up on the rise that formed a stony bank off to their left.

"Two down." She told him, her eyes closed and her face tilted up to catch the sun.

229

"What?"

"Two trees down."

He glanced up at the maple as they drifted under its canopy.

"I could have sworn . . ."

"That tree was smaller back then," she told him, then pointed up ahead and said, "There's the tree you're looking for."

"I don't remember it being that big." He frowned.

"And seventeen years ago, it wasn't. You've been away a long time, Ben," she reminded him.

"I guess I have." He studied the tree as they approached, then pointed upward. "It's still there. The tire swing. Just where we left it, I imagine."

"I'm certain you're right. I doubt anyone has jumped from that rope since you left."

"I'm sure that Nick—"

"Never touched it." She shook her head. "There were a lot of things that you guys used to do together, that Nick stopped doing after you left."

"You're kidding."

"No. He waited for you to come back. He always thought you would."

"I guess he didn't expect it would take so long."

"None of us did," she said softly.

"Least of all me," Ben replied.

"Was it that difficult, then, to come back here?"

"I was a very confused boy when I left here, Zoey. I guess in my mind I had built things up to . . . well, to be more difficult, more complicated than they really were. But once I was here, it was as if I had not left. Seeing your mother, seeing Nick, you . . . I really feel as if I've come home."

"You have, Ben. This is your home."

She stretched her bare feet toward him in the body of the canoe and he reached out to tweak her toes.

"You're right. It is." With his oar, he pushed off away from the tip of a rock that stuck out through the water like a raised fist. "And it's good to be home, Zoey."

"It's good to have you home." She sat forward as if to say something, when she was interrupted by the whoops and hollers from the passing canoe, manned by Nick and India. Corri hung all but completely over the side as she dove for something in the water and Nick grabbed the waistband of her jeans to pull her back in.

"We're 'sploring. Want to come?" Corri called to them.

"'Sploring what?" Zoey called back.

"The river," a wide-eyed Corri told them as Nick and India paddled to close the gap between the two canoes. "Nick says that there was a battle up there"—she pointed toward the far shore—"and that soldiers are buried there."

"Remember, buddy?" Nick asked Ben. "We used to camp there and sit up half the night watching for ghosts."

"Ghosts!" Corri exclaimed. "Did you ever see one?"

"Only in our imaginations." Ben laughed.

"And there was plenty of fodder for our active little minds, growing up in these parts," Nick grinned. "Remember all the days we set out, *positive* that today would be the day we'd find the highwayman's buried loot."

"We dug holes from here almost to Kennett Square." Ben laughed again, and this time, Zoey and Nick laughed with him.

"I remember one time you told me if I dug up the loot, that you'd give me a quarter," Zoey chimed in, grumbling with reproach. "A whole *quarter* for digging up Fitzpatrick's ill-earned treasure."

"Who was Fitzpatrick?" India asked.

"James Fitzpatrick was a blacksmith who used to haunt the taverns down around what is now Kennett," Nick told her.

Zoey tried to recall the local legend. "Wasn't he a member of the Continental army?"

"British army, I thought," Ben said.

"Actually, he fought on both sides at different times. He fought with the patriots for a while, but thought he was being mistreated, so he deserted and joined the Brits." Nick placed his paddle across his knees and leaned on it. "But he's best remembered for his exploits as a highwayman. He was, so the story goes, a master of disguise. One of his favorite ploys was to don one of his many disguises, seat himself in one of the local taverns, and join in the gossip about the exploits of 'that rogue Fitzpatrick.' Then he'd jump up, pull off his disguise, and proceed to rob the very fellows he'd been drinking and chatting with."

"And, of course, local legend would have had it that he buried his loot somewhere around here." India nodded.

"Of course. But I can assure you that it's not on Enright property," Nick told her, "because at one time or another, Ben and I sifted through every inch of it."

"What happened to the highwayman?" India asked.

"He was hanged down in Chester City," Zoey said.

"Now if we float down river just a little farther, we can drag the canoes out and leave them on the shore, walk a ways, and we'll come to an old Quaker meeting house where the American and the British troops skirmished outside while the meeting was in worship on the inside. Must have made for a heck of service."

"Most of the soldiers who dropped there that day were buried right there in the meeting cemetery," Zoey added.

"So." Nick turned to India and asked, "Shall we go in search of the highwayman's treasure, or shall we hike out to the old meeting house?"

"Actually, I would like to do both"—India glanced at her watch—"but I don't think we really have time to do either. Corri has school tomorrow, and I'd like to be back in Devlin's Light in time for dinner."

Corri made a face. "I want to see where the ghosts are."

"Next time, sweetie," Zoey told her. "Next time you come for a visit, you and I will go off on a trek and we won't come back till we have seen at least one ghost."

"Yay!" Corri yelled and started to jump up.

"No! Corri! We don't stand up in a canoe!" Nick cautioned as the canoe tipped periously to one side. Corri giggled, oblivious to the fact that she almost got the coldest bath of her life, and shot back to the middle of the canoe floor. Nick rolled his eyes to the sky and told Zoey and Ben, "How would you guys like to row back with Corri in your canoe?"

"Nah," Ben told him. "There's enough deadweight in this canoe as it is."

"Who are you calling deadweight?" Zoey leaned forward.

"Well, there's two of us here, and only one of us is paddling. . . ."

"I'll show you paddling." Zoey sat up and squared her shoulders, and dug into the water with her paddle, turning the canoe around in a circle.

"Ah, Zoey, we're going round and round in a circle," Ben noted.

"Shut up and row." She glanced over her shoulder at her brother and called, "Last one home is a rotten egg."

"If we can't go look for ghosts and we can't go look for loot," Zoey heard Corri ask as the canoe pulled away, "can I go for a ride in Ben's car when we get back? He said if it was a nice day, he would take me for a ride in his car. With the top off."

"Sure," Nick told her as he pushed his canoe past his sister's, "as long as we don't have to wait too long for them to catch up."

"Catch up?" Zoey croaked. "Catch up? You may not realize it, my beloved big brother, but you are messing with the paddleboat champ of Brady's Mill."

"Oh, well, then. Did you hear that, India?" Nick called loudly enough to be heard in the next boat. "The *paddleboat champ of Brady's Mill.*"

"Ummm. I suppose we should give up without a fight, Nick," India called over her shoulder. "How could we hope to beat the *paddleboat* champ of *Brady's Mill?*"

"Wow. Next time we issue a challenge, I guess we'd better find out who the competition is, wouldn't you say, India?"

Laughing, a full five feet behind the other canoe, Ben rose to the challenge. "Dig, Zoey."

"I'm digging, I'm digging!" She laughed, though they both knew that India and Nick would not be beaten at rowing. At least not on this day.

"Next time," Ben told Nick good-naturedly.

"Never," India told him. "Nick rows the bay every morning for a workout. He's unbeatable."

"Maybe I'll be a sport, though"—Nick grinned— "and we'll give you a handicap."

"We'll take it." Ben winked at India as they lifted the canoe and started up the incline from the river.

"What's a 'handicap'?" Corri skipped alongside of India and tried to keep up. Before India could answer, Corri asked, "And Indy, Ben didn't make us wait. So can I have a ride in his car?"

"That's up to Ben."

"Can we still go, Ben? Please?"

"Sure."

"Oh, boy, wait till I tell Ollie," she scampered ahead.

"Who's Ollie?" Ben laughed.

"Her best friend back in Devlin's Light," India told him as they reached the garage and leaned the canoes up against the outside wall.

"Indy, why don't you go inside and start getting your things and Corri's ready, while I hose down the canoes?" Nick asked.

"Good idea. Corri can go for a short ride with Ben while I do that and see if Aunt August is almost ready to leave." India nodded and set off for the house.

"Can Zoey come?" Corri asked Ben.

"Well, there's really only room for two people," Ben told her.

"Oh . . ." Corri seemed disappointed.

"It's okay, Corri. I can take Zoey another time. If she wants to go someplace with me sometime." Ben turned to her and asked, "Do you think you might want to go someplace with me sometime, Zoey?"

"Odds are that I could be persuaded." She nodded.

"Well, then, Miss Corri, you're on. Let's do it." He held her hand out to the little girl and they raced to the spot where he had parked his sports car earlier that day. In anticipation of the event, he had left the top down. Corri climbed in and fastened her seat belt.

While they were too far away for their voices to be heard in the garage, Zoey was certain that Corri's mouth was moving the entire time.

"She'll talk Ben to death, you know," Nick told his sister, and they both laughed.

"What a shame to lose your friend after finding him again after so long." She grinned.

"Yeah. Isn't that something? Ben turning up again after all this time?" Nick untangled a length of dark green garden hose. "I still can't believe it."

"Ummm." Zoey nodded happily.

Nick glanced at Zoey, wondering if he should ignore the obvious. Nah.

"So," he said meaningfully.

" 'So' what?"

"So what's up with you and Ben?"

"Don't know yet."

"Really?"

"Really." She sat down on the concrete apron of the driveway and asked, "What are you getting at?"

"There's a current."

"There's always been a current."

Nick frowned. "The last time we saw Ben, we were kids. Kids don't make currents." He sprayed one side of the canoe and turned the water off and said meaningfully, "Last night, there was current. Today there was current. I could feel it."

"Good." She grinned happily.

"I don't know about that." He shook his head.

"What do you mean?"

"I mean that as soon as his leg is better, he'll be off to

Monte Carlo or Monza or Silverstone or wherever the next Grand Prix will be run."

She sat and pondered this.

"No, he won't," she announced. "He won't leave."

"Zoey, don't delude yourself. This is Ben's life. He was just reaching a point in his career where he was about to make his mark before he had the accident." He sprayed the other side of the canoe, then turned it to dry in the sun. "If he can go back to it, he will. And besides, he told me that once he retires, he's planning on going into business with a friend of his back in England, Zoe. Ben has no plans to move back to the States. He's here to help Delaney out on a temporary basis, but as soon as he can, he'll be going back to the life he's made for himself in England."

"He won't," she said stubbornly, not willing to delve into *that* particular pot right then and there, then before he had a chance to add another two cents, caught him off guard by asking, "What was Mom crying about this morning?"

"What do you mean?" Nick turned his back and sprayed the second canoe.

"Nicky, don't play that game with me." She exhaled loudly. "I saw you in the garden with Mom this morning. She was crying, Nicky, and you know that she was."

"Well, you know how Mom is," he said, not looking at her. "She gets sort of overcome sometimes when she thinks about the wedding."

"Nicky, are you lying to me?" Zoey asked quietly. "Are you and Mom keeping something from me and Georgia?"

"Yippee!!" Corri called as the little sports car spun into a soft slow arc at the foot of the drive. "That was so fun! Zoey, it was so fun! We went all the way down the road, then back up around the pond!"

"Wow! I'll bet that was fun," Zoey's gaze was still fixed to the back of her brother's head. He still had not turned around to look her in the eye.

"Come on." Corri grabbed Zoey's arm, "Let's go tell Aunt August."

"You go on without me, sweetie," Zoey told her. "I'll be along in a minute."

"Go on up with her, Zoey." Nick turned around. "There's nothing I can tell you."

Zoey stared at her brother's eyes and could see there was something there, something he would not share. A chill of fear shot through her.

"Nicky," she whispered, "just tell me if she's sick."

"What? Oh, sweetie, no. No one's sick. I swear it."

"Then why won't you tell me, Nicky?"

"Sweetheart, there's nothing I can tell you," he repeated, then turned his back again. "Mom just has a lot on her mind, with the book tours and the wedding. . . ."

"Come on, Zoey. We have to get some apples from Mrs. Colson." Corri pulled her in the direction of the house, and Zoey followed her for a dozen steps or so before turning and calling over her shoulder, "You're sure that's it, Nick?"

"It's all I can tell you, Zoe." Nick turned back to the job of hosing down the canoe.

With absolute certainty, Zoey knew that her brother was lying to her, pure and simple. Nick was simply not an accomplished liar. He never had been. It was obvious to her that he was lying now. It would nag her until she found out the truth.

Why was he lying? And what in the world was he—and their mother—hiding?

Chapter

18

"Wow. Flowers for me?" CeCe grinned. "Can't say I can remember the last time someone brought me a bouquet of anything."

"Picked them myself." Zoey handed over the enormous bundle of lilac and followed her friend through the apartment door into the small living room.

"They really are beautiful." CeCe bent her face into the blooms and inhaled. "And the fragrance is heavenly. My mother had this color"—she touched the deepest of the several shades of purple—"and tons of the white. And she used to have this lavender growing along one side of the barn, but my brother, Schuyler, flattened it with the pickup the year he was learning how to drive."

Zoey laughed. "Now, Schuyler is your twin, right?"

"No, that's Trevor. Sky is a few years younger. Trevor and I are the oldest. Actually, I am the oldest by about seventeen minutes, which makes me everyone's big sister." CeCe dragged a cardboard box from one of the corners in the living room and pulled open the top. "None in there," she muttered.

"What are you looking for?" Zoey asked.

"A vase." CeCe poked into another box. "Maybe in here . . ."

"I realize I may be going out on a limb here, but it may be easier to find things if you unpack," Zoey dead-panned. "Now, it may not work the same for everyone, but I've definitely noticed an increase in success in locating things once the boxes were emptied."

"Very funny." CeCe made a face. "I'll unpack. Someday."

"If you need help . . ."

"Nah. It's just that I don't really want to stay here, in this apartment, but I haven't found anyplace else I'd want to live in, either." CeCe sighed. "I guess I just don't feel settled here."

"Didn't you sign a two-year contract?"

CeCe nodded somewhat glumly.

"Are you planning to live out of boxes for the next two years?" Zoey asked.

"I guess not."

Finding a vase large enough for the tall woody stalks of lilac, CeCe took it into the kitchen to fill it with water.

Zoey followed her into the small, all-white room. "Is it the apartment that you don't like?"

"The apartment is okay. It's smaller than what I'm used to, though."

"So find another one."

"I guess." CeCe shrugged, then said, "I think I'm just a little homesick today. I got a phone call this morning from my mother. All the family news makes me wish I was back there with them." She set the vase in the middle of the kitchen table, then passed a plate of cheese, grapes, and apple slices to Zoey, who took the plate and set it down on the table.

"Well, don't you have some vacation time coming up?"

"Next month. I'll be going back for my cousin's wedding."

"That should be fun." Zoey picked at a grape, peeling it absentmindedly with her teeth.

"It will be." CeCe nodded and took a pot down from the pot rack.

"Will the skating cowboy be there?"

"He's the best man." CeCe grinned.

"Ah, I see." Zoey nodded, then wiggled her nose. "By the way, that smells wonderful. What are you making?"

"Pasta primavera."

"You really should be doing the cooking shows." Zoey shook her head and popped another grape into her mouth. "I am so pathetic. My future sister-in-law's aunt called in this morning during the show to tell me that I had the flame too high on the chicken fryer and if I didn't lower it, I would most likely suffer burns from hot oil flying out of the pan when I put in those cold pieces of chicken." Zoey rolled her eyes. "How embarrassing."

CeCe laughed. "Well, the word is that your cooking show is gaining viewers at a faster rate than any other recurring show to date."

"And no one is more surprised than I am. Do you know they are planning to do a cookbook of the recipes that people have sent in to me?"

"How are they going to decide what goes in and what gets pitched?"

"I suggested that they give all the recipes to India's aunt August and pay her to do the editing. Which they are doing. She's a natural. And she calls in during most of the shows now, so the viewers are familiar with her. I asked if we could do a special from time to time and have her come on and be a guest cook. You know, at holidays, or for special events."

"What did Ted say?"

"He loved it. As a matter of fact, he asked if we might include her on the all-day Summer Wedding special they are planning. She said she would, as long as it doesn't interfere with India and Nick's wedding."

"The station is really getting into these all-day events, aren't they?" Without waiting for an answer, she continued. "And how are your brother's wedding plans progressing, by the way?"

"Great." Zoey recalled her mother's tearful face looking up into Nick's as if pleading for something. . . .

"Zoey, I said, what's your dress like?"

"My dress?" Zoey asked blankly.

"For the wedding." CeCe sliced first a green pepper, then a red one. "Did you just mentally *go* someplace?"

"I'm sorry. I'm afraid I drifted."

"Something on your mind?"

"A lot, actually."

"Want to talk about it?"

"Where to start?" Zoey sighed. "It was quite a weekend."

"How was the party?"

"Wonderful. The best."

"Really?" CeCe giggled. "Might that explain why Mr. Home MarketPlace was seen prowling the halls all week wearing a silly grin and mismatched socks?"

"Ben was wearing two different socks?"

"Yep. One blue, one brown. Where I come from, that's a sign of total distraction."

Zoey smiled happily.

"So. I take it your path crossed with Ben's this weekend."

"Ummm."

"Well, now. An 'Ummm'-rated weekend. My favorite kind."

"Mine, too."

"And I trust there will be more 'Ummm'-rated weekends in your future?"

"Oh, I sincerely hope so." Zoey grinned. "It was wonderful. The party was wonderful. We danced in the moonlight on my mother's porch. Did I say it was wonderful?" She sighed. "On Sunday, we went canoeing, and he stayed for dinner at my mother's. My mother invited his grandfather to come as well."

"You said that they knew each other from years ago?"

"More or less. It was fun." Zoey's lips tilted at the edges, as she remembered the way he had kissed her good night and left her standing in the driveway wanting more, her toes curled and her heart pounding. No one had ever kissed her like that. . . .

"I'll just bet it was." CeCe measured olive oil into a frying pan and turned on the burner. "Well, there's nothing like a perfect weekend to make you feel like all is well in the world."

"Not quite." Zoey shook her head.

CeCe turned to her, a puzzled look on her face.

"I don't know . . ." Zoey struggled with the words, as if afraid that speaking her fears aloud might give them a life of their own, and make them come true.

"Don't know what?"

"I don't think Ben's going to be staying here for too long. I think he's going to go back to England."

"When?"

"I don't know." Zoey unfolded the napkin at her place at the table, then folded it again. Then unfolded. Folded.

"Well, what did he say?"

"He said that if he couldn't drive again, he was going to go into business with a friend of his."

"What kind of business?"

Zoey shrugged. "Something to do with racing."

"When will he know if he can drive?"

"Probably not for a few months."

"Don't waste your time worrying about what might or might not happen, Zoe. Save your energy for the *now*, and deal with things as they happen."

"There's more," Zoey told her.

"More what?"

"More to worry about."

"Such as . . . ?"

"Something odd is going on with my mother. I saw her crying in the garden yesterday with my brother. Yet, when I saw her later, she was her usual charming self. As if she didn't have a care in the world."

"Maybe she doesn't. Maybe she and your brother were having a mother-and-son moment."

"You know, that's what I tried to tell myself. But it

doesn't feel right." Zoey shook her head slowly. "As much as I wanted to believe that it's nothing more than Mom being sappy about her little boy getting married and all that, I just know that there's more to it than that. You'd have had to see the look on her face. She looked so . . . sad. So . . . *lost,* somehow. *Frightened,* even. It's so hard to explain. My mother is always together, CeCe, I've never even seen her really afraid. And she is always in control."

"Zoey, no one is always in control."

"My mother is," Zoey insisted.

"Maybe that's what she would like you to think. But I'll bet there are times when she falls apart like the rest of us."

"Nah. I'd know if she did."

"Zoey, all you really ever know of anyone is that which they *want* you to know."

"CeCe, this is my *mother* we're talking about. We have no secrets. I know all there is to know."

"You can't really believe that."

"Sure. What's not to know?"

"Why did your father leave?"

Zoey's hand, wrapped around her wineglass, stopped in midair on its way to her mouth.

"I cannot believe I said that. Of all the insensitive . . . I'm so sorry, Zoey." CeCe cringed when she realized what she had said. "I'm sorry, it just came out."

"It's okay."

"It's not okay. It was thoughtless and it was—"

"No. Really. It's okay." Zoey looked up, her blue eyes clouded with uncertainty. "I have no idea why my father left. And you're absolutely right." She pondered the possibility for the first time. "I'm sure there are many things in my mother's life that I don't know anything about. It was a very arrogant assumption on my part."

For the rest of the evening, Zoey wondered just how many secrets her mother might have, and which one of them had driven her to tears on Sunday morning.

* * *

"Zoey, ah have to tell you how much ah enjoy this show. Ah look forward to Tuesdays just so's ah can watch you in the kitchen." The caller—June from Savannah, Georgia—giggled. "But ah have to say ah never did see anyone have such a dickens of a time making pie crust."

"Well, I know that there is a way to prevent this stuff from crawling up your arms. . . ." A flustered Zoey tried to keep her eyes on the monitor and away from the side of the set, where Ben stood laughing at her efforts to pick the sticky dough from her wrists.

"Sugar, if you would just flour your hands before you start, you won't have a lick of trouble next time," June confided.

"Really?"

"Really. Now, ah'm just going to hang up here and you can just go on with your show, there, Zoey," June told her with a touch of maternal warmth.

"Thank you, June. Ah . . . that is, *I* . . . appreciate your help." Momentarily off-camera, Zoey stuck her tongue out at Ben before continuing. "Now for the real challenge. I have to put this pie together." She attempted to pick up the round crust and place it in the bottom of the pie plate, but it ripped into two pieces. "Oh boy." She sighed and put the halves into the plate, trying to moosh them together.

"Zoey, you have another call," her producer told her through her earpiece. "And for crying out loud, you're burning the crap out of the strawberries. Take the pan off the stove!"

"Hello, Ruth." Zoey dropped the pie crust onto the counter and removed the pan of boiling strawberries from the burner. "How's your day going?"

She heard Ben chuckle but refused to look at him.

"Fine, honey, but it looks like you're having a little trouble there."

"I always do, Ruth." Zoey frowned.

"If I could give you a little suggestion . . ."

"Certainly. Please. Feel free."

"You can put that little torn section of crust back together with a little water."

"Water?" Zoey frowned.

"Just wet your fingers and sort of work the two pieces of the crust together."

"Like this?" Zoey signaled the cameraman to zoom in while her fingers worked the dough into a smooth and slippery disk.

"Exactly. That should be fine." Ruth's voice was soothing and patient.

"Hey! It worked!" Zoey beamed. "Well, I certainly thank you, Ruth."

"It was my pleasure, Zoey."

"Call back anytime," Zoey told her, pleased that she had been able to salvage the dough and make a presentable piecrust.

"Zoey, one more call," the producer told her.

"Hello, Zoey, this is Sharon calling from Boston."

"Hi, Sharon, how's everything in Boston?"

"Warmer than it was last week. I just wanted you to know how much I enjoy watching you cook—"

"Zoey, your oven mitt is on fire!" Ellen yelled.

"Oh!" A nervous glance at the monitor indicated that the burning mitt was off-camera. Zoey tried to inconspicuously knock the flaming mitt into the nearby sink.

She missed. The flaming mitt headed toward the floor.

"—and how thrilled I was to see you last week. I was lunching in the same restaurant as you and your mother. I sat three tables away."

"Really?"

Zoey dropped a thick towel onto the mitt, which had gone down in flames like a kamikaze.

"You're even prettier in person."

"Zoey, say thank you to the lady," Ellen instructed. "And see if you can stomp on that sucker to make sure it's out."

"Thank you," Zoey said as she slid one pump-clad shoe onto the smoking towel.

"And I loved that purple suit you were wearing."

"Thank you . . ."

"Sharon," Ellen supplied Zoey with the name she had clearly forgotten.

"Sharon. Thanks for calling."

Having gotten the fire out, Zoey glanced at the clock. Down to the last few minutes. She signaled the camera-man to run the promo shot and voice-over for one of the products to be offered on the next show while she retrieved the remnants of the burned mitt, dropped it into the sink, and turned on the water.

"Thanks for your help," she stage-whispered to the production assistants and product coordinator, who were all but falling on the floor in gales of laughter. "I could have burned the set down."

"We had a fire extinguisher ready, just in case," one of them told her, "but you were doing just fine."

"Zoey, please stop at my office when you're done here." Trying his best not to laugh at her, too, Ben turned away, nodding politely to the other employees as he walked off the set.

"Oh, boy." One of the prop boys rolled his eyes. "Poor Zoey. It's bad enough to mess up, but messing up with Pierce standing right there is not a good thing."

"Sorry, Zoey," another said as she walked off the set. "I guess you're really going to get it now from Pierce."

Ever hopeful that he might, in fact, be right, Zoey smiled to herself as she removed her microphone, stuck it into her pocket, and stepped down off the set.

* * *

"So, now you've seen firsthand what a buffoon I am in the kitchen, I guess you'll want to recommend someone else do the cooking shows, right?" Zoey cheerfully folded her arms over her chest and leaned against the side of Ben's desk.

"Not a chance. Everyone adores you." *Including me.*

Zoey sighed. "You'd think that people would want to see someone who knows what they're doing."

"They seem to like watching you." *I like watching you.*

"I thought maybe I had been summoned to the boss's office for a lecture."

He stood up from his desk, testing his foot. Therapy had helped a lot, but there were still times when his ankle seemed almost to freeze up. It didn't bode well, he knew, but he pushed the thought from his mind. "This has nothing to do with how many woks you can sell."

"What does it have to do with?"

"The way you look in that shade of blue-green." His voice grew husky as he walked toward her.

"Teal," she said.

"Teal." The corners of his mouth quirked into a grin. "Teal is a very good color on you, Zoey. It brings out that smoky blue of your eyes."

His fingers traced the outline of her face from her temple to her jaw and back again. "I haven't been the same since the weekend," he confessed. "I can't seem to concentrate on much of anything."

"Me, too," she whispered.

"All I can think about is kissing you, Zoey Enright."

"Well, then, I think you should stop thinking about it and do it."

"I think you just might be right."

He seemed to engulf her with his arms, which held her in an embrace both tender and powerful, and his lips, which caught her mouth and claimed it for his own. He seemed to siphon the very life from her, leaving her weak, short of breath, and dazed. But not totally defenseless, she discovered, as she parted her lips and felt his tongue, soft as a summer morning and hot as the midday sun, as it slipped into the corners of her mouth, and heard his breath catch in his throat. The pulse inside her head pounded like thunder and she lifted herself closer into his arms, drew his kiss deeper, until there was neither sight nor sound, only sweet hot sensation that spread downward from her mouth and showed no signs of stopping at her stomach. She wished she could be brazen, could act the way she'd seen women act in the movies, the ones that would pull their dresses up to their waist and slide on back to the top of his desk and just *do it.*

But she, Zoey Enright, had not been raised to seduce men on their desks in their offices in their place of employment.

Ben, however, had apparently not been as delicately taught.

He eased her back toward the slab of mahogany and pressed her against the front of the desk. *Oh, boy,* raced through Zoey's feeble mind. *Oh, boy!*

Finding that she did, in fact, feel much the seductress after all, Zoey pressed against the solid wall of Ben's body and the source of the heat that had risen so rapidly between them like a flash fire. She felt herself falling, falling backward, like a snowflake on a downward spiral, still held tightly by his arms but dropping back onto the desk, his lips still torturing her as they skimmed first her chin, then the long eager column of her neck. She heard her breath in short bursts, his heart beating wildly, her name as he whispered it somewhere between her waist and her collarbone. She heard the soft fall of items on the desk as they fled toward the floor.

She heard the voice of Ben's secretary announce through the intercom, "Ben, your grandfather is here."

It took a few seconds before he could react. But when he did, he was brilliant.

"My grandfather is here?" He raised his head and frowned. Looking down into Zoey's half-closed eyes, he repeated, "My granddfather is here."

"Just called from the parking lot. He should be up here in about, oh, my guess is three minutes. Providing he doesn't stop to talk to anyone."

The news seeped slowly into Zoey's brain.

"Did she say . . . ?"

"Ah, I'm afraid so." Ben eased himself back and drew her along with him until they were both standing upright and on their own two feet, and swore softly. *"Damn."*

"I guess I should just"—Zoey thought perhaps she'd just back on out the door, like a businesswoman whose business had concluded—"be going."

"There's no need for you to run away," he told her, his arms sliding from her shoulders to her elbows.

"I just feel a little awkward." She laughed nervously. "I mean, we were almost . . . that is to say . . ." She pointed to the desk, which, except for the phone, an appointment book, and one pen that managed somehow to remain in its place, was totally bare. "Oh, damn. Your desk." She bent and started to retrieve the pens, folders, and the small calculator that had been pushed aside, and handed them up to Ben, who replaced them on the desk. They had just finished when the door opened and Delaney O'Connor appeared.

"Hello, son, how's it going?" Delaney entered the room with his cane in his left hand and a leather folder under his right arm. He paused at the sight of Zoey down on one knee in front of Ben's desk. "Oh. Appears things are going very well. Very well indeed."

"Hello, Delaney." Ben chuckled and offered his hand to his grandfather.

"Hello, Delaney." A red-faced Zoey stood up and smoothed her short blue skirt. "I dropped my . . . pen." She held up the ballpoint she had retrieved.

"So I see." Delaney struggled to keep a straight face.

"Well, then, I'll just leave you to your business. It was nice to see you again, Delaney." She backed toward the door. "Ben, I'll see you—"

"At seven-thirty?"

"Fine. Yes. Seven-thirty."

Ben walked her to the doorway and leaned over to whisper in her ear, "And if you want to make it to dinner, do *not* wear your black dress."

She nodded somewhat numbly, her heart still pounding, and backed on out through the door. She stumbled out to her car and managed to drive from the parking lot to her house without being quite certain whether or not he had been giving her a choice.

Had he said dinner *or* the dress?

Chapter

19

Zoey stood in front of her open closet and pondered the possibilities. Maybe something casual, she thought, tugging on a long-sleeved red knit dress with a turtleneck. Maybe something sexy, she thought, searching for a little blue number she had bought in Paris three years earlier and hadn't worn since. She pulled it out and held it up.

Nah. Too blatant.

Debating the merits of safety as opposed to out-and-out seduction, she took one more look through the closet, hoping to find some forgotten favorite. She twirled a deep green suit on its hanger, then rejected it. Too warm for a suit. Besides, she longed for a casual evening, one spent in familiar chatter and easy smiles, with their heads dipped over glasses of wine the color of sunshine. She'd wear the red.

She paused and looked back at the suit, and the voice came back to her.

". . . how thrilled I was to see you last week."

Where had that call come from? Boston?

"I was lunching in the same restaurant as you and your mother." The caller's words, all but ignored at the time

251

while she had been in the midst of her firefighting duties, came back to her. *"I loved that purple suit you were wearing."*

Zoey began to tremble and her chest began to hurt.

She had not been in Boston with Delia the week before. And she had never owned a purple suit.

With shaking hands, she dialed Delia's number. She was not at all surprised when Mrs. Colson told her that her mother had left that morning for a long weekend at the beach. She was staying at a bed-and-breakfast called the Bishop's Inn right above Fenwick Island on the barrier coast of Delaware.

She no longer needed to debate what to wear. Tossing the high-heeled shoes off her feet and stripping off her panty hose, she reached for jeans and a sweater. Then she reached for the phone. Dinner with Ben would have to wait. She hoped he would understand.

Two hours and twenty minutes later, Zoey was parking her car at the curb two properties up from the Bishop's Inn, which was a rambling Queen Anne Victorian–style house on the corner of Sea View and Bay Boulevard. The air was thick with sea air, dense and salty, a telltale sign that the bay lay just a block or two in one direction, the ocean roughly the same in the opposite. She walked slowly up the brick walkway toward the neat house, which, for all its size, had a welcoming facade. Light poured from every first-floor window, behind several of which she could see diners at round tables. The inn had a casual but cozy elegance that would, Zoey knew, suit her mother just fine. She wondered how Delia had found it.

She wandered into the spacious entrance, where a large stairwell curved downward from the second floor and pots of greenery seemed to be everywhere. The inn keeper clearly was partial to African violets and gloxinia. The decor was eclectic, with handsome Eastlake tables complementing cozy overstuffed chairs. Dramatic sofas dressed in floral chintz with a black background were accented by small striped pillows of pink and white satin, and Victorian side chairs, upholstered in sage green velvet and holding a collection of needlepoint cat pillows, crowded a bay window dripping with lace. It was a beautiful room, well thought out, with lovely antique pieces and just the right touches of whimsy.

A young waitress crossing from one side of the entry smiled, then stopped and did a sort of double take before smiling weakly and continuing on her way.

Zoey frowned, wondering what that was all about, when someone asked, "Have you been helped?"

She turned toward the voice. Later, she would recall having had the momentary sensation that she had looked into a slightly older version of her own face.

Startled, the two women merely stared at each other while a great, undefined tension began rapidly to build between them.

From the doorway, Zoey heard a soft gasp, followed by, "Oh. Oh, no."

Delia stood at the threshold, the color rapidly draining from her face.

"Oh, Zoey . . ." she whispered, looking from Zoey to the other woman, shaking her head ever so slightly, as if in apology.

"Mother, what is going on here?" Zoey had to clear her throat to make the words come, so heavy was the sense of dread that began to surround her.

"Oh, Zoey . . ." Delia repeated helplessly.

"Come into the sitting room," the other woman said, taking Delia gently by the elbow and guiding her through the French doors off to one side of the entrance. She turned to Zoey and gestured to her to join them. "Please."

A confused Zoey hesitated, fear overtaking her, knowing instinctively that if she followed her mother into that room, her life would never be the same.

Looking through the doorway, she watched the woman turning on soft lights to illumine the room. It was as beautiful as the rest of the inn appeared to be, homey and warm. There were photographs on the piano top and all along the mantel, an older couple, a little girl, the woman herself, some with the older woman, some with the child, others with a handsome dark-haired young man. The thought occurred to Zoey that, whoever she was, this was a woman who cherished her loved ones.

Struck by the tenderness with which the woman now placed a pillow behind Delia's back, Zoey went into the room and closed the door behind her.

"Zoey, I was planning on telling you. I just needed a little more time. Please believe me when I tell you that I never would have had it happen this way."

"Tell me what? Time for what?"

Could Delia really be unaware that she was crying?

Zoey watched, fascinated, as the tears ran down her mother's face without any effort being made to stop them. The look on her face was the same as it had been when she had looked up into Nick's eyes on Sunday.

"Mother, please . . ." Zoey crossed the carpeted floor and sat on the hassock at the foot of Delia's chair. "Please, tell me. . . ."

"Would you like me to leave?" The other woman had poured water into a goblet of cranberry-colored glass and pressed it into Delia's shaking hands.

"Perhaps just for a little while." Delia nodded. "It might be for the best."

Avoiding Zoey's eyes, the woman left the room.

The only sound was the sound of Delia sniffing into her handkerchief.

"Oh, Zoey, where to begin?" She cleared her throat.

"Why don't you begin by telling me who she is?" They both knew who *she* was.

"Her name is Laura Bishop"—Delia took a deep breath and turned to look into Zoey's eyes—"and she is my daughter."

The knot inside Zoey's chest cavity suddenly grew bigger and threatened to burst out of her chest. She thought for a minute that she was going to be ill.

"How is that . . . how could she . . ."

"How is it possible that I have a daughter that you

knew nothing about?" Delia finished the sentence for her.

Zoey nodded, the shock continuing to grow and fill not only her body but, it seemed, the entire room as well.

Delia stood and began to pace, as if gathering her thoughts and her words carefully.

"I gave birth to Laura in November of nineteen sixty-three. I was seventeen years old," Delia said simply. "That's the short version."

Delia pulled a tissue from a box on a side table and dabbed at her wet face.

"This is the big deep secret in the Hampton family, my dear." Delia twisted the tissue into knots. "It would have been the biggest scandal had anyone found out." She paced a little faster. "If anyone had know that the daughter of the Right Reverend William Hanesford Hampton had had an illegitimate child, well . . ."

Delia stared out the window, both hands on her hips, the anger forgotten for so many years beginning to bubble and boil within her as the taps from one increasingly agitated foot echoed softly on the hardwood floor. "And Lord knows that William Hanesford Hampton was both *right* and *reverend*. And so when the unthinkable—the *unspeakable*—happened, well, there was a fast scramble to find a way to hustle me out of town in the fastest possible manner, you can believe that."

The tears had stopped momentarily and her voice began to harden.

"I was four months pregnant on the day I graduated from high school. And foolish enough to be happy about it." She turned and faced Zoey. "Can you imagine? I was happy about it. It never occurred to me . . . I never thought for a minute . . . what they would do to me."

She shuddered.

"Mother," Zoey whispered, horrified by the look of pain and loss on her mother's face. "Mother, you don't have to go on."

"Oh, but I do. I should have told you long ago." She

cleared her throat again. "You see, we had had it all planned, Edward and I. He would be home in July. No one really expected the war to escalate, you know. In the very early sixties, you see, Vietnam was just the name of a jungle somewhere south of China. And there was no fighting involved, there were only *advisers.*" She dabbed at the tears that started anew. "Edward's plane went down in the jungle on the first of June, and he never made it home."

"But, of course, there was his child. My child." She blew a long breath out from between softly pursed lips. "My mother's sister lived in Ocean City, Maryland, and that is where they sent me. Immediately. No time to think, no time to protest. Just 'Cordelia, how could you? You've disgraced us all,' and off I was sent. The adoption was arranged without my consent. They took Laura from me as soon as she was born and I never saw her again." She choked back a quiet sob. "They told everyone that I had gone to London for my first semester of college."

"Oh, Mother." Zoey's heart began to break for the young girl her mother had once been. "Oh, Mother . . ."

"You know, they never came to see me. Never asked about the baby. Never mentioned her. When I went home, it was as if it had never happened. For years, my mother almost had me convinced that it had never happened, till even I began to wonder if perhaps I *had* been in London." Delia squeezed Zoey's hand. "Except for the time I tried to tell Edward's parents. I thought they should know. He was their only child, you see, and I thought that they should *know.* But my mother convinced me that it would only bring shame to his family to know what he had done to me . . . My mother's words, by the way, not mine. I did go back to see them, a few years later, but they had moved away. I started to think that maybe my mother was right. Maybe it had never happened at all."

Delia sighed heavily. "I met your father when I was in my senior year in college. It was love at first sight. We married immediately after graduation, much to the relief of Reverend and Mrs. Hampton. We had Nicky right away, then you came along, then Georgia . . ." Her voice trailed off.

"And then Dad left us." Zoey said, knowing there was a connection, but not sure just what it was.

"Oh, my fault, darling." Delia shook her head vehemently. "I should have told him long before I did."

"You mean about the baby?"

"I should have told him sooner—before we were married—or not at all." Tears welled in Delia's eyes again. "There were complications with Georgia's birth. The doctors said I would not have other children. But it was okay, they kept saying, you have three beautiful children, and I kept telling them no, I had four, and they all thought it was some postpartum nonsense. But I knew that I could not go on pretending that it had never happened. I had a child somewhere in the world and I could no longer pretend that she wasn't out there. I had to tell someone. I had to talk about her." Delia sighed again. "Unfortunately, the person I chose to tell was your father."

"Dad left because you told him . . . ?"

"Almost immediately." Delia shook her head. "He simply could not accept it, could not understand how I could have deceived him for so long. He felt betrayed, Zoey, and he could not forgive me."

"For keeping it a secret?"

"A woman who could keep a secret like that, he said, was a woman who was capable of anything. Who knew what else she might lie about? He wanted nothing to do with me. He packed his things and left."

"I remember when he left." Zoey sat on the edge of the sofa. "It was early in the morning and you were crying. I heard you. I went into the hallway and saw Daddy going down the steps. I called to him."

"You never told me that."

"He didn't turn around. He stopped, but he didn't turn around," Zoey told her. "Over the years, every time I started to think that I missed him, every time it started to hurt, I remembered that moment, when he had heard me calling him, but he would not turn around to say good-bye. And then the hurt would go away again, every time."

"Oh, darling, I am so sorry." Delia met Zoey's eyes from across the room. "For everything. I am so sorry. And I will understand if you can't forgive me, either."

"Mother, how could you even think . . ." Zoey's eyes filled and she crossed the room to embrace her mother, and the floodgates opened as both sobbed like children.

"Sweetie, you haven't left little wet circles on my shoulders since you were teething," Delia said when it appeared that the worst had passed and that somehow, they had both managed to have survived it.

"Mother, pass the tissues." Zoey swabbed at her face. They both attacked the tissue box, sniffing back the last of the sobs.

"Tell me how you found her," Zoey coaxed her mother to continue.

"All those years, I had wondered about her, what had happened to her. Was she still alive? Had she been raised well? Had she been loved? Was she smart? Was she happy? Did she know about me?"

Delia stood and began to pace again. "So a few years back, I hired a private detective. At first, I just wanted to know if she was alive. I told myself that that would be enough. And for a while, it was. Oh, it had taken a while to find them. Laura's adoptive father died when she was two, and her mother remarried. It complicated things, but my detective was good."

"So you called her?"

"Oh, no. I didn't have the nerve to do that. I had checked with the agency, and found that Laura had made only cursory inquiries after her birth parents, so I wasn't certain if she had any interest in finding me. But through the detective, I learned a lot about Laura. One of the things I learned was that she was a member of the local historic society here. So I decided to set a book here, on the island, and I contacted the president of the historic society. One thing led to another, as I knew they would, and I managed to get myself invited as a guest speaker for one of their monthly luncheons."

"You're a clever devil, Mother." Zoey shook her head.

"Yes, well, I was a terrified devil that day, let me assure you. Terrified that she would come, terrified that she would not. I had decided that if she did not come that day, it wasn't meant to be. I would drop the whole thing."

"But she came."

"Oh, yes. I knew her the minute she walked into the room. As a matter of fact, my first thought was, what is Zoey doing here? She looks so much like you."

"There is a resemblance."

"It was uncanny, Zoe. She even walks like you. My heart just stopped in my chest, and for a moment, I thought I was going to pass out." She reached for another tissue and added, "I had never been that scared."

"What did you do?"

"Well, I couldn't very well walk up to her and say, 'Excuse me but I believe that you are the daughter I gave up for adoption thirty-some years ago.'"

Zoey smiled. Delia's sense of humor was slowly beginning to creep back.

"So you said . . . ?"

"I very cleverly managed to work my maiden name into my talk. I figured if she had looked at her birth certificate, she would know." Delia said simply, "She had, and she did."

The door flew open and a small flash of white buzzed past Zoey and flung itself onto Delia's lap.

"You promised to tell me a story tonight, Nana." The white flash landed long enough for Zoey to identify a little girl of perhaps three wearing a long nightshirt that identified her as the Princess of Quite-A-Lot.

"Why, is it your bedtime already?" Delia looked at her watch, pretending to be shocked. "Oh, my, it's well past your bedtime, Ally."

"Momma said I could stay up a little bit longer but . . ."

She stopped and studied Delia's face, then traced an errant tear with one small finger. Delia gathered her into her arms and rocked her, but the small body was not long still. She twisted around to face Zoey and pointed, asking, "Who are you?"

Before Zoey could answer, Laura called from the doorway, "Say your good nights, Allison. It's very late."

"Nana said she'd tell me a story."

"Nana has company, Ally. She can stop up later."

"But I'll be asleep then. And I want to tell her all about the fun stuff we're going to do at school for Grandparents' Day." She turned to Delia. "You didn't forget about Grandparents' Day, did you?"

"Not for a minute," Delia assured her. "You couldn't keep me away. Now run along to bed."

"But . . ." she protested.

"It's okay." Zoey stood up. All of a sudden, she was suffocating. It was all too much, had been too much for one night. "I have to leave."

"Would you like me to fix a room for you?" Laura offered.

"No!" Zoey answered, too quickly, she would later realize. "I have to work tomorrow. I need to go."

"Zoey . . ." Delia turned a worried face to her.

"It's okay. I just have to go." Her voice pleaded with her mother to understand. "Please, Mother, go with her." Zoey gestured toward the little girl, who was looking from one adult face to the other as if trying to read them all.

"I'll be here for another day or so, Zoey." Delia took Ally's hand.

Zoey nodded and gathered her purse.

"Zoe." Delia called to her from the doorway. "Are you sure you are all right?"

"I'm fine. I just have to go," she repeated.

"Nana, who is that lady?" Ally whispered. "She has hair like Mommy."

Laura followed Zoey into the lobby.

"Are you sure you won't change your mind?" Laura

asked. "It's getting late. There are some rooms available."

Zoey shook her head, knowing she should say something—at the very least, a simple *thank you* would be nice—but she could not speak. There were too many emotions fighting within her at that moment. As she passed into the hallway, she caught a glimpse of Laura in the mirror at the foot of the steps. Fascinated, Zoey's stride missed a beat and unwillingly, she studied the face of the woman who so strongly resembled her.

We have exactly the same eyes. And her daughter was right. We have the same hair.

Flustered, Zoey all but fled through the front door.

"Zoey . . ." Laura called to her from the top step.

Already halfway down the sidewalk, Zoey turned back.

"Please don't judge her too harshly," Laura said softly.

"She's my mother." Zoey stiffened, as if offended by the suggestion. "I don't judge her at all."

She had taken a wrong turn and ended up at a dead end, but Zoey knew that she was near the ocean. She could hear the rhythmic pounding of water upon sand, over and over. To her right were rocks. To her left, the road trailed off into the darkness. She parked her car under the faint glow of the lone streetlight and climbed over the rocks until she felt the soft shift of the sand beneath her feet. She walked until she knew the ocean was right there, and then she sat down, just beyond the touch of the waves.

She thought about her mother and the heartache she had kept hidden for so much of her life, and she thought about Laura. She thought about her father, who had been unable to see Delia's truth as anything less than a betrayal of his love for her. Of the years she and her siblings had missed their father, of all the years Delia had missed her child. Their faces all seemed to weave into a sort of blur, one into the next, until they were no longer distinct. All in all, it seemed like a long time before she stood and brushed the sand off the back of her jeans and walked back over the rocky ledge to her car, still thinking of the tangled web of *family,* and how strong that web was.

Zoey was hardly mindful of the drive home. It seemed she had gone into automatic pilot somehow, and before she knew it, she was coasting through the dark stillness of Brady's Mill, past the lake where sleeping ducks huddled on the banks and the long bare arms of weeping willow—just a few short late-spring weeks away from unfolding into green fronds—dipped into the water. The crunching of the stones in her driveway sounded loud enough to wake the dead, so complete was the silence behind her bungalow, and she almost regretted having to shatter the quiet by slamming the door of her car. The night was the color of pitch, the sky an enormous starry quilt, and the moonlight scattered itself here and there, on the white tips of the tulips that bore the luster of pearls, the pale trumpets of the daffodils that glowed like burnished gold, the heavy clusters of white lilac that hung like opaque clouds from the spindly branches.

The warmth and calm gentleness of the night garden were welcome after the turbulence of emotions that had threatened to tear her apart over the past several hours, and she picked a small white daffodil—Thalia, Wally had called it—and twirled it between her fingers. The peace of her surroundings soothed her, and she felt the tension that had settled in the back of her neck began to ease. She leaned her head back to inhale the heady fragrance of lilac, then smiled. There was another scent in the air.

Wally's pipe.

She leaned over the gate and peered into the garden, where Wally sat on the stone bench, the faint spark of the ashes in the bowl of his pipe glowing like a tiny flashlight.

"Work late?" he asked casually.

She shook her head, then realizing that he may not have seen the gesture in the dark, said, "No."

"Late for you to be out," he commented.

"Now, you weren't waiting up for me, were you?"

"Naw. Watched a movie on cable, then thought I'd enjoy a pipe before I turned in."

"Which movie?" Zoey smiled to herself. He could have enjoyed that pipe anywhere.

"Jurassic Park."

"Did you like it?"

"Would I stay up until two in the morning watching a movie I didn't like?"

"Is that what time it is? Two?"

"Yep."

They each wrestled with the silence, Wally not able to bring himself to ask, Zoey not having the strength to tell him. Not tonight, anyway. It was still all too jumbled.

"You going in soon?" he asked.

Zoey knew it was his way of asking her if she was all right. "Yes," she replied.

"Yep," he said, looking up. "A night sky like that is sure something to see. Makes you realize how inconsequential most things are."

"Yes," she said because she didn't know what else to say, but wanted him to know she got his drift.

"Well, don't be staying out here too long. Those raccoons have been wandering. Wouldn't want them to think you're a threat to their babies. They can be mean buggers."

"Okay. I'm going in now anyway."

"Me, too, in a minute."

"Thanks, Wally," she called to him.

"Don't mention it." His voice drifted through the dark much as the smoke from his pipe had snagged a ride on a passing breeze. "Sleep well, Zoey."

"You, too," she called back over her shoulder, wondering if she would sleep at all.

Chapter

20

Ben stood up and for what seemed like the fiftieth time that morning, walked to the window that overlooked the parking lot. The little red sports car had yet to find its way to its designated spot. He pulled the cord that controlled the drapes until he had the glass pane totally exposed. That way, he figured, he could watch for her without getting up every thirty seconds to peer out the window like the nervous father of a sixteen-year-old who was long past her curfew.

The message he had left on Zoey's answering machine the night before—and then again this morning—had been very simple. "Call me as soon as you get this message, Zoey. Please." Since he had not heard from her, he assumed she had not gotten the message, or was simply choosing to ignore it. Either way, he didn't like the possibilities.

His hand on the receiver, he debated on whether or not he should call her again. He dialed not her number, but his own, to play back the message she had left for him the night before. He had played it over and over, but had not erased it.

"Ben, I have to cancel tonight. I'm sorry. Something's . . . come up. I need to . . . I'll talk to you. I'm sorry."

Something's . . . come up.

The tremble in her voice, the hesitation, the shallow breathing—all told him that whatever that "something" was, it had her totally rattled. He realized that he knew so little about her life that he could not even begin to guess what could have prompted such a reaction in her. As children they had been as close as siblings. They had known how to make each other laugh, what could make the other cry. Now, as adults, they hardly knew each other at all. Except, he thought wryly, how to make each other sweat in the most primal and elemental way.

Well, that would change. He planned to get to know this grown-up Zoey every bit as completely as he had known the rough-and-tumble tomboy she had once been. Better, he told himself. I want to know her inside and out. I want to learn her dreams, and then, I want to make them come true.

He flipped on the radio behind his desk, then laughed out loud. Robert Palmer. "Bad Case of Loving You."

"Couldn't have said it better myself," he muttered.

Ben glanced out the window, then did a double take. Nick Enright was walking toward the building, his stride long and purposeful. Ben went to the window, then leaned closer to the glass for a better view. Nick's eyebrows all but ran into each other, forming a dark slash across his forehead. Something was definitely troubling him.

Something must have happened to Zoey.

Without thinking, Ben shot from the window and through the door, past his startled secretary and directly to the elevator that led to the lobby. He punched the button to close the door and counted the seconds until he felt the tiny lurch that signaled the stop. He was through the doors as they opened, and spotting Nick near the guard desk, called to him.

"Hello, Ben." Nick turned, trying, it would seem, to compose his features.

"Nick, what's wrong?" Ben asked immediately.

"That's an odd greeting." Nick extended his hand, and Ben took it uncertainly.

"You don't look as if you're making a social call."

"Actually, I wanted to see my sister." Nick smiled, and Ben saw right through it.

"That makes two of us."

"She's not here?" Nick tried again to be casual, but there was a definite edge behind his practiced nonchalance.

"And she's not returning phone calls." Ben led him by the arm toward the elevator. "I have several calls in to her."

"So do I," Nick said, and the facade began to drop.

"Well, obviously you must have some idea of what's going on, Nick. I don't recall that you've dropped in before just to say hi."

Nick sighed as if debating just how much to tell Ben as they walked from the elevator into Ben's office. Ben went directly to the window. Zoey's spot was as empty as it had been the last time he had looked.

He turned back to Nick, motioned for him to sit, then lifted the receiver and asked Beth for two cups of coffee.

"Oh, and Beth . . . can you check to see when Zoey Enright is scheduled today? Her brother stopped by and was hoping to surprise her. When? Oh, fine. Thanks."

To Nick, he said, "She's scheduled at noon. She's usually in by now. They expect her any minute."

Nick nodded and turned as the door opened and Beth came in with a tray bearing two mugs, a small creamer and sugar bowl, each bearing a Canadian goose in flight, and a tall black and gold carafe. She smiled at Nick and placed the tray on Ben's desk.

"Can I get you anything else?"

"Just ask the guard at the front door to have Zoey stop here as soon as she arrives, if you would."

"Sure thing." Beth smiled again at Nick as she left the room.

"So." Ben poured coffee into one of the cups and passed it to his old friend. "Are you going to let me in on what's going on?"

"Zoey's all right, Ben. I think she may have just . . ." —Nick seemed to struggle for a moment—"gotten some news that may have upset her."

"How upset?"

"Very."

"Is there anything I can do?"

"Just be there for her."

"I intend to."

Nick smiled. So, India had been right. Ben was, as she had phrased it, totally *end over end* over Zoey.

Ben turned to the window as the small red car pulled in and parked. "She's here." Zoey was out in a flash and, hoisting a large nylon bag over her shoulder, set off across the parking lot toward the building.

Oh, boy, Nick thought, watching the expression on Ben's face as he watched Zoey all but jog down the walkway, waving somewhat absentmindedly to a group of three or four who were headed toward the lot. *End over end* didn't begin to touch what he saw there.

Enamored?

Nick's eyes followed Ben to the door of the office, which he opened and peeked through, then leaned against the doorjamb, as if waiting. He *was* waiting, Nick knew. He was waiting for Zoey.

Besotted?

Nick saw the change in his old friend's face even before the elevator doors opened.

"Hi," Nick heard him say. "Are you all right?"

He couldn't hear his sister's response, but he could see the deep concern in every line in Ben's face as he watched Zoey's approach.

Yep, besotted pretty well summed it up.

"Someone's here to see you," Ben told her, and Zoey seemed almost to recoil.

"Who?" she asked, sounding uncharacteristically pan-icked.

"Nick." Ben took her arm, startled by her reaction.

"Nick?" She frowned, then entered the room just as her brother stood. "Nicky, what are you doing here?"

"That's a lovely greeting, Duchess." Nick tried to smile, but the look in her eyes drained the smile from his lips. "How are you, Zoe?"

"You've been talking to Mother," she said accusingly.

"Guilty." He nodded.

"Nicky, you *knew.*"

"Yes."

"Why didn't you tell me?" She was getting worked up.

"Zoey, it wasn't my place to tell you." He took her gently by the shoulders and tried to ease her into a chair but she would have none of it. "Mom wanted to tell each one of us herself."

The color drained from Ben's face as he watched the interaction between brother and sister. In Ben's experi-ence, only one thing had ever caused that kind of emotion.

Oh, no, please, no, he silently prayed. *Not Delia . . . please, God, not Delia . . .*

"I'm late for work, Nicky. I have to get changed."

"Zoey, I think we need to talk about this."

"We can talk while I put my makeup on." She lifted her nylon bag from the floor and said to Ben, "I know I owe you an explanation. And you will get it. Just not . . . just not right now."

She turned and all but fled from the room.

"Ben . . ." Nick gestured helplessly.

"Go with her, Nick. Whatever it is, you need to talk it out." Ben nodded, and watched as Nick followed Zoey out the door.

Ben closed the door behind them, then sat down on the small leather sofa and locked his fingers together as they dropped between his knees and fought the sick sensation of panic that welled up inside him. *Not Delia, too. Please, God,* he prayed, *please don't take Delia, too. . . .*

At noon he turned up the volume on the large overhead television so that he could hear, as well as see her. The first hour she hosted a collector's show, offering teddy bears, dolls, beer steins, and cut glass. The second hour she sold linens, and the last hour, jewelry set with semiprecious stones. She really was a pro, he conceded. No one watching her would have suspected that some terrible cloud hung over her. He glanced at his watch. There were ten minutes remaining in her last segment. He walked to the steps and took the long way to the studio, reaching the side of her set in time to watch her finish up with her last item. When she had said her goodbyes to the viewing audience and removed her microphone, she looked over and saw him there, sending him a smile that barely reached her eyes.

He waited for her, and as she came off the set, forced calm into his voice and said, "Since you stood me up for dinner, I figure the least you can do is have lunch with me."

She appeared about to protest, then looked up into his face. There was something there that she needed, and they both knew it.

"Can you wait until I get my things?" She pointed toward the lounge area.

"Take as much time as you need."

She didn't need much. She was back with the bag slung over one shoulder. She looked smaller, having changed from high heels into flat-heeled shoes, and the difference seemed to diminish her. She looked suddenly smaller, more vulnerable, and it was all he could do not to take her in his arms and hold her until that lost look left her face. Side by side they walked through the hallways, where the last shift of customer service representatives passed the incoming shift, and the delivery men congregated by the security desk, awaiting clearance to pass on through.

"Did Nicky leave?" she asked as they stepped into the fresh spring air.

"I am assuming he did. He didn't come back." His car was parked in the spot next to the one reserved for Delaney. He paused and asked, "What do you think, Zoey? Top down?"

"Sure." She shrugged as if it didn't matter, and got in as he unlocked her door for her.

He knew it didn't matter, top down or top up, considering the news. But he needed that openness, needed that feeling of freedom and flight, and thought that maybe she did too.

He stopped at his favorite deli and bought sandwiches, bottles of iced tea, and a bag of cookies. He grabbed straws and napkins and headed back to the car.

"Sorry there's no basket to carry our picnic goodies in," he told her, trying to act as if everything was normal. "We'll just have to pretend."

She smiled weakly and took the brown paper bag he passed in to her and settled it onto the floor.

Ben turned on the ignition and took one gently curving country road after another, slowing patiently for the occasional horse and buggy driven by a black-garbed Amish farmer. When he stopped, it was to turn into a small park overlooking a creek. He turned off the engine, saying, "This was always a favorite place of mine."

"How did you know it would still be here after all these years?" she asked.

"Intuition." He smiled and reached across her for the bag that held their lunch. "And the fact that this was one of the first places I checked out when I came back. I bring lunch out here at least once a week. It's a great spot. Come on."

Zoey got out of the car, feeling very tired and wondering why she was there, with Ben, instead of home, thinking through the fact that she had a sister she'd never heard of before last night and a niece she didn't know. Her stomach twisted again, thinking back to the scene at the Bishop's Inn. She still hadn't sorted it all out, still didn't know how she felt about the whole business.

"Are you coming?" Ben had opened her car door, and was waiting for her to get out.

"Oh. Yes," she mumbled.

Taking the hand Ben offered her, she followed him to the little grove where three picnic tables overlooked a swiftly moving creek. He took off his jacket and placed it on the bench closest to the water and motioned for her to sit.

"It's such a nice jacket," she said. "It's going to get dirty."

"Hence dry cleaning." He tried to smile, but knowing that he would most likely get bad news about Delia, the smile fell flat. Fortunately, Zoey was distracted enough that she didn't notice. He unwrapped a sandwich and handed it to her, watching her press down the crinkled white butcher's paper to make a kind of place mat on the wooden table. He shook up her iced tea, popped open the cap, and stuck a straw into the neck of the bottle before passing it to her.

"Thanks, Ben." She began to nibble at the edges of the round roll in tiny mouselike bites.

Ben, too, ate slowly, watching her face, knowing the pain she must be carrying inside. Had he not carried the same agonizing pain when he learned of his own mother's illness? Knowing the turmoil she must be feeling, Ben thought her a wonder for being able to function at all.

As a child, Ben had always felt that Delia had been an anchor. As an adult, she had welcomed him back without one word of recrimination for his having stayed away so long. Delia was loving and caring and giving in every way. The thought that she might be ill caused waves of pain to shoot through Ben's insides like carelessly aimed buckshot.

Finally, when he knew it needed to be said and dealt

with, he asked, "Nick told me you had news about your mother."

Zoey's blue eyes looked a paler shade from across the narrow wooden table.

"Yes." She cleared her throat.

"Would you share it with me?"

"I don't know if I can." She shook her head. "I don't know how to tell you, if she'd want you to know just yet. Georgia doesn't even know yet."

"I promise not to tell her, Zoey, but it's clear that you need to talk about it. Maybe I can help," he added.

"I have a sister, Ben," she said simply, not looking at him, but at a small red leaf that had dropped onto the table from a nearby Japanese maple.

"And I'm sure your mother will share her news directly with her." Ben hoped he could be as strong for her as she would need him to be.

"No. I mean I have *another* sister." She exhaled and looked up into his face. "Laura."

Had he missed something? Who was Laura, and what did she have to do with Delia's being ill?

"Who is Laura?" He asked.

"I just told you. She's my sister."

He stared at her, feeling incredibly stupid. "Georgia changed her name to Laura?"

"Ben, my mother had a child when she was barely seventeen years old. Her parents forced her to give the baby up for adoption. She recently located her. Her name is Laura."

It took a minute for it to sink in.

"You mean, that's Delia's news?" He held his breath, waiting for her response.

"Yes." She nodded, tears welling in her eyes.

"That's it? That's *all?*"

"That's *all?*" Zoey's eyebrows flew to her hairline. "I tell you that my mother had a baby out of wedlock when she was seventeen, that she has found this child that she gave up for adoption thirty-five years ago, and that I just found out that I have a sister I never heard of and you say 'that's *all'?*"

"Zoey, that's wonderful!" He lifted her off the old bench and swung her around.

"Wonderful?" Had he lost his mind? "Can you imagine what it's like to find out that you have a sister you never knew you had?"

"Well, to someone whose father died before he was born, has no siblings, and whose mother died when he was fourteen"—he stopped twirling her and set her down—"finding out *today* that I had a sister would be just about the most wonderful thing that could ever happen to me. And right now, you'll have to forgive me, but I'm so relieved I could just about pass out."

She continued to stare at him, still not quite understanding.

"Zoey," he said gently, "when you and Nick were talking about Delia having news—and judging by your faces, neither of you were happy about it—I . . . well, I'm sorry, but I just jumped to the wrong conclusion. I thought something was really . . . wrong with your mother."

"You thought that my mother was . . ." she said slowly, not even able to speak the last word.

He nodded.

"Zoey, for the record, I'd sell my soul if I could turn back the years and hear my mother tell me that she had found a child that she had thought she had lost, instead of hearing her tell me that she had six months to live."

Zoey sat back down on the bench and kicked at some dried leaves with the toe of her black leather flat. "Well, that does sort of put it into a different perspective, doesn't it?"

"I sure think it does. I don't mean to *minimize* this, not by any means, Zoey. But in the grand scheme of things, one could get worse news."

Zoey walked down to the creek and stared in. Small fish, minnows, fled to the safety of small rocks when they sensed her approach. Clumps of dark green skunk cabbage just starting to unfurl grew along the narrow bank, and harbored some small frogs, judging by the plops she heard as they, too, sought shelter from her presence.

"I just found all this out last night," she told him when he came and stood behind her. "I had thought that my mother was acting strange, but I passed it off as just being tired, touring with this new book. . . ."

Ben rubbed her shoulders gently, trying to ease out the tension.

"Then someone called in on one of my cooking shows and said something about seeing me in Boston last week with my mother. But of course I hadn't been there. I called her to ask about it. Mrs. Colson said she was away for a few days and gave me the name of the place where she was staying. The Bishop's Inn, right near the Delaware-Maryland border. So I drove down there, thinking I'd surprise my mother and find out what was going on." Zoey shuddered, recalling the moment she had turned to look into Laura's face. "I'm afraid I'm the one who got the big surprise."

"You met her? Your sister?" he asked gently.

Zoey nodded.

"What's she like?"

"She looks like me. A lot."

"She must be a knockout."

"She's taller than me by just a little, and our builds are a little different. We have different mouths, but the same eyes. . . ."

"How did you handle it?"

"Oh, badly." Zoey grimaced. "Couldn't have handled this much worse if I had tried. I just couldn't believe it, Ben. . . ."

"I'm certain it was a big surprise, Zoey, but surely—"

"Surprise? Try shock." Zoey turned on him, her face a map of desolation. "Ben, this is my *mother* we're talking about. About a part of her life that none of us ever even suspected existed."

"Poor Delia," he whispered. "It must have broken her heart, to have given her child away."

"It did, Ben. And it broke my father's too, when he found about it. That's why he left us."

"Your father left your mother, left all of you, because Delia told him she had had a child out of wedlock?"

Zoey nodded.

"Wow" was all Ben could think of to say.

"Yeah. Wow," she repeated. "At least I know now why he left."

"And now that you know the truth?"

"It certainly hasn't done anything to make me feel more kindly toward him, that's for sure. It's been bad enough all these years wondering why he left. To find out that he left because of something my mother did before she even knew him . . ." She wrapped her arms around herself and blew out a long-held breath from between clenched teeth. "I mean, that had nothing to do with us. He could have still been our *father*. He simply chose not to be. If anything, it makes me think less of him. If that's possible."

"Well, at least in the midst of all this, there is something to celebrate."

She cast a dubious look in his direction.

"Can you imagine what a joy it must have been for your mother to have found her? She must have ached so terribly, all these years."

"The Christmas angel," Zoey whispered.

"What?"

"The Christmas angel. When we were little, there was always an extra Christmas stocking. My mother always said it was for the Christmas angel. We'd fill it with all kinds of things and on Christmas Eve my mother would take it to the church and they would give it to a child who wasn't expecting much of a Christmas." Tears started down Zoey's face again. "I think that Laura was the Christmas angel. I think that Mother hung the stocking for her."

Ben encircled her in his arms and swayed with her gently, as if rocking a child from side to side to comfort her.

"Laura has a little girl," she told him through big long sniffs. "A little girl. Her name is Ally. She looks like she is maybe three or four."

"So. Delia not only found her daughter, she found a granddaughter as well," Ben murmured. "She must be beyond joy."

Zoey nodded. "I think she would be, if she wasn't so afraid of how we'd all react to the news. To Laura."

Ben reached into his pants pocket and pulled out a white linen handkerchief and blotted the fat tears from her cheeks.

"And of course, I'm afraid I didn't do much to help her through this. I sort of bolted and ran out the front door."

"But there's this thing about doors, Zoe," he told her gently. "They open out, but they open in, too."

She leaned back against him, dappled light sprinkling down through the maples that lined the clearing.

"I could go back," she said softly.

"You could."

"I could tell my mother"—she bit her bottom lip—"I could tell her how happy I am for her, that she's found her Christmas angel. . . ."

He held her very close, his heart swelling for her.

"And I could tell Laura"—she swallowed hard—"that I would like to get to know her."

"I think that would be a beautiful thing to do, Zoey." He kissed the tip of her earlobe. "And I think that Delia will be very proud of you."

"I wonder how Georgia will feel, when Mother tells her."

"What did Nick have to say, by the way?"

"Nicky met Laura last week. On Monday. He drove down to the inn to introduce himself. He spent the day there. He liked her very much."

"As I'm betting you will. And Georgia will too. How could you not?"

She looked up into his face, the question in her eyes.

"She's Delia's daughter, Zoey. How could she be anything less than wonderful?"

For her mother's sake, Zoey hoped he was right.

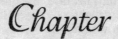

Chapter

21

Zoey sat in her car, motionless except for the light tapping of her fingertips on the steering wheel. She had, just the day before, polished her nails with a pale dusty rose shade, but already she had managed to chip and peel at the polish so that her nails looked blotched, like a pinto pony. Had she noticed, she would have fled to the nearest drugstore in search of nail polish remover and would have swiped her nails clean. Being distracted by other, more pressing things, however, the sorry state of her fingernails was low on her list of priorities this morning.

She had risen at dawn to drive back to Bishop's Cove. Now that she was there, she sat in the car, mentally running through all the reasons why she should stay where she was for a while. It was too early to knock on someone's door. Laura would probably be getting Ally ready for school. She probably had guests to tend to. Delia might be sleeping late. She recited this litany while watching the numbers blink on the digital clock on the dash of the car. It was interesting, watching time pass by, the seconds and the minutes of the day blinking away, and it held her attention for almost four minutes. Maybe, she thought, she should get a cup of coffee at that little store she passed on her way onto the island. She could get a newspaper, too, and read while she waited.

Waited for what? She sighed and looked across the street to where the Bishop's Inn reigned over the corner of the long block. This is silly. My mother is in there. There is no reason why I can't just—

Movement at the inn's front door caught her eye and she leaned over the steering wheel to watch. Ally bounced out onto the porch dressed in a dark blue jumper and a short-sleeved white shirt. Laura stepped out behind her and held up the backpack that Ally sort of backed into, sliding her arms through the straps and shrugging it up onto her shoulders. As Laura bent down to smooth her daughter's hair and plant a kiss on the little girl's forehead, Delia appeared in the doorway. She stood with her hands on her hips and watched as Ally readjusted the backpack. After exchanging a few words with Laura, who patted Delia on the back, Delia took Ally's hand and walked with her down the steps, down the cobbled walk, down the street toward the corner. Ally danced a step here and there, and their hands swung between them. Zoey felt her chest constrict just a little as she watched her mother walking her granddaughter to school.

It stung a little, and she was trying to figure out exactly why it should have, when she realized that Laura was walking toward her car.

She must think I'm an idiot, sitting here at eight o'clock in the morning, staring after my mother without speaking to her. . . .

"An idiot or an ax murderer," she muttered as she turned off the ignition.

"Good morning," Laura called to her as she crossed the street.

"Good morning," Zoey called back, her palms sweating and her heart pounding. Had she thought that any of this would be easy? "I guess you're wondering why I was just sitting there. Why I didn't let my mother know I was here . . ."

"Not at all." Laura reached a hand out to her through the open car window and touched Zoey's arm lightly. "I know you were just permitting Delia to have that time with Ally. And I thank you for it. That was very generous of you."

Zoey's cheeks flushed, knowing that other emotions— embarrassment at being caught watching the inn, combined with a sort of morbid fascination at watching her mother in a totally unfamiliar role—rather than any great generosity of spirit, had kept her from calling out to her mother.

"Actually, Laura . . ." Zoey sought to explain, not wanting to take credit for insights and sensitivities she hadn't had.

"Come in and have coffee with me." Laura had taken Zoey's hand, and had not released it. Now she tugged at it, and Zoey got out of the car and slammed the door. "The staff is already tending to the guests, so we can have some time together."

The inn was cool, in spite of the rising temperatures outside. Laura led the way into the big stainless steel kitchen where breakfast was being prepared by a young woman in her twenties.

Laura peeked over the cook's shoulder. "Ummm. French toast. Lucky guests. How many for breakfast this morning, Jody?" She reached into a tall cabinet and pulled out two dark green ceramic mugs emblazoned with the inn's logo and began to fill them with steaming, aromatic coffee.

"Sixteen. The Bartons in the Green Room left early to go crabbing with Larry."

"Do you have enough help?" Laura asked.

"We'll be fine. Jenny should be here any minute, and Clarence will be in before nine to help clean up."

The young cook turned and smiled at Zoey, then looked back at her again and said, "Wow. You two must be related."

Laura glanced over her shoulder and caught Zoey's eye, as if to ask permission. Knowing that she had to, Zoey said, "We are related. We're sisters," and found that the admission had not been as difficult as she might have expected.

The cup Laura had just filled rattled slightly as she set it on the counter. "Cream, Zoey?"

"Yes, please."

"I didn't know you had a sister, Mrs. Bishop," the young cook said.

"Until recently, neither did I." Laura forced a smile at the cook, then handed Zoey her coffee with a sort of sideways motion that permitted her to grab her own cup from the counter at the same time. "Shall we take our coffee down to the beach, Zoey?"

"That would be lovely. Yes. Thank you." The stiff formality of her response caused the cook to turn and look at her curiously, though Laura seemed not to notice. "But if you're busy here, I don't want to be in your way."

"I think breakfast is under control." Laura gestured for Zoey to follow her through a door that opened onto a brick patio over which a pergola of wisteria draped viney arms and long purple fingers of clustered flowers.

"Oh, they're so fragrant." Zoey reached up to touch the delicate blooms.

"And oh so attractive to the bees." Laura grimaced. "There are so many of them that the patio is pretty much off limits during the day while the wisteria is in bloom. But it does scent the back rooms on the second and third floors, and the guests seem to like it. I have an elderly couple who come every year around this time to stay in that room"—she stepped back into the yard and pointed to the corner bedroom on the left side of the house—"because the wisteria reminds them of their honeymoon cottage in the English countryside."

"The inn is yours, then?" Zoey fell into step with Laura as she walked down the driveway.

"Yes. Lock, stock, and the bats in the chimneys." She paused for a moment, then added, "My parents owned this inn, and their parents before them, and their parents. I'm hoping that someday Ally will want to run it."

Zoey stood on the curb and sipped at her coffee and waited for a lone car to pass before following Laura's long stride across the street.

"The beach is this way." Laura pointed to the right.

"I know," Zoey said. "I found it the other night, on my way home."

"I should have given you directions."

"I don't think I gave you the opportunity," Zoey said, slowing her pace just a bit. If she was going to get to know this woman, it would have to be on honest ground. And there was no time like the present to start. "I ran like a scared child."

"I don't know that I would have done any differently," Laura conceded. "As a matter of fact, given the circumstances, I thought you handled yourself admirably. I'm the one who ran, Zoey."

"You?"

"Right out the back door." Laura laughed wryly and kicked her sandals off at the edge of the beach.

"You're kidding." Zoey leaned over to untie her sneakers and pulled them off. "I thought you were so together, so cool. . . ."

"Me? Cool? I was so rattled about meeting you that I actually went looking for a cigarette. And I quit smoking almost five years ago."

"Did you find one?"

"No, thank heavens."

Zoey followed Laura down the wooden incline, a boardwalk of sorts, that led onto the beach. They walked in silence across the coarse sand toward the water. The waves slid onto the shore, gentle waves that left traces of foamy wash on the beach, and sea birds dipped and dug for sand crabs and other tender morning treats. The morning was still unfolding, but it promised to be a beautiful day.

"Do you mind sitting on the sand?" Laura asked. "I could go back and grab a few sand chairs."

"No, this is fine. I like it." Zoey plunked unceremoniously onto the sand and drew her legs up to her chest.

"Me, too. I love it here, particularly in the morning," Laura told her. "I can't imagine not living by the ocean."

"Did you grow up here in Bishop's Cove?" Zoey asked.

Laura nodded. "Lived here all my life except for the four years I went to college."

"Let me guess." Zoey grinned. "University of Maryland."

"How'd you know?"

"A woman called into one of my shows once and said I looked like her daughter's friend from college. She said they went to the University of Maryland."

"Gee, I wonder who that was."

"I don't remember her name." Zoey leaned back upon her elbows.

"I watch you now on TV all the time," Laura confided. "Whenever I can, anyway."

The two women stared at each other for a long moment, so much unspoken. Where to begin?

Finally, Zoey said, "You know, it was a caller that made me realize that something was . . ." Somehow, she couldn't bring herself to say *wrong,* so she said, ". . . that something was going on with Mom."

"The woman who said she saw you and Delia in Boston." Laura said.

"You saw the show?"

Laura nodded, "And I told Delia that she could not put off . . . talking to you and your sister—she had already told Nick. I knew you would put it together after that, and I was so afraid. . . ."

"Afraid for who?"

"For Delia," Laura's voice dropped slightly. "And for you and Georgia, too."

"Why?"

"Because it was no way to learn of such a thing." Laura stared straight out at the horizon. "I mean, Delia and I knew about each other, we both knew the other was out there, somewhere. And I think that we both knew that someday we'd find each other. But the three of you . . . you just didn't have a clue. I thought that for you to find out about me would be such a shock. For you to find out from someone other than Delia . . . I just couldn't imagine being blindsided like that." She shuddered. "I urged Delia to tell you that night."

"Why didn't she?"

"You'll have to ask Delia that."

"You don't call her Mother," Zoey observed.

"I have a mother," Laura told her. "I have the best mother a girl could ever have had." She dug her bare heels into the sand. "From the time I found out that I was adopted, I always wondered what she looked like, that woman who gave me away. I had this image in my head, when I was a child, of some very tall person in a long flowing robe tossing this baby bundled in pink blankets over the side of a cliff, and my parents jumping up to catch me, shouting, 'It's a girl! We'll take her!' I never for a minute regretted being adopted. My parents were wonderful, Zoey. I could not imagine anyone having better parents than I did."

Laura picked up a half-buried piece of clam shell and began to dig little valleys in the sand. "I never thought a whole lot about my birth parents when I was growing up. I had a mother and father who loved me and gave me all the love and security and sense of *family* that any child could need. My brother and I grew up here, on the beach and on the bay." She pointed back over her shoulder toward the bay side of the island. "I had a wonderful family. Yes, of course, it was always there, in the back of my mind, that there was *someone out there,* but please don't think of me as Delia's orphan child who prayed all her life that her real mother would come back and rescue her from a life of loneliness. I don't remember ever pining for her. I never felt that I had to."

Zoey protested, "Laura, I never thought for a minute that—"

"I just wanted to get that out of the way, Zoey. Some

people still have this misconception that all adopted children are desperate to find their 'real' parents. I have never felt that burning desire to confront my birth mother. I *had* real parents, all my life. My dad was a great man, and I've missed him every day since we lost him five years ago. I have a mother I adore. I'm not out to steal yours."

"Laura, if I gave you the impression that I thought that you—"

"It's just that I know that Delia is a well-known, wealthy woman, and I don't want you to think that I set off to find her hoping to cash in on the fact that she gave birth to me. I had no idea of who she was until that day she showed up as speaker at the historic society luncheon. I mean, I knew that my birth mother's name was Cordelia Hampton—it was on my birth certificate—but I had no way of knowing that *Cordelia Hampton* and *Delia Enright,* the famous novelist, were the same person. I cannot begin to tell you how shocked I felt, sitting in that room, all of my friends sitting around me, and hearing our illustrious speaker mention her maiden name. I thought I was going to have a heart attack and die on the spot. I just couldn't believe it. That she would show up like that . . . I later learned that she had managed to arrange to be there, that she had known how to find me." Laura looked at Zoey from the corner of her eye and said, "I'm just telling you this because I don't want you to think that I found out who my birth mother was and chased her to make her acknowledge me."

Zoey sat up and straightened her back. "Whoa, Laura. Where is this coming from?"

"I just don't want any of you to think that I'm motivated by the thought of material gain."

"First of all, I know that you hadn't set out to find her, that she came looking for you—Delia told me that. And I'm happy for both of your sakes that she found you. I am equally delighted to hear that you had wonderful parents and that you had a happy life." Zoey felt she had to add, "On the other hand, I am just beginning to understand how much pain my mother has suffered all these years. I can't imagine how terrible that must have been for her. You have to understand, Laura, she was *the best* mother, she has the most loving heart of anyone I ever knew. For her to have let you go must have been agonizing for her. I can hardly believe that she had the patience to wait this long to find you. Finding you is going to mean changes in all our lives. We're all going to have to take some time to get to know each other."

"I was so afraid that none of you would want to do that. Get to know me, I mean." Laura said softly.

Zoey touched Laura's arm. "You're as much Delia's child as the rest of us are, Laura. Right now, she needs you maybe more than she needs us. She's been without you for too long. Let her some spend time with you and with Ally."

"I've told Delia that she's welcome to stay as long as she wants to, but I was just afraid that you'd think I was trying to take her from you"—Laura swallowed hard—"that I was trying to use her. . . ."

"Laura, what are you talking about?"

"Well, I guess you'll hear about it soon enough, you might as well hear it from me." Laura turned to her and blurted, "Three years ago, right after my husband and I separated, we had to place my mother in a total care facility. I had to take a small mortgage out on the inn."

"So?"

"So, two weeks ago, before I knew what was happening, Delia paid it off."

"And you think we're going to hold that against you?" Zoey asked wide-eyed, and when Laura nodded slowly, Zoey almost doubled over with laughter. "And you think that *we'll* think that you're just after Delia's money?"

"Zoey, I swear, I didn't *want* anything from her. I didn't *ask* for anything from her. I never asked for a loan, I still don't understand why she did it. . . ." Laura, clearly confused by Zoey's laughter, was close to tears.

"She did it because she's Delia." Zoey proceeded to

explain about Delia's overly generous nature when it came to her children, about Nick's cabin and Georgia's condo. "I'm the only one who was able to outfox her where the house was concerned, but I had other reasons of my own, and besides, I've had more than my share of her generosity over the years. Her paying off your loan was just her way of—of being motherly, so to speak. It's just Delia's way, Laura. I think she can't help herself sometimes, she's a compulsive giver."

"And here I was thinking you would all think that I was somehow trying to make her *buy* me. . . ." Laura struggled to explain.

"Not at all. As a matter of fact, I think I'm just beginning to understand why she is the way she is. Mother always seems to feel that she has to take care of everyone, to do for everyone. I'm wondering if perhaps that might have stemmed somehow from her having lost you."

"What do you mean?"

"Mom always says that she does what she does for us so that we'll always know that she was there for us."

"Because she wasn't there for me?" Laura ventured.

"Possibly."

"But I didn't suffer, Zoey. My parents were there for me. Always. My mother, in particular."

"What does she think about Delia popping back into your life?"

"If she could understand, I would hope that she would be pleased about it. And knowing my mother, I think she would want to thank her." Tears beaded in the corners of Laura's eyes. "We have always been very close, my mother and I."

"You said, 'if she could understand' . . . ?"

"My mother has Alzheimer's. She really is no longer herself. I think she would have liked Delia. And I think if Delia had met my mother years ago, she would have liked her, too."

"Where is she, Laura?"

"She's in a home about eight miles from here. I see her

every week, but I know it's not really her. It's a terrible disease, Zoey. It takes everything that makes you what you are, and turns you into someone that you yourself would not recognize. If you could remember who you had been . . ."

"Laura, I am so sorry."

"So I guess you see the irony, Zoey. I lose one mother, I find another. I take out a mortgage on the inn to pay for my mother's care, Delia pays off the mortgage. . . ." Laura broke into sobs.

"Oh, Laura . . ." Zoey scootched closer and put her arm around Laura's shoulders. "Laura, I am so sorry."

"I feel so mixed up about the whole thing."

"That's perfectly understandable. Look, there's a lot going on in your life right now. Laura, if you need a friend to talk to . . . well, I can be your friend while I'm learning to be your sister."

"Thank you. You really are everything Delia said you were." Laura searched through her pockets until she found a wadded-up tissue in the back of her jeans. "She's so proud of you, all of you."

"I'll bet she's proud of you too, Laura." Zoey swayed her upper body, rocking Laura just slightly in the process. "And she must be totally beside herself to have a granddaughter."

"I think she really is, Zoey." Laura blew her nose in the tissue. "She just dotes on Ally, and Ally is just fascinated by her."

"That's because Delia *swoops,*" Zoey realized that her own eyes had filled up without her knowing it, and she wiped them on the sleeve of her sweatshirt.

Laura laughed. "What?"

"My brother's soon-to-be daughter, Corri, who is seven now, said that Delia *swoops,* like the character in a book she had read. Maybe Ally sees Delia that way, too."

The two women giggled together, holding the moment and feeling that first brick slide into the foundation of a relationship that was meant to last a lifetime.

"My mother never swooped," Laura told her. "She is a much more deliberate person than Delia seems to be."

"Oh, Delia is deliberate, all right," Zoey told her. "Don't let that carefree facade fool you. She rarely leaves anything to chance, and she is rarely caught off guard."

"She gives the impression of being so nonchalant about everything. I guess I have so much to learn about her. About all of you."

"Well, I'm looking forward to getting to know you, Laura." She thought back to Ben's words the day before, about doors opening in. "Tell me about your mother. And you mentioned that you have a brother. I want to hear about him. And about growing up in Bishop's Cove. My—*our*—soon-to-be sister-in-law, India, grew up in a shore town, too. In New Jersey. I think you'll like her. But I don't want to keep you from work. . . . I guess you have to get back to the inn and start the luncheon preparations."

Laura laughed.

"I have a cook. Actually, I have three cooks that I hired for different purposes." Laura lowered her voice, as if confiding a secret. "I'm a lousy cook, Zoey, and I hate it."

"What a coincidence!" Zoey laughed. "I hate to cook too!"

"I know. I watch you on TV and cannot help but think how alike we are in that respect."

"You know, I'll bet we have other things in common, Laura." Zoey gave Laura a little squeeze. "Let's walk down to those rocks and see what that fisherman just reeled in. It looks like a big something. And then maybe we can take the long way back to the inn and you can give me a little tour of Bishop's Cove."

Delia stood on the front porch watering the hanging baskets of fuchsia that Laura had hung just days earlier from the hooks around the roof line. It was turning into a fine day, sunny with just the faintest hint of breeze, warm but not yet humid. She hummed an old tune, the title of which escaped her. It was driving her crazy. She hummed the same part over and over, trying in vain to come up with the right words that would give away the name of the song, but it seemed hopeless. The sound of laughter from the driveway interrupted her train of thought, but one glance over her shoulder at the source of the merriment and the tune was forgotten.

I must be hallucinating, was her first thought. She went to the end of the porch, and watched the two beautiful dark-haired girls as they strolled, arm in arm, up the drive. Her left hand reached out to steady herself against one of the pillars, and her breath caught in her throat.

Laura and Zoey. Laughing and talking like . . . like *friends.* Maybe not quite like sisters, but certainly like friends.

Delia's right hand flew to her mouth and she covered the sob so that no one would hear. She had been so afraid that these two parts of her life would never come together. She knew she had been wrong not to tell Zoey and Georgia sooner, but it had been so damned *hard.* And until she had gotten to know Laura, how could she have asked her other children to accept someone that she, herself, did not know?

"Mom." Zoey stopped dead in the drive and looked up onto the porch where her mother stood with tears streaming down her face. "I . . . um . . . stopped in early and you were gone so Laura and I had coffee on the beach. . . ."

"It's a beautiful day for that." Delia sniffed.

"Give me your cup." Sensing that Delia and Zoey might need a few minutes alone, Laura took the mug from Zoey's hand. "I'll get you a refill. Delia, would you like a cup?"

"Yes, darling. That would be nice. Why not bring a pot out here on the porch and we'll sit in these lovely wicker chairs. . . ." Delia's eyes never left Zoey's face.

"So, you came back," was the only thing Delia could

think of to say as she watched Zoey climb the porch
steps.

"I needed a little time to think it through, Mom."
Zoey embraced her mother.

"I don't wonder that you did. I'm just amazed that
you're back so soon." Delia's words were soft against her
daughter's neck.

"At first I was angry that you had kept this hidden for
so long, that there was this big part of you that I knew
nothing about. But something that Ben said made me
realize that this was not about me and you. At the heart
of it, it's just about *you*. It's about you finding a piece of
yourself that's been missing for a long time. It must have
been so hard for you, Mom. I'm sorry that I wasn't able
to help you somehow, through all of this."

"Oh, sweetie, there was nothing you could do. When I
made up my mind to find Laura, I didn't know what I
would find. If I would like her—if she would like me.
But once that decision was made, I promised myself that
I would do my best to get to know her before I tried to
bring her into the family." Delia sank into the nearest
chair. "I don't know what I was expecting, but I don't
think I expected her to be quite so . . . so . . ."

"Terrific?" Zoey offered.

"Terrific works, sweetie. Terrific works quite well."
Delia smiled, knowing the worst had passed and she
hadn't even been there to witness it. She sat on one of the
wicker sofas and motioned for Zoey to sit in the opposite
chair, never letting go of her daughter's hands. "Once I
started to get to know her, I really did want to bring her
to Westboro, but I was afraid of moving too fast. So I
thought I'd talk to Nicky first."

"How long has he known?"

"For about a month."

"That long?"

"I'm sorry, sweetie, but I needed to take this slowly."

"How did Nick react?"

"At first? Much as you did. I think it's safe to say he
was similarly stunned."

Zoey thought back to the previous Sunday morning, to the gentle way her brother had ministered to Delia in the garden.

"Laura said she met Nick."

"And was totally charmed by him. As anyone would be. Nick is one in a million, Zoey. I still sometimes wonder that I have raised such a son." Delia's face lit up momentarily, then became somber once again. "But I should tell you that both Nick and India are insisting on having Laura at the wedding."

"Really?" Zoey frowned, wondering what that might mean for Delia. "Is she going to come?"

"Laura is very concerned that I would have to spend Nick and India's wedding day making explanations about who she is."

"Well, she may be right, Mom. Her presence is certain to cause talk."

"Which it will, whenever the truth becomes known, and it will have to be dealt with."

"True. But I think the question is, do you want to deal with it at Nicky's wedding?"

"I don't want my past to overshadow their day. Nick and India deserve this special day, and I have told them so. Nick, however, feels very strongly that Laura should be there."

"How do you feel about it?"

"It would mean the world to me to have all of my children there, Zoey, and damn what anyone would have to say about it."

"Then we should do whatever we have to do to see that Laura is there, Mom."

"The lemon poppyseed cake is warm. Jody just took it out of the oven a few minutes ago." Laura stepped onto the porch with a tray holding a carafe of coffee and a small cake sprinkled with powdered sugar. She set the tray down on a small table and said, "And you want to see that Laura is where?"

"At Nick and India's wedding." Zoey leaned over to nab a slice of warm, fragrant cake.

"I don't think that's a good idea." Laura shook her head.

"Sit, darling"—Delia patted the seat next to her on the small settee—"and let's think this through. Nick and India would both like you to be there. And frankly, nothing would please me more."

"Delia, people will be talking."

With a wave of her hand, Delia swept away Laura's protests. "Regardless of when they find out. I don't really give a damn. My first concern was Nick, and he is adamant that you be there."

"You don't know how Georgia will feel." Laura poured coffee with hands that trembled just a little.

"I will see Georgia on Thursday. I would be very surprised if she didn't show up on your doorstep, much as Zoey has, to ask her own questions and make her own connection with you."

"Zoey, how do you feel? Will you be embarrassed by my presence?"

"No. Mom and Nick are right. Family is family. I know you have your own family, and I think you need to decide if you can integrate us all, one into the other. But if it's up to the Enrights, we'd like you to be at the wedding."

"Thanks, Zoey. I'll think about it."

"And of course, that includes Ally. I'd like to get to know my niece, too."

"Now, about Matt . . ." Delia sampled a small piece of cake.

"Matt is . . . having some problems with this, Delia," Laura said in a soft voice. "I'm sorry."

"Who is Matt?" Zoey asked.

"Matt is my brother. My mother and father adopted him when I was about twelve. Matt was four at the time and a positive holy terror."

"Matt is disturbed by my presence here, Zoey. He wishes I'd go away and stay away."

"That's a bit more bluntly than I would have phrased it, but accurate. I think Matt feels threatened somehow by all of this, that somehow I'm betraying our parents." Laura looked pained. "And nothing could be further from the truth."

"I understand that, darling, and I think that, over time, Matt will come to understand as well. Give him time, Laura. Maybe he's afraid of losing you into a family where he feels he has no place. Though God knows there's room for him too, if he chooses."

Zoey laughed. "Mom, you should have had about twenty children."

"If things had worked out differently, I might have. As it was . . ." She spread her hands out in front of her, a gesture meant to imply that the choice had been taken from her. "And that's another issue we need to deal with, Zoey. Your father."

"Not today, Mom," Zoey told her. "Today is not a day to talk about absent fathers or brothers with a chip on their shoulders. Today is a day for the three of us."

"That's a lovely thought, sweetie." Delia kissed Zoey's cheek and turned to Laura, and asked, "Darling, you didn't by any chance see that box of Godiva chocolate I had last night?"

"I think you left it in the front hallway. Would you like me to get it?"

"If you don't mind. Then perhaps we'll just settle in for a chat . . . just us three."

Chapter 22

"Hi, Wally." Zoey cupped her hands to call across the lawn from the mailbox where she set about pulling out the morning's mail from the mailbox. "Don't you just love Saturday mornings?"

"Why, yes, I do." He nodded and puffed on his pipe. "But seeing as this is Wednesday . . ."

"To most people it's Wednesday. To people like me, who are off two days in the middle of the week and work on the weekend, today is my Saturday." She sorted absently through the mail as she walked toward him across the grass.

"I see." Wally puffed a little more. "And what have you planned for this 'weekend' of yours?"

"Not sure. Mr. Conley and his crew will probably finish working on the bathroom early this morning—can you believe it?—so unless I want to spend the day coughing up plaster dust and wheezing, I guess I'll have to find something to do out here. Maybe I'll prune or something."

"Might be a good day to clean out those flowerbeds and get yourself over to the nursery to buy your plants."

"Have you been talking to my mother?" she asked accusingly, her hands on her hips as she directed a suspicious glare at Wally.

He held his hands up in a gesture proclaiming innocence and laughed.

"Well, it just so happens that I thought about putting in a few things." Zoey flipped nonchalantly through the catalog featuring discounted linens that sat on top of the mail pile.

"Really? Well, then, you'll let me know if you need a hand."

"Sure. Thanks. But I think I've got it covered. I appreciate the offer."

"Well, I'll be spending much of the day over at my son's house. Promised the daughter-in-law that I'd help her rototill her vegetable garden this afternoon. Then, later this afternoon, I'll be watching my grandson play baseball. Little League, you know. But if you need me, you can give me a call."

"Thanks, Wally. I'll keep that in mind. You have a good time today with your family."

Actually, Zoey looked forward to a day spent alone—inside or out didn't really matter to her. As long as the carpenters and the plumbers were still working their magic on the second floor, she'd be content to work in the yard. It was a glorious June day, a day of china blue sky dotted with big fluffy clouds, a day of sweet outdoor smells and soft bird songs. After the emotional turmoil of the past week, such a day was to be treasured.

She had called Ben from her car on her way back from Bishop's Cove, only to find out that he had, at Delaney's request, gone to New York on business. She left a message on his answering machine: "You were right about everything. How'd you get so smart? All is well now, Ben—better than well. Give me a call when you get back."

She stood in the enclosed section of the yard—that section that lay within the arbor, the fence, and the wall running across the back. It was like a room—sort of.

Maybe she should get a few chairs—those big Adirondack chairs would fit nicely over in that one corner. And over there, in that far corner, maybe one of those wooden gliders that she saw out in front of one of the Amish farms where they made such things to sell. She pictured herself curled up on the glider, one foot on the ground to control the gentle back-and-forth sway, a good book in one hand and a glass of iced tea in the other. There were far worse ways to spend a summer afternoon.

But first, the beds needed tending. She unlocked the garage—which, judging from the cleanliness of its concrete floor, had never housed a car—and picked through the assorted garden tools that Delia had brought for her. Selecting what she thought might be the proper rake, she proceeded to clear the beds of dried leaves and new grass, then bagged it all to clear the walkway. By noon, the worst of the debris had been raked and the beds cleaned. The last of the spring daffodils and tulips remained, their once green leaves and stems beginning to go brown. She broke off the stems and bent back the leaves the way she had seen Delia's gardener do. She would need rubber bands or string to hold them but for now, just folding them back was an improvement.

She carefully inspected the plants that were left. Those tall, hardy-looking things that seemed to grow in every bed, she recognized as daisies. Judging by the number of buds, there would be lots of them that summer. She frowned as she bent to inspect something else, some dark blue spiky flowers the color of ink that danced in the breeze on sturdy stems that grew from ferny type leaves. What had Wally called them? She couldn't quite recall the name, but she liked them. They looked like dancing girls wearing hoop skirts. There were white ones in another bed, delicate yellow in yet another. Oh, columbine. That was what Wally had called them.

Those big tall ruffly dark pink things across the back fence were hollyhocks, she knew that too. They were a favorite of Delia's, who always had tons of them in her own garden. And along one side grew the daylilies—

everyone knew daylilies—in all colors and sizes. Cleaned up, the garden looked pretty, inviting. How much nicer still it would be when she planted her Shakespeare garden. She recited the names of the plants she would need: violets—got plenty of them; fennel—isn't that an herb? and columbine—no problem there. And then there was rue—Wally said that grew wild out back by the woods; and daisies—got that covered. Pansies . . . she smiled recalling Ben standing at the gate, reciting, "And there is pansies, that's for thoughts."

All she would need to buy for her Shakespeare garden would be fennel and pansies.

And, oh, of course. Rosemary. For remembrance.

"Pray love, remember," he had said.

Zoey sighed, remembering the touch of his lips against her mouth, her chin, the side of her jawline, her neck, and she shivered. Not much chance she was going to forget *that*.

Zoey drove to the nearest nursery with the windows down and the radio on. She grabbed several flats of pansies in what were being touted as heirloom colors—pale cream, pale dusty rose, soft yellow, and gentle lavender. Next, a flat of fennel, and two flats of rosemary. What she would do with all those herbs, she had no clue, but there were plenty of beds and she figured she might as well plan to fill in the empty spots.

A tall dark purple flower in the perennials section caught her eye and she stooped down to read its name tag. *Monkshood.* She had never heard of it but it was striking, so she grabbed a few of those. And a few of the soft silvery green of the Russian sage would look so pretty by the monkshood, she had to have a few of those. A rosy-colored delphinium looked interesting, as did the bright yellow coreopsis.

"Now, how are you fixed for annuals?" a young woman whose name tag identified her as Angelica asked Zoey.

"What?" Zoey frowned.

"You have all perennials there. You want to plant

some annuals that last through the end of the season, don't you? So that the garden's not bare come September?"

"Oh, sure." Zoey nodded, looking suspiciously at the flowers she had already pulled out and marked as hers. Would they not "last the season"?

As if reading her mind, the young woman told Zoey, "Perennials usually bloom earlier in the season, June or July, which is why all of those"—she waved her hand at the selections Zoey had made—"are already blooming. If you deadhead them all summer long, you'll still have some bloom come September, but to keep the color going until frost, you want annuals. They are slower to bloom—your zinnias and cosmos, for example, won't start blooming till maybe August, depending on sun and water conditions."

"Oh. Okay." Zoey nodded. "I'll take some of . . . those things that you said."

"Do you want your zinnias mixed or all one color?"

"Mixed, please."

"Flats?"

"Sure." Zoey shrugged as the woman pulled out several flats having what looked like several rows of small flowerpots, each holding several small plants.

"Now, you'll plant these in full sun and you'll have gorgeous blooms till November, if you're lucky," Zoey was told.

Zoey just smiled, not having any way of judging just how lucky she'd be in the garden, but willing, all the same, to make a go of it.

By the time all of her selections had been gathered at the cash register, she realized that little of it would fit into her little car. Not one to lose a sale, the young woman quickly offered to have the plants delivered to Zoey's house by two that afternoon.

That being done, Zoey took the long way back to Brady's Mill. When she arrived at the house, the work crew was just finishing up and preparing to leave. She walked with the contractor to the second floor to inspect her new living quarters.

"It's gorgeous, Alan. You've done an incredible job!" Zoey beamed as she glanced around the bedroom that had been created on the second floor of the bungalow. Once the plans had been agreed upon, the carpets and wallpaper selected, Zoey had deliberately avoided her new quarters, wanting to be surprised when the job was completed. The newly installed plush green carpet stretched before her like a well-mowed lawn, and the floral wallpaper with its strong colors seemed to bring the outside in, which was exactly what she had had in mind. The skylights would open to the sun by day, the moon and the stars by night. It would be perfect when she got that big canopy bed put together. . . .

"Come see your new bath." Pleased with her reaction, Alan grinned and pushed open the door.

"Wow!" she exclaimed. "Oh, wow! It looks exactly like the sketch! Oh, and doesn't it look sinful!"

Alan laughed and turned on the water in the oversized whirlpool tub to demonstrate its usage.

"Oh, just what I need after a long day." She smiled. "I can't wait to try it out."

"You can try it out tonight," he told her. "It's all set up."

"It's just what I wanted. You did a wonderful job."

"Thank you. I'm glad that you're happy. Now, what will you do about getting your furniture up here?"

Zoey frowned. She had thought to ask Nick to help her, but with the wedding three weeks away, she couldn't very well ask him to come to Brady's Mill to help her with a little interior decorating.

She bit her bottom lip. Wally was out. Lifting her big marble-topped dresser would just about kill him. Besides, how to get it from the basement, where it was stored, to the second floor of the bungalow would be a problem regardless of who was doing the lifting.

"Don't know," she replied.

"Look, my men are headed out for lunch, but we can

stop back in an hour or so and give you a hand with that. No charge."

"Really? Are you sure?"

"Positive. You've been a great customer, Zoey. It's the least we can do."

"Thanks!"

Zoey followed Alan downstairs, going into the kitchen after he left to fix herself a quick lunch of soup and crackers before going back up to her new room. She swung open the double doors on the space that would serve as a small dressing room and walk-in closet. She couldn't wait to begin to move her clothes in here, and she would do that tomorrow, taking her time to organize things. She went back into the bathroom and admired her new dark green fixtures, white tile accented here and there with small hexagonal tiles of deeply hued wildflowers. The course around the top was solid green and a stripe of ceramic dots in greens and blues ran around the wall halfway up. Even the whirlpool tub was dark green, and she envisioned how wonderful it would be with hanging ferns and baskets of flowering plants—maybe even orchids, she mused—on the window ledges.

She turned on the water and let it steam and bubble for a moment before turning it off. She sighed. Definitely luxurious, she thought. Lying in that tub would be a totally sybaritic experience. It would be a shame, she told herself, to bubble away alone.

"Zoey?" Alan called from the bottom of the steps. "We're back. Want to show us what you need done?"

"Yes! I'm on my way!" She ran down the steps excitedly, anxious to see her carefully sought and accumulated treasures once and for all where they had been intended to go.

Later, when the last of the workmen had followed Alan out the back door and Zoey had thanked them for the twentieth time for their help, she went back upstairs to look at her new room. It was perfect, exactly as she had seen it in her mind's eye. The canopy bed of verdigris stood angled in one corner, the skylights perfectly positioned overhead. All that remained to be done was for Zoey to make up the bed. She hummed as she fitted soft white sheets with a sprinkling of pale yellow roses onto the bed, and plumped the pillows after sliding them into their cases. Across the bed she draped a plush blanket of sage green that matched the old lamp she had found at a house sale some months before. How pretty it would be, she thought, when she bought fabric to drape around the bedposts and over the canopy. And how perfect a big bowl of fresh flowers will be on the dresser, maybe a smaller bouquet on the painted table next to the bed. . . .

She sighed with total contentment and peeked into the bathroom one more time. She had stacked some big fluffy towels on a wicker table and filled a small basket with lavender-scented soaps. She couldn't wait till she finished in the garden and could reward herself with a long, sensual soak amid the swirling waters.

A honk from the driveway drew her to the window.

"My plants!" she said aloud.

She ran all the way to the backyard.

"Right there will be fine! Thank you!" she called to the teenage boys who had been sent to deliver her purchases.

Zoey cast a concerned eye upon the rows of pots and flats that lined her driveway. Whatever had she been thinking when she had bought what now appeared to be miles of green things, all of which would be looking to her for survival?

With a groan, she swung open the garden gate and looked at the waiting beds.

"Oh, brother," she muttered. "What do I do now?"

The best place to start, she decided, would be to carry the plants into the garden and put the pots where they would be planted. An hour later, she was still moving pots around, but had pretty much decided where each would go. The tallest plants would go along the fence, so she moved the monkshood, delphinium, and hollyhock to places in the back of the garden. The Russian sage, she decided, would look nice in front of the tall things, so she moved those pots to the back also. The rosemary and fennel would go with the daisies and the columbine in the Shakespeare bed. The coreopsis with its bright yellow color would be pretty along the outer edges of the long beds. That left the pansies—low growers, they would go in the front of the beds—and the annuals. She didn't know what to do with them. The zinnias and the—she looked at the tags again to check the name—*cosmos*—how tall would *they* get?—would wait until everything else was planted.

Searching in the garage for a shovel, Zoey attacked the warming earth and turned it over, just as her mother had cautioned her to.

"Air out the soil, Zoey. It's been covered up all winter," Delia had told her.

"Okay, Mom, the soil is aired," she announced after another hour of backbreaking work.

On her hands and knees she planted, wishing she knew a better way of getting the little buggers out of their pots besides digging them out with her fingers. Too late, she realized, she should have been wearing gloves. Her fingernails were a mess—and she would have a full hour of rings to sell on Friday morning. She inspected her nails with a frown.

"Oh, well," she muttered. "The damage has been done. Looks like it will be fake nails for me for a while." She continued going from one bed to the other, until all but the annuals were planted, before stepping back to admire her work.

"Not bad for someone who has absolutely no idea of what she is doing."

Newly planted, all would need water. Zoey unwrapped the hose and attached it to the spigot at the end of the garage, soaking all the new plants. She stripped off her old sneakers and ran the cold water over her hot, tired feet, then washed her hands before turning the hose onto her face. The water felt like ice as it ran down the front of her old T-shirt, but Zoey could not have cared less. It was wet and it washed away the sweat and the grime and cooled her hot skin that had soaked up more sun than she had realized.

"I have a farmer's tan," she smiled to herself as she rolled up the sleeves of the shirt and ran the hose water over her arms. One more spray on her feet and she turned off the water.

"Oh, *duh!*" she exclaimed. "No towel to dry off with."

She stood in the middle of the yard with her hands on her hips. Well, she would just have to dry off in the sun. There was no way she was going to drag her sloppy wet self into her nice clean house and her beautiful new bedroom. She dropped with a tired sigh onto the grass and stretched out. She would just lie here in the sun, just for a little while.

She hadn't realized how tired she was.

Zoey folded her hands behind her head and rested the back of her neck on them and looked up into the sky. The clouds were so big and puffy. *That one looks like Mickey Mouse,* she thought, *and that one looks like a train. That big one looks like a great big bird, with a nasty sharp beak.*

Nasty bird took a big bite out of Mickey and Zoey watched in fascination as cloud faded into cloud.

She stretched with satisfaction at having completed so much hard work in one day.

"Mom would be proud," she told a small bird that landed on the edge of the concrete birdbath.

She wondered where Delia was, if she was still in Bishop's Cove. Maybe on her way to Baltimore; she said she wanted to talk to Georgia this week.

Zoey rolled over onto her stomach and poked at a clump of clover. When they were younger, she and Georgia would spend hours searching through the grass for four-leaf clovers. She wondered if Laura had done the same.

There were lots of things she wondered about this newly found sister of hers. What books did she read? What kind of music did she like? Did she enjoy movies? And did she ever play sports? Did she bite her nails? Like

Chinese food? Drink Coke or Pepsi? Was she organized, like Georgia, or was she more of the whirlwind type, like Zoey herself? Did she sing in the shower? In the car? What had her husband been like? What had caused them to split apart?

So many, many things to learn about Laura.

She found herself wanting to know, not just for Delia's sake, but for her own. Zoey had made the trip to Bishop's Cove with the intention of offering her hand in friendship to Laura for Delia's sake. If she found she didn't like the woman, she would ignore that fact as much as possible. But for her mother's sake, she had been determined to make the effort. That she had found Laura so, well, *nice,* had made it easy to like her, easier to make her mother happy. That she and Laura could be friends would lift a terrible burden from all of them, and she said a little prayer of thanks that she genuinely liked this woman who had suddenly been thrust into her life.

"Ha!" she exclaimed and plucked the puny stem from the plant. She raised the four-leaf clover and twirled it around in her fingers. *This is my lucky day.*

Zoey started to roll over, then groaned as her muscles, worked beyond reason that day, began to protest. She lay back down and rested her face on her folded arms and turned slightly sideways toward the sun. The warmth spread through her like molasses, slow and thick and complete, and she drifted languidly from one random thought to another.

It wouldn't hurt to just lay here for a little while longer. I've earned a little rest, and besides, the sun feels so good, and the grass smells so like a new summer. And the flowers smell so good . . . what is that, anyway? Roses? Peonies? Whatever . . . it smells like heaven must smell at the beginning of June. I wonder if Laura likes to garden. I wonder when her birthday is. I have a niece. Ally. I want her to call me Aunt Zoey and I want to buy her useless, sentimental little-girl things for Christmas. Listen to that sweet little bird . . . Wally would know what it is . . . I'll have to remember to ask when I see him . . . and I have to remember to call Mrs. Colson and find out if my brides-maid dress for the wedding has come yet . . . I'm so glad that Ben will be at the wedding. He's not going to leave, I don't care what Nicky thinks. I can't believe that he would leave, now that he's found me . . . Surely he has to know that we belong together. . . .

* * *

"Zoey?" Ben pushed open the back door of the bungalow and called in. "Zoey, are you here?" He tried one more time. No answer.

Maybe she's at Wally's. Ben bounded down the steps and across the lawn to the house next door, where he noticed no car and no one answered the door.

Her car was in the drive, he noticed as he walked back toward his BMW, and there were rakes leaning up against the garage wall. He opened his mouth to call into the garden when he leaned over the gate and stopped in his tracks.

Zoey lay sleeping on the grass like a fairy princess from an age-old tale. From a haphazard ponytail, strands of her dark hair had worked their way loose to fold gently around her face.

"Sleeping Beauty," he whispered. No doubt about it.

As quietly as possible, he eased open the gate and as quietly closed it behind him. Zoey lay on her side, her feet were crossed at the ankle and her face turned up just slightly. Her lips were parted just the tiniest bit, and her black lashes lay on her cheeks like feathers from a small bird. She looked so totally innocent, so totally beautiful, that Ben sank to the ground next to her without even realizing he had done so.

How a gawky preadolescent had grown into so magnificent a woman was a mystery that he knew would never be solved.

He took the four-leaf clover from her fingers and twirled it between his own, much as she had, though he could not have known that. Lying down beside her, he touched the clover to her face and watched the corner of her mouth on that side twitch into a tiny smile. He traced the outline of her jaw, and her eyebrows, the tilt of her nose and the tip of her chin. Her nose wiggled once, and she giggled in her sleep, like the laughter of a tiny enchanted creature.

It was a joy just to watch her, and for almost half an hour, Ben did just that. He watched as the fading day played light and shadow off her face, watched as she turned slightly and snuggled toward him as the air began to cool. The light breeze was heavy with the sweetest scents—peony, he knew, having recognized the same fragrance that had surrounded a house he'd rented outside of Glasgow one year—and all was quiet, save for the birds and a cricket or two. He wondered if he'd stumbled accidentally into Paradise.

Zoey stirred in her sleep, and he twirled the clover under her chin to speed her awakening. He'd waited— and watched—as long as any sane man could.

"Hi," he said when she opened her eyes.

"Hmmm." She smiled in her sleep and inched closer to him, and he laughed.

"Come on, lazybones. Time to wake up."

"Lazybones?" Her eyes shot open. "I worked like a dog today, Ben. I dug and carried and raked and planted. Didn't you notice how beautiful my garden is?"

"Nope." He shook his head. "I didn't notice anything but you."

He lowered his head to kiss her, and Zoey drew his mouth to hers and his body down closer to her own. His tongue traced the outline of her lower lip and her hands tangled in the collar of his shirt.

"I'm such a mess," she whispered. "I need a shower and I smell like—"

"Springtime," he told her. "You smell like springtime." He nibbled at the corner of her mouth and she turned her head slightly to pull his mouth back to hers and kissed him the way she needed to. Again and again and again, deeper and deeper and deeper until there appeared to be nothing beneath her skin but molten liquid that molded with his touch.

His lips slid to the point of her chin and lower, down the gentle slide of her throat to the neck of her T-shirt, then over it, his teeth lightly picking at the soft fabric until he reached the swell of her breasts. Her hands ran through his hair, and his hands ran over her body, as if to touch all of her at once, because if he did not, she might disappear with the sun that was just about to dip behind the trees. She arched to his touch, urging him on, every inch of her skin craving the feel of his hands, her breath coming in tiny bursts. Crossing her hands in front of her, she pulled the shirt over her head, and drew him back to her. She moaned as his mouth tasted and teased her waiting, eager skin, and she slid her hands up and down the smooth firmness of the muscles of his back. She could not get close enough to him, could not seem to get enough, of his mouth, his hands, his body.

"Ben, please," she had whispered, and he had responded immediately to her plea. She felt him inside her, felt the sweet, tortured rhythm mount between them, and followed where he led her until they had both reached the end and it crashed down around them like thunder.

Later, lying in his arms, she tried to remember how—and when—she had gotten out of her clothes, but she could not. She giggled, and he moved against her just slightly, as if afraid to put too much distance between them.

"I hope you're not laughing at what I *hope* you're not laughing at," he muttered.

"I don't know where my clothes are." She laughed and nuzzled his throat with the side of her face. "We're in my backyard, buck naked, and I don't know where my clothes are."

"You don't need them yet," he told her, running one hand up her back. "Unless you're cold."

"A little chilly, but not cold." She lay flat back on the ground and looked above them to the sky. "The moon is out, Ben. Just a piece of it."

"Mmmm," he replied.

"It's all silvery, you should see." She poked at his back. "Turn over and look at it."

"I can't," he sighed. "I couldn't move if I wanted to."

"Ben, sooner or later, you will have to move. I heard Wally's car drive in."

"When?"

"When you were just about to . . . well, it doesn't matter when. The point is that he could very easily decide to stop in."

"Won't old Wally get a surprise?" Ben murmured into her ear.

"I think we should go in," she said, having thought about the very real possibility of her next door neighbor peering over the gate and finding them entangled in each other. "Besides, I really would like to try out my new whirlpool."

"You have a whirlpool?" He opened one eye.

"Well, I guess we know how to get your attention, don't we?" She traced his eyebrows with her index finger. "And yes, I have a whirlpool. It was just hooked up today."

"Really?" He opened the other eye. "We should break it in, so to speak."

"We have to go into the house to do that, Ben. And to go into the house, we need our clothes."

"There's always a catch, isn't there?" he muttered. "Okay, I'll help you find your clothes. I might even help you put them back on. But you better be thinking about this, Miss Enright. There are lots of great games to play in a whirlpool tub, and I know every one of them. So you might want to grab a bottle of something cold to drink as we pass through the kitchen, because a body can get mighty thirsty after a few hours in a whirlpool."

"A few hours?" She asked.

He nodded slowly. "I told you, I know a lot of water games, sweetheart, and we're going to play every one of them."

Chapter

23

Staring up through the open sky light at the stars that glimmered so high above like the lights from tiny Christmas trees, Zoey shifted slightly and sighed. It had been a night to remember. The corners of her mouth crinkled. Ben had been true to his word—he certainly knew a lot of . . . water sports. Oh, yes, it had certainly been a night she would never forget.

Ben stirred in her arms, his head still under her chin and his arms still wound about her. She caressed the side of his face lightly, unable to resist the urge to touch him. She had waited so long for this night that she wanted to hold on to every second of it. If she could have made time stop, she would have done so. One night could never be long enough to fill all of her fantasies—though Ben had, she acknowledged, done his best.

"What time is it?" he asked sleepily.

"Almost three."

"A.M. or P.M.?" He mumbled.

"A.M."

"Did we have dinner?"

"No."

"That explains why our stomachs are singing in two-part harmony." Ben rolled onto his back. "I don't suppose there's any food in that fancy new refrigerator of yours."

"Some leftovers, maybe," she told him.

"Let me guess . . . Chinese or Mexican?"

"Chinese." She grinned.

"Chicken lo mein? Some fried rice? Shrimp with cashews?" he asked hopefully.

"Close. Shrimp lo mein and some steamed dumplings."

"Sold." He kissed her forehead at the hairline and swung his legs over the side of the bed. The moonlight drifted down and played across the muscles of his back.

He pulled on his boxers and turned to her, leaned back across the bed, and kissed her mouth.

"Are you going to throw something on, or are you planning on strolling through the house just as you are?"

"I think I'll dress."

"Nothing formal, though."

She laughed and climbed out of bed, trying to remember which dresser drawer held her nightshirts. She found them in the third drawer on the left and pulled out a long soft gray T-shirt and pulled it over her head.

Ben was halfway to the kitchen by the time she found a pair of fluffy white slippers to slide onto her feet and followed him down the steps.

"Let's see here"—his head disappeared into the refrigerator—"here's two cartons of something. . . ." He passed the cartons back to her.

"This is it. The leftover Chinese." She set the cartons on the kitchen counter.

"Sweetheart, that small amount of lo mein wouldn't fill a soup bowl. And one steamed dumpling is not 'some.' We're talking major hunger here."

"Hmmm. I might have some soup. . . ."

"Homemade, of course," he quipped. "Something you whipped up just the other day, I'm sure."

"Right." She opened the cabinet door and pulled out two cans.

"Ah, yes. The old red and white cans of chicken noodle soup." He juggled the two cans and said, "Break out the crackers, sweetheart. We're about to do dinner."

Three bowls of soup later, Ben leaned back and smiled. "I feel so much better now. You really worked me over tonight, Zoey. And if you plan on a repeat performance, we're going to have to do some serious grocery shopping. Man does not live on chicken noodle soup alone, you know."

"Well, then, I guess I'd better find out where the nearest grocery store is."

"You mean you don't know?"

She shrugged. "I think there's a little general store in town but I can't swear to it."

"Where do you buy things like milk and bread and butter and stuff like that?"

"Convenience store." She grinned.

He laughed and shook his head. "Tomorrow, we go to a real grocery store and do some real food shopping. And I feel I should warn you, I am a breakfast eater. I will need toast and eggs—which I'll make myself, by the way—or at the very least, a big bowl of shredded wheat."

She bit her bottom lip, thinking about other nights, other mornings, he alluded to. She pinched herself on the inside of her arm just to make sure she wasn't dreaming. A small red spot rose up just north of her elbow and she gazed at it with satisfaction. Not a dream, she told herself gratefully. It really was happening. She really was there, in her kitchen, at 3:45 in the morning, with the sexiest, handsomest, most gentle man in the world. Ben. Her Ben.

". . . was she like?" he was saying.

"What?"

"I asked, what was she like?"

"What was who like?" She frowned.

"Delia's daughter."

"Oh. Laura." She sat back into the kitchen chair and pulled her knees up to her chest. "She's really very nice. You know, I had promised myself, no matter what, that I was going to get along with this woman. I didn't know if I'd like her, and quite frankly, that was immaterial to me when I went there, whether or not I liked her. But I was determined to get along with her and to give her a chance. I owed my mother that much."

"And . . . ?"

"And I really liked her, Ben. I want to get to know her."

"That must have made your mother very happy, Zoey." He folded his arms on the table and gazed across at her. "She must have been very proud of you."

"I think she was happy. And relieved. I don't think I can really appreciate just how difficult this has been for her. I can't even imagine what it's like to have to introduce yourself to your own child, then try to get to know her and forge some type of relationship with her. Add in the dynamics of three other children and all of the emotions involved there and it must have been overwhelming for Mom. While I can't resolve any of her personal issues for her, at least I could try not to make things any more difficult, any more painful for her than they already were."

"And you found that you liked Laura?"

"Yes. I liked her. We sat on the front porch and drank coffee and ate chocolate and dished."

" 'Dished'?" he asked.

"Girl talk." She grinned. "Laura's good at it. Almost as good as I am."

She toyed with her soup spoon, moving the one remaining noodle around in the bottom of the bowl. "Nicky liked her too. He invited her to the wedding."

"She must be something, then. I'm glad for you, and for Delia. And for Laura, that you've all been so supportive."

"Well, not all. Mom still has to talk to Georgia, but I can't imagine her not being open-minded."

"When is Delia planning on seeing her?"

"Thursday." Zoey glanced at the calendar on the far wall, where she had marked her work schedule. "Today."

"So I guess I'll get to meet your new sister at the wedding."

"She hasn't decided to come yet. She's afraid it will cause too much talk on Nick's wedding day and distract people. But Nick doesn't seem to be concerned about that, nor does India—and Mom isn't worried about the gossip either, so I guess Laura shouldn't *not* come because of that," Zoey said thoughtfully.

"Did you tell her that?"

"Pretty much." She chopped at the remains of the lone noodle. "It would have been nice to have had some time to visit with Georgia and Laura both before the wedding, which is only three weeks away, you know. But I don't know how I could fit that in, since I'm scheduled to work a lot between now and then."

"Speaking of which, don't you have a cooking show today?"

"They changed it to Friday since I'm off today." She grimaced. "I get to make apple butter tomorrow. Who makes apple butter in June?"

"When do you normally make it?"

"I don't normally make it at all, but Aunt August says that the fall is the time."

"Then why are you doing it now?"

"Because they have this new pot in inventory and someone thought it was just right to make apple butter in."

Ben laughed. "Well, I for one will be watching."

"You and about a million other people." She groaned. "Can you imagine having to pretend to enjoy something with a million people watching?"

"Aw, sweetheart, you're just so damned cute in that apron."

"Watch it, Pierce, I have never done 'cute' . . . and I hate that I have to wear an apron. Did you see the one they made me wear last week? It said, 'If Momma ain't happy, ain't nobody happy.'" She shivered. "And everyone thought it was so funny."

"We'll just have to get you an apron that expresses a more apropos sentiment."

"I'd be happier if you just got someone else to do these stupid cooking shows."

"Unfortunately for you, it's become wildly popular. And I'm afraid you are grossly underestimating your appeal, sweetheart."

"What do you mean?"

"I mean that there's been a lot more than a million TVs tuned in to 'Zoey's Cookbook.' A whole lot more, according to the numbers I saw a few days ago."

"Really?"

"Yup." He stood up and set both his and her bowls on the counter nearest the sink, rinsing first one, then the other.

"I don't think I want to know how many."

"Then I won't tell you." He leaned over her and kissed the end of her nose. "I need to get moving. I have an early appointment. Want to show me how to work that new shower of yours?"

"No." She groaned. "No more water. My hands and feet still look like prunes."

He lifted her from her chair, effortlessly swung her over his shoulder, and headed toward the stairwell.

"Ben, did you hear me? No more water," she pleaded, to no avail, as he climbed the steps, humming quietly.

With a mischievous smile, he turned on the shower, and stepped into the stream of cold water, plunked her down.

"You won't need this." He tugged at her nightshirt.

"No more than you'll need these." She tugged at the boxers.

And they were both right.

*　*　*

"I think you could use just a tiny tuck right here at the waist." Mrs. Colson frowned, her glasses slipping down on her nose just a bit as she tugged on the midsection of

Zoey's bridesmaid gown. "Otherwise, the dress is perfect."

"But you, miss"—Mrs. Colson pointed a finger at Georgia, who had just slid her dress on and was twirling in front of the mirror—"if you get any thinner we'll be missing you when you turn sideways."

"I think they sent the wrong size," Georgia told her.

"I think you've lost about another eight pounds," Zoey said accusingly.

"It was only two."

"Hold still, Georgia," Mrs. Colson admonished, measuring the excess fabric around the thin young woman's waist. "Not nearly as bad as I thought. Less than half an inch. I think Zoey's actually needs more taken in than yours does."

Georgia grinned and stuck her tongue out at her sister.

Mrs. Colson motioned for her to take off the dress, and Georgia placed the pale gold silk dress in Mrs. Colson's hands at the same time she placed a kiss on her cheek.

"Both of you . . . fade away to nothing," Mrs. Colson muttered as she hung the dress up and left the room.

"So. What's new?" Zoey asked.

"What's new?" Georgia pretended to ponder to the question. "Gee, I don't know, Zoey. I just found out that my mother had a child out of wedlock when she was fresh out of high school . . . that I have a sister I never knew about. . . ."

"I'm sorry. I shouldn't have been flip about it. Obviously you've spoken with Mom."

"Yes."

"And?"

"I don't know how I feel, Zoe."

"Neither did I, at first." Zoey sat down on one of two loveseats in the small sitting room on the second floor of her mother's house.

"And now?"

"Now I've had time to think it through. Have you met her yet?"

"No. Mom said you and Nicky have, and that you both liked her."

Zoey nodded.

"Well, I'm driving down tomorrow to make the visit. I don't know that I want to, but I feel that I have to. It would hurt Mom too much if I turned down Laura's offer. I called her last night—mostly because I think Mom expected me to—and she invited me to dinner."

"Give her a chance. I don't think you'll be sorry, Georgey."

"Damn, I hope not." Georgia shook her head. "Mom doesn't have enough on her plate, with Nicky's wedding in two weeks." She went to the small refrigerator and took out a bottle of water and a diet Pepsi, which she tossed to Zoey, who caught it with her right hand. "How do you feel about her coming to the wedding?"

"I feel it's right." Zoey popped the lid of the soda can. "Mom desperately wants her there. I think she needs her there."

Georgia sat down opposite her sister and took a long drink of water.

"You know, it just occurred to me that Mom's little refrigerator there is better stocked than the brand new, oversized, kick-butt model in my kitchen," Zoey mused.

"You're a mess, Zoey. And you talk about my eating habits," Georgia chided.

"What's in your refrigerator right now?"

"Carrots, apples, zucchini, green peppers, and some plums. All organic, of course. Some yogurt. Oh, and a bottle of cranberry juice."

"That organic too?" Zoey asked, and Georgia just grinned.

"Now you. What's in yours?"

"Half a dozen eggs, some cream for my coffee, about four slices of bread—"

"Wimpy white bread, I'll bet."

Ignoring her, Zoey added, "An enchilada, two beef burritos, and some refried beans, all leftover from last night."

"Just thinking about all those chemicals makes me ill." Georgia turned slightly green.

"Well, we meant to do some grocery shopping the other day, but I got called in to work Thursday night because someone called in sick and—"

"*Who* meant to?"

"What?" Zoey froze.

"You said 'we' meant to go shopping." Georgia leaned forward and grabbed Zoey's sleeve. "Who is 'we'?"

"Oh. Did I say 'we'? I meant 'me'."

"Oh. You *meant* to say, 'Me meant to go shopping.'" Georgia laughed. "I don't think so." She picked up a magazine from the basket and smacked her sister with it. "Spill."

"I don't think I really want—"

"Spill." Georgia smacked her again. "And don't leave out any of the good parts."

Zoey sighed. "Do you think Mom might have left a box of Godivas up here?"

"There's a box in the fridge. I'll get it. You, talk."

"It's Ben." Zoey sighed.

"No. Really? You and Ben? Now, this would be Ben *Pierce,* right?" Georgia deadpanned. "My, my, what a surprise."

"It's that obvious?"

Georgia rolled her eyes.

"Really?" Zoey asked.

"Only since you were, like, ten years old."

"You were only seven. How could you have known?"

"I read your diary." Georgia shrugged.

"You didn't."

"Yup."

"You *read* my *diary?*" Zoey frowned.

"Don't worry, there was nothing in there that interested me much, as I recall." Georgia opened the box of chocolate and stared into it, as if mentally tasting every piece.

"But my *diary,* Georgey?"

"That's what little sisters do, Zoe." Georgia appeared to be debating.

"Georgia, when you're finished drooling into the box, I'd like a piece."

Georgia took a slim wafer of chocolate and passed the box.

"That's it? You can gaze into a full box of Godivas and come out with one piece?" Zoey asked in disbelief.

"I only want one. There's all sorts of *stuff* in these things, Zoey." Georgia wrinkled her nose. "For one thing, there's preservatives. . . ."

"Don't tell me. I don't want to know." Zoey settled for the dark chocolate walnut. "Ignorance is bliss."

She nibbled at the side of the walnut. "I wonder if I would have snuck into Laura's diary," she mused.

"Absolutely. Little sisters always want to know what their big sisters are up to." She took another sip from the bottle of water. "Which brings us back to the subject at hand. Do I have to break into your house and hunt down your diary, or are you going to spill?"

Zoey spilled.

* * *

Ben dropped tiny grains of fish food into the top of the tank he had recently had installed in his office. He might not have bothered to look for more permanent living quarters beyond his grandfather's condo—which was, after all, spacious, close to the office, and fully equipped with all manner of technological gadgetry—but he needed some kind of living thing to keep an eye on. Delaney was allergic to cats, and dogs demanded more of a routine than he could keep on any regular basis right then. Fish were just right.

Ben still hadn't given up on getting a dog. He had missed having one since he had lost Hercules. He wondered if he could talk Zoey into getting a dog. Maybe not as big as Herc had been, but surely, living out in the country as she did, it wouldn't hurt for her to have a decent watchdog. He pictured them walking down that old country road together, Zoey, the Big Dog, and him. Or maybe just him and the Big Dog, exploring those woods back behind Zoey's house early on a January morning, trudging over frost-covered grasses that crunched and bent beneath their feet.

What if Zoey didn't like big dogs?

He dismissed the thought as one having no merit. Zoey was definately a Big Dog kind of woman. She'd love an Irish setter . . . maybe a golden retriever or a Chesapeake Bay . . . or a Newfoundland. Or a Great Pyrenees. Yeah, that might be the one—big, like a Newf, but golden and soft. . . .

He frowned. Sharing a dog with someone was a big commitment, a life-changing event.

But then again, so was loving Zoey.

Ben wasn't exactly sure when it dawned on him that he was in love with Zoey, but he suspected it had been somewhere between that last game of Hide the Soap and the chicken noodle soup. But love her he did, and there was no getting around it. He had thought it would frighten him more, this falling in love business, but he found it barely scared him at all . . . not at all what he'd been led to believe, if in fact he'd believed what he'd heard from other guys over the years. It had pleased him, actually, the way she had just sort of slid right into his life and assumed her place there, as if that place had been waiting all along for her to fill it. And perhaps it had been. It was a spot inside him that no one else had ever occupied. Maybe it had in fact always been hers. . . .

"Ben, there's an Anthony Chapman on the line for you." Nancy's voice broke through his reverie.

He grabbed the receiver eagerly. "Tony!"

"Ben, old man. How are you?"

"Couldn't be better! And you?"

"Great. Wonderful. How's the foot?"

"Coming along. I've found a therapist here who's a miracle worker."

"Splendid. That's exactly what I was hoping you'd say."

"Why's that?"

"Well, because I have a little something in the works here that I thought perhaps you'd be interested in." Tony paused briefly, then asked, "Wouldn't be thinking about going to Magny-Cours at the end of the month, would you?"

"You mean for the French Grand Prix?" Ben looked at the calendar on his desk for the date.

"Right."

"Not a chance. I have a wedding to attend. One I wouldn't miss for anything."

"Not your own, I hope." Tony chuckled.

"No." Ben laughed. "Not this time, anyway."

"Now, should I be looking for a hidden meaning there? Ben, mate, you haven't gone and done something foolish, have you?"

"Nothing at all foolish. And you'll meet her soon enough."

"Ah, so there *is* a she. Any chance you'll be coming to Silverstone in mid-July, then?"

"Hmmm . . ." Ben flipped the pages of the datebook. The British Grand Prix was held at Silverstone, a former airfield in Northamptonshire, England. This year it would be run two weeks after the wedding. "That's a possibility. Very doable."

"Great. Wonderful. There's something I want you to see."

"You've got my curiosity piqued, buddy. Let me see what I can do."

"Wonderful! I'll be counting on it." Tony said. "And Ben . . ."

"Yeah, buddy?"

"Bring her with you."

"I'd planned to." He laughed as he hung up the phone.

His Big Dog would have to wait. He was taking Zoey to Silverstone.

Chapter

24

"What are you thinking about?" Propped up on one elbow, Ben stretched his legs a little to the right to entwine with hers. It was just slightly after seven o'clock in the morning on the morning of the twenty-seventh of June.

"My big brother getting married," Zoey answered without hesitation.

"Ummm. The big day. Do you suppose he's nervous?"

"Nick? No." She shook her head. "It couldn't come fast enough for Nick. He can't wait to marry India. And who could blame him? They were meant for each other."

Meant for each other. The phrase repeated itself over and over in Ben's mind. He wondered if in fact it could be true, that certain people were meant to be together. It was a thought worth pursuing. And he would do just that. Later, when Zoey wasn't so close, when she was wearing something more than a sheet. It was just too damned difficult to think important thoughts when she was all snuggled up close to him and warm from sleep. Later, maybe, he'd think about the designs of fate. Right now, they had a wedding to go to, and he had promised Delia they'd be there nice and early.

"Don't we have to be leaving soon?" he asked.

"Yes. We need to be on the road to Devlin's Light by nine."

"Don't you think you should be getting up?"

"Yes." She did just that, abruptly.

"I'll bring you a cup of coffee while you're in the shower." Ben watched her as she walked toward the bathroom, covering a yawn with her right hand and scratching the back of her head with her left. "And then while I'm in the shower, you can make me a nice breakfast. Eggs over easy, home fried potatoes . . ."

Without turning around, she made an obscene gesture in his direction with the hand that had been scratching her head.

Yup, she sure was a little charmer first thing in the morning.

"Where's the dress you're supposed to wear?" Ben frowned as she stashed her bag in the trunk of his BMW. "Aren't you wearing some long bridesmaid thing?"

"Mother took it down on Thursday, mine and Georgia's. Mrs. Colson was afraid we'd let them get wrinkled, so she wouldn't let us take them. She'd take it quite personally if anything was less than absolutely perfect, Mrs. Colson would." She slammed the trunk. "Well, are you ready?"

He opened the car door for her and she muttered her thanks.

Following her pointed directions, Ben managed to drive toward their destination in a mostly silent car. He tried to engage her in conversation on several occasions, but she seemed distracted and edgy.

"You know, I've never been to a wedding in a lighthouse before," he said as they crossed the bridge from Pennsylvania into New Jersey.

When she didn't reply, he continued. "Why do you suppose they decided to get married in a lighthouse?"

"The lighthouse has been in India's family forever," she told him. "And India's brother was killed there."

"Oh. Well then, that makes perfect sense." He nodded. "Who would want to get married in a church when they can exchange their vows at a murder scene?"

Zoey glared at him. "India was very close to her brother. And he—Ry—was a very close friend of Nicky's. They just wanted to feel that he was there with them."

"Speaking of invited guests, what's the latest on Laura? Is she coming today?"

"The last I heard, she was still on the fence. I called the inn this morning, but the person who answered the phone was apparently one of the college students hired for the summer. She didn't know where Laura was and wasn't sure where to look. It sounded as if they were really busy so I didn't want to press. Laura could have been with a guest, she could have been walking on the beach." Zoey shifted in her seat as if to find a better spot. "Or she could be on her way to Devlin's Light."

"Is that what's bothering you? Worrying about what Laura is going to do?"

"What makes you think that something is bothering me?"

"You're edgy and grumpy and that's not normal for you."

"And you're the expert on what's normal for me?"

"As a matter of fact, I am." He reached a hand over and took one of hers, having to unclasp them from the death grip her right hand had on the left.

Finally she said, "I want everything to be perfect for Nicky. He's the best brother in the world. He deserves a perfect wedding day."

"And it looks like he'll have it. The weather is beautiful—not a cloud in that baby blue sky."

"I wasn't referring to the weather."

"Ah, all of a sudden, you're concerned that maybe convincing Laura that she should be there today maybe wasn't such a great idea?"

"It isn't that, not really. Mother thinks that some reporter or two might attempt to crash the wedding."

"Why would reporters be interested in Nick's wedding?"

"Probably just 'cause it's Mother, you know, internationally famous writer and all that. I'm afraid that if they find out about Laura, they'll make a big deal out of it, and that's what people will remember about my brother's wedding day . . . that Delia's secret was publicly revealed."

"So what?" He shrugged. "Delia's not afraid."

"I didn't say I was afraid. I said I was concerned," she snapped.

"Same thing," he said under his breath and she shot him a dirty look.

"Zoey, sweetheart, relax. Delia is a big girl. She knows what she's doing." He smiled. "Have you ever known Delia to not know what she was doing?"

Zoey thought about it for a minute, then shook her head. "Not really."

"Everything will be fine. Delia's handling this thing exactly the way she wants to. Who are you to second-guess a woman like Delia Enright?"

In spite of herself, Zoey laughed. "You're right. Everything will be fine. I guess I'm just looking for something specific to worry about, since I'm nervous."

"What are you nervous about?"

"Just the whole thing. That everything goes right. India's Aunt August has everything planned down to the last second, so I guess there's nothing that could go wrong. India's friend Darla is catering, so the food will be out of this world."

"Isn't she also the matron of honor?"

"Yes."

"Isn't that going to be a bit of a stretch? Getting the food ready while she's part of the ceremony?"

"Mom said she and India planned mostly cold dishes so that almost everything could be prepared ahead of time. Darla apparently also has hired some capable help who will be there today. No one seemed worried."

Zoey checked the handwritten directions she had jotted down the night before and pointed to the light just ahead.

"I think this is where you turn left. Georgia mentioned that gas station there on the corner, and that little picnic grove next to it, since the road is not marked."

Ben made the left and Zoey continued her chatter. "Georgia also said that she helped August with the flowers. Mother had bunches of things brought in, but August wanted to do the table arrangements. My sister seemed to enjoy it. I'm glad. Georgey doesn't have enough fun in her life. All she does is work."

"You mean dance, don't you?" Ben asked.

"I'm getting the feeling that it's becoming more of a job and less of a joy for her. And don't ask me why, because I can't explain it. It's just a feeling I have. So I'm really happy that she is away for a few days and is relaxing and having a good time." Zoey rolled the window down and sniffed at the air. "We're really close to the bay. Can you smell it?"

Ben pushed the button to lower his window.

"Ummm. Oh, yes. I can smell it. Salt with just a hint of decaying matter. Just the perfect atmosphere for a romantic wedding in a lighthouse that just happened to be the scene of a murder."

"You stop that." She smacked him lightly with the rolled-up directions. "It isn't like that at all. Devlin's Light is one of the most peaceful, beautiful places I've ever been. You'll see."

"I'm confused. Is it the town or the lighthouse that's called Devlin's Light?"

"Both. The town was named for the lighthouse."

She leaned forward and said, "Now, slow down, we're coming into the town limits. 'Welcome to Devlin's Light. Speed limits strictly enforced.'" She read the sign as they passed by it.

Ben slowed just slightly as they drove into the small

bayside town of Devlin's Light on the shores of the Delaware Bay. Long ago, India Devlin's ancestors had settled here. The lighthouse that overlooked the bay, as well as many of the town's landmarks, still bore the Devlin name and benefited from the proceeds of the Devlin Trust.

"Turn here." Zoey pointed to a small gravel road on the left.

Ben eased onto the brake as he crept up the stone drive, carefully avoiding kicking up stones that would mar the finish of his car. At the end of the drive through salt marsh heavy with the scent of salt and sea, Zoey instructed him to park next to the white Pathfinder and pointed to the cedar-shingled cabin in front of them and said, "This is Nicky's place."

Ben got out of the car and stretched his legs, at the same time taking in his surroundings. The cabin sat on stilts at the edge of the marsh, facing the bay, which was perfectly calm that day. Grabbing his things from the back of the car, Ben followed Zoey along the wooden walkway that ran from the back of the structure to the front. By the time they were approaching the small dock and the steps leading to the cabin, Nick had burst through the door and leaped down the steps to the walkway that served as a floating dock, to pick up his sister and spin her around.

"You crazy man!" Zoey shrieked. "One wrong move and we'll both end up in the bay!"

Nick set her down, kissed his little sister on the forehead, and hugged his old friend.

"Ben! It's good of you to offer to give me a hand here this morning." Nick slapped Ben on the back.

"Hey, someone had to keep an eye on you, just in case you were thinking of backing out."

"Not much chance of that." Nick took Ben's bags and gestured for them to follow him into the cabin. "When you get to know India, you'll understand. She's one in a million."

Zoey's eyes misted as her brother bragged about his

soon-to-be wife, about her accomplishments as a prosecutor, about how beautiful she was, how she so perfectly adapted to becoming a mother to the little girl her brother had adopted before his death.

"She sounds like the perfect woman," Ben told him.

"Perfect for me, anyway." Nick nodded, then turned to his sister. "Zoey, don't you think you should be getting over to the Devlin house? Mom and Georgia arrived Thursday night, but I'm sure they could use an extra set of hands."

"Okay." She turned to Ben and held out her hand. "Keys, please."

"What?"

"I need the keys to your car. I'm not about to walk from here into the town."

"You want me to turn over my car—my BMW roadster—to a woman who knows two speeds—stop and 'whoa, baby'?" Ben blanched.

"Come on, Ben. I'll be careful. I promise." She smiled sweetly.

"How 'bout if I drive you over to . . . wherever it is you're going."

"That would be a waste of time. Nicky needs you, don't you Nicky?"

Before her brother could answer, Ben said, "Zoey, unless you go real slow up that drive, you'll kick up stones. Stones will pock my paint job."

"Oh, far be it from me to *pock* your *paint.*" She grinned and proceeded to search his pockets for the keys.

"What's going on here?" Observing his sister's antics, Nick frowned.

"I'm trying to get the keys so that I can . . . Whoops!" She laughed. "That wasn't your key ring, was it?"

Ben laughed and dangled the keys in front of her face.

Zoey grabbed for the keys and Ben let her take them. She kissed Ben on the chin, saying, "I'll be very careful, Ben. I promise. And I'll make it worth your while later."

"What's that supposed to mean?" Nick's eyes narrowed another notch.

Zoey turned to her brother and kissed his cheek. He was still frowning. "Get over it, Nicky. Your little sister is all grown up. I'll see you at the wedding."

As she skipped down the wooden walk toward the car, she heard her brother say, "Ben, I think it's time that you and I had a little talk."

Zoey laughed out loud.

She was still smiling when she pulled into the driveway of the Devlin house on Darien Road and parked at the rear of the property.

"Zoey!" The screen door slammed and Zoey knew without even looking that young Corri Devlin—soon to be Corri Devlin-Enright—had spotted her car.

"You're just in time for brunch! Delia said you'd get here on time! Darla made the wedding cake. It's the biggest, bestest cake I ever saw! It's three different cakes and they stand on top of each other. And all white outside and chocolate inside! It has real white flowers on the top and they sort of fall down the sides. And it has some roses made of frosting. Darla made a few tiny ones just for me and Ollie to taste."

Corri flew across the yard and Zoey caught her. As always, the child brought an enormous grin to Zoey's face.

"Is everyone here already?" Zoey asked.

"Georgia and you and me. And Darla will be here soon, she's taking some food things out to the lighthouse." Corri stopped and looked at the car Zoey had driven. "Why do you have Ben's car?"

"Because Ben and I drove here together today. I dropped him off at Nick's so he could keep Nick company."

"When I get big enough to drive," Corri said thoughtfully, "do you think Ben would let me drive that little car? With the top down? If I promised to be very, very careful?"

"Well, if he still has it in ten years or so, maybe he'd let you take it for a spin. As long as you don't pock his paint job."

"I wouldn't . . . what you said."

"Then you could probably work something out." Zoey winked at her and unlocked the trunk. Corri leaned it to help take out Zoey's overnight bag.

"Mrs. Colson came down this morning in Delia's limousine," Corri chatted away. "Randall, Delia's driver, brought her down. She brought your dress and Georgia's and Delia's. Mine and Darla's were here. Mine is just like yours. Only Darla's is different, 'cause she gets to be the honor."

"The maid of honor. Or matron, whichever," Zoey corrected herself, wondering how Darla was holding up.

Darla Kerns had been India Devlin's best friend since their grade school days, but Zoey knew that Darla was much more than just an old friend of India's. Darla and India's brother, Ry, had been deeply in love. Had the fates been kinder, Darla would have been India's sister-in-law by now. As it was, they were as close as sisters, and even Ry's death had not shaken their relationship.

"And Zoey! Guess what!" Corri asked wide-eyed.

"What?"

"I have a cousin," she announced solemnly.

"A cousin?"

Corri nodded vigorously. "Her name is Ally and she's almost four." Corri added, "And she calls Delia Nana."

"Oh, does she?" Zoey nodded. So Laura had decided to come, after all. She wondered how that was going. Well, soon enough she'd see for herself. To Corri, she explained, "That's because she is the daughter of one of Delia's daughters. That makes Delia Ally's grandmother."

They walked in silence to the back porch and up the steps.

"You know, Delia is going to be your grandmother too," Zoey told her.

"She is?"

"Sure. You're going to be Nicky's daughter, right?"

Corri nodded.

"And Nick is Delia's son, right?"

"Right." Corri was beginning to catch on.

"So, that would make you . . ."

"Delia's granddaughter." Corri grinned and opened the back door, pushed past Zoey, and ran into the house yelling, "Hey, Ally, guess what . . ."

"Corri Devlin, for heaven's sake . . ." August Devlin bustled into the kitchen shaking her head. When she saw Zoey, she opened her arms to embrace her and said, "Oh, Zoey, good, you're just in time for brunch. Here, give me that bag, and go into the dining room and join your mother and sisters."

Your mother and sisters.

"Mother"—Zoey leaned over and kissed the side of her mother's face, then went down the line to Georgia, India, and Laura, kissing and hugging each with the same affection. Laura's grateful eyes followed Zoey as she seated herself at the opposite side of the table. "Sisters." Zoey raised her water glass casually in a toast, then added, "and soon-to-be sister." She tilted the glass in India's direction. "What have I missed this morning? Georgia, have you filled India in on all of Nicky's bad habits? India, are you getting cold feet?"

"Me? Nah." India laughed. "But if I don't stop eating, I'll have a devil of a time getting into that dress."

"What's your dress like? How are you wearing your hair?" Zoey asked, and the room immediately filled with lively chatter. From time to time, Zoey or Georgia would direct a comment to Laura, to include her in the conversation.

"Don't think I didn't notice how you skillfully kept Laura in the loop." Delia cornered Zoey and Georgia in the kitchen, where they were washing up the brunch dishes to spare August a little time. She kissed the sides of their faces. "You do me proud, every time. Never more than you have today. I love you both so *terribly.*"

"Aw, Mom, you love us just fine." Zoey squeezed Delia's hand. "And we adore you, too."

"Well, then," Delia said, patting at her eyes with a tissue, "I suggest we get ourselves ready to make that little journey across the bay. The wedding's in just about two hours and we all need to get dressed in our wedding finery."

"How are we getting over to the lighthouse?" Zoey asked.

"Captain Pete is loaning us several boats for the occasion," Delia told her.

"Captain Pete?" Zoey grinned. "You mean Captain Pete who has the charter boats? Captain Pete, who we think has the hots for August?"

"So delicately put, Zoey." Delia rolled her eyes.

Zoey laughed. "But he does."

"Ummm." Delia nodded. "So it would appear. Rumor has it that they were an item in their younger days."

"Really?" Georgia dried wet hands on a dish towel. "August and the salty old sea captain, eh?"

"I heard that, Georgia Enright," August called from the dining room.

"She heard it, but she didn't deny it," Georgia whispered as they sneaked up the back steps to the second floor to help India get her things together for the short boat ride to the lighthouse.

India, however, was ready.

"Just give me a hand carrying these things downstairs," she told them. "Our dresses are already out at Devlin's Light. The flowers are there. Darla and Mrs. Colson should be there as well. I think we only need to get ourselves there."

"What's in here?" Georgia grabbed a small suitcase.

"Stuff for the honeymoon." India took a garment bag from the back of her bedroom door.

"Where are you going?"

"Not telling." India shook her head.

"Well, where are you spending the night?" Zoey asked.

"Not telling." India grinned.

"What if something happened and we needed to get in touch with you in a hurry?" Zoey persisted.

"Darla knows where we'll be." India laughed. "Come on, you two. Oh, where's Corri?"

"Laura went out to look for her and Ally," Delia said when they reached the bottom of the steps.

"I hope they're still clean when she finds them," India muttered. "Okay, this stuff all goes out to the limo. Does everyone have their things?"

Laura had managed to round up the three little girls—Corri, Ally, and Darla's daughter, Ollie—short for Olivia—before they had gotten too dirty. The six women and three children piled into the limo. Randall, Delia's longtime driver, headed directly to Captain Pete's dock four blocks away.

True to his word, Pete had the boats ready for the ladies, and though slowed by an eternally bad leg, he gallantly helped each of them into the cabin cruiser he'd reserved from his fishing fleet for the purpose. Scrubbed down, the deck sporting white ribbons, the boat was to be manned by Pete's oldest son, Tucker, to the point where Devlin's Light rose from the beach to keep watch over the comings and goings on the bay. Pete himself, being Nick's choice for best man, would drive over later, with Nick, Ben, and Randall who for now would stay behind on the dock to await the arrival of the guests.

The bay was as clear and calm as glass, the sunlight glistening off the water like diamonds and the breeze as gentle as a sigh. Georgia, the only Enright without sea legs, sat with her head between her knees, tended to by her mother, India, and August. The three little girls huddled in the cabin with Tucker, who let each of the little girls take a turn steering the boat.

Laura stood against the railing at the back of the boat and stared out at the sea.

"Isn't it a perfect day?" Zoey touched Laura on the back and leaned against the rail next to her.

Laura nodded. "Perfect," she whispered.

"Laura, are you all right?" Zoey asked, concerned.

She nodded.

"Is it the boat? Are you feeling seasick?"

"Me?" Laura laughed. "I grew up on a boat just a little smaller than this one. No, I don't get seasick."

"Well, then . . . ?" Zoey waited for an explanation.

"It's just a lot to handle all at once, that's all." Laura told her. "I do want to thank you, though, for everything you've done to make me feel . . . well, to make things less awkward for me. I know that you're doing it for Delia's sake, but I appreciate your kindness."

"Initially, yes, my first concern was for my mother. I—we, Georgia and I—would be nice to you even if you were awful." Zoey poked Laura playfully, adding, "Which I'm so happy to say, you aren't. I'm glad that you decided to come today. It means so much to Mother to have you here. I know it's not easy for you, but I'm so happy that you did this for her."

"I don't want anyone to hurt her," Laura whispered.

"None of us do. Anyone who tries will have to get through all of us to get to her. Nicky, India, Ben, not to mention her daughters."

"Count me in," Laura told her.

"I was." Zoey swung an arm around Laura's shoulder. "Let's go see if we can make Georgia laugh."

"The last thing you want when you're seasick—except of course for a big bowl of chili—is someone in your face trying to make you laugh." Laura put her hand on Zoey's arm to stop her.

"Really?" Zoey tapped her foot on the deck. "Well, then, let me tell you about the time I went on a bird count out here at Devlin's Light with Nick and India. And Corri, who can identify more birds than I even knew existed. It was on Christmas Day. . . ."

The boat rolled up to the newly constructed dock on the far side of the lighthouse and the passengers piled out, assisted by Tucker Moreland, who with great affection helped both India and August from the boat before lending a steady hand to an obviously weakened Georgia. Zoey jumped over the side by herself, as did the three little girls. Last to leave the boat was Laura, who blushed deeply when Tucker took her hand and despite her protests, helped her off the boat.

"Tucker, the guests will probably be arriving at the dock in about an hour or so."

"I know, Miss Devlin"—Tucker grinned—"no one comes over till you say they come over. Got your cell phone?"

August laughed and held it up.

"Aye, aye, then. We're at your service, Miss Devlin." He bowed gallantly, trying not to appear obvious that he was in fact looking beyond her to where Laura stood gazing out across the bay.

"Off with you, you young pirate." August shooed him back toward the boat, debating whether or not she should ignore the fact that he had barely taken his eyes off the oldest of Delia's girls since they had arrived at the docks. She could not.

Having once, many moons ago, taught him Latin, she leaned over to Tucker and lowering her voice, said, "Fortes fortuna juvat."

He laughed, then translated, "Fortune favors the brave."

"A more contemporary reading might be 'go for it.'" August smiled.

"Now, Miss D. . . ." It was Tucker's turn to redden, and he did, clear down below the neck of his cotton T-shirt.

August laughed again, then lowered her voice and touched his arm. "You won't forget, now, Tuck. No one gets on that boat without an invitation."

"Don't worry, Miss D." Tucker gave her arm an affectionate squeeze. "No one will."

The wedding party oohed and ah'ed over the transformation of the downstairs rooms of the lighthouse from the once rustic home of India's ancestors to a perfectly beautiful spot for a wedding reception. Long buffet tables wearing white linen cloths and swagged with palest pink tulle draped with long arms of ivy ran along the two inside walls of the largest of the two downstairs rooms. Large white pottery crocks brimming with white peonies, roses, stock, and lilies served as centerpieces and perfumed the air with the scents of early summer. Round tables with chairs for eight, with smaller but similar centerpieces, were scattered throughout the downstairs rooms and out onto a deck that overlooked the bay. The windows, draped with filmy white gauze held back with bunches of fresh flowers tied with pink and white ribbons, were opened to allow the gentle sea breezes in. Outside, several newly constructed decks and patios had room for dining and dancing.

In the two corresponding rooms upstairs, freestanding mirrors and several small loveseats had been arranged for the bride and her attendants. The newly installed bathroom held a series of double sinks, allowing everyone room to apply their makeup and fuss with their hair without elbowing each other in the face.

"This is some lighthouse," Georgia said as she admired the newly finished rooms.

"I was beginning to fear that the renovations would not be completed in time," India told her, "and we really only just made it by a few days."

"What are you going to use it for after the wedding?"

"Darla is going to have a little restaurant here, as well as a home for her catering business. We're thinking of maybe even renting out for other weddings."

"How will people get back and forth?"

"Pete will run a shuttle." India set her makeup case on one of the loveseats. "Darla's even thinking maybe she'll do luncheons during the bird migrations next spring. It would offer a comfortable place to observe the birds without getting in their way. Oh, Darla, there you are. We were just talking about the plans for the lighthouse."

Darla hugged her friend and said, "The only plans I have right now are to get through this day without a snag. I hope Jason gets here in time to get the grills started for the fish. And I hope that that new generator doesn't pop and blow out the refrigerators. And . . ."

"Enough!" India laughed. "I forbid any more talk of what could go wrong. Come into the bathroom and fix my hair and stop worrying. Everything is going to be just perfect, Dar."

And it was just perfect, from the simple ceremony on the dock overlooking the calm inlet to the music and the incredible buffet. India and Nick's wedding could not have been more perfect than it was.

"You really are the most beautiful bride." Delia had sniffed back the tears as she fussed with India's veil of gossamer tulle held in the front by combs covered with fresh flowers.

"Thank you, Delia." India kissed her on the cheek. "And you are the most elegant mother of the groom I've ever seen, in that pale champagne-colored silk dress."

"I didn't want to clash with the decor." Delia sniffed and her daughters all laughed.

"Mother, you're the only person I know who would take orchid petals with her to shop for a dress," Zoey said.

"I wanted the photographs to be balanced," Delia defended herself archly, then laughed good-naturedly. "Your dresses are such a pale shade of gold, and August is wearing a deeper color. I thought my dress should complement the overall color scheme."

"And you do, exquisitely." August squeezed her arm. "Ahh, are those violins I hear?"

Laura looked out the window. "Yes. There's a string quartet, just warming up."

"Oh, good, they made it." India peeked out the window and grinned.

"I guess violins make an easier crossing than an organ," Zoey commented. "Or a five-piece band."

"Oh, we'll have a regular band later, but we had to have violins for the ceremony." India smoothed her gown of creamy white satin. "Did you know that on the night Nick proposed to me, he had arranged for a string quartet to serenade us?"

"Oh, how romantic." Laura said. "No wonder you said yes."

"I would have said yes anyway." India began to puddle

up. "How could I not have loved him? He's sweet, loving"—she sniffed slightly—"kind, thoughtful . . ."

"Who is she talking about?" Zoey stage-whispered from the doorway.

"I'm not sure," Georgia pretended to frown. "But Nicky had better not hear about it."

"I'm talking about Nick," India told them.

"You'll have to pardon us, but the man you're describing doesn't sound anything like the Nick we grew up with." Zoey's eyes began to gleam. "Georgey, do you remember the time that Nick—"

"Don't you dare," Delia warned her daughter sternly. "No 'bad-Nicky' tales on his wedding day. Now, girls, let me take a last look at you. . . . Zoey, let me fix those flowers, they're hanging half out of your hair. Laura, would you please straighten the back of India's dress?"

"Is everyone ready?" August asked from the doorway. "Tucker has just brought over the last boatload of guests."

"Then it's time," Darla said simply. "India?"

"Let's do it."

And with that, one of the most unusual weddings ever to be held in Devlin's Light began. A blend of tradition and improvisation, the marriage of India Devlin to Nicholas Enright would be talked about for years.

When asked "Who gives this woman?" Augustina Devlin, the bride's aunt, stepped forward and announced, "I do," in her customary crisp fashion.

The Enright women had come properly prepared for the emotional ceremony with handkerchiefs hidden in the hands that wrapped around bouquets and tissues in Delia's purse. There was barely a dry eye among those who stood in the sunlight and witnessed the exchange of vows between the lithe golden-haired young woman— the last of the Devlin descendants—who had so recently returned to the town in which she had been raised, and the tall, broad-shouldered man who made a place for himself in Devlin's Light.

"Do you, India Sarah Devlin, take this man, Nicholas Burton Enright . . ." Reverend Carlton Douglas began what Zoey always thought of as the *real* ceremony, the only part that *really* mattered.

Nicky really is so handsome, he really is such a love, Zoey thought as she watched her big brother, who stood so straight and solemn before all of their family and most of the town of Devlin's Light as he exchanged his vows with the woman he loved. *I'm so glad he found India, she really is just right for him.*

And Ben really is just right for me. We belong together just as surely as Nick and India do. If he leaves now, I think I'll die. . . .

The fear tugged at her heart—as it had, more and more, begun to do lately—that he would, in fact, return to England, to the life he had known before he had come back.

He's driven in Grand Prix races. He's traveled all over the world. His life has been filled with fast cars and, I would guess, fast women. What man would trade all that—France, Italy, Monaco—for Chester County, Pennsylania?

Ben would.

Wouldn't he?

The inner dialogue went, back and forth.

He belongs here, he'll stay.

This is just a diversion for him, he'll go back as soon as he's able.

It was beginning to make Zoey slightly ill. She tried turning down the volume on the taunting little voice and tried to concentrate on what was going on.

She turned slightly to look for Ben in the crowd that had gathered on the dock, and found him standing just slightly in the shadow of the lighthouse, between Laura and Mrs. Colson. She caught his eye and winked, earning a broad smile from the only man who had ever turned her blood to fire and caused her palms to sweat. He looked so handsome, in his navy blue blazer and white linen slacks, though surely no more alluring, she reasoned, than he had looked in a green and white checkered sheet earlier that morning.

He couldn't—wouldn't—leave her.

Zoey turned her attention back to the ceremony—"Do you, Nicholas Burton Enright, take this woman . . ."—to see her mother dab at her eyes. What a day this was for Delia. Gaining a daughter . . . Zoey glanced back to Laura . . . make that *two* daughters. Ben lifted Ally, who had been straining to see, onto his shoulders.

Make that two daughters and one—no, two granddaughters, counting Corri.

"By the power invested in me by the state of New Jersey, I now pronounce you husband and wife. You may kiss your bride, Mr. Enright," Reverend Douglas was telling Nick.

And kiss her he did, while the guests tossed birdseed and rose petals, as requested by the aunt of the bride. Cheers rang out and violins played a lively tune and, as the bride had wished, waiters appeared instantly, carrying trays of fluted glasses bubbling with champagne to lift a toast to the lighthouse, and to the spirit of the bride's late brother.

The buffet was both sumptuous and inspired, with mounds of icy cold shrimp and delicate lobster salad, tureens holding cold strawberry soup, and large porcelain bowls of chicken salad plump with pineapple and grapes. Then came the trays of summer salads—minted rice, potato salad with lavender, green beans and mushrooms in a mustardy dressing, and a fruit salad garnished with fresh tender violets. Later, Darla's crew grilled salmon and swordfish and shrimp wrapped in bacon, a favorite of Nick's. The wedding cake—exactly as Corri had promised—was a three-tiered delight of rich dense chocolate covered with white buttercream frosting. From the top tier cascaded white lilacs, and around the base of each layer, buttercream roses grew. The dessert buffet was a staggering testimony to Darla's ability, with chocolate-covered strawberries, creampuffs with mocha filling, and every variety of fruit tart imaginable.

"What a staff you must have, Darla!" Zoey exclaimed as the waiters passed by with trays of tiny cheesecakes and miniature soufflés. "To prepare so much of so many different things."

"Thanks, Zoey, but I'm afraid that you're looking at most of the staff." Darla dropped wearily into a chair.

"How could you possibly have done all this?"

"It takes a lot of organizing. And you'd be amazed at how much can be prepared ahead of time. For the last-minute assembly, it helps to have people whose skills you have confidence in. And of course I did have some help . . . just not the dozens of people everyone assumes I have."

"Well, everything is exquisite, Darla." Delia joined them on the deck. "I will never use another caterer for anything. We'll simply have to bring you to Westboro for the next party."

"Thanks, Mrs. Enright." Darla put her hand over her mouth to stifle a yawn. "Please forgive me. I'm starting to wind down."

"It must be really difficult to do so much." Georgia shook her head. "I'm just amazed at it all."

"Actually, one of the most difficult things has been to find the quality of herbs that I like. If I could grow them myself, I'd do it." Darla stifled another yawn. "I just don't have the time, but I often think about it."

"Where do you buy from now?" Georgia asked.

"I buy from several farmers, but it makes for a lot of driving around. This one grows rosemary, that one grows sage, someone else grows the best dill. It would be a great business to get into, growing top-quality fresh herbs for resturants and caterers. If I had the time, I swear I would do it."

"Ah, there you are, Zoey." Ben wandered through the door leading from the lighthouse onto the deck.

"Where did you disappear to?" Zoey stood and went to him.

"Corri took my grandfather and me out to the end of the jetty to show me how Devlins look for birds," he told her. "And while we were out there, we noticed a boat circling around between the inlet and the bay side of the light. Captain Pete's son has gone to investigate, but it looked like a fisherman."

"So, Mother, it would seem that there was no great influx of nosy reporters after all."

"Isn't that a pleasant surprise." Delia smiled.

"And while Laura's strong family resemblance certainly is noteworthy, I haven't heard a lot of speculative whispering," Georgia noted.

"That's because I told everyone in the family in advance." Delia smiled and sipped at her wine.

"What?" Zoey and Georgia both asked.

"I said, I already told everyone. I called all of my cousins over the past two weeks and told them everything. I decided that I'd be damned if I was going to waste a minute of my only son's wedding day worrying about how anyone would react to finding out about Laura. So I called them on the phone and I just figured anyone who had a problem with it could stay home."

Georgia and Zoey exchanged surprised glances.

"So?" Zoey waited for her mother to elaborate.

"So, you will notice that everyone is here except for my cousin Carolyn." Delia shrugged. "She was oh-so-shocked in an oh-so-pleased sort of way. But I don't care. It's been a beautiful wedding and a wonderful day—one totally *perfect* day. All the people I most love are here with me." She stood and tilted her wineglass in the direction of the dock, where Laura stood with Ally watching the gulls circle. "The circle is complete, children, and my cup, indeed, runneth over."

Chapter

25

"So, what's this I hear about Nicky having offered you his cabin for the night?" Zoey nuzzled closer to Ben as they danced yet one more slow dance on the patio that looked out over the inlet. In the distance the lights of the houses back on shore were just going on for the night, and the moon was just beginning to peek out of the clouds. Someone—probably India—had turned on the spotlight that now shone from the top of the lighthouse, and the pale yellow glow spilled into the bay like warm butterscotch. Zoey sighed. Everything about this day had been filled with romance, from the minute she had opened her eyes to see Ben watching her to this exact moment, when they danced together in the moonlight.

Ben sighed too. If she snuggled any closer, they wouldn't have to worry about whether or not Nick had offered to let Ben stay in the cabin that night. Ben would be tossing her over his shoulder and heading for the deck of that cabin cruiser that was tied to the nearest dock.

"Yes, my love, he did," Ben told her.

"Oh, goodie, when do we leave?"

"I think it's customary for the bride and groom to

leave first," he told her. "I think it would be considered a serious breach of etiquette for—"

She kissed him, a long, serious kiss.

"Then again, I suppose if one could slip out discreetly, so as not to be missed . . ." He nibbled at her bottom lip.

"Zoey, come on, India's waiting for you. She's ready to toss her bouquet."

Zoey looked up to see Darla standing on the deck.

"You catch it for me, Dar." Zoey smiled dreamily at Ben.

"You get your butt up here, Zoey Enright," Georgia called down to her. "If I have to stand there and play catch, you have to stand there and play catch. Besides, Mom said you have to."

"Why?" Zoey frowned.

"She said she wants to see who's next. Now come on."

"I guess we're stuck here for a while," Zoey told Ben.

"There are worse things that could happen." Ben kissed the side of her face near her ear and led her toward the lighthouse. "At least there's still some of those little fruit tarts on Darla's dessert table."

"How many of them have you had?"

"Who's counting? Darla has given gluttony a respectable name, raised it almost to the level of virtue," he confided as they walked inside the lighthouse where the party was still in full swing.

India stood on the third step holding her bouquet of white roses and palest pink lilies. She winked in Zoey's direction, and Zoey winked back.

"Nana, why is India throwing her flowers away?" Ally asked Delia. "Doesn't she want them anymore?"

"It's customary for the bride to throw her flowers to all of the unmarried women at the wedding," Delia told her, smoothing the child's hair affectionately. "Supposedly, the one who catches it will be the next one to get married."

Ally pondered how this might work while all of the single women in the group gathered at the foot of the steps. India looked around and, satisfied that all were present and accounted for, turned her back, counted to three, and tossed the bouquet.

It hit Georgia right smack in the chest.

"Wow!" Corri jumped up and down. "Georgia will get married next."

Delia laughed, watching her youngest twirl the bouquet she'd caught, knowing that Georgia's devotion to dance had left her with precious little time for a social life.

But a little romance would be good for her.

And wouldn't she make a beautiful bride someday, Delia mused. *Won't each of my girls make beautiful brides? I would suspect Zoey might actually be next, judging by the way she and Ben are panting—discreetly, of course—after each other.*

She smiled. Ben Pierce. Almost as dear to her as her own son. To think that he and Zoey were in love. Her daughter and Maureen's son . . .

"And oh, Maureen, he's grown into such a fine young man," Delia whispered to the night, "you'd be so proud. As proud as I am, of all of them."

The circle that had once held only Nick, Zoey, and Georgia had widened, and now Laura, Ally, India, Corri, Ben—and, of course, August—had stepped inside. Delia smiled with pleasure, wondering who else, as yet unknown, would someday join them. Someone for Georgia, someone for Laura . . . and maybe, a tiny voice inside her whispered, just maybe, someday, someone for me. . . .

The guests whooped and hollered as Nick withdrew his hands from beneath India's long skirt and held up her garter, then, without ceremony, tossed it directly to Ben, who caught it easily with one hand. Laughing, he caught the eye of his grandfather, who stood in the doorway with his guest for the occasion, the stalwart Pauline, who looked pleased as punch to be there.

"Does this mean that Georgia has to marry Ben?" Ally tugged at Delia's skirt.

"No, sweetheart." Delia patted her on the head, then

signaled to the photographer to keep busy. She wanted lots of pictures of this very happy day, so that someday when she was older, when she needed something to remind her, she would be able to see every bit of it again and again.

Ben had had a devil of a time explaining to Zoey that Nick's invitation to sleep in his cabin that night had not included an invitation for Ben to sleep with Nick's sister.

"I wouldn't feel right," Ben told Zoey reluctantly when they got back to shore.

"It wouldn't bother me a bit." She laughed.

"What are you going to tell your mother?"

"Hmmm. My mother." Zoey frowned. "Hmmm. You've got a point there. Could be sticky."

"How 'bout if we leave early tomorrow?" Ben suggested.

Zoey nodded. "You're supposed to come to the Devlins' for brunch in the morning, and then we'll just leave from there."

It had sounded like a good plan, but now, alone on the narrow porch overlooking the dark bay, Ben almost wished he'd been a little less honorable. He'd changed into jeans and a cotton shirt upon returning to Nick's cabin, grabbed a beer from the refrigerator, and sat himself down in one of the rocking chairs to watch the stars. Now and then something splashed out in the water, and the night cries of owls and other, unknown birds of prey echoed over the marshes. He rocked and drank his beer and reflected. Maybe it was time for that trip to a breeder of Big Dogs. For now, he wished he had already made the trip so that his Big Dog would now be lying by the rocker, sharing the night sounds and smells in this most perfect of places.

Nick Enright was a very lucky man to have such a life here on this peaceful bay, and a beautiful new wife to share it with.

Ben thought back to catching India's garter. That Nick had thrown it directly to him was, he thought, Nick's way of giving his blessing to the relationship between his sister and the man who was still, after all these years, a treasured friend. Ben smiled, happy that Nick approved. He intended to be around for a long time.

He leaned back in the chair and placed his feet upon the railing. Watching Zoey that day had been a joy. She was beautiful and animated and it made his heart ache and his chest tighten just to look at her. He could barely remember how it had felt not to have her in his life, although it hadn't been that long ago that he was in his flat in London, cursing his luck and wondering if his life would be worth living again.

Meant to be together. That's what Zoey had said about Nick and India, but the phrase had never left Ben's head. It was how he felt about her now, and from the minute he had heard her say the words, he had known it was true.

Funny, after all these years, after all the women I've known, to come home and get knocked on my butt by a girl who used to follow me through swamps to catch tadpoles. Ben laughed out loud. *That will be something to tell our children, won't it?*

And there would be children, he mused. Lots of them. They would live in a big rambling house in the country, like Delia's, and they would spend their summers in Devlin's Light, playing with their cousins. And he and Zoey would build a house like this one, and at night they'd send the kids over to their Uncle Nick's house, and he and Zoey would make love on the back porch, on nights just like this. Oh, yes, life will be wonderful, full of love and rich with laughter.

He rubbed his chin thoughtfully, and wondered when he should tell Zoey.

* * *

"Wasn't it a wonderful weekend?" Zoey cooed as she curled up next to Ben in her bed where, overhead, a soft rain made gentle taps on the skylight. "The most wonderful wedding ever."

"Wonderful." He nodded. *Almost as wonderful as ours will be.*

"And wasn't India the most beautiful bride you ever saw?" She sighed.

"Ummhmm." He ran his fingers along her forearm, a vision of Zoey draped in white lace playing in his imagination.

"And wasn't it funny when they walked into August's this morning?" She giggled. "Imagine them spending their wedding night in Captain Jon's."

"I'm still not certain I understand what Captain Jon's is."

"It's an old mansion in Devlin's Light. It was built by one of India's ancestors, Captain Jonathan Devlin, and kept in the family till a few years back, when the Devlin family gave it and the surrounding grounds to the town. The historic society maintains it and rents it out for weddings and parties and every year they have several big fund-raisers there. Fancy costume balls and stuff like that."

"And that's where India and Nick wanted to spend their wedding night?"

Zoey laughed and said, "I have the feeling there was more to it that just that, like there's some secret between her and Nick. Darla made some joke about revisiting the scene of the crime, but neither the bride nor the groom made any effort to clarify that so I let it pass."

"Is it like a hotel?"

"Nope. Just a big old house, beautifully furnished and impeccably maintained. My mother and I went to a concert there last year with August. I'm pretty sure they don't, as a rule, rent rooms out for overnight. I think it was just a concession to India, because she's administrator of the Devlin Trust, which kicks a goodly portion of the money that maintains the grounds and the building. But there's certainly no room service. That's why they came to August's for breakfast this morning." Zoey turned and stretched in Ben's arms. "And don't you love Devlin's Light?"

You, Zoey. I love you.

"Ben, I said—"

"Yes, of course. It's a wonderful place. I wouldn't mind owning a summer place there myself."

"Really?" She squirmed happily. *Yes! He is staying. Nicky was wrong, wrong, wrong.*

"Really." Ben noticed the little smile that had turned the corners of her mouth upward. "And what, may I ask, is that little grin for?"

"It's for you, Ben." She pulled him back down to her. "Now, come here and *really* give me something to smile about."

And of course, he did.

* * *

"Ben, the oddest thing happened today," Zoey told him the following Wednesday when he stopped at the bungalow with three bags of groceries and a six-pack of beer.

"What's that?" He leaned over and kissed her. It was seven-thirty at night and he had been in a meeting since four that afternoon. Just being here—just walking through that door—had taken it all away. He smiled. This was how he'd heard it was supposed to be but had never believed it.

"There was a note in my mailbox at work. My request for a week's vacation was approved." Zoey was frowning.

"Yes, I can see why you're upset," he said thoughtfully. "How dare they approve your vacation. Tell me who signed it, Zoey. I'll have them fired first thing in the morning."

"Ben, I don't remember asking for a week off."

"Oh. Well, let's take advantage of the week and go someplace special." He reached into his jacket pocket and withdrew an envelope. "Like maybe to England to watch the British Grand Prix." He opened the envelope and said, "Fancy that! I just happen to have two tickets for the Concorde."

The smile spread slowly across her face. "We're going to England . . . ?"

349

"That's what the ticket says."

"And we're going to watch a race?"

"Yup."

She frowned. "You're not driving in this race, are you?"

"No, no." He laughed and folded her in his arms, swayed with her slightly to the tune on the classic rock station on the radio. "Even if I wanted to, I could not. But I do know a few of the drivers, and it will be fun to see some old friends."

"Are you sad that you're not driving?"

"Yes. Of course I am. I really love the sport, Zoey. Maybe not as much as you love your cooking show"—he earned a jab in the ribs—"but I love it. I love the cars and the camaraderie, I love the noise and the speed. I even miss the smells of the track . . . exhaust and expensive cigars and gasoline."

"You miss the smell of exhaust and gasoline?" she asked incredulously. "Well, we could always take you out to Interstate 95 down there by the Philadelphia airport a few times a week and let you inhale the fumes from the tractor trailers as they go screaming by."

"It's not the same." He laughed again.

"What, gas fumes are not gas fumes?"

"Nope. Race cars use special gasoline."

"What's different about it?"

"It's specially formulated for high performance, no nitro, and the oxygen content is limited to a certain percentage. Like everything connected with the sport, the regulations are very specific."

"Who regulates it?"

"The FIA World Council is the legislative body for Formula One racing. They make the rules and develop standards. They determine the specifications for tires, for example, and how wide the cars have to be."

"Why would they care if one car is wider than another?" She poked behind him into one of the grocery bags and said, "Oh, we're having steak?"

"Just another form of high-performance fuel." He took the package from her hand and placed it on the counter. "Here"—he handed her one of the brown paper bags—"try to make a salad without slicing off one of your fingers. Now, to answer your question, the width of the car will have an impact on the cornering speeds. FIA wanted to reduce the cornering speeds slightly as a safety factor—the faster you take the corners, the more likely you are to lose control."

"Is that how you had your accident? Going around a corner too quickly?"

"No. One of my brake discs disintegrated and locked my right front wheel. I lost control and slammed into a wall."

"I didn't know that brake discs could disintegrate." She wondered how the brakes on her little red number were holding up.

"Under normal conditions, they don't. But keep in mind that these cars run at average speeds of one hundred twenty to one hundred thirty miles per hour for a sustained period of time. You might do fifty laps on a three-mile track. That's one hundred fifty miles, Zoey, at a very high rate of speed. And you're running for an hour or better, with just a few pit stops—the fewer the better, since they cost you valuable seconds."

"Seconds? Don't you mean minutes?"

"I mean seconds. A really good pit crew can get you in and out in maybe eight or nine seconds. That's changing tires, refueling, everything."

"That's hard to believe." She shook her head.

"That's why the pit crews are so important, why each man has to be the best at what he does. There's a lot of money at stake here, Zoey."

"You mean when you win a race?"

"Not just the individual races. You get points for every race—ten for winning, the runner-up gets six, the third-place driver gets four, fourth place gets three, fifth place gets two, and the number six finisher gets one. They are tallied throughout the season, and the driver who has accumulated the most points at the end of the racing season is the world champion for that year."

"What's the most points you ever got in a race?"

"Three. At Monte Carlo last year. And they were hard won. That race is run on the narrow streets of the city, with tiny turns and spots where it's almost impossible to get your speed built up before you have to make a hairpin turn. It's a fun race for the spectators, and of course, it's Monte Carlo, with all its glamour and mystique. But it's a devil of a run, and I was lucky to finish in fourth place."

"You miss it," she stated simply, and an alarm began to ring inside her head. She tried swatting at it mentally to turn it off, but it wouldn't go away. His eyes took on a sort of gleam when he spoke of the races he had driven, of his old life, that was becoming increasingly difficult to ignore.

Clearly, racing was in his blood. But was she?

"I miss it every day," he was saying. "But I can't change what is. I don't see my ankle making a full recovery. Sometimes I think it's fine, and then it sort of locks up, unexpectedly. You can't have that happen when you're screaming around a track at a hundred twenty miles per hour. If you don't kill yourself, you'll be damned lucky if you don't kill someone else. It simply isn't worth the risk."

Zoey turned on the sink and rinsed the lettuce, then tore it into small pieces. So. He couldn't go back to racing if he wanted to. She wondered how badly he wanted to, but didn't ask. It made a difference somehow, that he was there, stayed there, because he had no choice. She wondered what would happen if the choice was his to make. Part of her didn't want to know.

"So, no, I won't be driving again, but I intend to stay close to the sport. And it will be great to see some of my old friends again. I can't wait to introduce you to Tony. He'll be going with us to Silverstone, which is near

Towcester, Northamptonshire, for the race. You'll like Tony, by the way. He's quite the character. He was the first friend I made when I came to England for graduate studies."

"Does he still race?"

"No, no. He, too, was forced to quit following a bad accident that made him stop and count his blessings. But he'll never be out of the sport completely, either. We've talked for years about going into business together someday, you know. Recently he's been looking into several possibilities. When I spoke with him some weeks ago, he hinted that he has some new venture he wants to talk to me about." Ben laughed and slid the slab of beef onto the broiler pan. "Could be just about anything. Who knows what he's come up with?"

A chill passed through Zoey and she shook it off, refusing to acknowledge it. Not now. Later, there would be time. . . .

"We'll have a wonderful vacation together, I promise." He turned and smiled at her. "You'll love the whole race experience. It's fast, it's loud, and it's fun."

"Will this be the first race where you've been a spectator, not a participant?"

"Yes." He turned back to the stove and fiddled with the broiler switch. "And yes, it will be difficult for me not to be driving. Very difficult. But that's how it is."

Later, after Ben had fallen asleep, Zoey thought back to his words. Having herself taken so many years to find her place in this world, her heart hurt for Ben, who, having found his place, was now denied that which he loved to do. It was sweet of him to want to take her to this big English race with him, and to introduce her to his friends. It should be a fun holiday—it had been years since she had been to London, one of her favorite cities for shopping, and she mentally made a list of all the boutiques and little shops she would have to check out before they came home. She had always loved London's pace, the pomp of Buckingham Palace, the extravagance that was Harrod's, even the imagined sense of eerie foreboding she had experienced in the Tower of London. It would be a treat to spend a week there—a week, she reminded herself, she would be spending with Ben.

Then why—she twisted in his arms slowly, so as not to awaken him—did she feel so uneasy?

Chapter
26
~

"Ben, where are you going?" Zoey turned in the small front seat of the sporty tan Jaguar Tony had left for him at the airport for Ben to make the drive between London and Northamptonshire, where the British Grand Prix would run in two days. "The sign for Towcester pointed that way."

"Just a little detour, my dear." Ben glanced in the rearview mirror to make certain that no car had emerged from one of those little hidden driveways, thinking to pass him on this narrow road. Seeing no other cars, he eased into the left turn, whistling a happy tune. There was something absolutely wonderful about speeding along a country road in a spectacular car, on a superb summer day, with a dazzling woman at your side. He smiled. Sometimes life was as good as it could possibly get.

"Slow down," Zoey told him. "I'd like to see a little of the scenery."

"You can do all the sight-seeing you want on the way back."

"I thought the race wasn't till Sunday."

"Right."

"Then why are we flying through the English country-side like a couple of whippets?"

"We're supposed to be at Tony's in time for tea."

"Now's a fine time to tell me. I could have changed into something less wrinkled at the airport." She frowned. Why do men always overlook little things like that when they make plans? Had she known they'd be making a social call, she would have worn something other than the pale green linen suit, which, after hours of traveling, looked like she'd found it under the bed.

"You look fine, sweetheart. Beautiful."

She didn't feel beautiful. She felt travel worn and travel weary, and had spent the past several hours dueling with a tight edginess that had settled under her rib cage. As much as she longed to spend time here with Ben, something had set her instincts on alert. This was *his* territory, and she didn't know how strong the pull might be.

She leaned back against the seat and told herself to concentrate on the scenery as it zipped by. Fields edged in stone walls, randomly set, picturesque churches and neat, tiny towns, spacious estates surrounded by mani-cured grounds—all flew past in a blur of shapes and colors.

Ben slowed as they entered a small town with rows of stone town houses lining both sides of the street. A small marketplace with several magazine-perfect shops—or *shoppes*, as several of the signs declared—outlined the square in the middle of town, and a lovely old stone church and vicarage defined the outermost limits of the village.

"Pretty place," Zoey told him.

"Very." He nodded, and accelerated just slightly as he took the soft turn in the road onto a straightaway.

A mile or so down the road, he pointed to an old stone house that sat back a bit from the road and was surrounded by gardens and told her, "J. D. Borders, the rock singer, and his family live there," as they whizzed by.

"I'm sure it was lovely," Zoey grumbled, "had I been able to see it."

"I promise, on the way back, I won't even take the car out of second gear. I'm just anxious to see my friend, that's all. I'm sorry, Zoey. I will make it up to you on the return trip."

Twenty minutes later, Ben made a slow right turn up a narrow, tree-lined lane.

"How much farther?" Zoey asked.

"We're here."

"We're where?"

"At Tony's."

"Where's his house?"

"About another quarter mile up the lane."

"Tell me more about this Tony person."

"Tony Chapman and I went to graduate school together. He was majoring in engineering, I was majoring in business. We roomed together, became the best of friends. He was the one who introduced me to the racing. We've worked pit crews together, we've test-driven cars together." Ben smiled. "We've even talked of owning our own cars someday, maybe even having our own team."

"But not to drive . . ."

"No. We would build."

"Build the cars?"

He nodded.

"Doesn't that take a lot of money?"

"Tons."

"Well, if it's not too personal to ask, do you have tons of money?"

"When I turned twenty-one, I inherited the money my grandfather had set aside for my mother. I invested it well—acting as my own broker, I am pleased to say— and that money paid for my cars. Of course, I had sponsors to back me financially as well. I don't know of anyone who could completely fund their own cars without a few sponsors." He broke into a grin. "Except maybe Tony."

"Is he terribly wealthy?"

Ben merely pointed to the large stone house that rose majestically from behind the trees. "Stowe Manor," he said simply.

"I've seen that house before. In magazines!" Zoey leaned forward.

"Tony's sister is a fashion photographer. She often uses the estate for her shoots."

"It's beautiful!" Zoey exclaimed. "And look at that fountain! Wow! A real English country manor house! Wait till I tell Mom!"

Ben came to a stop in front of the house and turned off the engine. Almost immediately the wide front door opened and a tall, lanky man with wavy brown hair pulled back into a short ponytail stepped out. Ben was out of the car in a flash, and Zoey watched as Ben greeted his old friend.

"Zoey"—Ben opened her car door—"please say hello to Anthony Chapman, the twelfth earl of Stowe."

"An earl," she repeated as Tony offered her his hand and helped her out. "What do you call an *earl?*"

"Tony," he told her. "You call me Tony. And I'll call you magnificent." He kissed her hand, his eyes twinkling. "You're far too beautiful for this rake. You should be with me."

Zoey laughed, charmed by his easygoing way and flirtatious manner. The twelfth earl of Stowe was adorable, with baby blue eyes and deep dimples.

"Leave your things." Tony took both their arms. "Mrs. Bridges has been holding tea, waiting for you, and you know how she hates to serve a late tea, Ben."

"Mrs. Bridges is still with you?"

"Could you imagine this place running without her? Mrs. Bridges is a distant relative of my mother's and has been with the family since, oh, roughly seventeen twenty-two or thereabouts," Tony confided to Zoey.

"We've offered her a handsome retirement on several occasions, but she's convinced that it is she, and only she, who holds Stowe Manor together. She firmly believes that should she turn her back for more than ten minutes, the entire estate would collapse. And the truth of the matter is that she's most likely right. She's like a little army drill sergeant, our Mrs. Bridges is, and we wouldn't have things any other way."

Tony led them into a wide hall with black and white marble squares on the floor and rich wood paneling on the walls. The eyes from rows and rows of what surely must have been family portraits followed them down the hall. They passed through a maze of rooms until they reached a sunny sitting room overlooking the expansive grounds.

"Well, then, and it's about time." The formidable white-haired woman wore a blue and white polka dot dress that fell two inches below her knees and sturdy sensible oxford shoes, and she actually *clucked* as they entered the room. "You have never been on time for tea in this house before and it's no surprise to me that you're late today, Bennett Pierce."

"Ah, Mrs. Bridges." Ben embraced her fondly, and the stern folds of the woman's face softened in spite of herself. "You remembered. I'm flattered."

"It's not meant for flattery." She shooed him away even as the smile touched her lips. "Your scones are getting cold and so's your tea."

"I'd cross the ocean for your scones and tea"—he kissed her forehead—"cold or otherwise."

"Sit down, then, and I'll pour you a cup." She pointed to a small settee. "But you won't have it until you introduce me to your lady friend, you ill-mannered young pup."

"Mrs. Bridges, this is Zoey Enright." He took Zoey's hand. "Zoey, this is Mrs. Bridges."

"I'm pleased to meet you," Zoey told her.

"Come sit here, miss"—Mrs. Bridges pulled a small lady's chair forward and gestured to Zoey—"and leave those two be. Heaven knows neither one of them's fit company for a lady like you."

Zoey sat in the chair without being told twice, sticking her tongue out at Ben as she did so.

"And you, sir, may sit there." Mrs. Bridges indicated where Tony should sit.

Amused by and apparently accustomed to her dictatorial manner, Tony sat without protest.

"And where is Miss Sibyl?" Mrs. Bridges asked.

"I don't think she was joining us. I think she's working," Tony told her.

"And your other guests?"

"Won't arrive until this evening."

Having established that there would be no more late arrivals, Mrs. Bridges poured the tea with little additional ceremony. She served the tea sandwiches, then left the room to return with a tray of scones fresh from the oven and a porcelain plate of fancy little tea cakes, which she set upon the table. With a wink in Ben's direction, she left the room at a dignified, if someone slow, pace.

"Wow. She is something." Zoey laughed.

"Runs Stowe Manor with an iron fist." Tony grinned. "And I don't know what I'd do without her. She keeps us all on track."

"So, bring me up to date on all the news," Ben said, and the two men slipped into a conversation filled with names that meant nothing to Zoey. She didn't mind, however, having nibbled on watercress sandwiches and tiny confections before pouring herself another cup of tea, which she took out onto the verandah that ran across the back of the handsome country house.

Wait till I tell Mother. She smiled to herself. *And Georgia—wait till she finds out that I met a real British earl. She should be so lucky—she has no social life anymore.* Thinking about Georgia's lack of a life banished the smile from her face. She worried about her little sister and her total dedication to dancing. *What will happen to Georgia when the day comes that she can no longer dance? She has nothing else in her life that I can see . . . no real friends that I know of, except for Lee Banyon.*

Zoey followed the stone steps down to a path that led toward the grounds that spread out before her, sipping thoughtfully at her tea, wondering just how much company Lee was these days, having lost his longtime companion to AIDS a few months back.

The path led through a gate over which white roses spilled like gallons of paint from an endless can. Letting herself into the garden she wandered aimlessly, pleased to find that she recognized so many of the flowers that lined the beds and wound around the paths like rivers of color. She bent to touch a columbine of palest pink, a tall spike of deep rose veronica, a tumble of something magenta that grew from fat leaves of deep green.

"That's geranium," a voice from behind announced, "or did you know that?"

Zoey stood and turned. A slight young woman wearing slim black jeans and a cropped yellow T-shirt, large round framed glasses, and bare feet had come quietly into the garden.

"No. I wouldn't have recognized it as geranium. The geraniums we have back home look nothing like that."

"I thought they might be new to you, the way you were looking at them so curiously." She stepped forward and extended her hand. "I'm Sibyl, Tony's sister."

"I'm Zoey Enright. I'm a friend of Ben Pierce's."

"Yes. I know. I just saw him inside. He and Tony are deep into conversation, so I thought you might like some company."

"That was very thoughtful. Thank you."

"Would you like a tour of the grounds while Tony and Ben discuss business? They're apt to go at it for a while, what with the new engine on the boards and all." Sibyl smiled. "You know."

Actually, she didn't know, but Zoey let it pass. She'd find out later. Right now, she wanted to get a closer look at that geranium. And those lavender-colored roses along the back fence were like nothing she'd ever seen.

Beyond the garden was another fountain, and a lake with water lilies and swans. There was lots to see here. Ben could have all the time he wanted with his old friend. It was a perfect late afternoon, a lovely time for a stroll through the grounds of an ancient estate in the English countryside.

"So, Sibyl, tell me all about Stowe Manor. . . ." Zoey smiled to herself, knowing that Delia would grill her for details once they arrived back home, and she'd better have the answers to all of the questions her mother was certain to ask.

* * *

The British Grand Prix has run on the Silverstone Circuit since 1948, and only seventeen times in all those years had the race been run on a track other than the former airfield in Northamptonshire. Over the years there have been modifications to the course, tightening this corner and lengthening that, adding a new complex of curves—a right-hand turn here, a double of left turns there, all efforts to slow the cars down.

"But I thought that the whole idea behind the Grand Prix was to go fast." Zoey had said as Ben showed off the track upon their arrival early on Sunday morning. "To see who could go fastest, to win."

"Well, the object is to win, certainly," he had told her, "but there's a strategy involved. Being fastest all the way around the track is more likely to get you to the morgue than the winners' circle."

"I don't understand."

"Look, here." He took her hand and walked her to the fence between the track and spectators' area and pointed across the track. "There's a series of curves there—they're called, for the record, Bridge, Priory, and Luffield—"

"They give names to the curves on the track?"

"Yes. Now, picture, if you can, coming into that first curve at, oh, let's say, one hundred and twenty miles an hour, then moving into Priory without slowing down."

Her jaw dropped contemplating it. "You'd die."

"Highly probable. But if you reduce the speed, you lessen the chance of a crash. There are far too many vehicles on the track during a race to risk the kind of accident that can result from driving at too high a speed for a sustained period of time. So they have modified the circuits to force the drivers to drive a smarter, more thoughtful race. You have to time your stops more carefully, you have to maneuver more intelligently."

"And here I was thinking it was merely a pedal to the metal game," she mused.

"I think that's what most people believe." He tugged at her arm. "Let's catch up with Tony, Zoey. I see someone he's been wanting to talk with."

Zoey smiled a smile she didn't really feel. If Ben took off with Tony, that would mean that she would get stuck playing buddy-buddy with Tony's date for the weekend, Greta, a Dutch model whose only real interest appeared to be keeping track of how many times her picture was taken and whether or not anyone else in the crowd was wearing the same hat. Zoey figured the hat—being black and white straw sporting a blood red feather flat across the brim—to be one of a kind, and found herself shrugging indifferently every time Greta asked, in her thick accent, "Did he just take my picture? Was my mouth open? Is my makeup all right?" which seemed to be the outer limits as far as her command of the language was concerned.

Zoey strolled through the well-dressed crowd, marveling at the number of beautiful young women, all fashionably attired, in attendance. She had recognized several high-fashion models, a number of movie actors and musicians, and several international celebrities. *Mom would get a kick out of this,* she mused as she passed a group that included Meryl Webb, a British actress who had starred in the film version of one of Delia's books, and several aging stage actors whose names Zoey could not recall. She wandered back to where she had last seen Ben, only to find him deep in conversation with Tony and an older man who appeared to be drawing some sort of diagram on a small notepad. *I wonder what all that is about,* Zoey thought as she walked toward him, trailed by Greta, who was keeping an ever watchful eye out for the press.

At her approach the older man smiled and closed the notebook, gesturing toward Tony as he slid the slim leather book into his pocket.

"Ladies." he smiled gallantly.

Tony made the introductions. "Zoey, Greta, this is an old friend of Ben's and mine, Darryl Beckett. Darryl used to design for Ferrari."

"And who do you design for now, Mr. Beckett?" Zoey had asked.

Beckett smiled broadly. "A new company. One you will, undoubtedly, be hearing a great deal about in the near future." To Ben and Tony he said, "I'll have that chat with Nigel Vale, gentlemen, and I'll get back to you within the week with his decision. Ladies, it's been a pleasure." He tipped his hat and disappeared into the crowd.

Ben and Tony exchanged a look of satisfaction, and Zoey couldn't help but think that there was more going on than just old friends catching up on old news. A shot of apprehension shot through her.

"It's almost time for the drivers to come onto the track," Ben said, taking her elbow. "Let's get some good fence position, and I'll tell you who's who and what to watch for during the race."

The overwhelming impression that Zoey took away with her from Silverstone was that car racing had to be the loudest sport on the face of the earth. Long after they had left the track, she could still hear the high-pitched whine of the engines as they streaked past in a blur, one amazing, incredible machine after another.

"I guess you really have to be familiar with the sport to be able to follow the strategy," she remarked later to Ben as they strolled into a tent that had been set up on the grounds for an after-race meet-and-greet. "I guess you have to know what to look for. Everyone's talking about

WONDERFUL YOU

the winner having driven a brilliant race, but it still just looked like a lot of fast driving to me."

Ben laughed. "The winner—Jacques Villeneuve is his name, by the way, he's Canadian—drove smart, but he got a bit of luck there, too, when Michael Schumacher's wheel bearing failed and forced him out. That Ferrari was a big favorite coming into the race."

Ben seemed to know almost everyone in the crowd, and was greeted with welcoming slaps on the back from the men and kisses from—to Zoey's mind—far too many women, who all seemed to have names like Ursula and Luciana and Astrid and who wore dresses that were Spandex versions of what might pass for a tank top in the States. Waiters in summer white passed silver trays of champagne and spring water and delicate sandwiches of watercress and cucumber. Wondering what Mrs. Bridges would have to say about the propriety of serving bubbly with tea sandwiches and all the while watching the posing and preening of the women—and some of the men, she did not fail to notice—Zoey wandered a bit through the crowd of drivers and celebrities and politicians, all of whom appeared to know each other well.

Tony touched her shoulder. "So, what did you think of your first Grand Prix?"

"It was loud." She laughed. "But exciting."

"Yes, to both." He gave her a pat on the small of her back and stopped a waiter, asking Zoey, "Champagne, or perhaps some of that sparkling water you Americans seem to like so much?"

"Water would be fine, thank you." She sipped gratefully for a moment, the warm English morning having eased into a hot English afternoon.

"Is this your first time in England?"

"No, I've been several times before, a few times with my mother, twice with my sister."

"Ah, right. Ben told me that your mother was a writer. And that you are a celebrity in your own right back in America. We don't get Ben's television channel here, though Mrs. Bridges was working on him after breakfast.

365

She rather fancies the idea of seeing the latest merchandise without having to leave her apartment to do so."

She nodded. "It's an interesting concept."

"Ben seems keen on it. Of course, we do know that Ben's keen on you, as well. And I can't say that I blame him. You're a delightful woman, Zoey Enright. Are there more like you at home?"

She laughed. "Actually, I have a sister"—she corrected herself—"*two* sisters."

"And you left them both at home?" He appeared crushed.

"Left who at home?" Ben joined them.

"Zoey was just telling me that she has two sisters."

"Two beautiful sisters," Ben told him. "And the older sister—probably just your age, Tony—looks a great deal like Zoey."

"Dark hair, gorgeous face and smile, long legs . . ." Tony pondered the possibilities.

"That would be Laura," Ben told him.

"And you left her behind?"

"I thought perhaps it would be safer, with Greta on the prowl. Nope, if you want to meet the fair Laura, you'll just have to travel to Maryland, Tony."

"Hmmm. Maryland, you say? I believe we have a cousin who lives in Virginia. Maryland is not beyond the realm of possibilities. And for someone who looks like your Zoey, it would be worth the trip." He grinned. "After we get Chapman-Pierce off and running, of course."

"Chapman-Pierce?" Zoey's eyebrows rose.

"Oh, surely Ben's told you about the company we're starting?" Tony patted Ben on the back, and Ben appeared to sputter. "To build engines?"

"Ah, Zoey, remember I told you that Tony and I had talked about going into business together."

"I remember you mentioning it in an offhand sort of manner. I don't remember you saying that there was a company." Her stomach turned. She did not like the sound of this.

"We have the design for an engine that will be so technologically innovative, everyone will want one," Tony whispered in her ear. "We're working on something that will keep the engine cool at speeds up to two hundred miles per hour."

"Well, that does sound like something everyone will want to have." Zoey tried to be light, all the while watching Ben's face. "And what role will the Pierce, of Chapman-Pierce, be playing?"

"Ben will be setting up the business from the ground floor."

"What Tony means is that I've agreed to help him put together the team he needs to run the business, to help locate the accounting and marketing staff, to make sure the business gets off to the right start."

"Do you know how to do that?"

Ben nodded. "Tony and I have been discussing this for the past two days. I already know who I'd like to bring on board to balance out the team."

Tony slapped Ben on the back affectionately. "This will be the biggest news in racing. We'll produce the best engine that can be built. And we'll be in business together, just like we've talked about for the past eight years or so." He winked at Zoey. "This is one of those dream come true things for me, Zoey. I'm glad that Ben brought you over this weekend, so that you can share in the fun."

"The fun?" She raised her eyebrows. Did he think she was having fun, watching her own dreams go down the drain?

"We're going to have a press conference tomorrow out at Stowe Manor to launch our new venture, since Ben is here and all that. Oh, look, Ben, there's that bloke from that new racing magazine. I think I want a word with him. Excuse me."

Zoey and Ben stood silently in the wake of Tony's zippy departure.

Finally, Zoey said, "So. Tell me your version of this new venture that I'm fortunate to be here to witness."

"It's pretty much as Tony said. He finally found an engineer who, he believes, can build this engine."

"Why didn't you tell me before?"

"Well, I did tell you that we had talked about going into business together someday. Of course, I didn't realize that *someday* was so close at hand. When he called last month, he did tell me that he had something to show me, but at the time I had no idea of what he had up his sleeve."

"The engine design?" She asked.

"Yes. Zoey, I had no idea—" Ben began, and she interrupted him.

"What did he think you were doing in the States, Ben, that he thought you could just drop your job and walk away?"

"I don't know that Tony really understood that I was working for my grandfather, Zoey. I think he thought I was on an extended holiday while my ankle healed. Which is partially true. Delaney asked me to come on board with him until I was ready to go back to racing, Zoey. It wasn't intended to be a permanent job. I thought you understood that."

"And you're going to do this? Come back to England to work with Tony?"

"Zoey"—he sighed—"this is something we've talked about doing for years."

"When were you going to tell me?" She frowned, fighting the urge to cry.

"As soon as the details were straightened out."

"You could have mentioned it last night, Ben. We were together all night." *I am going to handle this in an adult fashion,* she told herself. *I will be mature about this. . . .*

"We weren't really talking last night, if you remember. . . ."

"We could have been. You could have told me." *I will not whine, I will not whine. . . .*

"I was going to. But the moonlight came in through the window and you were wearing that little slip thing. . . ." He leaned closer, nuzzling her ear.

Zoey frowned, and he stopped. Bad timing. She wanted answers.

"Zoey, I owe you an apology for not having discussed this with you sooner. Tony just moved far more quickly on this whole thing than I ever expected him to. I thought it would take him a year to pull this together. As it turns out, he's had things outlined for months. I just wasn't aware how far he'd gone with it."

"You're supposed to be his partner and you weren't aware of what he was doing?" *I will not be bitchy, I will not be bitchy. . . .*

"He thought he'd surprise me. Zoey, Tony knows how much I love to race, and he knows how disappointed I am that I will not drive competitively again."

"Is that final? Has anyone told you that?"

"The doctors I've been seeing back in the States are the best we could find. They have all told me that my ankle's mobility will never be one hundred percent. But more importantly, *I* know it. I can feel it. Sometimes my ankle almost feels as if it's sticking, somehow, that it's reluctant to bend. I could never get behind the wheel of a race car knowing that my ankle could freeze up and endanger the lives of everyone on the track. I don't need anyone to tell me that I can't drive again, Zoey. I know that I can't."

"I'm so sorry, Ben. I know how much you love it." She turned to him and put her arms around him.

"Well, it's the way the cards fell, Zoey." He swayed with her slightly. "And besides, it's not the end of the world. I love driving, yes, but nowhere near as much as I love you. And if it hadn't been for the accident, I wouldn't have been available to come home when Delaney asked me to and I wouldn't have ended up at the HMP to find you again. All in all, it's not a bad trade-off. And if you want to know the truth, I'm beginning to think that maybe I am getting a little too old for this."

"Ben, do you really?" She bit her lip.

"Yes. I really do. I was thirty-three in May, you know."

"No. I mean, you said you loved me." She leaned back and watched his face. "Do you really love me?"

"Yes, Zoey. I really love you. More than anything on the face of this earth. Didn't you know?"

"I wanted you to. I hoped that you would. I dreamed that someday you would. . . ."

"One of my goals in this life is to make your dreams come true, Zoey. We'll start with that one." He kissed her. "What else might you be longing for?"

She forced her fears into that small place she reserved for things she could not deal with at the moment, and she tugged on his lapel. "Take me back to the hotel, and I'll show you."

"We're on our way."

Later, she told herself as she watched Ben drift into slumber. *Later, I'll think about what all this means. Later, I'll worry about when he will leave and when we will see each other and I'll deal with it. Right now, I want these hours and I want his love and I want him to know how much I love him. And later, I'll worry about what comes next.*

Chapter

27

Delaney O'Connor cursed softly while he fiddled with the tangled cord of his telephone. *They can put a man on the moon, why can't they make a telephone cord that doesn't wrap itself into a little plastic ball?*

"Pauline . . ." he grumbled as she entered the room on quiet feet.

She smiled and removed one end of the cord from the socket that fit into the handset, let the cord dangle free until it was straight, then plugged it back in. Without so much as looking at him, she placed a stack of mail on the center of his desk and said, "Peter called while you were on your last call and wanted to know if he could move up the two o'clock meeting. He's running a bit late today."

Delaney responded with a sort of half grunt, half nod, and Pauline glanced at her watch.

"Ben will be here in ten minutes. Shall I have coffee brought in for him?"

"Please." Delaney nodded and sank into his chair. "And thank you, Pauline. I don't know what I'd do without you."

Pauline smiled her ever patient *neither do I* smile and left the room as quietly as she had entered it.

Delaney managed to remain in his chair for almost three entire minutes before the tension wound tightly around his gut and compelled him to walk it off. He grabbed his cane and began to pace.

For the twentieth time, he flipped open the newspaper that had been express-mailed to him from his London office just the week before. The photo at the top of page five had caused the initial onset of restlessness that had kept him awake every night since he'd first seen it. The camera had captured two handsome men, a beautiful dark-haired woman between them, leaning against the fence right before the start of the British Grand Prix. It was the caption that had stirred such unease within him.

"Anthony Chapman, the Twelfth Earl of Stowe, and former Grand Prix driver Bennett Pierce met at Silverstone on Sunday to announce the formation of Chapman-Pierce Motors, a new venture which will manufacture engines specially designed to hold up under the rigorous strains of Formula One racing. It is rumored that Nigel Vale, formerly of Ferrari, has accepted the challenge of designing what is being touted as the engine that will set the standard on the European circuits into the next millennium. Earl Chapman is pictured above with Mr. Pierce and Miss Zoey Enright, of the United States, who was the guest of Mr. Pierce at Silverstone."

The London *Times* had run an article in the business section speculating on how much of the new company's stock might be made available by the principals, and how much it might sell for. The head of Delaney's London office had called him immediately upon seeing the article, and had followed the call with a fax. Delaney had read it over and over, wondering how long it would be until Ben himself told him the news. He had felt a perverse sort of pleasure when Ben called him the previous Friday, upon his return to the States, and had asked if he could speak with him first thing on Monday morning.

Well, you knew when he came back that it wasn't going to be permanent, Delaney reminded himself as he stared at the shifting clouds in an open sky through the plate glass window.

I just didn't expect him to leave so soon.

Delaney sighed heavily and turned to the portrait of his daughter that hung on the wall behind the sofa. *I tried, sweetheart. I tried.*

"Ben is here, Delaney." Pauline told him from the doorway.

"Send him in."

"Delaney!" Ben entered the room and filled it with his enthusiasm.

"Son. It's good to see you." He politely shook Ben's hand and offered him a seat with a gesture of his hand. "How's the foot doing?"

"As well as it's going to do, I guess." Ben shrugged. "It appears that it's reached maximum medical improvement. The doctors don't expect that full range of motion will ever return."

"I'm sorry to hear that, son. I know how you wanted to return to racing."

"I'm probably lucky that it's healed as well as it has. And as for racing, well, I have to accept the fact that those days are behind me now."

"Well then." Delaney cleared his throat, wondering how to play this. "Perhaps you'll be looking for permanent employment now. How would you feel about taking over as president of the HMP? All the reports since you started there have been positive, Ben. Sales have increased, our viewing audience has expanded. The ideas you've suggested have all been solid ones—offering credit cards to members to charge directly with us, bringing in more celebrity endorsed products . . . and those interactive segments have been very successful, I am told."

"Thank you, Delaney. I've enjoyed every day that I've

spent in your employ. I don't think I expected to, but I can honestly say I've enjoyed working at the HMP. It's a challenging concept, the market is totally without limit. There's no end to where you can go with it. And you've some really fine people working there . . . from the producers to the warehouses."

"I had heard you had tried out just about every position in every department. Drove the managers crazy." Delaney chuckled in spite of the sense of disappointment that was welling up inside him.

"It was time well spent." Ben smiled. "I learned a little about what everyone did. I even took some orders over the phone. It was good experience for me to see how it all fit together."

"Like the pieces of a puzzle," Delaney nodded, "or of an engine . . ."

He slid the newspaper across the desk, and without glancing down, Ben knew what story it told.

"I wanted to tell you myself, Delaney. I came here this morning to tell you," Ben said softly. "I'm sorry. It didn't occur to me that this would have made the papers so soon, though with Tony involved, I should have expected it."

"This Chapman fellow—"

"—is an old friend. For years we talked about doing something like this, but I had never really given much thought to it. I always figured when I retired, we'd sit down and talk about it, Tony and I. After my accident, he assumed I'd not be returning to driving, so he proceeded to move ahead. I have to admit it came as a bit of a surprise when I found out he'd lined up this whole thing." Ben tried to laugh, but it sounded hollow, even to his ears.

"Which was when . . ."

"When Zoey and I arrived at his house on the Friday before last." Ben locked his fingers together in his lap and stared at them with more intensity than they warranted.

"Ah, yes. Zoey." Delaney nodded.

Ben met his grandfather's eyes and for the first time since Ben had entered the room, Delaney found reason to be hopeful.

"Now, will you be taking my best sales host from me, Ben?" Delaney tried to inject a light tone into the conversation.

"Zoey?" He frowned, the lines deepening in his brow and around his mouth. "No. She isn't inclined to leave the HMP, Delaney."

"I take it you have asked her, then?"

"I did. Zoey really likes what she does, Delaney. She's exceptionally good at it, and she's happy. She isn't ready to give it up. And I can't blame her. I *don't* blame her." The lines seemed to deepen, and he asked, as if intending to joke, "You wouldn't be planning on expanding the HMP to the British Isles, would you?"

"Not in the foreseeable future." Delaney shook his head. "So, when are you planning to take your leave, Ben?"

"As soon as you feel you can let me go."

"I've no intentions of holding you, son. You came here as a favor to me, and I'll always be grateful for the time you gave me." He glanced out the window. It simply hurt too much to look at the boy's face. He loved him too much.

"Delaney, I was more than happy to be here when you needed me. There's really no way that I can ever repay all you've given me over the years. I don't know if I've ever even really thanked you." Ben leaned closer to the desk. "But I'm thanking you now. I'm grateful for all the years you cared for me when I was having a hard time caring for anyone, including myself. I'm grateful to you for somehow knowing that I would never be whole until I came back to Westboro. I'm thankful to you for finding Zoey for me, though I have no idea how you managed to do that. I'm grateful to you for bringing me back, and I'm grateful to you for letting me leave."

"I'd keep you with me if I could, son." Delaney fought the lump in his throat.

"If you asked me to stay, I would."

"I know that, son. And it's not a good enough reason to stick around. You have to find your own way, Ben. If going into business with Tony Chapman is what you need to make you happy, then that's what you have to do."

"It's what I want. I mean, it's what I wanted. . . ." Ben looked thoughtful for a long moment. "It's what we planned on. . . ."

"Then it's what you must do. A man has to follow his dreams, Ben," Delaney said softly.

"Thank you for understanding that, and for supporting my decision."

Both men rose from their seats at the same moment. Delaney leaned on his cane and walked around the desk to where his grandson stood.

"You'll always have my understanding and my support, son," Delaney told him, then added, "and my love."

"I love you, too, Delaney." Ben embraced his grandfather and held on for a long time.

"Well, then," Delaney said, when he could finally speak. "Don't be a stranger."

"Don't worry." Ben patted him on the back, "I'll be a regular visitor to Lannings Corner. I'm leaving the company, but I'll be seeing you on a regular basis. And besides, I'm not giving up Zoey."

"I'm glad to hear that, son. She's one in a million." Delaney walked him toward the door.

"She certainly is." Ben paused before he walked through it. "I'll give you a call before I leave."

"When do you think that will be?"

"As soon as you can replace me."

"I'll send Peter down to fill in for the time being, so that should not be a problem." Delaney hung on to Ben's elbow for just a moment longer. "When would you like to leave?"

"I'd like to leave by next week, then, if you're sure." Ben took the old man's hand. "Tony found a building he'd like to lease for the factory. He wants to produce all the parts right there in England."

"You wouldn't be looking for investors, now, would you?" Delaney asked.

"I think Tony's got that covered, but I'll ask him. I don't know if any company ever has enough starting capital. Maybe we can work out something, if you're sure you're interested."

"I definitely am interested." Delaney nodded.

"Then we'll be in touch." Ben paused, then hugged his grandfather again, briefly this time, but it was still a hug.

"Have a safe trip." Delaney called as Ben headed for the elevator. "And Ben . . ."

"Yes?"

"If you ever want your old job back, all you need to do is ask."

* * *

"You can still change your mind, you know. It isn't too late," Ben whispered in Zoey's ear.

"You have the damnedest timing, Ben Pierce." She leaned back against the pillows, wrapping her legs around him to take him with her.

"I thought I'd wait for a weak moment." He nibbled on her ear.

"I have no weak moments." She nipped at his chin. "At least, as far as that particular conversation is concerned. And you're wasting time."

"Oh, a bit anxious, are we?" His brows slid together in a frown. "You know, it really isn't ladylike to be quite so insistent, Zoey. As a matter of fact, I think—"

Whatever it was that Ben was thinking at that particular time was lost when she took his earlobe between her lips and her hands went seeking the length of his body.

When she had finished with him—for the time being—she asked, "You were saying something about my lack of inhibitions."

"Was I?" Ben seemed dazed.

"Something that started with the letter *i*, I believe," she sighed and rolled over on him.

" 'Incredible' was probably the word I was looking for." He scraped his teeth lightly along the side of her jaw line. "Or maybe it was *ay carumba.*"

She laughed and kissed him soundly, then snuggled back down against him, closing her eyes tightly to impress every one of these last seconds with him deeply into her heart. The thought of his leaving, even if only for a few weeks, terrified her. How long before the life he would make for himself would consume him and begin to edge her out, bit by bit? How long would it be before a Greta or an Ursula found him at a lonely, vulnerable moment? How many more nights like this would there be for them to share? If she thought about it, she would grow cold inside and her hands would start to quake and she would want to cry, so she would not permit herself to think about it right now. Later—tomorrow, after his plane had taken off and he was safely on his way to England—she would think of it. But when he left, it would be a smiling, confident, understanding Zoey who would be seeing him off, not the sobbing red-eyed woman she would be if she gave in to the tears now.

"I guess it would be overstating my case to remind you that it's still not too late to change your mind," he told her the next morning in the shower, taking his sweet time soaping her back. "My grandfather might never forgive me for stealing you away from the HMP, but I'll take my chances."

She ignored his plea, however cavalierly it had been delivered. "Do you think Delaney is really all right with your leaving?"

He thought for a moment before responding. "I think he is. At least, if he was upset, he hid it well. As happy as he had been to have me here, he was still supportive of my going into business with Tony." He turned his back to the steady stream of hot water to rinse off the soap. When he was finished, he stepped out of the way to permit Zoey to rinse her hair. "But it's been a very good thing, being here."

"You found something to your liking amidst the rolling hills of Chester County?"

"You could say I found a lot to my liking here." Ben kissed her shoulder blade before stepping out of the shower and into a large fluffy white bath sheet. He grabbed a second towel and held it open for her to step into. "Everything I love best is here in these rolling hills."

"Then why are you moving to England?" Zoey pulled a towel from the rack and blotted her hair with it.

"I'm not moving to England." He frowned.

"What do you call it?"

"I'm just working there."

"And living there."

"I like to think I live here, with you." He opened the bathroom door and pointed across the room to the tall oak armoire they had found at an antique store three weeks before. Over the past month or so he had spent more and more time at Zoey's, less and less at Delaney's condo. They had both fallen in love with the Empire-style piece and thought it would be just the place to hold his clothes, and so they had struggled together to carry it up the narrow steps from her first floor to the second. "My clothes are—"

"Packed, Ben," she told him flatly. "Most of your things are packed."

He turned and watched her comb out her straight dark hair.

"Ben, you can call it anything you want, but you will not be living here with me. You'll be thousands of miles away, living a life that has nothing to do with me."

"Everything I do has to do with you," he told her.

"I know you think that, but things change, Ben."

"That won't change, Zoey. I love you. I've never loved anyone else. I can't imagine my life without you."

Then why are you leaving me? she wanted to ask, but

could not make the words come out. Instead, she said, "I love you, too, Ben. I think I always have. I always will."

"You could still come with me."

"You know that I can't do that. As important as it is for you to have this business with Tony, that's how important it is for me to be where I am. Maybe more so." She picked up the hair dryer and held it loosely in her right hand. "You've always known who you were, Ben. I never did. It wasn't until I found this job that all the pieces began to fall into place. I love what I do. I get up in the morning and look forward to going to work. I love the people I work with and the people who call in to talk to me. I love being on camera and I love working behind the scenes with the buyers. I'm good at what I do, Ben. It makes me happy, it's helped define me. And it took me so long to find myself, that I'm afraid I wouldn't know who I'd be if I left now. I love you with all my heart, and I hate the thought of your leaving, but just being with you can't make me what I am."

"I understand, of course I do. So we'll just have to make the most of our time together—you know, quality over quantity. And we'll find a way to work this out. I promise you, it will work out. We'll spend as much time together as possible, and we will take things one step at a time. But it will work out."

Ben stood in the doorway, wishing he knew for sure just *how*.

As did Zoey, when three hours later she stood in the airport, her arms wrapped around her chest, the warmth and strength of his last kiss still fresh on her lips, her face pressed up against the glass as she watched his plane taxi down the runway.

"I'll be back in two weeks," he had whispered, "and I'll miss you every minute of every one of those days."

"Me too," she had told him, her bottom lip starting to quiver as he kissed her.

"Don't worry, Zoey," he said as he turned to go through the gate. "It'll be fine. Other people have done this and survived. We will, too."

She had nodded and forced a smile. "I know."

And then he was gone. She had started to sniff a little when she realized she didn't know where on the plane his seat was. She should have asked. She wanted to know if he was by the window, on the side of the plane facing the building, so she would know if she waved, he might see her. A silly thing to think about, she chided herself, but the thought only made the lump in her throat get bigger.

For all the years Zoey had lived here and there, in this city or in that, as she had tried on first one job, then another, she had never been lonely. Alone, yes. Lonely, no. she had never known the meaning of the word until Ben had taken his shirts out of the armoire that morning and packed them in his suitcase. The space looked so empty when she went home and opened the door and stood in front of the handsome piece of furniture as if to measure the space in terms of something more than how many shirts had so recently hung inside. She closed the door quietly and sat on the edge of her bed.

Before Ben, everything had been easier. It didn't matter if she ate alone or slept alone, watched a movie alone or not. But her daily routine would be different now. Reading the morning paper alone would mean there was no one there to share the outrage over some reported miscarriage of justice or a chuckle over a particularly witty column on the op-ed page. Having someone to share these things, she had only recently begun to discover, was better than not.

And they had shared so much over the past few months—their secrets, their dreams, their fears. In the hush of an early July morning, he had told her why he had stayed away so long, and she had immediately understood. She had told him of her long journey in search of her own place in this world, and he had cheered her for having found it.

She sat on the edge of the bed and smoothed the pillow on what had become Ben's side. Knowing it would go unused for two full weeks made the fist in her gut turn and twist just a little. She wondered what he would have said if she had asked him to tell Tony he wasn't interested in this company he was forming. Or if she had been willing to quit her own job and go with him. She sighed, knowing neither option was right for them.

Ben would be back, every two weeks, Friday through Monday. Every six weeks Zoey would fly to London and spend four days. They had carefully marked it all off on the calendar.

And, she reminded herself, there were lots of people whose relationships survived greater hardships. Whether or not theirs would be one of them remained to be seen.

Only time would tell.

Chapter

28

Zoey eased slowly into the only available parking space in front of CeCe's apartment building and turned off the ignition. She carefully lifted the lemon meringue pie she had bought in that pricey little dessert emporium outside of West Chester, Helen's Hamper, and slid out of the car, balancing the white bakery box flat on the palm of her hand. Nothing, not even chocolate, raised her spirits like a truly great lemon meringue pie. Tonight she needed all the help she could get.

CeCe met her at the door, her new puppy, Elvis, at her heels. "Come on in. Watch she doesn't trip you."

"Hi, Elvis." Zoey handed the pie box to CeCe and lifted the pup with both hands. Elvis covered Zoey's face enthusiastically with sloppy puppy kisses. "If she's a she, why is her name Elvis?"

"Well, there were only four pups that survived the litter. And the hands on the ranch had already named them John, Paul, George, and Elvis. Unfortunately, only John and George were males."

"Tell me again what kind of dog she is?"

"She is what we call a 'barn dog' back home. A mix of

whatever was in the barn when her momma came into heat." CeCe grinned. "Elvis's mom was a Labrador retriever, and we think her daddy might have been a visiting weimaraner, but we're not sure. And watch her, Zoey, she will lick the freckles right off your face," CeCe warned her. "I'm not having much trouble housebreaking her, but teaching her not to lick is near impossible."

"I kind of like it, to tell you the truth"—Zoey smiled wryly—"since it's the most action I'll see for three more weeks."

CeCe frowned. "I thought it was supposed to be every other weekend."

"It was. It is. But there's a big meeting in Germany that's supposed to determine whether or not certain types of somethings in the engines can be bigger than a bread box," she shrugged. "Ben told me about it, but all I really heard was 'three weeks.'"

"How's it working out?"

"It's great and it's horrible." Zoey settled into a wooden chair in CeCe's small kitchen, noting that only a few more, if any, of CeCe's packing boxes had been emptied. "It's great when we're together and murder when we're not."

"You're really in love." CeCe sighed.

"Totally. Terminally." Zoey nodded.

"How long do you think you will be able to keep this up?"

"For as long as we have to. Ben is the love of my life, CeCe. The absolute love of my life. If this is the most I can have of him, I'll just have to take it."

"If you had to choose—"

"Between Ben and my job?" Zoey answered without hesitation. "There'd be no decision to make, not really, if I could only have one. I couldn't lose him now, I just couldn't. But I've found so much of myself through what I do, that I worry about who I would be without it. Would I be the same person he fell in love with?" She shook her head. "I don't think I would be, and I'm afraid to take that chance. But I do know that I'll fight to keep him. Even if it's myself I have to fight."

"Let's hope it doesn't come to that." CeCe handed her a tall green glass of iced tea. "Let's hope it doesn't become an either/or situation."

"Let's change the subject. Let's talk about something fun. Tell me all about your vacation back home."

"It was so great, Zoey. I got to spend a whole day with my mom, just the two of us. I can't remember the last time we had that much time alone together. Oh, and I went on an overnight camp out in the hills. . . ." CeCe's eyes took on the sheen of a highly glazed doughnut, a fact that Zoey did not fail to recognize.

"Oh? I think that's the part I'd like to hear more about."

"Oh." CeCe shrugged it off noncommittally. "It was just with my brother, and a few of his friends. Just for a few days, up to the lake."

"The skating cowboy." Zoey tapped a finger on the table. "He was there, wasn't he?"

"Oh. Well, he is a friend of Trevor's." CeCe blushed and turned back to the sink, where she was rinsing bay scallops for their dinner.

"Well?"

"Well . . ." CeCe nodded, as if giving great thought to her response. "It was an interesting few days."

"Interesting?" Zoey raised an eyebrow. "A few days? You went camping with the cowboy for a few days and you call it *interesting?* Were there any other women on this little camping trip?"

"My sister Liza. She's the baby of the family. She came home at the last minute and she wanted to come along."

"So what did you and . . . what is his name?"

"Dalt."

"Dalt." Zoey tested it aloud. "Nice. What did you and Dalt do for those few days?"

"Oh, it was so great." CeCe's eyes began to sparkle.

"We went swimming every morning and we hiked. We went backpacking into the hills and sat on rocks overlooking the canyon and watched the baby bald eagles learn to fly. It was breathtaking."

"Oh, I can see that it would have been." Zoey tried not to grin.

"Zoey, you haven't lived until you've wakened at dawn to watch the sun come up over the Montana hills, to start the day with a cold dip in a mountain lake and head back to camp to make pancakes with the wild blueberries you've picked along the way."

Zoey watched her friend's face fill with wonder, then asked, quietly, "What are you doing here, if all that is waiting for you back there?"

CeCe thought it over, then replied, "The same thing you're doing here, when Ben is on the other side of the Atlantic. It's a question of where you are, but it's not necessarily a matter of where you'll stay."

"Does that mean you won't be renewing your contract when it comes up next year?" Zoey asked softly.

"There's a good chance that I won't."

"Is it because of Dalt?"

"It's because of me," CeCe said simply. "Yes, I admit that it's a consideration, knowing that he is there. I'll never get to know him better, never get to explore those possibilities from here. But it really has more to do with me, Zoe. I am a child of the hills. I miss my family, and I miss Montana. It's where I belong, Dalton or no Dalton."

"That's why you still haven't unpacked."

"There's nothing in those boxes I need on a temporary basis," CeCe acknowledged. "Every bit as much as you need to stay, I think I need to go home."

"I can't even think about what it would be like without you there, at the HMP. You're my best friend, CeCe."

"I always will be. If you can maintain a long-distance romance with Ben, you and I shouldn't have much of a problem holding our friendship together."

Zoey sipped at her drink thoughtfully, hoping that she would, indeed, be able to do both.

* * *

"Ben, I said it's after seven. Are you coming to dinner?" Tony Chapman stood in the doorway of Ben Pierce's office and waved the newspaper he held in his hand to get his friend's attention.

"What?" Ben frowned. "Oh. Dinner. No, no thanks. I'll grab something on the way home."

"Not much of a life you're living these days, mate," Tony observed.

"Well, I'm not here to socialize," Ben told him. "I'm here to work."

"All work and no play, all that," Tony chided.

"I play when I go home." Ben grinned.

"And you work your tail off while you're here. Not much of a balance, old friend. You're bound to tire of it soon." Tony said. "It worries me."

"Why 'worry'?"

"Because we both know what you're doing."

"What's that?"

"You're working nearly around the clock so that when you go back to the States, you can go with a clear conscience and you don't have to feel that you're taking advantage of our friendship when you leave for four days at a time. And it's okay. I don't mind, Ben. If I had someone like your Zoey, I'd be doing the same thing. But it worries me that all you do these days is work."

"I want to pull my own weight."

"I know you do. And you are. More than you need to."

"I don't want to let you down, Tony."

"You never have, Ben. You never could." Tony took a small breath, then added, "If you left tomorrow, I'd still consider you my best friend."

"Why did you say that?" Ben frowned. "I've never said a word about leaving."

"No, no, you're right. You haven't." Tony's voice softened. "But there's something in your eyes, when you come back from a weekend away. You're totally in love with her."

"Absolutely."

"And you miss her terribly."

"Terribly," Ben agreed.

"Maybe you should think about bringing her over here."

"I've asked her. She won't come."

"Well, then, I guess it's up to you to solve that little dilemma, isn't it?" Tony smiled a half smile and swung himself through the door. "As for me, I've dinner waiting at Greta's."

"Why'd you ask me to join you, if you were going to her apartment?"

"Because I knew you wouldn't come." Tony saluted his friend as he left the room. "You never do."

Well, he's right about that. Ben nodded as he shuffled through the latest stack of design specifications that the engineers had dropped off that afternoon. Dinner out or dinner in, alone or with friends, it was all pretty much the same to him these days. The only time he felt alive was when he was back home with Zoey, in her little house on Skeeters Pond Road. The rest of the time, he could be anywhere. Since the last time he'd been home, he'd traveled to Paris to interview test drivers and he'd gone to Spa-Francorchamps for the running of the Belgian Grand Prix. He'd been to Monza for the Italian race and to Nurburgring for the Luxembourg circuit. In two weeks he'd travel to Japan to watch the race at Suzuka. More and more, he was beginning to suspect one thing. There was a world of difference between *racing*— strapping into one of those sleek, incessantly whining cars and driving as if your life depended on it, because in so many ways, once the race started, it did—and *watching*.

Ben had never been much of a spectator.

He sighed and swung his chair around to face the open window behind him. On the other side of the building,

Tony had had a track built so that they could test their own engines right there where they built them. Even though it was well after hours, the sound of an engine's whine rattled the windows. Someone else was working late.

Ben pushed his chair back and walked the short hallway to the small lobby, then out through the front door and around the building to the track. A small vehicle—more engine than body—sped around the dry track in a cloud of dust. After seven more laps, the test car coasted to the edge of the field and stopped and its driver hopped out. As the young man unstrapped his helmet, Ben recognized him as a test driver they had hired just several weeks before.

"How's she feel?" Ben called.

"Like silk." The young man called back. "Try her yourself."

He walked to within ten feet of Ben before tossing him his helmet. Ben caught it with both hands, then stood staring at it for a long time. Once upon a time, not so very long ago, he'd have strapped on the helmet and slid behind the wheel in one motion, without a second thought, and taken flight. Now, he realized, he was debating whether or not even to drive, wondering what the consequences might be if his ankle got stubborn at the wrong moment. He twirled the helmet for a long moment, then popped it on his head. Tossing his sport jacket onto the nearest fence post, he slipped behind the wheel and turned on the ignition. That the engine purred was no exaggeration. Ben eased his right foot onto the accelerator and glided onto the track.

She was fast, she was easy. *Silk* had said it all. Loud, whiny, but definitely silky. Their engineers had done one hell of a job. Ben was lost in the sound and the speed, and lost count of how many times around the track he had taken her, until the engine began to sputter. Disconcerted at the sound of distress from their perfect machine, he tried to ease up on the gas pedal, but his foot did not want to cooperate. Braking with his good left foot, he had to slide his right foot from the accelerator, exactly what he had feared. As the car slowed to a stop, he realized two things. The stutter coming from the engine was due to a lack of fuel, and the decision to retire had been a wise one.

He sat in the car long after he turned off the ignition. He looked up to see the young driver approaching him, a smile on his face.

"What'd I tell you?" He grinned.

"You didn't exaggerate," Ben called back.

"Nothing like it, is there?" The young man patted the side of the car.

"No." Ben nodded slowly. "No, there isn't. Nothing at all."

Later that night Ben sat in the small sitting room in the suite he'd rented at an old inn about a half mile from the factory. The year was slipping into an early fall, just like last year. And it was hard not to remember that this time last year he had been preparing for the race that ended his career.

"Nothing like it, is there?" the test driver had said.

Nothing but *driving* is driving. Nothing but *racing* is racing. Not designing the cars, not building the cars, not owning the cars. There was no worthy substitute, he acknowledged. Everything else connected with the sport was, for him, just another form of spectating.

Then why, he wondered, *was he here?*

"A good question," he said aloud to the empty room. "A *damned* good question."

* * *

Zoey stood on the deck of her house and sniffed the air. Definitely a scent of fall there. Of course, she mused, all one had to do was look at her lawn to know that. The leaves had begun falling early, lining the paths of her still colorful garden with gold and russet droppings, but she just hadn't been motivated to rake. On this Thursday morning in late October, she still lacked motivation, but faced the unpleasant truth that the longer she put it off, the harder the job would be.

"Sort of looks like the yellow brick road," she muttered as she hauled a rake out of the garage.

"What's that?" Wally asked from the corner of the garage.

"I said, it looks like the yellow brick road." She narrowed her eyes. "Where did you come from?"

He nodded toward the garden. "Just sitting on your bench watching the crows and wondering when you were going to get around to doing some raking."

"Obviously today," she told him archly.

"Glad to see it. Don't want to smother your grass." He sat himself down and took out his pipe.

"Smother my grass," she mumbled.

"Doing a lot of talking to yourself these days, aren't you, missy?"

"No more than usual."

"Did a real nice job with your garden this year. I know that Addie must be pleased."

"You think Addie keeps her eye on this garden?" Zoey began to rake, pulling the leaves toward her with long strokes.

He nodded. "I don't think Addie's missed a thing."

"There's a scary thought," Zoey said, looking up to the house and the second-floor bedroom where she and Ben had spent so many nights. Even here, in the garden, they had made love on more than one occasion. Why, right here where she raked, they had . . . She blushed at the thought of Addie Kilmartin keeping tabs on the goings-on at her old home.

As if reading her mind, Wally laughed out loud. "I sure had you going for a minute there, didn't I?"

"Yes, you did." She laughed in spite of herself.

"Good to see you laugh, Zoey." He puffed on his pipe.

She understood what he was saying—that she didn't seem to laugh as much anymore—but couldn't bring herself to acknowledge it. To do so would invite conversation about why, and they both knew why. There was no point in discussing it.

Wally apparently didn't agree.

"So. When's the boyfriend due back in town?" he asked.

Zoey shrugged as if it wasn't of consequence, though they both knew differently. "I'm not sure."

"How's that?"

He just wouldn't let it drop. Zoey leaned on her rake and said, "Something came up and Ben couldn't make it home last week. And no, he can't make it home this weekend either." She started to rake a little more fiercely, stabbing at the leaves as if they were somehow responsible for her present situation. "And don't ask, Wally, 'cause I don't know when he'll be here, okay?"

"I hear you, loud and clear." He nodded. "Course, that probably means that you don't have a partner for the paddleboat races this year."

"Is that this weekend?" She frowned.

"It is," he told her.

"Has it been a whole year since I met you?" She stopped again, confounded by the realization that a whole year had gone by since she had first seen the house that had become her beloved home, a whole year since Wally had befriended her. And in that one short year, Ben had come back and, miracle of miracles, he had loved her.

"Yup. The sixtieth Brady's Mill Pumpkin Fest will open at eleven A.M. on Sunday." Smoke puffed from the bowl of his pipe. "So. Whatcha say?"

"About what?"

"About the paddleboat race on Sunday. Want to make it two for two?" He grinned. "Word around the post office has it that Clifford and Nancy are just itching to challenge us."

"Well, then, Clifford and Nancy had better practice up this week"—Zoey grinned—"because the reigning champions will be back to defend their title on Sunday."

The reigning champions of the Brady's Mill paddleboat race scored an easy victory, and as she stood on the dock with Wally to accept the prize, Zoey felt a certain satisfaction. She loved this little town. She fit in here— *fit like a glove,* Wally would say. And later, as she lined her front porch steps with the pumpkins she had bought that day at the Brady's Mill Pumpkin Fest, she wished that Ben had been there to share the sheer fun of it, the camaraderie, the laughs, the simple pleasure of drinking a cup of cool, fresh apple cider, and the warmth of the sweet autumn sunshine. Maybe next year Ben would be there.

Sure. She shrugged without enthusiasm as she went into the house and locked up for the night. *Sure he will. . . .*

On the following Tuesday afternoon, she walked off her cooking set—peanut satay ("Okay, who's the wise guy who thought that it would be fun to watch me do Thai?") and was flagged down by her producer, who told her, "You're wanted in the boss's office."

"Whoops, I guess there was a little too much lime juice in the dipping sauce for good old Petey." She grimaced as she took off her apron and folded it under her arm. Made of heavy black cotton, it loudly pronounced "To hell with housework" in red block letters. Ben had sent it to her his first week in England and it had become a show favorite.

She took the steps two at a time, wondering what Peter wanted to see her about. *Maybe he's had enough of my cooking.* She grinned to herself, having instructed the show coordinator to make sure that a serving of whatever it was she had cooked went to the man who sat behind the big desk in the executive suite. Maybe he'd get the message and let her off the hook, she reasoned.

She smiled at Beth, the secretary Peter had inherited when he took over Ben's old job.

"Go right on in," Beth said without looking up. "He's expecting you."

"I never thought I'd say this, but you're really turning into a good cook."

Her head snapped up at the sound of his voice and she stopped dead in her tracks.

She must be hallucinating.

She must want so badly to see Ben behind that desk that she had conjured up his image.

"This really isn't all that bad. Did you taste it?" Her vision held the fork out to her, as if they were in some small, intimate restaurant somewhere sharing a romantic dinner for two.

She shook her head dumbly.

"No?" He grinned. "Don't trust your own cooking? Well, then, maybe you'd rather go out for lunch?"

She still could not speak. He was acting as if . . . well, as if he'd never been gone, as if the past few months had been an unpleasant dream.

"I personally can vouch for the satay, but . . ." He glanced at his watch. "Oh, gosh, we're going to be late. We'd better get going."

"Late?" She managed to get out the one word in a sort of squeak.

"For our appointment." He walked from behind his desk, and took her elbow, pausing to kiss her gently.

"What appointment?" she asked, not bothering to close her eyes, although her lips were tingling at the touch of his mouth and it would have been oh so easy to wrap her arms around him and lose herself there.

"Beth, take a long lunch for yourself. Leave early if you like," he told his secretary as he escorted Zoey through the doorway and into the hall.

"There's no place in this world like Pennsylvania in the fall," he said as they strolled toward his car, Zoey still wide-eyed and wanting to pinch herself. "And don't you think," he said as he started the car, "that the trees are particularly beautiful this year? Have you ever seen such a shade of red before?"

"Ah, no." She shook her head.

"And how 'bout that one, that Japanese maple," he pointed to a small graceful tree with leaves like coral-colored lace. "Gorgeous."

"Ummm," she nodded, sneaking a glance at him from across the console.

Ben slipped a CD into the stereo, pausing to ask, "How do you feel about Pink Floyd?"

She nodded. "Fine."

He hit the button and "Dark Side of the Moon" filled the small car with music and maniacal laughter.

Why, of course. That's it, she reasoned calmly. *He's lost his mind. That would explain his bizarre behavior.*

"Where are we going, Ben?" she asked in cool, soothing tones.

"It's a surprise," he told her, grinning as if very pleased with himself.

"Give me a hint."

"Well, you see, when I was in England—"

"Oh, good. So you *do* realize that you've been away."

"Of course I realize I've been away." He frowned at her.

"Go on." She gestured.

"Well, when I was away, I had time to think about it. To put it all into perspective, you know?"

She didn't, but she nodded anyway.

"And I came to the realization that if I wasn't doing what I really loved to do—which is racing—then what was I doing *there,* alone, when I could be *here,* with you?"

"I give up. What were you doing there?"

"I was running a business. Which in itself is not a bad thing to do. But then it occurred to me that if I was going to be a businessman, I didn't need to be there."

"You didn't?"

"No. Tony could hire anyone to do what I was doing. He didn't need me to do that job. But Delaney, now that's a different story altogether." He peered in the rearview mirror, then made a quick right-hand turn down a narrow two-lane country road. "Delaney needs me. I'm the only grandson—the only living relative—he has. And besides, I had started to like the HMP. It's not quite the same as *driving,* but then again, neither is building engines. So Tony and I had to sit down and talk about where the company was going and where I was going."

"Which was . . . ?"

"Back here, of course."

"Back here?" Zoey's heart flipped over. "To stay?"

"Of course, to stay." He took her hand and squeezed it, then said, "Hey, I think we're here."

He made a left into a wide driveway and stopped in front of a three-car garage that sat well behind a white farmhouse. Without another word he hopped out and was around the car to open Zoey's door before she could ask *where*.

Which she did, as soon as she got out of the car.

"Ben, where are we?" She grabbed his arm.

He took her hand as the back door opened and a trim woman in her mid-fifties stepped out onto the small porch.

"Hi." He smiled as he led Zoey toward the steps. "I'm Ben Pierce. I called earlier."

The woman smiled at Zoey and said, "They're all awake now, but you know how babies are. Awake and playful one minute, napping the next. Come in, come in." She stepped back so that Ben and Zoey could follow her into the house.

"This way." She beckoned to them.

Zoey stopped and sniffed at the particular smell of the house, something vaguely familiar that she just could not place.

"They're in here," the woman told them as she opened a door, and a flood of yellow fur spilled out onto the tiled kitchen floor.

Ben's laughter filled the room as a dozen balls of pale gold rolled onto the floor in a moving heap.

"Puppies!" Zoey exclaimed. "They're puppies!"

"They certainly are," Ben picked up first one, then the other, as if silently evaluating the merits of each.

"What are they?" Zoey asked.

"Golden retrievers," the woman responded, then bent

over just slightly to scratch the head of the much larger lump of lumbering pale fur. "It's okay, LuLu," she crooned. "No one will hurt your babies."

Zoey's head was spinning, much as the yellow lumps were spinning around her feet and licking at her legs. One, two, three runs sped down the side of her leg as her pantyhose fell victim to a platoon of tiny puppy toes. She leaned over and picked up the pup who had started an assault on the heel of her shoe.

"What do you think you're doing?" Zoey laughed as the pup merrily slurped her face with an eager pink tongue.

"Which one do you think, Zoe?" Ben asked, holding up a waggy-tailed specimen who looked a bit brawnier than the one that was still washing Zoey's face.

"Which one what?" She asked.

"Which one do we want?" He spoke as if they had discussed it.

Zoey thought that she could hear the crazy-man laughter from "Dark Side of the Moon" all over again.

"Which one do we want?" she repeated.

"Which puppy. Zoey, are you feeling all right?"

"I feel fine."

"Good. Which puppy do we want?"

"Do we want a puppy?" she paused to ask.

"Why, yeah. We do. Definitely." He nodded.

"Oh, well, then, I guess maybe . . ." She looked down at the soft bundle of fur that squirmed in her arms and the rollicking mass that rolled at her feet. How did one decide such a thing with so many to choose from?

"Several have been sold," the woman told them, and she proceeded to point out five that had already been spoken for.

"How can you tell them apart?" Zoey asked. "They all look alike to me."

"They all have their little differences," the breeder said. "Now, that one there, that you're holding"—she pointed to the pup in Zoey's arms—"she's going to be a real pistol. She's the one who starts the others into scratching at the door to go outside. She likes the fresh air. But she's the runt. She'll always be small, small-boned and small at the shoulder. Now that one"—she pointed to the pup Ben picked up—"he's the biggest male in the litter. He'll be a real bruiser when he's full grown."

Ah, yes, Ben sighed. His Big Dog. He could see them now, taking off through the fields this time next year. Maybe even do a little duck hunting . . .

"I think I like this one, Ben."

Ben frowned. The pup Zoey was holding up was not his Big Dog.

"Zoey, she's the runt," he said out of the corner of his mouth.

"So?"

"So, she's not going to grow to be that big. Now, this little guy here . . ."

"Why does she have to be big?" Zoey frowned.

"Because that's what a big dog is, Zoe," he explained as if speaking to a child. "It's supposed to be . . . well, *big.*"

Zoey stared at him as if she hadn't understood one word. The pup in her arms licked at her chin, then nipped it. Zoey laughed. "I really like her, Ben."

"But . . ." Ben looked down at the puppy that had settled down to chew on his shoelaces. The pup's paws were enormous, a sure sign that he'd be a *big* Big Dog.

"Ben, you asked me which puppy I wanted"—she smiled at him—"and I'd like this one."

Ben glanced reluctantly at the big pup, the visions of autumnal boy-bonding-with-dog slipping away. He glanced at Zoey's face. Clearly, she was smitten with the smaller female. And she *was* a cutie, he had to concede, with those black button eyes and that dark brown nose. She was still buff colored, not yet golden, but she would darken up, he knew. For a minute, he all but regretted having brought Zoey along. Maybe he should have just picked out his puppy and brought it home. But that would have defeated the purpose of picking out a pup together, of making the commitment together. And that was at the heart of this trip. Judging by the way Zoey was looking at him, he suspected she already knew that.

"She'll be a great little dog," the breeder told them.

At the sound of the words—little dog—Ben's heart sank even further, but Zoey held the puppy out to him and he took it. Little Dog wagged her tail excitedly and tried to nip his ear.

"Does she already have a name?" Zoey asked.

"She's Wagonwheel's Lucky Diva," the breeder told her.

"L. D.," Ben said, sighing. He just couldn't get away from it. Lucky Diva. Little Dog. It was all the same.

"Ben, why can't you buy both?" Zoey asked.

"Both?" His eyebrows rose as he contemplated the thought, then nodded happily and smiled at the breeder. "We'll take both."

He lifted his Big Dog pup, who proceeded to wash Ben's face. *Ah, the fields we'll walk through, the days we will share* . . .

"When can we come back for them?"

"They need two more weeks with momma, but after that"—the woman began to herd the puppies back through the small gate to their mother—"they're all yours."

All yours, the words repeated in Ben's head as they got back into the car. *All yours.* He stole a glance at Zoey as he turned the BMW around and pulled back onto the road. She was all his, too. He wondered if she knew.

"I can't believe you just bought me a puppy." She grinned at him.

"Bought us puppies." He corrected her. "We'll be sharing them."

"We will?"

"Definitely." He nodded. "It's part of the plan."

"The plan?" she asked curiously.

"Sure. You know, I thought maybe we'd stay in your house, since you just fixed it up and everything, and besides, we both love that house, and it's big enough for us and a dog or two. Now, we might have to think about an addition, when we start having children. . . ."

"Children?" She leaned back in her seat, terribly amused. "Are children part of the plan, too?"

"Why, sure." He grinned. "Don't you remember that old kids' rhyme, 'First comes love, then comes marriage, then comes—'"

"'Ben with the baby carriage.'" She was laughing out loud now.

"Well, yeah," he nodded. "Someday."

"Someday." She repeated the word softly, rolling its meaning around in her mind like a lone marble.

Ben reached across to take her hand, driving a few more miles down the road before he pulled over at a pond that stood like a large puddle at the side of a large field. The crops—soybeans maybe—had been harvested, and a large flock of Canadian geese picked enthusiastically at the smorgasbord of plant debris left behind by the farmer. Tall cattails, already gone to seed, waved wheatlike arms from the edge of the pond. Ben rolled down the window and let the cool late-afternoon air drift in.

"Yup. Nothing like a Pennsylvania autumn." There was true satisfaction in his voice.

"Does Delaney know that you're back to stay?"

He nodded. "I went to see him in New York yesterday, right from the airport. He's delighted that I made the decision to come back to work for him. He didn't seem quite as surprised as I thought he'd be, but he's very happy."

"Are you happy?"

"Happier than I've ever been in my life."

"Happier than you were when you were driving race cars?"

He hesitated for just a moment. "It isn't the same, Zoey. That was a part of my life that's over. It was great while it lasted, but it's over." He stroked the side of her face with his fingers. "But you and me, we'll never be over. No matter what happens, Zoe, it'll never be over between us."

"And you're willing to stay here? No more Silverstone? Monte Carlo? Monza? Wherever?"

"We can always go just to watch, if we wanted. That's all I'd have done if I'd stayed with Tony anyway."

"Aren't you afraid you'll miss the lifestyle?"

"Not for a minute. And anyway"—he kissed the tip of her chin, before settling in on the corners of her mouth—"who needs Monte Carlo when I get to spend the rest of my life with someone as wonderful as you?"

"I just don't want you to feel that you're giving up something that you love. . . ."

"I love you, Zoey. I love you and the life we'll have together, the home we'll make and the children we'll raise together, the life we'll build." He leaned back and smiled. "Besides, before I left, I was starting to get used to the routine."

"Which routine was that?"

"You know, Mexican on Monday, Thai on Tuesday . . ."

"Wanda on Wednesday." She laughed.

"Wanda?" He frowned. "Who's Wanda?"

"Mrs. Colson. I've been making it a point to have dinner with my mother one night each week. It's been falling on Wednesdays lately, so *Italian* has been moved to Thursday."

"We should go see your mother." Ben thought of Delia, and all she had done to make his homecoming a real one over the past few months. "There are things I need to thank her for."

"Can it wait till tomorrow?" Zoey leaned across the console and scraped her teeth lightly along his bottom lip. "Today's only Tuesday. . . ."

"Hmmm. That would give us a full twenty-four hours to spend together."

"Let's go home, Ben. I have an idea or two on how to spend some of those hours. Maybe all of them."

"Home it is." He kissed her full on the mouth and started the ignition, taking the shortest, most direct route back to the house in Brady's Mill. He pulled into the driveway and looked around at the little house with its trees and its garden, its welcoming front porch, and was overcome with the feeling that he had finally, once and for all time, come home.

Home. It had such a beautiful sound. He'd been trying to come home for years, and hadn't even known it. Now that he was here, he was going to take pleasure in every minute of it.

Starting now.

Epilogue

_∾_

Delia Enright stood at the top of the first-floor landing overlooking the gaily bedecked entry hall of the Bishop's Inn and smiled as the front door swung open yet again and another of her children entered into the crowd that had begun to gather earlier that morning. Nick and India, along with August and Corri, had been the first to arrive, followed by Zoey and Ben. Now that Georgia was there, the circle was finally complete. Delia sighed a sigh of wonder, that she would, at long last, celebrate a holiday with all of her children gathered around her. That Laura had closed the inn to paying guests to permit the family to share this Christmas Eve had been a gift without measure, the most welcome gift Delia had ever received.

The joy of the moment filled her and she leaned over the railing just enough to see Ally hand Corri a tray of hors d'oeuvres and to instruct her on who to serve first. Budding little hostesses, both of them, Delia smiled to herself. Ah, and it's such fun to be a grandmother, such fun to have two little girls to spoil again.

There should always be children in the family on

Christmas Eve. They help us to keep the joy of the season alive in us all.

She turned on the landing, an old worn red felt stocking with an angel on the front in her hands, and thought back to so many other Christmases, when this stocking had hung with three others on the mantel at the old house in Chester County. The angel's halo of glittery gold trim had lost some of its sparkle, and the wings, once proud puffy mounds of white feathers, looked as if a moth or two had come to call. But the love that it had held for all these years was just as bright as it had been when Delia had bought it, so many Christmases ago, to keep the memory of her own Christmas angel close to her heart.

What a joy it would be to see it hang there, with the others, on the mantel at the Bishop's Inn. From her place on the landing she could see the stockings hung across the long wooden mantel in the front hallway below. One for each of them. There was Nick's old stocking, a tall affair in the shape of a tin soldier, thick blue felt trimmed with gold epaulets and a tall hat. Then Zoey's, shaped like a Christmas tree, with its garlands of glitter and fancy buttons and shiny silver and gold balls, and a fat, broad bottom that held lots of presents. Delia smiled, recalling a time when Zoey had thought the carol "Oh, Christmas Tree" had been written about her stocking. And there was Georgia's dancing girl, her arms reaching high above her head, her stiff pink tutu flared around her hips. Delia had had them made when her children were just small, and had carefully preserved each one over the years. Delia's own had been made in the shape of a book, *A Christmas Carol* stitched across the front and bits of felt holly sewn here and there. Tonight there would be no thoughts of Christmas Past. Christmas Present and Christmas Future, however, were blissfully welcome.

There were so many stockings this year, she noted, that they would not all fit across the front of the mantel, and so she had hung some down each side of the fireplace. With much love and a great deal of satisfaction, she had had each one specially made for the newest members of her growing family. There was India's, with its appliquéd elves standing in front of a lighthouse, and August's, with cross-stitched shells decorating a hand-embroidered tree. And Corri's, with its little girl peering out a window onto a starry sky, awaiting, no doubt, the arrival of a sleigh filled with goodies. Ben's was next; deciding to cut his in the shape of a car had been easy. Ally's stocking was decorated with little felt animals, appliquéd raccoons and bunnies, foxes and a squirrel, all around a holly bush. Delia had even had a stocking made for Matt, Laura's brother, hoping that he would accept his sister's invitation to share the holiday with the entire clan. He had apparently declined, and none too gracefully, Delia had surmised, having watched Matt leave the inn by the back door, which he had closed behind him with a resounding smack, before any of Laura's Enright siblings had arrived. *Well, then*—Delia had pursed her lips as Matt had backed his pickup down the driveway—*perhaps next year* . . .

The last stocking to be hung would be Laura's. It seemed that Delia had waited forever for this moment, and she wanted nothing more than to savor it.

All in all, it had been a very good year.

Zoey's laughter floated above the crowd. Ah, there she was, with her Ben, at long last and for always by her side. The fates had been kind, Delia smiled, in bringing them together. Ben, so like a son to her, had taken her aside earlier and shown her the emerald-cut diamond he would be giving an unsuspecting Zoey before the night ended.

Delia's eyes narrowed as she watched her youngest child move gracefully from one side of the room to the other. *Tiny Dancer,* Delia recalled the old pop tune.

Maybe a little too tiny. Zoey's right, Georgia is working much too hard and enjoying life far too little. And life was, after all, so very short. . . .

Delia tapped her foot impatiently at the thought of her

little girl working her life away for a career that seemed to be giving her less joy than it had promised, and that she, Delia, was powerless to do anything about it. She sighed. Georgia would bear watching over the coming year.

Her eyes searched the gathering for her daughter-in-law. Was it her imagination, or was India's tummy just a tad rounder than it had been even a month ago when they had all made the trip to Devlin's Light for Thanksgiving at August's? Hmmm. Might there be yet another reason to give thanks come next year?

That would be lovely. She sighed, thinking how wonderful a father her Nicky would be, how lucky the child born into a family so filled with love.

And then there was the miracle of Laura. . . .

Oh, yes—Delia grinned, her heart all but singing as she started down the steps—it had been a *very* good year.

POCKET BOOKS
PROUDLY PRESENTS

MOON DANCE

MARIAN STREET

Georgia Enright leaned over nimbly to tie first her left, then her right running shoe, then stood and stretched from side to side to limber up. Though in top athletic form after nine years of dancing on a daily basis, she still performed an exacting ritual before setting out for a run. Side-to-side stretches, forward lunges, jumping jacks, leg lifts—twenty of each. Her warm-up completed, she left her sixth-floor condo, locked the door securely behind her, tucked the key into the pocket of her dark green hooded sweatshirt, and set off for the ground floor. On foot.

Taking the steps only prolonged her prerun warm-up, she rationalized. It was good exercise, good for her heart, good for her lungs. Why ride when you can walk? And besides, elevators made her claustrophobic.

Georgia skipped through the lobby, but once outside the imposing front door of the building she had called home for the past five years, she broke into a measured trot and took to the pavement. At the corner, she turned onto Pratt Street and set a pace that would carry her to her destination within her allotted twenty minutes. Despite the day's sunny disposition, a late winter chill still hung about Baltimore's Inner Harbor. Filling her lungs with air heavy with the faint, tangy scent of the sea, she jogged past lingering piles of snow that huddled in the shaded areas around the Convention Center.

At the corner of Gay and Pratt, she stopped for traffic, then began her cool-down pace for another few blocks until she reached the small restaurant with the red-and-green awning under which several small round tables for two had been set with plaid tablecloths and some healthy optimism that the day would in fact warm up.

It still being early, the last of the breakfast crowd remained inside. Georgia pushed open the curtained door and stepped inside to the warmth of clean brick walls and the smell of fresh bread. She winked at the young man who stood chatting with a customer at the cash register as she strolled to the back of the restaurant.

"Ah, there she is," a male voice called out from behind immaculate stainless steel counters. "Maria, didn't I tell you that Georgia would be here before nine this morning?"

"Why, yes, you did." The young waitress nodded. "Maybe you really are psychic, Lee."

"Don't let him fool you," Georgia laughed. "I called him at eight to let him know I'd be stopping in."

"Fake." Maria flashed dark eyes good-naturedly at the tall man with the clipped graying beard and the mildly amused expression.

"Spoilsport," he stage-whispered to Georgia, who laughed again. "So, what can I get you?"

"Water is fine," Georgia told him, "and I can get it."

"Help yourself," Lee Banyon gestured toward the refrigerator. "I have one last omelet to fix, then we can sit down and chat. Can I make something for you? I have some lovely ham. . . ." he added, knowing full well that Georgia was what she termed a semivegetarian—eggs, dairy, occasionally even fish, but never meat.

"I'll think about an omelet. No ham." She frowned at him teasingly as she lifted a glass from the counter and filled it with chilled spring water.

Leaning back against the cool steel, Georgia watched Lee effortlessly chop green peppers and mushrooms and slide them into the pan, all the while moving with the grace of a dancer, which he had been until his self-imposed retirement eighteen months earlier. The death of Lee's longtime companion, David, had brought home the fragility of life, and Lee had quit his position as the male lead with the Inner Harbor Dance Troupe and had taken over running the restaurant David himself had opened six years earlier.

Tall, lanky, dark-haired, and handsome, Lee Banyon had been Georgia's best and closest friend from her earliest days with the Troupe, but her support and compassion during David's illness had won her a place in Lee's heart for all time. There was no question that Lee would walk through fire for her, would slay her dragons, if need be. Right now, judging from the look in her eyes, a dragon lurked somewhere nearby, and as soon as he finished this last order, he would make it his business to find out where.

"So, Miss Georgia," he said as he garnished the plate with thin slices of orange and wedges of cantaloupe. "What's on your mind this morning?"

"What makes you think that anything—"

He held up one hand to stop her.

"Please, we've known each other far too well for much too long to start playing games now. I can see it in your face, *cara.*" He guided her through the kitchen door into the now-emptied dining room and to a table near the window, pulled a chair out for her with one hand, and placed her plate before her with the other.

"Ummm." She bit into a piece of broccoli and sighed. "Heaven. No one makes a veggie omelet like you do, Lee."

"Right. It's my secret combination of herbs and spices." Lee sniffed at a pot of coffee and, convinced of its freshness, poured two cups, which he brought to the table. "Don't try to change the subject. Tell Uncle Lee what's bothering you."

"Did you know that Mallory Edwards is in the hospital?" she asked.

"Yes, I had heard."

"I went to visit her a few days ago." She was avoiding eye contact and he knew it.

"I don't recall that you and Mallory were friends." A frown creased his brow. "Now that I think about it, I don't recall that Mallory had any friends at all within the Troupe."

"We're really not, and I don't think she does."

"Then why the act of mercy?"

"I felt sorry for her, Lee. I was there when she collapsed. It made a big impression on me. One minute she was dancing, and the next minute she sank to the floor like a marionette whose strings had all been cut at exactly the same time." Georgia shivered at the memory of it.

"Surely you've seen people faint before."

"I have, but this was different. This was . . ."—she struggled for a word, then shook her head and repeated—"different. Everyone saw her fall, and no one helped her. Ivan stood over her yelling at her to get up. . . ."

"Ah, yes, Ivan would be the very soul of compassion," Lee murmured.

"Finally, one of the girls checked her pulse and had a real hard time finding one. At first Ivan didn't want to call an ambulance; he kept insisting that she just wanted attention, that she would get up on her own. Of course, she didn't, so we called 911."

"Over Ivan's objections, I would suspect."

Georgia scowled. "He didn't want paramedics coming into the studio. He wanted us to carry her into the lobby. . . ."

"I've always said that Ivan was a prince among men."

"Here's the scary part." Georgia sighed and put her fork down quietly. "Everyone knows that Mallory collapsed from malnutrition. We all know that she suffers from eating disorders. I'm not certain which one, but we all know there's something seriously wrong. She is a very ill young woman. In the hospital, she was hooked up to skatey-illion tubes and IVs, and yet she was talking about coming back in six weeks and taking over her old spot."

"And she probably will." Lee shrugged. "Surely you know that she's not the only member of your troupe who thinks she's found an easy means of weight control?"

"Easy?" Georgia's eye's widened, recalling the hollow cheekbones, pencil-thin fingers, and large eyes in the gaunt face. "If that's the easy way, I'd sure as hell hate to see the hard way."

"Well, I do not have to tell you, of all people, how unreasonable Ivan can be at times when his dancers' weights are concerned."

Georgia met his eyes across the table but did not answer. Those whose weight fluctuated by a pound or two might be ridiculed in front of the other dancers, but those whose weight gain might exceed that would be subjected to humiliation of the cruelest form. Ivan could indeed be terrible.

"No," she told him. "I know that a lot of the dancers do dreadful things to themselves to keep their weight down. Not just in our company, but in just about every one that I know of."

"Eating disorders are as old as the dance, Georgia. Consider yourself fortunate that you never were afflicted."

"I do. But, Lee, there's more." She averted her eyes again.

"Isn't there always?" Lee sighed and gestured for her to continue.

"Yesterday Ivan announced his choice to fill Mallory's spot. He made a big deal out of it in front of everyone."

"Let me guess." Lee narrowed his eyes and pretended to think. "His choice was . . . Georgia Enright."

"How did you know that?"

"Ivan is a petty, wicked little man and is as transparent as a beam of light. Somehow he must have found out that you had visited Mallory in the hospital. Ivan being Ivan, he will want to punish Mallory for disrupting his routine. How best to punish her? By replacing her with the only person who has shown her any kindness."

"I didn't realize that you knew him that well," she said softly.

"I've known Ivan for more years than I like to recall. We were in the same company in Boston, and then again in Houston. It was only coincidence that we both ended up in Baltimore together. Oh yes, we go back a very long way. But that's old news, and nothing interests me less than yesterday's news." He leaned back in his seat and crossed his arms over his chest. "Did he give the other dancers the opportunity to challenge you for the role?"

"You do know him well, don't you?" she asked glumly.

"He's done this before—set several dancers against each other. Offer one a part, then ask if any of the others would like a chance to win the role away. Divide and conquer, so to speak. It's a means of maintaining control, you know. And it never fails to create a little drama, a little tension. Ivan, as we both know, thrives on tension."

"Well, so far, only one dancer has asked to audition. Sharyn Heffern. She was new last year. She's a wonderful dancer, Lee. She deserves the role much more than I do."

"What is the role, by the way?" he asked.

"Giselle."

Lee rolled his eyes to the heavens. "A very important ballet. A challenging one, and definitely not a role for novices. What in glory's name could the man be thinking? *Giselle* is demanding, it's difficult. It's dramatic ballet at its best, and it's . . ." He paused. "Did you accept Ivan's offer?"

"I didn't accept or not accept. I was stunned. I couldn't respond. And he did his usual, you know, drop the bombshell, then turn heel and leave the room."

"Well, how do you feel about it?"

"I feel like . . . like I'm being used. It's just like you said. Like he's trying to hurt Mallory. And at the same time, he's humiliating me. He knows I don't deserve the position; he knows I'm not good enough. Sharyn can dance circles around me. I wouldn't be surprised if he had suggested to Sharyn that she audition."

"What are you going to do?"

"I don't know." Her voice dropped to a whisper, and she looked into her friend's eyes, hoping for guidance. Georgia knew no one who could better understand her predicament. "On the one hand, it's the chance I always dreamed of. On the other, I know I will make a complete fool out of myself because I know that I don't deserve the role."

"And of course, to decline, you would have to publicly admit that you don't feel you're good enough, which will give Ivan sufficient cause to never offer you another shot at moving out of the corps."

"Which I probably would not ever get anyway." Georgia's shoulders sank a little farther. "If I accept, my limitations will be glaringly evident. There's no way I could ever best Sharyn, Lee. She's young—eighteen—but she is exceptional. She's the one who deserves the big break."

She frowned, then added, "And there's one other thing that's bothering me on a different level."

He gestured for her to go on.

"If I accept this offer, I will be knowingly assisting him in hurting Mallory."

"Of course. That would be Ivan's intent." Lee rubbed his chin thoughtfully. "Quite a dilemma for you, Georgey-girl."

"What would you do if you were in this situation, Lee?"

"Me?" He nodded thoughtfully, tapping his fingers lightly on the polished wood tabletop. "Well, actually, I was in a similar situation once."

"And?" She waited for him to continue.

"And I think that whatever I say will influence your choice, and I don't want that responsibility, Georgia. Whatever you decide to do, this is your call, *cara.*" He paused and watched her face, knowing that for Georgia, this was both a moral decision as well as a career decision. "Maybe it would help if you took a look at your goals at this stage of your career."

With a slightly rounded fingernail, she traced the delicate embossed motif on the white paper napkin on the table. "All I ever wanted to do was to dance. From the time I was a little girl, all I ever wanted to do was dance."

Her eyes drifted toward the front window and the clouds that were forming in a lazy gray sky.

"It never mattered to me that I had to work hard at it. I loved that part of it. Working toward the goal was very important to me. I was very proud of myself when I met that goal, Lee. But I always knew that I would have to work harder than some of the other girls, and my dream of becoming a prima ballerina died when I was about nineteen. It didn't take me too long to realize that some dancers are just gifted, and if you didn't have that gift, you would be limited in how far you could rise within the troupe." She smiled a lopsided smile. "I've known for several years that I did not have the gift, Lee."

"You are a lovely dancer, Georgia." He told her honestly, wishing that he could, in all good conscience, assure her that she could one day be a star. But caring much too much for her to lie about something so important, he simply took her hands between his and gave them a squeeze.

"But I will never rise to that next level, and we both know it."

"So, then. This is leading somewhere. . . ."

"I think I need to decide where I want to go from here. If I want to stay in dance, or move on."

"That's pretty drastic, Georgia."

"I'm twenty-six years old, Lee. I have no education to speak of. I started dancing professionally when I was sixteen. I had a tutor for my junior and senior years in high school and have a GED. I never gave a second's thought to college. I've never known anything but dancing. I never wanted to."

"And now?"

"Now I'm wondering if there isn't something more for me somewhere."

"All this because of Ivan?"

"Yes, and no." She shook her head. "Let's just say he's given me cause to evaluate my situation."

"And what have you found?"

"That I am a very good dancer in a world of very good dancers. That I am as good as anyone else in the corps. But I will never go beyond where I am. And I will never be

Giselle, Lee." Her green eyes began to glisten with tears. "At best, I have maybe five or six more years when I can realistically expect to make my living as a dancer. And the question I have to ask myself is: What then? Where do I go from there? And will it be easier to get there if I start now, instead of when I'm in my thirties?"

"I don't know what to say to you, *cara*." Lee reached across the table and wiped her tears away with his thumb. "Did you ever see one of those movies where the earnest young understudy finally gets her chance to prove her stuff when the star breaks a leg or gets pneumonia or something equally dramatic?"

"Yes, but in the movies the understudy always knocks 'em dead. I'm afraid that won't happen in my case, Lee, but it will for Sharyn." Georgia sniffed and forced a smile. "Ironic, isn't it? *Giselle* is my favorite ballet, the role I waited a lifetime to perform."

"Perhaps if I worked with you at night . . ."

"You are a sweetheart and my best friend, Lee, but no amount of rehearsal will give me what I don't have."

"Another dance troupe, then," he suggested. "I know several directors who would surely be pleased to give you an audition."

"I don't know that things would be different anywhere else."

"You wouldn't have Ivan to contend with."

"True, but is that really the issue at this point? I'll never be better than I am, and I'll still have the same questions in my mind." She spun her spoon around on the table in slow circles. "Maybe it's just time for me to move on, Lee."

"Move on to what, *cara?*"

"I have no idea. I have no training to do anything except dance. I hardly even know anyone that I haven't met through dance. I exercise. I cook. I read. I dance. I lead a mostly solitary life, Lee." She shook her head. "Scary, isn't it? That I've lived for twenty-six years, and I've never seen much of anything beyond the edge of the stage. Even my first love was a dancer."

"Mine, too." He deadpanned, and she laughed in spite of herself.

"I think you should perhaps discuss this with your family—your mother, your sister," Lee said. "This is a very big decision, Georgia, one you should not make in haste."

"Actually, I've been thinking about it for a long time now."

"What's a long time?"

"Since last summer."

"Really." He took one of her hands in his and rubbed the top of her wrist. He had suspected that something had been bothering her for the past few months but had not realized it had been anything this serious. "Tell me."

"I feel restless. Besides the fact that I feel more and more that it's time to move on, I also know I'm missing so much in life. It didn't used to bother me. Now it does." She swallowed hard. "My brother Nicky got married last summer."

"I remember. He got married at a lighthouse or some other such unlikely place."

"Yes. Devlin's Light. His new wife's family owns it . . . has owned it . . . forever. To get to the lighthouse, we had to go by boat. Lee, I had never been on a boat like that before. I got seasick and panicked, and I was scared half to death."

"A lot of people get seasick, *cara.*"

"This wasn't just seasick. I was so out of my element that I was frightened. And after the wedding, I walked up to the top of the lighthouse. You can see all the way to Delaware from the top of Devlin's Light, and way out toward the ocean. It made me realize just how narrow my own boundaries are, how limited my own little world is. It's bothered me ever since, Lee. That's when I began thinking that maybe it's time to push the boundaries back a bit."

"And how might you go about doing that?"

"I'm not sure, but I'm thinking a good place to start might be to take some time off to think things over."

"An excellent idea. When was the last time you had a vacation?"

"I haven't had one since I started dancing professionally. Not a real one, anyway."

"Then I would say you're overdue." He clapped his palms together. "Didn't you tell me that your 'new' sister owns an inn near the beach somewhere?"

Georgia smiled at his use of the word *new* to differentiate between Laura Bishop, Georgia's half-sister—the child Georgia's mother had been forced to give up for adoption many years before—and Zoey Enright, Georgia's "full" sister.

"Yes. Laura owns the Bishop's Inn."

"Well, this might be a good time to pay her a visit. Take a week off. Talk to her. See what she thinks. Walk on the beach; it's wonderful this time of year. It'll help clear your head. Things always look so much clearer when you take a step back."

"Ivan isn't likely to give me a week off." She frowned.

"Just how unhappy are you, *cara?*"

She looked up at him and allowed her normally cheery facade to fall away. Lee saw a beautiful young woman with hollow cheeks and circles under her eyes.

"Then take an indefinite leave," he said softly. "No one, especially Ivan, is worth your health or your happiness."

Lee watched her face as his words sunk in, and waited for her reaction.

"These other directors that you talked about." She drew the words out slowly, as if weighing every one of them. "Where might their dance companies be?"

"I have friends in Boston, Princeton, Savannah, and New Haven."

"Supposing I asked for time off and Ivan refused and I left the company. Supposing that after some time off—a few weeks or a month or whatever—I decided that what I really wanted was to stay in dance for however many more years. Is there any reason to think that any of these other directors might be willing to give me an audition after . . ."

"After having walked out on Ivan?" He dismissed her fears with a wave of his hand. "I'm certain that I can arrange that for you. Ivan is brilliant, but he is known to be difficult. He has the well-earned reputation of being a son of a bitch. You would not be the only dancer to have left a troupe because of him." And then he winked and added, "And besides, the director of the Princeton company is an old and dear friend of mine. No, *cara,* you need not fear that leaving Ivan the Terrible behind will close the door on your career. Should you decide you still want one."

Georgia played with her flatware, stacking spoon onto fork onto knife, contemplating Lee's words. It had not occurred to her that there might be other real choices, not just abstract possibilities. The thought that there might be many other options both warmed and confused her.

"You know, I'll think about it. I will." She leaned across the table and kissed Lee on the cheek. "Maybe I'll give Laura a call later and see if she has time for me to visit."

"It may turn out to be the best thing you've ever done for yourself." Lee's chair scraped against the wooden floor as he pushed it back from the table and stood up. "Give me a hug, Georgey-girl."

Georgia hugged Lee and thanked him for breakfast, then zipped up the front of her sweatshirt; and promising to let him know what she decided to do, she left the friendly warmth of Tuscany for the crisp cold streets of Baltimore.

She walked, rather than ran, back to her condo. Maybe Lee was right. Maybe a leave of absence would be best. Time to think and time to search her heart. Time to step back and take a good look at the big picture—something she had never done—and put things into perspective.

She tried to imagine what it would be like to go a whole week without dancing. Two weeks. Three. Unthinkable. What on earth would she do with her time?

Georgia passed through the lobby of her building mechanically, her mind clearly someplace else. She twirled her door key around on its chain absently as she climbed the six flights of steps to her floor, then unlocked the door and entered into her own white world.

Her whole life had revolved around dance for so long that she wasn't sure she could fill even a week's worth of time if she was not dancing.

And yet, the last time she had visited Laura, there had been a pull toward the beach, where she had sat in the sun and just watched the rhythmic roll of ocean onto sand. And later, there had been pleasant hours spent curled up in one of the little sitting rooms where she had read a book, cover to cover. It had been a delightful day. Laura, an avid reader, always had lots of books available for her guests. Georgia thought about that as she washed her hair in the warm shower water, picturing herself lounging in one of those oversized chairs pulled up near to the fireplace . . . or maybe snuggled amid the many cushions on the window seat that overlooked Laura's gardens. Not that she would expect there to be anything in bloom this time of the year, but it would still be a pretty view. Laura had bird feeders outside of just about every window of the inn, and there would be nuthatches and titmice at the feeders, cardinals and blue jays on the ground below pecking at the spillage.

Georgia glanced at her watch. Her mother would be working in her spacious office on the first floor of the carriage house on her "gentleman's farm" tucked amidst the hills of Chester County, Pennsylvania. A mystery writer, Delia Enright kept a meticulous schedule, particularly when she was just starting a new book. Georgia recalled that her mother's latest project was now a healthy three weeks old, and she would be allowing herself a leisurely lunch hour around one, the best time of the day to reach Delia by phone. Georgia knew that Delia would support all her children in absolutely any endeavor that made them happy. If Georgia felt she needed a break from dance, Delia would encourage her to take one. If dance was no longer fulfilling, Delia would be the first to urge her to move her life along. Georgia needed to hear her mother tell her exactly that before she spoke with Ivan later that afternoon.

Georgia knew, of course, exactly how Ivan would react. He would get that malicious little gleam in his eye, and it would all go downhill from there. Very publicly—and very loudly.

Her face burned at the thought of the ordeal, of the humiliation Ivan would heap upon her right before dismissing her. There was, however, no way around it, other than to just never show up again. As much as she dreaded the very thought of the certain confrontation, she could never be that much of a coward. She would tell Ivan, face to face, of her plans to take a leave of absence from the troupe. And she would take the consequences. She just prayed that it would, in the end, prove to be worth it.

Matthew Bishop stood at the passenger side of his battered black pickup truck and waited until Artie, his dog, had climbed in before slamming the door with a vengeance. His sister Laura made him crazy, pure and simple. Ever since she had found her birth mother, things had just not been the same. He just couldn't understand it, why Laura would feel this need to get to know this stranger, who had, after all, given her away as a newborn and hadn't bothered to look for her until thirty-five years had passed.

And hadn't Matt and Laura been raised by the sweetest woman God had ever placed here on His green earth? Who could ever need more *mother* than Charity Bishop had been?

Matt himself had never felt the need to go looking for his birth mother. He had memories enough of her—hazy though they might be—to know that he never wanted to so much as hear her name spoken aloud. In his mind and in his heart, Charity Evans Bishop, who had taken him in as a terrible-tempered toddler and had loved him fiercely, *was* his real mother. It had been Charity who had loved him before he had been lovable, had rocked him when he screamed with rage and frustration, and had held him while he sobbed out his fears.

Having been mostly neglected and ignored since birth, Matt had come to the Bishops' home as a four-year-old who, having rarely been spoken to, could not speak beyond a very limited vocabulary. The social workers who had found him living in squalor when his drug-addicted mother had overdosed that last time had immediately declared the boy to be retarded, but the cop who had been called to the scene had apparently sensed something else in the child, something fierce and alive. The officer had called his cousin, Tom Bishop, from the hospital to ask if Tom and his wife still wanted that son they had talked about adopting. From the minute she had laid eyes on Matthew, Charity had declared that there was nothing wrong with the boy that a loving family could not cure. And, for the most part, she had been right. Matt had gone from the hell of abandoned houses to the luxury of a historic inn, from near-complete solitude to a loving family that had included the daughter the Bishops had adopted twelve years earlier. Laura had adored Matt from the day he had been brought home. She had played with him and read to him, taught him the things that a child living with the bay on one side and the ocean on the other needed to know. She had become his big sister, and together they had been the children that Tom and Charity had prayed for.

Charity Bishop had given Matt a home and a family, a name and a sense of self-worth, and most importantly, she had given him unconditional love. No, there was no need to seek out his past. He knew exactly who *his* mother was. Laura should have just told that Enright woman to take a hike when she first showed up. And for the life of him, he couldn't understand why she hadn't.

"Damn stubborn woman," Matt mumbled as he shot into the driver's side of the cab and caught a glimpse of his sister Laura in his rearview mirror.

"Matt, I just wish you would be a little more rational about this. I can't understand why you are so closed-minded—"

"Closed-minded?" He rolled down the window and stared into Laura's face. "Because I can't understand why you'd need to be bothered with this woman who claims to be your birth mother, when your real mother is wasting away over at Ocean View?"

"Matt, I'm not ignoring Mom. I still go to see her the same number of times each week; I stay just as long as I always have—"

He scowled. "Save it. Maybe it helps that your *real* mother is the most widely read mystery writer in the world and that she's a millionaire how many times over."

"Matthew Bishop, I have half a mind to drag you out of that truck and drop-kick your ass from here to the Atlantic. That's a *terrible* thing to imply, and I really resent—"

"Yeah, well, I really *resent,* too. . . ." he muttered as he shifted the truck into gear and prepared to pull out of the driveway.

"Matt," she called after him. "If you would only spend just a little time with Delia, talk to her, get to know her, you'd see that she is—"

"Oh, I think I know what she is. And I don't have the time or the inclination to spend with *Delia,* or anyone else named Enright." He hung one arm out the window and waved.

In his rearview mirror, Matt could see Laura standing where he'd left her, her hands folded across her chest. That one foot tapping on the asphalt surface of the parking area behind the inn left no doubt in his mind that his sister was *really* angry. Well, he was none too happy with her, either.

Laura turned heel and stomped up the back steps leading to the inn.

Forced by oncoming vehicles to stop abruptly about ten feet from the entrance to the narrow lot, Matt waited as both a light blue jeep and an oil-delivery truck prepared to pull in. The jeep drove past him briskly and swept into a spot to his left, but the driver of the oil truck had cut too wide an arc, and Matt had to back up to permit the truck to enter the parking lot. Mumbling oaths under his breath, he sat and watched the truck slowly maneuver through the entry.

He heard the slam of a car door and shifted his eyes to the sideview mirror in time to see a young woman round the back of the jeep and open the cargo door. She was a tiny thing and looked as delicate as spun glass.

A trim little bottom wrapped in denim leaned into the

back of the jeep, and the woman dropped a canvas bag at her feet. As she bent to retrieve it, unbelievably long hair, pale as cornsilk and reaching near to her waist, slid over her shoulders in a thick wave. She turned and in one motion slammed the cargo door and pushed the hair back from her face. From clear across the parking lot, Matt could see big, wide-set eyes, a pert little nose, and full lips that bore no trace of lipstick. It was a face a man wasn't likely to forget.

"Nice." He nodded objectively. "Very, very nice."

The blond hoisted her bags over her shoulder and walked toward the inn.

She moves like music slipped unbidden through his mind, and he wondered where the thought had come from.

"Looks like we left one day too soon, Artie," Matt said aloud.

The dog panted noncommittally.

"Probably a tourist making her way up the coast. Ummm, maybe Florida to New York—what do you think?" Matt said, playing with his dog the game he had, as a child, played with his sister, trying to guess who the inn's patrons might be, where they were from, and where they might be going.

Artie thumped his tail loudly on the black leather.

"Yeah, that's what I thought, too." Matt peered in the rearview mirror for one last glimpse of long blond hair and faded blue denim as he prepared to make the left turn, but the woman was out of view.

He shrugged. Not that it mattered. Their paths weren't likely to cross again.

Matt made his left and headed for the road that would take him back to the highway.